FROM

CHARRED REN

ALSO BY SUSANNA CALKINS

A Murder at Rosamund's Gate

FROM

—THE—

CHARRED
REMAINS

Susanna Calkins

MINOTAUR BOOKS ❧ NEW YORK

FROM THE CHARRED REMAINS. Copyright © 2014 by Susanna Calkins. All rights reserved. Printed in the United States of America. For information, address St. Martin's Press, 175 Fifth Avenue, New York, N.Y. 10010.

www.minotaurbooks.com

Map by Rhys Davies

The Library of Congress has cataloged the hardcover edition as follows:

Calkins, Susanna.
    From the charred remains / Susanna Calkins.
        p. cm.—(Lucy Campion mysteries; 2)
    ISBN 978-1-250-00788-9 (hardcover)
    ISBN 978-1-250-00789-6 (e-book)
    1. Great Fire, London, England 1666—Fiction.   2. Women—England—
History—17th century—Fiction.   3. Murder—Investigation—Fiction.   4. Great
Britain—History—Restoration, 1660–1688—Fiction.   5. London (England)—
History—17th century—Fiction.   I. Title.
    PS3603.A4394F76 2014
    813'.6—dc23

                                                                2013047140

ISBN 978-1-250-06051-8 (trade paperback)

Minotaur books may be purchased for educational, business, or promotional use. For information on bulk purchases, please contact the Macmillan Corporate and Premium Sales Department at 1-800-221-7945, extension 5442, or write to specialmarkets@macmillan.com.

First Minotaur Books Paperback Edition: March 2015

10 9 8 7 6 5 4 3 2 1

To Matt, Alex, and Quentin

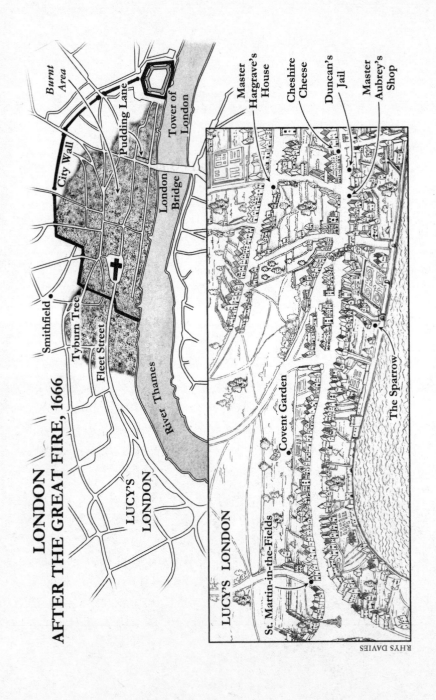

LONDON
AFTER THE GREAT FIRE, 1666

Burnt Area

Pudding Lane

City Wall

Tower of London

London Bridge

Smithfield

Tyburn Tree

Fleet Street

River Thames

LUCY'S LONDON

Master Hargrave's House

Cheshire Cheese

Duncan's Jail

Master Aubrey's Shop

LUCY'S LONDON

St. Martin-in-the-Fields

Covent Garden

The Sparrow

RHYS DAVIES

ACKNOWLEDGMENTS

There are many people who helped transform *From the Charred Remains* from a series of scrawls into a real book. In particular, I deeply appreciate the invaluable insights and feedback provided by my beta readers, Maggie Dalrymple, Margaret Light, Steve Stofferahn, and Shyanmei Wang, as well as Greg Light for our many conversations about writing. I must also thank my chief medical correspondents, Larry Cochard, Marian Dagosto, and Gary Martin, who painstakingly answered all my questions about corpses and bones. I'd also like to thank the lovely towns of Wolcott and Chalmers in Indiana for giving me the idea for one of my favorite character names (Wolcott Chalmers). And without coffee, I don't know if the book would have been written; so to this end, I must thank Amy Touchette and Jill Gross for allowing me to write for hours on end in Arriva Dolce, the best coffee shop in Highland Park.

I will always be grateful to my agent, David Hale Smith, for helping make this dream a reality and for connecting me to this new world of writing and publishing. I so appreciate, too, my wonderful editor, Kelley Ragland, for her talent in helping me reflect on plot points and character motivations. I feel extremely fortunate that she cares about Lucy Campion and her world as much as I do. I'd also like to thank Elizabeth Lacks and the rest of the St. Martin's/Minotaur Books team, including David Rotstein, the amazing artist who designed my cover, for their commitment and hard work on my book.

As always, I'm grateful for the love and support of my family, especially James and Diane Calkins, Becky Calkins, Monica Calkins and Steve Wagner, Vince Calkins, Robin Kelley and Angie Betz, and Jennie Bahnaman. To my wonderful children, Alex and Quentin Kelley, it's been so much fun to share the silly and entertaining parts of being an author with you!

Most of all, I'd like to thank my dear husband, Matt—keeper of the thousand monkeys all typing at a thousand typewriters—for his boundless enthusiasm and love. It is to him I dedicate this novel.

LONDON

---·◆·---

September 1666
After the Great Fire

· I ·

At the clanging of the swords, Lucy's stomach lurched and her hands tightened on her rake. The sound still made her cringe, even all these years after Cromwell's war.

No soldiers now, but two boys garbed as knights, pitching at each other with heavy swords, their underdeveloped bodies encumbered by breastplates and armor made for men. Lucy watched the boys play for a moment, as they slid about in the rubble—the aftermath of the Great Fire—trying to stay atop the mountains of debris that once comprised London's bustling Fleet Street.

Barely a fortnight had passed since the Great Fire of 1666 had devastated London in the three days between September 2 and September 5, leaving a sprawling, still smoldering, wasteland. Ludgate, Cheapside, St. Paul's—all unrecognizable. Where dwellings had once pressed in on each other, like old women clinging together in market, now all was leveled. The moment one medieval structure had fallen nearly all had collapsed, as the centuries-old timber could not withstand the mighty blaze. Here and there, a few structures remained. St. Giles-Without-Cripplegate. St. Katherine Cree. London Bridge. The Tower. Perhaps licked by flames, but not destroyed.

Lucy had heard that, by King Charles's reckoning, more than thirteen thousand homes, churches, and shops had been destroyed, leaving thousands of people without shelter or livelihoods. The real miracle was that scarcely few had perished outright, even though Lucy herself had nearly died in the early hours of the blaze. Everyone had missing neighbors though, people who'd not returned, so the death toll might still grow.

And the Fire was still not yet quenched, despite the unceasing fire brigade. In their panic, when the Fire had first started, Londoners had dug into the network of elm pipes that lay under the streets, to get at the water pumped in from the Thames. With so many punctures, the pipes did not work as they ought, and the water had ceased to flow. The horses and the pumps could not get through the narrow streets, particularly as they grew more jammed as people tried desperately to flee with as many belongings as they could carry in small carts and on their backs.

Even now, buckets of water drawn from the nearby Thames were still being passed hand to hand, from soldier to butcher to child to soap-seller, throughout the day and night, as they had been since the wind had changed on the third day and the fire had at last begun to subside. The smell of smoke still hung heavily in the air, stinging Lucy's eyes and nose, and making her petticoats and bonnet reek.

Like hundreds of other Londoners, Lucy had been pressed into service by the King and the City government to help clear away the rubble, for a few pence a day. It was a far cry from what her life had been like up until the Fire had broken out. For the last few years, she'd been serving as a chambermaid in the household of Master Hargrave, a local magistrate, who spent many hours presiding over the assizes and other court sessions.

Well, no longer a chambermaid exactly, she reminded herself. Lucy had risen to be a lady's maid, excepting now there was no longer any lady in the household for her to serve. Mistress Hargrave, bless her soul, had been taken by the plague last summer, and the magistrate's only daughter, Sarah, had turned Quaker, traveling to distant lands. Since then, the master, a good and kindly man, had kept Lucy in his employ.

Truth be told, there was no clear place for Lucy in the household. Annie was the chambermaid now, having taken on Lucy's old scullery duties, emptying chamber pots, laundering clothes, and keeping the house tidy. Cook prepared the small family's meals, while her husband, John, tended to the needs of the magistrate and his son. Lucy did what she could, helping Cook and John keep the household running with godly order. But the knowledge that she had no clear place in the household remained heavy on her thoughts.

Clinging to order was all they could do—or so it seemed—in this world gone mad. The lawlessness and looting, rampant even before the Fire, when the great plague of the preceding two years had torn social and familial ties apart, threatened to grow worse. During the plague, many servants who had survived their masters had simply seized what they could. Some took just food or trifles, others new clothes or more luxurious items, but many had taken everything, in a quest to start their lives anew. They stole their masters' carts, horses, homes, livelihoods, and, in some cases, even their titles. In an instant, barmaids could become fine ladies, apprentices could become masters, with no one the wiser. Most seemed to have gotten away with these deeds too. Some areas of the city had been so hard hit by the plague that there were few left alive who could gainsay these usurpers' outrageous claims. No gossiping neighbors, no knowledgeable parishioners, no bell-men keeping careful watch. The ties of community that had so long bound Londoners to order and authority had been shattered when the plague was at its height. Only after the members of gov-ernment had returned to the city had communal order and au-thority slowly been restored.

Yet with the Fire the world, once again, seemed completely askew. As before, people were quick to take what did not belong to them and to seek a new place in society. The ponderous thefts that had occurred during the plague had only been worsened by the Fire. Property records, wills, legal testaments, and other such documents had been swallowed by the flames, leaving many prop-erties, trades, and livelihoods in dispute, opening the door even wider to looters and squatters.

Although Lucy would never have betrayed the Hargraves in such a base way, as so many servants she knew had done to their masters, there was something about the way these thieves had liberated themselves that she admired. The apprentices who had taken over their masters' shops, and the servants who were now sleeping in their masters' beds, had seized the opportunity to bury their old identities and livelihoods deep within the ashes, and to craft new lives for themselves.

For now, Lucy was just grateful that her family and most of the Hargraves had survived the plague and the Fire, although that survival had not come without cost. The chaos, the suffering, the aftermath of both events were still the stuff of nightmares.

Perhaps the prophets and soothsayers were right, Lucy thought. Maybe 1666 *was* the devil's year, as so many people fearfully whispered. Surely a judgment was being passed by the Lord.

Yet even as the thought occurred to her, Lucy pushed it out of her head. "Fantastical stuff," she could almost hear the magistrate say. "Utter foolishness. I'm surprised at you, Lucy."

Lucy returned to the tedious work before her. Rake. Scoop. Bucket. The men would first dismantle and carry away the fallen beams, and then remove the remains of furniture, doors, shutters, and other large materials. It was up to the women then to fill sacks and pails with debris, and empty them into the waiting carts. From there, the carts would dump everything into the Thames. Buckets of water coming up to cool the embers, buckets of debris going back.

The clanging sound of the boys started up again. "Stole that armor, I'd wager," said the young woman at her side, commenting on the antics of the two boy knights. "Don't you suppose, Lucy?"

Lucy glanced at Annie. As the magistrate's chambermaid, Annie was certainly growing up, no longer the gawky scrawny girl she'd been when Lucy found her on the streets of London two years before. Though still small, her arms and cheeks were round now, and her smile was no longer so sad.

"I don't know," Lucy shrugged. The armor donned by the boys had likely come from a church, a family monument perhaps. Who could know? The Fire had disturbed as much as it had secreted and destroyed. "Maybe."

Certainly, the Fire had been fickle, incinerating some objects while gently charring others. As she and Annie had raked through the rubble over the last few days, they had seen many things surface, giving little hints about the people who may have lived and worked there. A bed frame, a spinet, children's toys, fragments of clothes, some tools, a dipper, some buckets, a laundry tub, a few knives, all a jumble of life and humanity. They had even uncovered a pianoforte. With one finger, Annie had tapped on one of the grimy ivory keys, and Lucy had winced at the discordant jangling sound that had emerged from the once precious piece.

Here and there they found bits of treasure too. A silver mirror, blackened and peeling. Some gold coins, blackened and distorted from the flames. All those involved with the shoveling and the raking had been warned not to pocket any items they found. Strict laws against looters had been passed and the King's soldiers monitored the ruins to ensure that merchants, landowners, and tenants did not lose their property or their rights. For her part, Lucy wanted nothing from the Fire, seeing that it had only brought misery, despair, and chaos.

Meanwhile, the two boys were still playing, oblivious to all that was going on around them. The helmet of one boy had slipped over his eyes. "I'll slick you to bits, Sir Dungheap," he called to his friend, his voice somewhat muffled under the heavy iron mask. They heard him make a wretching sound. "Hey, this thing stinks!"

"Not so fast, Lord Lughead," Sir Dungheap retorted. "First, you shall have a taste of my sword." The other boy struggled to lift the sword, but only succeeded in toppling them both over, a great mash of arms, legs, and rusty armor.

Although Lucy was hot, tired, and greatly in want of an ale, a smile tugged at her lips. Clearing the rubble was backbreaking work, but it had already brought in a few extra shillings that she and her brother could sorely use. Besides, there was a funny sort of camaraderie that had arisen among the group she was with, some friendly jesting and singing had helped pass the long hours. Most people blamed the Catholics for the Fire. Papists, they called them. This notion united them a bit as they labored, even though by some accounts the inferno had started on Pudding Lane when a baker had failed to douse his ovens before his slumber.

Others hysterically claimed that the French had set London ablaze. Even before the Fire, it was customary to mock and jeer the French. After all, King Charles had been at war with France for a number of months now. Why they were at war, Lucy could not really say. She thought it had something to do with the Dutch and shipping routes, but was otherwise in the dark. At first, when the war was going well, the French were just the source of many tavern jests. Who hadn't laughed at the French "dancing men," who dared fight the valiant English soldiers? Who hadn't heard the tale of the French sailors who had looked down the barrel of a cannon to see if the gunpowder had been lit? As the war dragged on though, and the English began to suffer actual damages, the mood toward the French had grown steadily more poisonous. In the weeks leading up to the Fire, rumors abounded about Frenchmen plotting to blow up Parliament, just as Guy Fawkes had tried to do some sixty years before.

Since the Fire, though, all foreigners but especially the French were looked at with heavy suspicious eyes. As rumors worsened, Lucy knew that at least a few French merchants had fled London with their families for fear of a mob being set upon them. Just yesterday, they'd heard of a Frenchman in Smithfield being run out of London with a pitchfork.

But it wasn't just the French or the Catholics who were being blamed. A lot of griping, though, and surly words were being directed toward the King himself. No matter that the monarch had helped fight the flames with his own hands, many Londoners were still quick to claim that King Charles had not done enough to help the survivors. Last Thursday, the monarch had stood at Moorfields to declare that the Fire had been an act of nature. "Not foreign powers!" he had proclaimed. "Not subversives! Not the Catholics! Not even our enemies across the Channel. An act of God!"

This pleased the soothsayers and almanac-makers to no end, of course, particularly as people began to buy their books and seek more hidden prophecies. Still, most people were not convinced. "Looking for a scapegoat, they are," the magistrate had told her. "I can tell you, Lucy, this worries me." She remembered how last year, when the full-blown plague had finally descended on London, Master Hargrave had called his servants together. "If ever you see a mob forming, you run the other way!" he had warned them. "Bad things happen when a crowd takes leave of its senses." The same was surely true in these tense days.

Thinking of the magistrate's kindness, Lucy smiled. She could never put into words the fortune she had received when entering service in Master Hargrave's household. Not only was he a just and godly man, but he was not one to diminish an idea simply because it came from a servant. As she learned later, he had not minded that she secretly listened to his daughter's tutors, so long as she had polished, chopped, swept, and laundered as she ought. When he would read texts to the members of the family, fulfilling his moral duty as the head of the household, he would allow her to ask questions. He was only required to read them the Bible to assure the salving of his conscience, but over time he began to read from other texts he enjoyed—Locke, Hobbes, and the like. Even Shakespeare, since the ban against frivolity had been lifted by the King six years before.

How shocked his son, Adam, had been, when he first returned to his father's household upon completing his legal studies in law at the Inns of Court. Not only that his father would question his chambermaid about some fairly difficult pieces, but, as he told Lucy a long time later, he was deeply struck by her ability to answer his father's questions in a lively and imaginative way.

Thinking of Adam now, Lucy bit her lip. For so long, there had been nothing between them. Like his father, Adam had always treated her respectfully, not being a man to abuse or force himself upon his servants, as so many men of their station were wont to do. He'd always been courteous, but generally aloof, seemingly paying her little mind. From time to time, though, they had shared curious fluttering exchanges that had revealed that she was in his thoughts, but she did not know what to make of it.

Then, when the family was beset by several tragedies over the last year, including the death of her mistress, Adam's mother, something between them all had begun to change. To the magistrate, Lucy had become something like a daughter. To the magistrate's daughter, she had become a sister. To Adam, well, she became something more dear, although for the longest time, as she recently learned, he had struggled with his feelings for a servant. Social convention claimed that there could be no honorable match between gentry and servant, and she knew he had not wished to dishonor her.

The night of the Fire though, Adam had seemed to cast convention aside. She shivered, remembering his fervent promises. Even in the immediate aftermath, their future together, not quite stated, had seemed possible. But what would that future be like, she couldn't help wonder. Would she be accepted by Adam's peers? Certainly not by those who knew her to have been a chambermaid. Would such a poor match hurt Adam's career? And more insidiously, a little voice whispered inside her, did she even want to get married? The world of dawning opportunities beckoned. Marriage, children—could they wait? The magistrate had told her once how much he had admired several of the petticoat authors, women who had dared take up a pen and promote their own views. Had he been suggesting something to her? She could not be sure.

With a slight sigh, Lucy remembered her last conversation with Adam, a week ago, in the magistrate's kitchen. He'd been pressed by the Lord Mayor to help survey the wreckage and assess the scope of the property claims, and had barely slept or eaten for three days. Sitting at the bench, resting his head on his fist, Lucy had never seen him so overwhelmed and distracted. The disaster that had befallen the City was clearly taking his toll.

Exhausted, he'd barely spoken to her, and seemed to be only half-listening when she broached the topic of her leaving service to look after her brother, Will, a smithy in his own right. "It's not as if I have a place here. Not truly," she'd whispered. "Not since Annie has taken on my old responsibilities."

At that, he had opened his eyes and frowned. "She's done so for a few months now. Nothing has changed. There's no need for you to leave."

"Nothing has changed?" she had asked. "It no longer feels proper for me to live here. That's what changed. Or perhaps you don't agree?"

The words came out differently than she intended, and for a second he looked hurt and puzzled. "I was not aware that I had dishonored you," he said.

"No, no. You haven't," she said, fervently wishing she had not spoken. "Please, you're exhausted. Let us discuss this at another time."

He had closed his eyes. "Yes, I am quite weary. The madness that is out there, Lucy. The beggars, the looters, the liars. So many at the mercy of some truly godless wrongdoers. I should not like you to see it." Then he trudged up to his chamber to sleep, as he was leaving early the next morning. Given her work cleaning up the rubble, their paths had barely crossed and they had found no time to resume this delicate conversation.

Watching Sir Dungheap and Lord Lughead again, tilting aimlessly at each other, Lucy was reminded of this promise of a new world. At what other time could ragamuffins become knights, she pondered with a smile.

Again, Annie was following a different thought. "Those lads best not let them soldiers see them with those swords. They look valuable, fancy-like," she said, sniffing. "Those boys are going to get hauled off to Newgate. Well, not Newgate, since that's been burnt, but another jail."

Lucy shivered, remembering the long terrible months during which her brother Will had wasted away in Newgate jail, the stinkhole of London. Mercifully, he had been released before the plague had taken hold. Not for the first time, Lucy wondered what had happened to the rest of the prisoners during the Fire, for surely the jailers she had met would not think twice about running off without setting the denizens free. The official word was that no one in the prison had died. She had heard whispers, though, that the prisoners inside had simply been left to the inferno and their eternal damnation. And if Will hadn't been set free—. She thrust the thought away.

"Oh, sorry miss, I didn't think," Annie said, awkwardly patting her arm. "They won't be off to jail. More likely they will get their ears boxed." She set her shovel down, as if she were about to start moving debris again. Instead, she took a half-step closer to Lucy. "Someone's watching us," she whispered. "Just yonder, past the stones there." She discreetly pointed her finger.

Lucy followed her gaze. Sure enough, a young man was looking at them, not raking as he ought to have been. "Not working too hard, is he?" Lucy commented. Catching her eye, the man began to saunter toward them. "Oh, no! He's coming this way. Ignore him, Annie. We've work to do."

The young man planted himself in front of them. "'Tis a shame your pretty hands are getting dirtied in this muck." When he grinned, his face lengthened, making him look a bit devilish.

In that instant, Lucy recognized him and rolled her eyes. Sid Petry. She'd seen him once pick a woman's pocket and later being tried at court for another misdemeanor. Like the other laborers, Sid was wearing heavy wool breeches and a jacket, but somehow he didn't seem quite as raggedy or dusty as the rest of the men, although a light grime covered his features. He wasn't wearing a hat, and his dark blond hair looked fairly well kept. His hazel eyes danced with mischief.

Her own eyes narrowed. "Shouldn't you be working, *Sid?*" she asked. Annie looked at her, surprised Lucy would know the former ragamuffin.

Sid's smirk grew. "So we've met, have we?" he asked, looking more interested. Not wanting him to recall the exact circumstances of their first meeting nearly two years before, when she was just eighteen, Lucy repeated her question.

He winked. "Who's to say I'm not working?"

Remembering Sid's penchant for petty theft, Lucy hid a smile. "Looting is a bad business," she warned. "The justice of the peace may not be so lenient this time. You might get more than the stocks, should you do anything the law might not like."

Sid puffed up his chest. "So, you've seen me work, eh?"

"Seen you get caught."

"Ah, you cut me to the quick." He looked around. "Don't see no Redcoats nearby, do you? They must have pinched off for a pint, I'd wager."

"They're around. Take something. You'll see." Lucy warned him again. She looked around. Sure enough, there weren't any soldiers around anymore. For heaven's sake, she thought. The looting that could happen if the others realized that the soldiers were no longer paying attention. She turned back to Sid. "You're familiar enough with the stocks, aren't you?"

Sid stepped closer to her. Being close to seventeen or eighteen now, he'd grown taller since she had last seen him, and now loomed over her a bit. "Ah, miss. I don't even know your name?"

"She's Lucy," Annie piped in, even as Lucy elbowed her in the ribs. "I remember you too, Sid. From the streets."

Sid turned his attention to the younger girl, slapping his head in mock dismay. "Now I must be going daft. Not to recall two lovely lasses such as yourselves."

Annie looked pleased. "Oh, get on with you."

Lucy was about to wave Sid off when she noticed one of the boys, Sir Dungheap, suddenly drop his sword, and rip off his helmet. Looking horrified, he began to shout, making an odd gurgling sound. He pointed downward at something hidden on the other side of the mound of debris. Lord Lughead was nowhere to be seen. For a moment Lucy felt sick. He probably had run his mate through with a sword.

But then the boy started to call. "Help! Help! A body! A body!"

Hearing the boy's cry, Lucy and Annie dropped their rakes and buckets and raced over the rubble, their skirts catching in the debris, Sid a few steps ahead of them. Lucy wondered sickly what they would find. She had heard of a few bodies that had been found here and there. A young woman, too afraid to jump from a burning building. An elderly woman found huddled in St. Dennis, probably thinking the great stone pillars and God would protect her. And most miraculously of all, the corpse of a saint who had died some hundreds of years before, perfectly preserved after being displaced somehow from his crypt.

But when Lucy reached the boys, she gagged. A man's body was spilling from a great wooden barrel, where it lay on its side on the ash-covered ground.

"He knocked it over, he did it," Sir Dungheap said, a bit resentfully, pointing at the other boy. "Standing on top of that barrel, 'til he toppled it over, he did."

Sir Lughead, who looked a little pale, tried to muster a cheeky grin. "Not my fault the body was in there, though, was it?"

Ignoring the boys, Lucy took a closer look. From the vermin crawling all over him, he'd clearly been dead for a while. Lucy dimly noted a shock of black hair and brownish skin before her eyes fixed on the handle of a knife protruding from his chest. His eyes—mercifully—were closed. She saw Sid turn away in disgust.

At the sight of the corpse, a great buzzing began to rise in Lucy's ears. Annie said something, but Lucy could not hear her. For a moment, the vision of a different gruesome death she had recently witnessed rose before her eyes, and she began to shake. Lucy forced herself to speak. "We must summon a constable," she heard herself say. Her voice sounded tinny and flat.

No one moved.

"We have to get the constable!" Lucy repeated, her voice sharpening. She looked about at the handful of people who had gathered. Annie looked a bit queasy but, like Lucy, she had seen far too much death in her young life to be very moved by a corpse. Murder, though, that was different. Lucy put her hands on Annie's shoulders and gave her a little shake. "Annie, you must fetch a constable. Or a watchman. Quickly."

Fortunately, Annie seemed to regain her senses. She had lived long enough in the magistrate's household to know better. "Right, miss," she said, unconsciously deferring to Lucy, before running off.

The crowd began to murmur among themselves. Most were the people Lucy had been working alongside all week, but there were a few she hadn't met.

"Looks like a foreigner. Probably a sailor."

"Dunderhead!"

"Poor man. What a way to go."

"Like as not, he had it coming." This verdict came from a small rotund man, who Lucy remembered from before the Fire. He used to sell perfumes and spices in the market. "A chap don't get knifed through the chest for no reason."

"Where's his finger pointing?" a former seller of pies cried, balancing a babe on her hip. "He's surely pointing to the one who done him in." Everyone knew that victims who had been monstrously killed would point to their murderers. A few people nodded, but others scoffed.

"Daft woman," the perfume-seller spoke again. "Can you see his hands?"

"Now how can I? They're all tucked up inside the barrel, ain't they?"

"Well, dump him from the barrel then. See where he points."

Hearing the crowd hum its approval, two men moved to dump the corpse out. But that would mean the murderer was there. It made no sense.

"Wait!" Lucy called out, finally finding her voice. "I don't think we should move the body!" She could almost hear the physician Larimer complaining, as he had many a time while sup-ping at the magistrate's household. "Bloody fools! I need to look at the body where it lays to determine cause of death." She shook her head. The cause of death here looked easy to see; the big knife through his chest was a dead giveaway.

As if reading her thoughts, the man standing at the barrel frowned at Lucy. "He's dead, ain't he? Not going to hurt him none, are we?"

Lucy thought quickly. "Yes, well, his soul might not like be-ing disturbed. He might decide to haunt you."

At that thought, a few people crossed themselves quickly, the gesture a holdover from their distant Catholic past, and backed away. No one wanted a spirit following them home, especially with so few crossroads that could confuse the ghost and send it in the wrong direction.

Luckily, the constable arrived just then, Annie at his heels, panting slightly. A second man, a soldier, followed them both. Lucy recognized the constable. Duncan. Lucy had first met him two years ago when he had brought news to the magistrate of a terrible murder. And just two weeks ago, on the night of the Great Fire, she had stood before him, sobbing out the story of another terrible death that had occurred.

Taking in the scene at once, Constable Duncan spoke, his York-shire accent setting him apart from the Londoners around him. Though young, he commanded respect. "Who found the body?" he demanded.

Lucy pushed the two young boys forward. "These two, Con-stable Duncan. They were playing atop the barrels."

Duncan glanced at her, his face registering slight surprise at seeing her there. "Indeed, Miss Campion? Alright then. The rest of you. Back to work."

Grumbling, sneaking glances over their shoulders, the small group returned to their shovels and carts, resuming the seemingly endless restoration of London. The soldier moved closer, keeping an eye on their work. Lucy noticed that Sid seemed to have disappeared. Not surprising, seeing how he disliked any representative of the law.

Duncan looked sternly at the boys. "Now, lads, tell me how you came to find the body."

In sullen tones, Sir Dungheap explained. "We was just playing, climbing about on the barrels. Just there."

They followed his finger. A few more barrels were still stacked against a bit of a stone wall. The rest of the dwelling must have been made of wood, as only a few burned timbers remained. The stone wall, probably once connected to a much older structure that had survived the flames, must have protected the barrels stacked alongside.

"We was rolling on top of the barrels. Dunno there was a stiff in it," the boy said sullenly.

Duncan held out his thumb, looking in the distance first at the ruins of St. Paul's Cathedral, and then did the same thing to the remains of St. Faith's. Turning, he did it a third time, looking at the structures at the end of Fleet Street that were still intact, having been just out of reach of the Fire.

"What are you doing?" Lucy could not help but ask.

"Measuring distances," Duncan said. "A trick I learned from painters. They call it 'perspective.'"

"Why?"

"Well, Miss Campion, I'm trying to determine which tavern this was. There were several on Fleet Street."

"How do you know it was a tavern?"

Duncan pointed at the barrels. "Those are malt barrels."

Lucy frowned, trying to remember what the street had looked like before the Fire. Surely, she had walked along here enough times, to and from the market. Right now, without the shops with their signs, she was at a bit of a loss.

Duncan, however, had figured it out. "The Cheshire Cheese!" he said.

With a flash, Lucy remembered the old sign that had hung out front. She couldn't remember ever having been inside, not because she didn't enjoy a pint from time to time, but because that tavern hadn't seemed to draw the most respectable sorts. She said as much to the constable.

"Hmmm," he said, not listening to her. "Now the question is, when was this poor sot put in the barrel? I assume before the Fire, since the soldiers have been patrolling this area. But how long before?"

"The physician should be able to tell you that," Lucy said. "What he can't tell you, though, is who murdered the poor man. Or why."

·2·

Later, as the sky grew dark, all the Fire workers were given a few coins and sent home. The Lord Mayor had imposed a curfew on the City to help restrict lawlessness. He had also temporarily restricted travelers from carrying lanterns, for fear another fire would start again. The fog and smoke still lingered, making the early-September evening look as black as a smithy's forge.

Feigning a bravery she did not feel, Lucy took Annie's arm. "Come on. We've got to get home within the hour, lest we break curfew."

As they walked, the two young women clung together, making their way cautiously through the dark. Lucy had never longed so deeply for a lantern. Fortunately, some kind souls had placed candles in their windows to ease the path of nighttime travelers. This charitable act allowed them to keep to the main paths fairly easily. Only when they approached the last desolate field they had to pass through before reaching the magistrate's home did Lucy feel a bit anxious.

Hearing a step behind them, they both froze. "Did you hear that?" Annie whispered, gripping Lucy's arm painfully.

"Who's there?" Lucy called, trying to keep her voice from wavering. For a long moment, she held her breath. When a man stepped out of the shadows, they both gasped. Instinctively, Lucy pushed Annie behind her.

"Afraid are you?" a familiar voice asked. "Nay, calm your fears. 'Tis only me."

"Sid!" they cried out in unison.

Though she relaxed a bit, Lucy was still wary. She had learned the hard way that a friendly grin could easily mask a murderous heart. "What are you doing here?" she asked.

Sid's grin was wide as he regarded them. "I wanted to talk to you some more. Get to know you a bit."

Clearly relieved, Annie smiled back. "What about that stiff today?" she asked, seemingly eager to make conversation. "Gaw! That nearly scared me witless."

Lucy shot her a reproachful glance, and the younger woman fell silent. "Where'd you get to, Sid?" Lucy asked, frowning at the young pickpocket. "Earlier? When the body was found? I looked around and you were nowhere to be seen."

"You were looking for me?" His tone was suggestive.

"Oh, for heaven's sake!" Lucy said, annoyed. "Enough already!" She took the younger woman's arm again. "Come, Annie. We must make haste." To her vexation, Sid started walking with them. "Hey, what are you doing? You know we're almost at curfew. We'll hear the bellman toll the warning any moment."

Sid had fallen into step with Annie, and seemed intent on walking with them. "Oh, I was going this way anyway," Sid said, pointing vaguely in the direction they were going. "I'll just keep you company. You need a man to make sure you are alright."

Lucy ignored Annie's gratified look, and pressed him a bit. "And where are you living these days, Sid?"

Sid had no cheeky reply. "Nowhere, truly," he mumbled.

Lucy sighed. "You lost your home in the Fire, didn't you?"

Annie squealed. "Oh, Lucy, Sid should come home with us. Right, Lucy? Surely, he could use a bite to eat. The master won't mind." To Sid, she added, "The master's a magistrate, you know. We live in a fine house. Though not as fine as the house we used to live in."

At Annie's mention of the magistrate, Lucy saw Sid grimace. A pickpocket staying under the magistrate's roof. An absurd idea. Apparently, Sid had come to the same conclusion. He gave Lucy a sidelong glance. "But I have been a bit starved of late. I'll have a bite, and then I'll be on my way. Quick as a wink."

Lucy relented, and soon they were relaxing around the kitchen fire in the magistrate's new home. Fortunately, the magistrate and Adam were both out for the evening, having been invited to dine by the Lord Mayor, Thomas Bloodworth. Cook had taken one look at Sid and thrust some lye soap at him, gesturing toward a small basin that she had filled halfway with water. Grimacing slightly at the rancid smell, he nevertheless rubbed his face vigorously with the bit of cloth she'd handed him. Clearly, Cook had not let him use the more precious soap she made with lavender; instead, he had been given the more pungent soap that smelled like dog piss.

The grime gone, they could see he had light whiskers on his chin. While they ate, Sid launched into a full tale of life in the streets, largely embellished, Lucy thought, for Annie's benefit. Seeing Annie hang on the pickpocket's words made Lucy vaguely nervous. At twenty, she felt far older than both of them.

Right now, Annie was teasing Sid about his coat. "Just look at those rips, here and there. It shan't take me but a moment to sew these. Give me your coat."

Lucy studied his coat. "Those don't look like rips. They look like someone cut through the jacket. Could it be so you'd have extra pockets?"

Sid closed his arms protectively around his coat. "It's alright, isn't it? Who do I need to look all spruced up for? I ain't no gentleman."

"That may be so," Lucy agreed. "However, Sid, given that the magistrate has provided you with a meal, in his very home, at his own table, I think a bit of honesty is in order. Don't you? Are you, by chance, hiding something?" She leaned forward, examining the front of his coat.

Sid jerked away. "I didn't take nothing," he growled.

"No one says you did," Lucy soothed him. "Come, like Annie says, let's have your coat off."

Grunting a bit, Sid eased off his coat. Quick as he was, Lucy still caught him slipping something from an inside coat pocket, into a pocket of his shirt. She exchanged a glance with Annie.

"I knew you were hiding something," Annie crowed. "Come on, show us."

"Yes, Sid," Lucy added more sternly. "Surely you'd like to enjoy the magistrate's fire and food a little longer. If not, I'm sure

John would be happy to escort you out." More likely, put you out on your arse, she thought to herself.

Sid glanced at his mug, now drained of the warm mead. Catching the hint, Annie ladled some more of the hot drink from the pot she'd removed from the hearth just moments before.

For good measure, Lucy added another biscuit to his plate as well. "Show us," she said firmly. Both women looked at him expectantly.

Sid made a face. "As you like." He tossed a leather bag out onto the table. "Nothing much here. I already poked inside."

Lucy picked up the leather pouch. "Where did you get this?"

Sid yawned.

"Did you pick it?"

"Nah, I don't pick pockets no more."

Lucy wasn't sure if she believed that, but seeing that he was a bit down on his luck, she didn't pursue it. "Well, where did you get it then?"

"In the barrel. Well, alongside it," he muttered, adding defensively. "I found it."

"You found it at the Fire site? Oh, Sid!" Annie cried. "You've broken the law!"

Lucy rubbed her chin, unconsciously adopting the magistrate's gesture when he was puzzling over an idea. "Are you saying, Sid, that you found this pouch with the dead body? When did you take it?"

Sid grinned wanly. "I'm quick, ain't I?" He looked from one to the other, clearly expecting to be turned out any moment. "It was at the edge of the barrel, just beside the poor fool. No one noticed when I nicked it."

"You know you can't keep it," Lucy warned. "We'll take it to the constable first thing in the morning." She ignored Sid's dour look.

"We can still see what's inside the bag," Annie pleaded, curiosity getting the better of her. "No harm in looking, right?" Without waiting for Lucy to agree, she shook the little leather bag, dumping an odd assortment onto the wooden table.

Against her better judgment, Lucy leaned closer, peering at the hodgepodge of objects. Some playing cards, an elephant elegantly carved in translucent green stone, a ring, a few coins which Sid immediately snatched up, a fluff of wool, and a small oilskin packet that seemed to have been once sealed with wax. Lucy turned the packet over in her fingers, while Annie pulled at the fluff.

"There's something in here," Annie squealed. From beneath the layer of wool, Annie extracted a woman's brooch made of a smooth white wood. Three roses interlocking with a heart had been carefully carved from a single piece. An iron pin in back had been attached, so that one could hold a cloak together with the piece.

"Oh! How beautiful!" Anne breathed. She traced the delicate lines. "So smooth! What kind of wood is this, do you suppose?"

Peering over her shoulder, Sid looked at the brooch. "Not oak, cherry, or ash, I'd say. Ivory?"

"It does look like the pianoforte keys," Lucy said, reaching for the brooch. She certainly owned no jewelry as fine as this. Like Annie, she could not resist running her fingers along the heart and flower petals. "What an odd jumble this all is. It's amazing this pouch survived with the miscellany intact. I suppose the leather protected it."

"Or it was divine providence," Annie ventured. "The body should have been burnt up too, but the flames skirted the barrels."

"I suppose you're right," Lucy said, wrapping the brooch carefully back in the wool. She was always uncomfortable with the notion of providence. Why should some people have lost everything, while others lost nothing? She shook her head; twas not the time to question the way of the world. "We must take this to the constable in the morning," she declared. "Someone must be missing these things."

Sid's face dropped. "Everything?" he asked, disgruntled.

"Everything," she said. "I mean it, Sid." She looked at him meaningfully.

Reluctantly, he put two coins back on the table, near the pouch.

"And the rest?" She drummed her fingers on the table.

Sid laid out the other coins. Altogether, there was a gold sovereign, two shillings, and four coins of a type she'd never before seen. Lucy fingered them. "I wonder where they're from."

"These two are French," Sid said, with surprising authority. Seeing Lucy raise her eyebrows, he defended himself. "What? I know a gent who collects coins. I, er, come across French coins from time to time."

"But these two." He tapped the coins on the table. "I've never seen the likes. I know they're not German or Dutch, or even Spanish."

"Look at this," Annie said, examining the ring. "Look, it flips, see?" she put the ring on her finger where it easily slid around. It fit a little better on Sid's hand when he tried it. Clearly, it was intended for a man's hand.

Sid passed the ring to Lucy. She studied it carefully. The ring was unusual, completely unlike anything Lucy had ever seen. The surface swiveled so that the ring's wearer could choose to display either side. One side seemed to be a coat of arms, while the other showed a hunter chasing a boar. Surrounding each surface was a blue dial, allowing the owner to flip the ring as he chose.

Setting the ring aside, Lucy picked up the elephant. Painstakingly carved from a bit of green rock, the elephant's smooth surface suggested it had been much handled. It reminded her of the door above the comb-seller's shop, down by Cloake Lane, which sold beautifully carved ivory combs and pendants, far too costly for Lucy to ever imagine buying. Or at least, it had sold combs before the Fire. Now, the sign and shop were probably burnt away, or buried under the rubble like so much of that part of the City.

Sighing, Lucy picked up the oilskin package again. The seal was definitely broken. Carefully, Lucy withdrew a bit of paper, with Sid and Annie watching closely. Unlike the paper used by printers for broadsides, ballads, and pamphlets, this paper was thicker and smoother to the touch. Slowly, she unfolded it. Right away, she could see it contained a bit of verse. Having lived in the magistrate's household for several years, Lucy had learned to read very well, beyond the capacity of most servants. Glancing at the words, however, she was at first excited, then puzzled.

"What's it say?" Sid asked. "I'm not so good with my letters."

Annie leaned forward, as Lucy read the words aloud.

Now, Dear Hart—
As the poet says, come to the garden in spring. There's wine and
  sweethearts in the pomegranate blossoms.

Remember!
If you do not come, these do
Not matter.

If you do come, these do not matter.

My rose will bloom, among the
Hearty pineapples,
even in the first freeze of autumn.
Rose, my love—.
Even kings can wrong a fey duet.

Sid stopped chewing on a piece of rye bread. "What's that mean?"

Lucy shrugged. "I have no idea. A love letter I guess. No one signed it."

"Pfff," Sid said, unimpressed. "Not much point if the bird don't know who's writing them fancy words, now is it?"

"Sometimes people have to hide their love, I suppose," Lucy said, putting everything carefully back into the little leather pouch. "Now off to the woodshed with you. You'll be off in the morning. And Sid," she added sternly, "we'd best not find anything missing. The magistrate's not likely to take a theft in his own household very kindly."

Ignoring Sid's protestations of innocence, Lucy pushed him outside. Before she went to bed, she carefully wrote down a list of everything that had been in the small leather bag, including the words to the letter. As she drifted off, her last thought was that she'd never seen a pomegranate or a pineapple, but the garden sounded lovely.

At the site of the Cheshire Cheese the next morning, she found Constable Duncan scribbling notes in his book. The body had been removed, and he was carefully sifting through the timbers and stone. He looked like he hadn't gotten much sleep. For a moment, she wondered what his home life was like, whether he was married, had children. She'd seen him in court, when he had presented a devastating case against her brother. For her part, she'd only had three or four conversations with him over the last three years—two in which she'd protested her brother's innocence, and a more recent conversation she preferred not to think about.

"Constable Duncan," Lucy called, his name ending in a bit of a cough. Her throat was a bit scratchy from the smoke she'd been breathing in all week. Not surprisingly, he didn't hear her above the din. Moving closer, Lucy called his name again.

Hearing her, he gave her a quick harried grin. "Coming to tell me who killed the poor sot?" he asked.

"Do you know who he was?" she asked.

"No, not yet. But I've sent word to the innkeeper—he might know something about him." Duncan paused. "I tell you, Miss Campion, this is a bad business. I've had the physician look at him. He was fairly well beaten before being stuffed in that barrel. A couple of bones and ribs broken. And he was definitely killed before the Fire, but probably not long before."

"That makes sense," Lucy agreed. "Otherwise, I would think

his body would have been discovered when they had to refill the barrel with malt."

"I'm afraid of what London is becoming." He shook his head. "Since the plague, and the Fire. 'Tis as if men can't control themselves." Duncan glanced at her. "I assume you didn't come to chat about murder. You were coming to see me though?" He looked wary. "Not another death to report, I hope?"

Lucy laughed. "No, but I've come across something that may be of interest." She held out the bag. "This was found by the barrels. It may well have been on the body."

Duncan scowled. "Miss Campion. Looting is a serious crime—"

"I know, I know," she said hastily. "'Twas a mistake. One of my young acquaintances sort of, ahem, just walked off with it. By happenstance, I assure you. Thus, I brought it back."

"By happenstance. Hmmm." Duncan looked skeptical. "Alright. I'll try to ignore that part. What's in the bag?"

"Some odd stuff. A ring, some coins, an ivory brooch. A poem. Or perhaps it is a letter. I can't rightly tell."

Duncan turned two of the barrels over. "Here. Sit." Thoughtfully the constable pulled each item out of the pouch, turning it this way and about in his hands. Silently, he examined the brooch and the coins. He whistled when he looked at the elephant carved in the green rock. "This is a rook. From chess. Made of jade. Quite valuable, I should think." Setting the rook aside, he went on. "Five playing cards. A jack, a queen, a ten, a king . . . a winning hand?" He carefully opened the letter, skimming its contents. "Nothing identifying here." Carefully, he placed everything back in the bag and retied the strings. "Thank you, Miss Campion. And no more of your friends accidentally walking off with items from the Fire."

"Of course not, Constable Duncan." Lucy stood up. "Well, I'll be off now. I'm not working at the Fire site anymore. The master thought that Annie and I needed some time to rest."

"Still working for the Hargraves, are you?"

Something about his steady gaze made her flush unexpectedly. "Um, yes. I enjoy working for the magistrate. He's a kind man. He treats me well."

"I'm sure Master Hargrave does treat you well. How does his son treat you, if I may ask?"

"Adam? I mean, Master Hargrave?" She said in a stumbling away, aware of the constable's raised eyebrow. "He treats me well. Very well. I don't see him very much these days, of course. He's been helping out with the Lord Mayor's surveyors. He may even advise the King," she added proudly, before flushing even more deeply. Why had she added that last part? She sounded like she was boasting.

"Has political ambitions, does he?" the constable asked drily. "I guess that's the way of men of his station. Secure a good post, marry well, and he'll be all set."

"It's not like that! He's a good man. He's trying to help!" Lucy protested, hotly. Then she stopped, seeing the constable's pitying gaze. His mention of Adam "marrying well" made her stomach lurch. Without thinking, she added, somewhat defensively, "I'm going to be leaving the Hargraves myself, soon, though."

"Oh?"

Duncan's keen look disconcerted her. Her next words came

out in a rush. "Yes, I'm to keep house for my brother, as soon he finds some rooms to let. He's a journeyman now; he received his letter for the smithy's guild just before the Fire."

For a moment her thoughts flashed to her brother Will, laughing and handsome. Fortune's wheel had surely spun in Will's favor recently. No longer was his life so wretched as it had been the year prior. During the fire, Will had worked ceaselessly to save his master's tools and goods, and in exchange the smithy had released Will from his apprenticeship, which, truth be told, should have run for three more years. In addition, his former master had written a coveted letter to the guild, proclaiming her brother a journeyman in his own right. With that letter, her brother would be officially recognized by the guild, once Guildhall was restored. This meant too that as a journeyman, he could now work for more than one master, and could live where he pleased. "He's doing very well for himself," she said.

"Is that so? I'm glad to hear it. Very glad," the constable replied. "There's a world opening up out there, Lucy. You can see that, can you not?"

Hearing him call her by her first name startled her for a moment, but she found she didn't mind the familiarity. Duncan seemed to be studying her, waiting for her to respond. When she nodded, he added, "A dangerous world too. I hope you'll let me know where you set yourself up." He coughed slightly. "I would rest easy, knowing you are safe."

As she walked away, Lucy kept her head high in case the constable was watching her. His comment about Adam needing to marry well rankled her. Her thoughts swirled. Only two weeks before Adam had assured her that he had no interest in marrying for political gain. Or to enhance his career. Yet a sneaking little voice tugged at the back of her mind, saying that the opposite was also true. Wouldn't marrying poorly hurt his career?

The wind picked up, and unexpectedly, a tear slipped from her eye. "Dratted smoke," she muttered, not looking back.

Since she did not have any particular duties to attend to, Lucy decided to venture down Fleet Street to see how far the damage from the fire had extended. Within a few steps, she thought the bellman had surely turned the clock back, to the day before the Fire. Halfway down the street, she could see that along with a dozen other narrow three-story dwellings, The George had remained intact. Will would be glad to know this, The George being one of his favorite alehouses. Next to it, the apothecary and bakery were open, their painted signs depicting their wares as they had for a hundred years.

Several of the printers' shops were open, and booksellers were hefting packs of broadsides and ballads to hawk their tales throughout London. Mercifully, Master Aubrey's shop had not been touched. Indeed, the man himself was standing atop his customary wooden box, narrating the details of a broadside. As always, his face seemed a bit flushed, and his balding head was glistening with sweat. "Hear the story of a most fantastic birth, here among the ruins!" Master Aubrey boomed.

Lucy ventured closer. That story didn't seem to be particularly interesting—why did he think anyone would pay a precious penny for this tale? Of course, she had not taken into account Master Aubrey's considerable skill at weaving in details, making even the most banal story exciting. She'd also forgotten his penchant for a final twist—with the rest of the crowd, she discovered that the baby was not a human child, but rather a monster born of a witch and a papist.

Clapping and laughing, even the poorest among them was soon coughing up a penny to bring the story home to share with their families. Others would just paste the woodcut on their walls, to have something to enjoy during the long winter nights that lay ahead.

Lucy hung back while Master Aubrey was collecting his pennies. When the crowd dispersed, she followed him into his shop. Inside, she breathed deeply, always surprised at how the whiff of the printing press gave her such pleasure.

Master Aubrey, returning to his press, glanced at her when she came in, but did not stop what he was doing. Fascinated, Lucy watched him unroll a sheet, lay it down, and then roll it over the inked typeset letters.

"What brings you to my shop, lass?" he finally barked out, not bothering to modulate his voice despite the cramped confines of the shop. Lucy wondered if the noise of the printing press had deafened him over the years. "Did the Hargraves send you again?" He was referring to another time when she'd come seeking important broadsides related to a murder, claiming that Adam had requested she do so.

"Er, no." Lucy paused, wondering how to proceed.

"Is there something you want to buy? Astrological predictions for love? Dr. Pumphrey's cures for warts?" When she shook her head, the printer added, not unkindly, "I can't have you reading all my tales for free, lass. You understand. Besides, I'm busy. Today was the first day the Stationer's Company allowed us to print—those of us printers who survived the Fire, that is."

Lucy took a deep breath. "I thought you'd need some help, Master Aubrey. Selling books, or even working here in the shop."

"Already got a lad. 'Sides, I thought you were working for the Hargraves."

Lucy didn't answer, and wandered over to the other press. It was open and it looked like the letters were waiting to be inked. Though backward, she could see they all related to the Fire. She read the titles: *An Elegie on the late Fire And Ruines of London,* by E. Settle. One by R. L'Estrange, called *An Anagram on the Citie London.* She read it out loud.

"The Citie *London* when I now behold it
In its true Anagram *Then I Condole it.*
But when't revives, whose Triumph shall transcend
Turning the Anagram, *Let Ioie contend.*"

Seeing her quizzical expression, Master Aubrey laughed. "Oh, that Roger L'Estrange, I despise him, but he is a witty one. See this line, 'Then I Condole it.' How about you find the letters for 'The Citie London.' That's the anagram. You get it?"

Lucy frowned, not wishing to admit she didn't quite understand. He pointed to another one. "Lass, try this one. 'London's Fatal Fal, an acrostic.' Here you can just read the letters down. L-O-N-D-O-N."

Lo! Now confused Heaps only stand
On what did bear the Glory of the Land.

No stately places, no Edefices,

Do now appear: No, here's now none of these,

Oh Cruel Fates! Can ye be so unkind?

Not to leave, scarce a Mansion behind . . .

Master Aubrey looked at the last page of his collection. Lucy could see a great white expanse without any text or picture. " 'Tis a shame to leave it blank. Just one or two more short pieces, is all we need."

Lucy only half heard him, murmuring the words of another poem.

One Merchant swears the Elements conspire

Rescu'd from Water to be wrackt by Fire.

Finding more mercy in the rageing Waves

Whose sinking billowes but present their Graves

Which here too true he finds: His Merchandise

In a confused Chaos buried lies.

She tapped it. "A 'confused chaos' is right," she said. "I was helping clear the debris yesterday and there was all manner of odd stuff popping up out of the ashes." Thinking of the poem that had miraculously survived the fire, Lucy pulled her copy from her pocket. "Perhaps you might be interested in this piece. It came from the Fire. You could say 'From the charred remains, here is a poem.'"

The master's apprentice walked in then. He was the same redheaded boy who had worked there long ago, although not so pimple-ridden as he'd once been. Even though he'd been a bit rude to her in the past, Lucy was glad to see he had survived the plague and the Fire.

Master Aubrey and the printer's devil read the poem. "Pomegranates, roses, pineapples . . . Makes no sense," the apprentice sniffed. She thought she remembered his name was Lachlin, or some such Scottish name.

Lucy frowned, but watched Master Aubrey count the lines of the poem. The master printer grinned. "Yes, it will work. Let's get to it, so we can make the next printing. See to it, Lach."

Lucy felt absurdly pleased, as if she had written the poem herself. "We could mention the body that was found nearby too."

Master Aubrey swiveled around, and Lachlin stared at her. "Body?" the printer asked. "Lass, have you lost your senses? What body?"

"Oh, yes. I suppose I forgot to mention that. When I was working, clearing away the ashes and rubble and such, someone found a body stuffed in a barrel."

"And you didn't think to mention that?"

"Well, no," Lucy stammered. "I didn't think—"

"Woman, poems don't make pennies, corpses do. Tell me, was he murdered?" Master Aubrey asked, looking hopeful.

"Had to have been, unless he hid in the barrel," Lachlin piped up. "Afraid of the Fire, he must have been."

Master Aubrey swatted the back of his printer's head. He looked heavenward. "Lord, what I must put up with."

Lucy answered the printer's question. "Verily, he was murdered. He had a knife through his chest."

"How'd I not hear about this? I've been cloistered in here like a damn nun." Aubrey rubbed his hands together. "Never mind!

Murdered, you say? All the better! Lucy, tell me all about it. I'll
write it, and we can set it tonight. Print in the morning."

Lucy smiled at him, as engagingly as she could. "How about I
write the tale myself? I could recount how we found the body,
and the poem. There was a fair assortment of bits and pieces too—a
ring, some coins." She paused. "Although, on second thought,
perhaps we shouldn't mention that part. I don't want to look like
I was looting. How about I give you the account for a price? Maybe
it's enough to waive my apprentice fee?"

"What?" For a moment the master printer seemed stunned.
"Waive your apprentice fee? Woman! Is your mind completely
addled? Or is this some sort of jest?" he asked, hopefully. "Did
your master put you up to this?"

"No, not at all," Lucy said quickly, with what she hoped was a
reassuring smile. "I should like to enter the printer's trade. I should
like to learn to make books as you do, and sell them."

Still, Master Aubrey stared at her, now at a loss for words.
Lucy rushed on. "I know I could do it, I know I could! I'm strong
and I work hard! I know my letters too."

Master Aubrey blinked under the full force of her smile. "Well,
what about Master Hargrave? I thought you were in his service."

"I am, I was—" Lucy stumbled. "I mean, I think he would
not mind. He has Cook and John and Annie, and three servants
are more than enough help. It is just him, and," she paused, "young
Master Hargrave. I think they will not take it amiss should I leave
them."

Master Aubrey scratched his head, considering her. "One True
Account will not cover the cost of an apprenticeship. Young Lachlin's father, well, he paid me twenty pounds three years ago to

teach this rascal my honorable trade. Meals, clothes, training. That's what the fee is. Twenty pounds. That's what the Stationer's Company established and I'm not going to lose my printer's license for a chit of a girl."

"Twenty pounds?" Lucy repeated, her heart sinking. She had nowhere near that amount. "I see."

He gave his apprentice a sidelong glance. "I could use another set of hands around here, though. Ever since my daughter off and got married, I haven't had anyone to put supper on," he admitted grudgingly. "That is, someone who doesn't always burn the porridge." Here he glared at Lach, whose face reddened slightly.

Lucy nodded, suddenly feeling more encouraged. She didn't dare to interrupt Master Aubrey as he spoke, more to himself than to her.

The printer went on, his tone still musing. "I *could* use a bit of help selling. And sometimes I have to buy more supplies from the paper-maker, and Lach can't very well run the press and sell at the same time."

Aubrey then turned back to Lucy. "Let me hear you sing." He handed her a ballad, a cockamamy tale of a lass cuckolding her sweetheart, an earnest potter, with a thief looking to steal everything from the home.

Lucy groaned. Of course, a bookseller's apprentice must be able to sing. She looked at the sheet. The ballad's author, R.A., had noted the words were to be sung to the tune of "Three Merry Maids at the Aylesbury Fair." A common enough tune.

She sang the first line in her regular alto, trying not to feel uncomfortable. Lach snorted, not helping her confidence any.

"You're not in St. Michael's, lass!" Master Aubrey exclaimed. "Sing so people can hear you!"

Lucy thought about how the soap-seller called her wares. She sang the lines again, this time so that it sounded more like a chant.

Master Aubrey grudgingly nodded. With the air of someone making a great decision, he said, "You'll not be an official apprentice, you understand? You won't be with me seven years. You'll be keeping the shop clean, cooking, doing a bit of selling, helping a bit with the presses. And I'm not sending your name to the Stationer's Company, you understand? You've not paid the apprentice fee."

Lucy nodded, her heart beginning to pound.

"I'd need you here at dawn every day."

"I can do that!" Lucy said, growing even more eager.

"That's a bit of a walk from the Hargraves'," Master Aubrey hesitated. "Unless you'd want to be letting a room here? You've got a brother, haven't you? I've got two rooms. You can have them for two shillings a week. My other tenants just left. Their whole family is going to Suffolk." He scratched his elbow. "Mind you, make your mind up quick. I've got many bodies clambering for the space."

"Two rooms? For my brother and myself?" Lucy quickly calculated her brother's take and the coins she'd saved from the Hargraves'. Now that her brother was a journeyman, surely he could make enough to keep them. She gave the printer a bright smile. "I'll take them both!"

As she was turning to go, Master Aubrey added, not unkindly, "Make sure that true account is good. If it don't sell, I won't keep you on."

After she completed her duties that evening, Lucy sat down in the little chamber she shared with Annie to write the true account.

For a long moment, she stared at the white piece of paper, unsure how to begin. She had written some penny pieces before, but had never dared submit them to be published. This piece, though, was important. She needed it to be good to sell a lot of sheets for Master Aubrey. After a few dozen scratched out beginnings, she sighed, feeling a little at a loss.

She'd already sent a quick note to Will to tell him her news, leaving out the part about her being a petticoat author. "He can find that out later." She hardly liked to think of what her brother would say about her apprenticing herself to Master Aubrey either, but he might be glad she was leaving service.

Leaving service. What a strange way to think about leaving the Hargraves' household. To leave Cook and John, and little Annie. To leave the magistrate, who had come to treat her as his own daughter. To leave Adam. She shook her head. "He'll understand," she whispered fiercely. "There's no place for me here. I have to leave." For a moment, tears blurred her eyes. "He'll understand. They all will."

She stared down at the paper again, looking at the scratched-out sentences. "The words are jumbled because I am jumbled," she muttered to herself, standing up. Picking up her candle, she made her way down to the master's study. Without giving much thought to her words, she knocked. When she heard the master's assent, she went in.

The magistrate was seated in his old wooden chair, a great leather-bound book in front of him. He was chewing on the end of his pipe, but Lucy could see it was not lit.

"Ah, Lucy," he said, his eyes brightening a bit. "What may I do for you, my dear?"

Taking a deep breath, she told him in a rush. "I talked to Master Aubrey today. He told me he would be glad to take me on as an apprentice. Well, not truly an apprentice since I do not have twenty pounds to pay the apprentice fee. But I'm hoping to learn the trade, and maybe in time, I will be able to pay the fee . . ." Her voice trailed off, seeing the sorrowful look on his face. "I'm sorry, sir, I did not think . . ." Her voice dropped off again, and she looked at him, misery tightening her stomach.

"Sit down, Lucy," he said, regaining his usual equanimity. "Tell me all about it."

After she explained more slowly, he nodded in his grave way. She was grateful that he did not press her to further explain her decision to leave his employ. He did ask her a few questions about her living and working arrangements though.

"You'll be staying at Master Aubrey's, then? Above his shop?" At her murmured assent, he went on. "I know Master Aubrey has a daughter, but she's long been married off. There's a lad there too, his apprentice. Is that correct?" There was no judgment in his look, but she could see a faint fatherly concern about her going off to live with two men.

"That is why I've asked my brother Will to live with me too."

That bit of information seemed to put him at ease, and he said, "Well, Master Aubrey is an honorable man, and I've known him a very long time. I imagine he would keep his apprentices behaving in a proper manner."

Thinking of the skinny redheaded Lachlin making advances on her, Lucy had to hide a smile.

The magistrate then had continued. "Lucy, so you know. You are always welcome here. You must understand that. If you don't get on at Aubrey's, or if my son—" Here he stopped, looking uncomfortable.

Lucy was glad he did not continue. She had a feeling he was about to say something about Adam. *Or if Adam doesn't marry you, you'll still have a home with us.* "Thank you, sir," she said, smiling with slightly misty eyes.

The magistrate wasn't done. "If you are determined to leave, I do have two small gifts for you. As tokens of my high regard." He cleared his throat.

Hesitantly, Lucy held out her hand, expecting a few shillings. It was customary for a master to reward his servants when they left service, if they had been loyal and trustworthy.

He shook his head. "For your wonderful service to my family these last few years, I have held ten pounds for you." He smiled when she gasped and drew her hand back to her side.

"Ten pounds! Oh no, sir, I couldn't take such a sum! It is too much."

"No, it is not nearly enough. Call it a dowry if you like, or perhaps a way to begin a living. Perhaps you will wish to pursue the apprenticeship with Master Aubrey in earnest. Printing is a noble profession, to be sure. How about I hold it for you, for a while, until you are ready. I should not like you to carry such a sum upon your person."

"No, sir, no indeed, sir. Thank you, sir," she said, her words stumbling over themselves as she tried to express her heartfelt gratitude. Ten pounds would set her up in trade or, as he said, certainly set her up with a comfortable dowry. Tears pricked at her eyes, as she regarded the magistrate in awe.

He patted her hand. "It's alright, Lucy, I understand." He

smiled again, this time more sadly. "I have something else for you as well." He seemed more reluctant. "My wife's clothes, I'd like you to have them. Perhaps save a dress or two for Annie, now that she's older."

Lucy's eyes widened. His late wife, the Mistress Hargrave, had exquisite taste in clothes. Such a bequest! She'd look very fine for sure. Her thoughts flew to Sarah, the magistrate's daughter. Hesitantly, she asked, "Shouldn't Sarah inherit her mother's clothes?"

A shadow passed the magistrate's face and in that glimpse, she could see that he had not forgiven his daughter for joining the Quakers. For disobeying the law. For leaving England. For disobeying him. "Quakers do not wear fine linens or taffeta," he said stiffly. "I'll not have her selling them to promote their *cause.*"

"Thank you, sir," she said hastily, vowing, in that instant, to never take her mistress's clothes. "I'll collect them another time."

At the door she smiled again at Master Hargrave, but could not speak. He nodded and bid her good night.

Standing at Master Aubrey's shop the next morning, Lucy watched as the printer and his apprentice laid out a great shallow wooden box and set it on the large table between them. The box was sectioned into a hundred different compartments, with each compartment containing an assortment of tiny metal blocks.

"This is the typecase," the printer explained. "This box contains the font we are going to use for this folio. We are only setting eight pages, so it should not take very long." The printer gestured toward a tray. "Pick any letter out, look at it. Ah, do you know what that is?"

Curiously, Lucy looked at the tiny metal piece she had se-lected at random. It did not seem to be a letter at all. "I don't know the word for it. I know it means 'and.'"

"That is an ampersand. There are several others too, like these," he gestured to the bottom row, "which I mainly use for texts in Latin." He went on. "You'll see that I have already set the title, using roman type, thirty-six point. I put spacers, these blank ones here, between every word, with two spacers between each sentence."

To her surprise and delight, she read the title. *The London Mis-cellany.* Underneath, in slightly smaller text, she read *From the Charred Remains, a Body found among the Flames.* He had moved the other pieces so this would be the first story seen. He was will-ing to believe, sight-unseen it seemed, that her true account would be good enough to print.

Then a shiver of fear and excitement wafted over her when he held out his hand. "Let me see the true account now."

Nervously, she watched the printer read her words. From time to time he grunted, but didn't say anything out loud. Finally he gave her a gruff nod. "A little long, but we can work with it."

Lach scowled. Clearly the apprentice was none too happy that his master had taken someone new on. Lucy wanted to say some-thing about how pleased and honored she felt, but the printer held up his hand. "That's enough, Lucy," he said. "I'm a busy man and we need to get this finished. So I beg you to pay attention and be silent. The quicker you will learn."

He turned the pamphlet over, half explaining, half thinking out loud. "Here, I've added the poem, discovered with the body, on the last page." He continued, "The first letter of every paragraph will begin with a larger size. For words we wish to emphasize, we will use italics. This will be in twelve-point roman. Like so."

He proceeded to rapidly lay the text into a small box he held in his left hand. "Notice that I am putting the letters in—"

"Backward!" Lucy interrupted.

Master Aubrey beamed at her. "Quite right," he said, cuffing Lach lightly on the ears. "Took this one a while to get that straight. Just lay them in each row, keeping your thumb below. This will keep them in place until you fill in with larger spacers. The side that will be inked is called the 'face.' Now, Lucy, go ahead and read your account. I'll put it in as you speak, and Lach will work on the back page with the poem."

Watching their practiced hands fly, placing the tiny letters into the wood blocks, Lucy was amazed. Although she still felt a hard lump in her throat from her conversation with Master Hargrave the night before, the excitement of seeing her words built line by line was pushing her sadness aside.

For the next few hours, they worked steadily. From time to time, the printer would shake his head. "No, that won't work," he'd say. "That line needs to be shorter." Once he stopped and stared at her. "I can little believe you wrote these words." But mostly she would read each word and he would build it into place without speaking.

Lucy's throat was parched and dry, but she did not dare ask Master Aubrey for a break. The printer seemed excited, as if he couldn't wait to finish the piece and sell it. Like the printer, Lach never let his fingers stop moving, setting part of the middle document, although from time to time he directed a baleful glance toward Lucy. She supposed that they usually stopped when necessity called.

The *Miscellany* was quite long now, but no matter. At last, they were done setting the type. Master Aubrey let Lach run out back to piss in a pot by the door, and began to dab black ink onto the letters himself with a soft leather pad.

When his apprentice returned, together they placed the paper onto the typeface and lowered the lid while Lucy watched. Pushing a great lever back and forth, the two men finally stopped. With great excitement, Lucy watched them open up the press. There was the first page. "From the Charred Remains," and a woodcut of the Great Fire. The woodcut had already been used in the L'Estrange piece. As she had learned a year ago, it was common for printers to use the same images repeatedly, once they had asked an artist to carve the block. Reusing the pieces saved both money and time.

After a quick lunch of bread, cheese, and mead, the three continued. They finished the four sheets and hung them to dry. By early afternoon, they had cut and folded the first few. They were ready to sell.

Master Aubrey stepped outside of his shop with Lucy and Lach following, the latter scowling. The printer began his customary call. "A murder! A true and most terrible account of a barbarous murder committed before the Great Fire. From the Charred Remains, his corpse emerged from a malt barrel."

Within a few minutes, a crowd had gathered eagerly. Remembering what Master Aubrey had said about the presses being delayed by the King, many townspeople, milling toward the market, seemed eager for a new story. And as Master Aubrey liked to say, "Everyone loves a good murder."

After they'd read it once, the crowd was clearly growing. Those toward the back clamored for the story to be read again.

Lucy was quite surprised, though, when the printer put his arm around her shoulders and proclaimed to the crowd, "This fair lass here was the one who did find the body. A foreigner from a far-off land! Found with a poem, now printed on the back sheet."

People oohed and ahhed, eyeing her curiously. Londoners' natural cheerful morbidity began to show. "Tell us, lass, was he truly stuffed in a barrel? A knife through his chest?" one called out.

Lucy nodded.

"Was there a lot of blood?" another asked.

"Of course there was, you idiot," another crossly answered. "What, think you that a knife in the chest there won't be a lot of blood?"

The crowd murmured about this. "Let's hear the poem!" someone called.

Master Aubrey straightened up, and with a great booming voice, read the poem. The crowd shuffled back and forth. Not quite the doggerel they were used to, but some nodded approvingly. Master Aubrey then recounted the story of how the man was found stuffed in the barrel.

"Say, that's an interesting tale to be sure," another man called out, moving forward. He handed Lucy a penny for the collection, and put the pamphlet in his cloak. "Who was this poor sot, do you know?"

"Why, I have no idea," Lucy said.

"Where was this body found, exactly?" the man persisted.

"As likely as not," Lucy said, "the constable thinks it must have been near the Cheshire Cheese. You remember the tavern. He's sent word to the tavern owner, but I don't know if he heard back from him. If he even will. A lot of people don't seem to have returned yet." She saw a few people nodding.

"Where did you get the poems from?" another woman asked, her hands on her cheeks. She looked to be about Lucy's age, or a little older. A gentlewoman, likely enough. If Lucy didn't know better, she would have thought the woman was nervous.

Master Aubrey shrugged. "Oh, well, authors send them to me. Their names are on them, of course. Roger L'Estrange writes a lot for us, of course. Sometimes we get anonymous pieces, slipped through a slot in the door. Don't always use those tales, of course. No telling from whence they came. I like to know who I'm getting in bed with."

"Except for the one Lucy found, in the leather bag. The funny love poem," Lachlin said. "All kinds of odd stuff in that bag, isn't that so, Lucy?"

"I suppose," Lucy said, giving Lach a hard look. She didn't want to give out any details, to keep thieves from trying to claim the more valuable items.

"Alright, enough of that," Master Aubrey said. "I'm sorry, ladies and gents, it's time for us to get back to work." On the way back in, he said to Lucy, "Nice job, lass. Why don't you head over to the Golden Lion. Or maybe the Bell." He rubbed his hands together. "We'll see how murder fares there."

·3·

Her pack now full of pamphlets and broadsides, Lucy headed down Fleet toward the Strand. Master Aubrey had told her that she wouldn't miss the Golden Lion, housed as it was in the midst of some elegant noblemen's homes. As she walked, she looked about curiously. One of the more refined areas of London, with very few shops, it was certainly not a place she'd visited very often.

Thankfully, she spied the tavern and started toward it. Filling her pewter cup with water from a nearby well, she watched a few men and women walk into the tavern with a picture of a lion above the door. No time to lose. Lucy quickly relieved her parched throat, and scurried over to the tavern, positioning herself just left of the hanging sign.

She found her heart was beating quickly. Taking a deep breath, Lucy read the title of the pamphlet that she had helped Master Aubrey put together. "From the Charred Remains," she croaked.

"A London miscellany of warnings, poems, and astrological predictions." A few curious looks from passersby, but no one stopped to listen. This was much harder than she had thought it would be. Setting down her pack, she hopped atop the low stone wall in front of the inn and called again. "A most unnatural death!" Ah! Good. A few passersby stopped this time. "A body found in a barrel, a knife through his heart," she half-sang, half-shouted through cupped hands, "his corpse having survived the fiery inferno that did engulf London this September 1666."

Within the hour, Lucy had sold most of the pamphlets. As Master Aubrey had warned her to do, she slipped the coins out of sight to lessen the attention of pickpockets. Her feet were aching from standing on the hard stone walk for so long, and her throat, still scratchy from inhaling the smoke at the Fire site, was feeling worse. Sipping water from her little cup did not seem to help. Grimacing, she decided to go inside, which appeared decent enough. She took an unoccupied table, in the corner, but still toward the front of the establishment, where respectable ladies might be found.

Lucy ordered some warm mead from the tavern keeper, thinking the honey would soothe her throat. As she waited, she slipped her feet from her pointed leather shoes to rub some life back into them. A moment later a serving lass banged a steaming mug of mead down in front of her, not bothering to wipe up the drops that spilled out. Gratefully, she took a sip. Nearby, some men were pulling apart a bit of roasted pig; the smell of pork and apples made her think of Master Hargrave, as that was one of his favorite dishes. Sighing, she hoped it would not be folly to leave the comforts and security of the magistrate's home. Feeling quite sorry for herself, she closed her eyes.

"Excuse me." Someone touched her arm.

Lucy's eyes flew open. A woman, just slightly older than herself, was standing at her table, a worried expression on her face. She looked familiar, but Lucy couldn't place her. She looked to the woman's clothes for some indication of her station and rank. She wasn't the tavern maid, that was certain. Her kirtle was a soft gray taffeta, unstained, but slightly dusty as if she'd been traveling.

Finishing the last sip of her pint, Lucy stood up, dropping a slight curtsy. "Yes, miss? What can I do for you?"

"I should like to purchase the *London Miscellany*," the woman said, her clipped, slightly haughty words confirming her gentlewoman's status. She thrust out a coin. "Now, if you please."

Lucy looked around. She saw the innkeeper direct her a warning glance. Master Aubrey had given her strict instructions. "No hawking inside. No one wants to share their customers' coins."

Lucy pushed out one of the wooden chairs at her table. "I'll sell it to you if you sit and have a pint."

"I don't want a pint."

"At least sit down. Please, miss. The owner will throw me on out on my arse—pardon!—if he thinks I'm hawking inside his shop."

"Oh, I see." Looking about, the woman sat down. She slid over a coin, which Lucy quickly palmed before pushing the Fire poem across the table. The innkeeper started over, a baleful look on his face.

Lucy smiled pleasantly up at him. "Some mead for my companion if you please, sir." She glanced at the woman, who was staring at the first page of the pamphlet, and made no attempt to pay for her own drink. Reluctantly Lucy handed the innkeeper a coin, mentally counting what she had left. She prayed that he would not expect her to buy another drink for herself, for she could not spare any more.

Thankfully, the barman nodded, satisfied. "Hannah!" he called gruffly to the serving maid. "Another mead here!" He even took the dingy towel hanging from his waste to wipe away the little pool of liquid that had spilled on the table, before moving off.

Now, the woman had begun to anxiously page through the *Miscellany*. At the pamphlet's last page, the woman's face grew pale; indeed, she looked quite ill. Belatedly, Lucy wondered if the woman had taken sick. She edged back in her chair, lest the woman should sneeze upon her. She cursed herself for not carrying a posy that might ward off the sickly vapors. Although the physician Larimer had declared London well-rid of the plague, the ague and other deathly maladies never truly went away.

To Lucy's dismay, the woman's eyes had filled with tears. "You said this poem was found with the body?" she whispered, pointing at the woodcut on the front. Lucy could barely hear her over the din of the inn.

Lucy nodded. "I saw him myself. Poor sod. He was killed through and through with a knife. Before the Great Fire. A wonder his body survived, and that's a fact."

The woman's shoulders slumped. "Thank you." She stood, turning quickly on her heel. Before Lucy could say anything more, the woman turned and walked unsteadily out of the tavern.

Without thinking, Lucy raced after the woman, who had gotten a few paces down the street. "Miss! Wait!" Lunging forward, she grasped the woman's arm. Something was clearly amiss. "Pray, you are not well. Let us sit back down. Have your drink."

Lucy led the woman back into the Golden Lion, almost as one

might lead a child. The serving maid, Hannah, was standing by the table they had just vacated, looking bemusedly at the steaming tankard in her hands. "Oh, you came back," she said. "I was about to dump this back in the kettle."

The woman still looked dazed, and a bit teary, but seemed to revive slightly when she placed her hands around the warm tankard.

"Drink," Lucy urged. She wondered if the woman's wits might be addled, given her odd countenance. Then she recalled the woman's clear and elegant speech. Distraught as the woman might be, she did not seem touched.

The woman dutifully took a sip, breathing in the fragrant liquid. Lucy took the moment to study her. Looking to be in her late twenties, the woman had dark circles under her eyes that added to her years. Her mouth was pinched and drawn, her dark brown hair pulled in a practiced way under her soft blue cap. Again, Lucy was struck by her pallor. She scrambled for something to say. "I'm Lucy Campion."

The woman looked up from the woodcut. "Thank you." She hesitated. "I'm Rhonda."

"Do I know you, Miss—?" Lucy asked, noticing the woman had not provided her last name. Clearly she did not want to be too familiar, and yet even servants did not introduce themselves with just their first name. Truth be told, only ladybirds and doxies kept their last names to themselves, and that was only to keep from further shaming their fathers and brothers. Or so Lucy had been told. She did not have any prostitutes among her own acquaintance.

The woman seemed to realize this at the same time. "Rivers. Miss Rivers." The way she hesitated made Lucy suspect that was not her real last name. "No, we've never met." "Miss Rivers" took another sip of the hot liquid. The sustenance seemed to calm her, as it had Lucy a half hour before when she first sat down in the tavern.

"How did you know I was," Lucy paused, "a bookseller?" For a moment, she forgot the woman's obvious turmoil, savoring the ease with which she had proclaimed her new identity. Bookseller! Then her natural curiosity resurfaced. "Did you see me selling the miscellany outside? I did not see you, though." She searched the woman's face. Something about the woman's sad eyes prompted her memory. "You heard Master Aubrey tell the story, back at his shop!" she said, snapping her fingers. "I remember you now."

"Yes, I was there. I'd been to the market with my father, hoping to bring some provisions to some of my father's acquaintances who'd been put out by the Fire," Miss Rivers admitted. "I heard the printer say you would be selling them at the Golden Lion on the Strand. I needed to read the pamphlet myself. So I followed you."

"Then why didn't you buy the pamphlet there? Save yourself the trouble?" Lucy asked. Miss Rivers looked to be a woman of means; it was unlikely she had not possessed sufficient coin. Truly, the woman's actions made no sense.

"I can see you are wondering at me." Miss Rivers's chin trembled. "I didn't want to believe it. Then I found I could not bear not knowing."

"I'm sorry," Lucy said, clasping her hands at the table. "I don't know what came over me. I know I do not always heed my tongue as I ought. You do not owe me any explanations. Truth be told, you seemed so distraught."

Miss Rivers looked down at her tankard, which was still about half full.

Lucy continued her stilted amends. "The Fire, you must have lost—" That didn't sound right, so she tried again. "The body, I mean, the man who was murdered—" Seeing Miss Rivers's face blanch, she stopped again. After a moment, Lucy settled on the most tactful question she could muster. "Did you lose someone in the Great Fire?"

Miss Rivers spoke, her tone flat and colorless. "Yes, I'm most certain I did. My great love. He came for me. Now he's dead!"

Lucy shook her head. "I'm sorry. I don't understand. How can you know he was the one who died? I mean, no one knows who the body could have been," she stumbled again. "I mean, who the man was, not even the constable."

"I know," Miss Rivers declared, with the same chilling certainty. She pointed to the poem that Sid had found in the wooden barrel. "He wrote that poem. For me." Despair rising in her voice, she repeated again, "He's dead! I know it!"

"How could you possibly know that?" Lucy asked, hoping to stave off the woman's growing agitation. "It just says 'Dear Hart.' Surely, that could be for anyone. And the poem is unsigned. Aren't poems signed? Even if just with 'Anonymous'?"

Miss Rivers smiled, a sad pitiful smile. "I know you mean well. But I can prove the poem was intended for me." She smoothed out the woodcut. "See, it's an acrostic."

Like the London Fire poem, Lucy realized. She watched as Miss Rivers put a delicate finger on the first letter of each line.

Now, Dear Hart—
As the poet says, come to the garden in spring. There's wine and
sweethearts in the pomegranate blossoms.

Remember!
If you do not come, these do
Not matter.

If you do come, these do not matter.

My rose will bloom, among the
Hearty pineapples,
even in the first freeze of autumn.
Rose, my love—
Even kings can wrong a fey duet.

"N-A-S-R-I-N-I-M-H-E-R-E," Lucy spelled out loud. "I still don't get it."

" 'Nasrin, I'm here.' That's what it says. He was speaking to me." Seeing Lucy's puzzled look, Miss Rivers continued in a more hushed tone. "My name *is* Nasrin, in Persian. You see, my name, 'Rhonda,' actually means 'wild rose' in Welsh. My parents' tribute to my Welsh lineage, I suppose. When I told my sweetheart that, he wanted to give me a special name, which also meant wild rose, which only he and I would know."

"Nasrin?" Lucy tasted the name. "How did he come up with that, I wonder."

Miss Rivers smiled slightly, her voice thick with tears. "You see, my sweetheart he is—was—Persian, from the land of the Shah." She shook her head. "He must have traveled here. 'Nasrin, I'm here.' " She dabbed at her eyes. "He must have been hoping to surprise me. Now he's gone!"

"Yes, it would seem so," Lucy said, chewing on her lower lip.

"However, the poem was only published by mistake—because I had asked Master Aubrey to include it in the *London Miscellany*. Why didn't he just tell you he was here? Why did he need to inform you by poem?"

Miss Rivers was silent for a moment. When she spoke, it was with the air of someone seeking to share a heavy burden. "My father would never allow him to see me, I'm afraid. Certainly, he would not let me be courted," she said. "I met Darius, you see, in the court of the Persian shah. My father, an Oxford scholar, wanted me along because of my expertise with languages. Not that he would admit to that completely, of course." She took a sip. Revived, she continued. "Even though we lived graciously, my father could never quite view the Persians as his equals. I am ashamed to say it. He was keen enough to study their culture and their literature, but become connected by blood? This he could not do." Her voice shook a bit. "We had traveled to Persia with another of my father's colleagues from Denmark. I think my father may have hoped the Danish gentlemen would become smitten with me, or I of him, to keep that valuable connection close to our family."

Lucy grimaced. She knew well of the expectations that gentry had about marriage. They married for property and connections, usually giving little thought to love and friendship.

Miss Rivers continued. "Instead, I met Darius, one of the translators at court. We fell deeply, madly in love. From him, I learned about life, love, and the poetry of the great mystics." She gulped. "We often wrote poems to each other. My sweet Darius must have intended to send this poem to me. To let me know he was here."

"So he wanted you to know he was here in London," Lucy said gently. "Yet he doesn't say where he is, or how to meet him." She paused. "Or does he?"

Miss Rivers studied the poem again. "I'm not entirely sure. In the first part, Darius is referring to the words of Rumi, an ancient poet. This passage was one I loved most deeply. When I heard the poem read, I just knew he had written it." Closing her eyes again, the woman recited, " *'Come to the garden in spring. There's wine and sweethearts in the pomegranate blossoms. If you do not come, these do not matter. If you do come, these do not matter.'* " She smiled at the distant memory, perhaps remembering her love-drenched days in a garden with Darius.

"You did not say the word 'remember,' " Lucy noted, dragging Miss Rivers from her reverie, having followed the words written on the paper with her index finger. "That's what Darius wrote in the poem."

"No, I supposed Darius must have added the word to make sure my name was easily spelled in the acrostic."

"Was this second part also written by this poet, what did you say his name was, Rumi?"

Miss Rivers frowned. "I don't know. It doesn't sound familiar." Musing, she read the last line of the poem again. *"Even kings can wrong a fey duet.* I wonder."

"Wronged by a king." Lucy repeated. "You said 'land of the Shah' before. Is the Shah a king? That's what he must have meant, don't you think? And a 'fey duet.' That must be you and him. Rather sweet, truly." Though she tried to sound comforting, Lucy could not help but blink away tears thinking of poor Darius spilling out of the barrel, knife through his chest. Perhaps he had come to London to challenge Miss Rivers's father and seek her hand in marriage, only to wind up murdered in an old seedy tavern. She looked away.

"Yes, you must be right," Miss Rivers said, but she didn't seem convinced. Lucy was thankful when she passed Lucy a coin for the mead. She pressed Lucy's hand. "Lucy. Dear. Thank you."

Lucy found herself unexpectedly drawn to this dignified and sad young woman. "I think you should tell the constable about," she hesitated, "your young man. Darius." Seeing Miss Rivers's mouth turn down in protest, she added, "Constable Duncan does not know who this man is. The law should be apprised."

"Lucy, I can see you mean well, but talking to the constable will not bring my Darius back. Nothing will bring him back to me."

"Surely you would want his murderer brought to justice?!" Lucy said. To think otherwise was too painful. She herself had spent more than two years trying to bring a monster—the murderer of her most dear friend—to justice.

"I cannot explain. Pray, do not press me any further." With one final sob, Miss Rivers fled from the Golden Lion. This time Lucy made no attempt to follow her, stunned and saddened by what she had just learned. It wasn't until much later, when it was far too late, that Lucy realized she had not asked Miss Rivers about the other items in the leather bag.

·4·

His name was Darius," Lucy said. Duncan looked up from a stack of papers, squinting at her in the bold streaming light of the setting sun. In the hours since she had last been on Fleet Street, the constable had made a sort of makeshift jail near the site of the Cheshire Cheese. It looked to have once been a candle-maker's shop. She remembered now a chandler had worked there but had succumbed to the plague or the ague, or some other such malady rampant in London before the Fire. Evidently, the City had appropriated the shop as one of the many jails temporarily designed to hold criminals while they figured out what to do without Newgate or Fleet Prison. She could see they had lost no time, however, in putting up bars across one side of the old work-room, to lock up the riff-raff and other nefarious sorts that the constable wanted off the street.

"What?" Duncan asked.

"Darius," Lucy repeated. "The dead man. In the Fire. His name was Darius. He was Persian."

The constable stared at her. "How on earth do you know that? Lucy, tell me you haven't been doing something foolish!"

Quickly, she related her encounter with Miss Rivers.

"Although I don't believe that's her real name," she added. Then she showed him how the acrostic spelled the woman's name. "Nasrin."

Duncan gave a low whistle. "I would never have seen that." He read the poem again. "Persian," he mused. "That makes sense, actually. Dr. Larimer thought the victim's features looked like those of a man from the Near East. He thought he might have been Arabic."

Lucy nodded. "Part of the poem, Miss Rivers said, was also written by a poet they both enjoyed. She thought it was a bit of a message for her. Rumi, I think she said his name was."

"I'm not familiar with that verse-maker," Duncan admitted. "Well, truth be told, I only know the Bard and Marlowe. But Miss Rivers didn't think the second part was from this Rumi fellow?"

"No, she seemed confused by the poem. If there was a message there, she didn't know what it was."

"Let's think about this for a moment." Duncan paused before rereading the first part. '*Come to the garden in spring. There's wine and sweethearts in the pomegranate blossoms. Remember, if you do not come, these do not matter. If you do come, these do not matter.*'"

"It sounds to me like he's inviting her to meet him. In a beautiful garden. If she doesn't come, she won't see the beauty of the garden, and neither will he, since he will miss her. If she does come—"

"He will revel in her beauty, and hers alone," Duncan finished. "No mere flowers will be able to compare, when she is beside him. A lucky man that." Lucy looked at him in surprise. He looked lost in thought, as if thinking of someone far away. Then, he caught himself. "Well then," he added brusquely, "a shame the poor fool is dead. He had a romantic soul."

"His name was Darius," Lucy reminded him.

"So you say." Duncan sucked in his cheeks. "Well, did you ask her about any of the other things in the bag? Whether they meant anything to her?"

Lucy felt her moment of triumph rapidly deflate. "No," she said, hating to disappoint him.

"Ah, no matter that. I should, of course, like to be able to inform his family, but no one else has come forward. If they're all in Persia, 'tis hardly likely we will locate his relations."

"We could look up the coat of arms on the ring, don't you think?" Lucy asked. "Darius may have been connected with that family?"

"I doubt it," Duncan answered. "I'd wager that's an English family emblem."

For a moment, Lucy looked out the window, watching the men dump buckets of ashes into the waiting carts. Just then a strong breeze came by, causing the top layer to swirl about the air and choke the men standing nearby. Sometimes she wondered if the ashes would ever be gone, whether the ever-present filmy grime could ever be lifted. When some ashes blew inside, Duncan shuttered the window, making the room seem much darker.

Coughing a bit, Lucy turned back to the constable. "I know

we do not know Darius's last name. However, there cannot be so
many scholars at Oxford who study the Persian language. His
name could be Rivers, but all we know for sure is that his daughter's name is Rhonda. Perhaps we could learn who Darius was if
we could identify the scholar. I could ask the magistrate?"

But Duncan was not listening, hearing a clamor at the door of
the jail. A bellman popped his head around, tipping his cap. He
may have been twice Duncan's age. Once again, Lucy noticed the
respect the constable had garnered in his men.

"Begging your pardon, sir," the bellman said. "There's a doxy,
er, a woman outside, demanding to see you, sir. Says you've got
something of hers. From the Fire."

"This is why we need the Fire Courts in place! I can't look into
all these claims!" He half-rose in his chair. "Hey! What do you
think you are doing?"

The woman had burst in, pushing past the bellman as he attempted to block her.

"Alright, Hank. It's all right." He turned to the woman, taking in her wild red hair. "Woman! What do you want?" Duncan
asked. Unlike his bellman, who could not keep his eyes from the
woman's rather ample bosom, the constable directed his gaze toward the woman's face.

To Lucy's surprise, the woman pulled out the *London Miscellany* and pointed to the very poem they had just been discussing.
"This! This is what I'm here about!"

Duncan's eyes widened slightly, but he did not otherwise be-
tray his surprise. He did, however, smile at the woman. He had
quite a friendly grin, when he wanted. "Sit down." He pulled a
bench toward her. Lucy moved to go, and without looking at her

he said, "No, Lucy. Why don't you stay?" Turning back to the woman he said, "Now first things first, my dear. What is your name and occupation?"

"Tilly Baker, since the day I was born and until the day I marry," Tilly simpered, warming under Duncan's attentions. "Although I'm still quite young, so that day's likely some time off. Not that I don't have my fair share of suitors, don't I?" She looked at Lucy then, as if daring to be contradicted. Since Tilly was well into her thirties, a spinster now, Lucy doubted this statement. "You can call me 'Tilly,'" she said, fluttering her eyelashes.

"Thank you," Duncan said. He took out some paper, and began to sharpen his quill, with careful deliberate strokes of his knife. "Tilly, you must have them dancing on a stick. Tell me, my dear, where do you live and work?"

"The Fox and Duck. Over in Smithfield. Before that wretched man set fire to London, I was tavern maid at the Cheshire Cheese, wasn't I?" Tilly had a funny way of ending her statements with questions. "I had a room there, just above the tavern. Didn't I just?"

Lucy found herself leaning forward. That's where the body had been found.

Tilly's face darkened. "Now I've nary a coin to speak of, my fortune and dowry all burned up." Having arrived at the heart of the matter, her fawning manner ceased. "That's why I've come. To get what's mine."

Duncan's smile remained friendly, but his eyes narrowed. "What, pray tell, Tilly, would that be?"

"A small leather bag, full of belongings valuable only to myself, I can assure you. I know that you have it. I heard her"—she bobbed her head at Lucy—"say so. And I can see my poem has been printed too. I aim to get my fair share for that, don't I?"

"*You* wrote the poem?" Lucy asked, trying to hide the disbelief that threatened to creep into her voice.

"Nah, I didn't say I wrote it now, did I? 'Dear heart,' it says, right? That's from one of my suitors. I put it in a bit of oilskin and silk for safekeeping. And my brooch in the wool. And my coins. And my ring." Reading their exchange of glances correctly, Tilly added, "You didn't think I'd know what was in the bag, did you?"

Duncan was silent a moment. He appeared to be thinking. Lucy waited for him to tell Tilly that knowing the contents of the bag did not mean she was the bag's owner. Instead, his reply was mild. "Yes, of course. It sounds like it must be your bag." Duncan said. "Perhaps you'd care to explain first how your bag came to be found with the body of a murdered man?" Tilly opened her mouth, and then promptly shut it. Duncan continued. "Because I can't think of many good honest reasons why the belongings of one person might be found on the corpse of another? I'm sure my bellman can't. I wonder how the magistrate would look up such evidence. It doesn't look good, hey, Lucy?"

Lucy solemnly shook her head.

Tilly began to look afraid. "Whatcher mean? I ain't have nothing to do with no murder! I don't know nothing about no dead man, do I?"

"Well, let us start from the beginning, shall we?" Duncan soothed her. "Tell me what you know about this bag and the contents."

Somewhat mollified, Tilly sniffed. "I saw the bag during the card game. Someone read the poem out loud. That's when I heard it. That's all I know." She stood up. "I'll be off now."

"Hold on a moment, Tilly." The constable's voice was mild, but firm. "I need to understand this. So, there was a game of cards being played at the Cheshire Cheese?"

Tilly rolled her eyes. "Yeah. The night of the Fire. A few hours before the bells."

"September first," Duncan said, scratching something down on the paper. "So you were serving ale, I take it? Not playing? And a few people, what—three, four, five?—were playing cards at the table?"

" 'Twas four or five, though I'm not sure if they were all playing. A few others just drinking their pints, weren't they?"

"The items that were in the bag were—what?—the winnings?" Duncan asked. He furrowed his brow. "Someone wagered a poem? That doesn't make sense."

"They were playing for what was in their pockets. The poem was wrapped up. Later, one of them opened it up and read it." Tilly explained as if to a dullard.

"Can you tell us anything about these men?" he asked. "Did you know them?"

Tilly considered for a moment. "One didn't speak English right. He was a foreigner." Tilly hesitated. "Probably a bloody papist, wasn't he?"

"Foreigner?" Lucy glanced at the constable. "Did he have darker skin, and black curling hair?" At Tilly's muttered assent, she went on. "Could he have been Persian, do you think?"

"From Perton?" Tilly shrugged her shoulders. "I dunno about that. Staffordshire's a while away, isn't it? I got a niece who works at the manor there."

"No, she meant *Persian*," Duncan clarified. Seeing Tilly's uncomprehending look, he tried again. "From the East?"

Tilly yawned. "Now how would I be knowing that? He looked Italian-like, but not too, you know what I mean. I just heard him say that where he came from, the game was an-*nas*. Nasty, I say." She chuckled at her own joke. "Bloody foreigners. Not taking to our English ways. What do they expect? No wonder he got himself killed."

"How did you know he was the one who had been killed? This foreigner?" Duncan countered. "I thought you didn't know about 'no dead man.'"

Tilly shrugged again. "I just guessed. That's all." She rushed on. "I don't know who killed him now, do I?"

"Tilly, this is important," Lucy looked sideways toward the constable. He shrugged slightly, which she took to mean he didn't mind her asking the woman questions. "You must know something; you just don't realize what you know. Who called him a 'bloody papist'?"

"Don't remember," Tilly said sullenly. Lucy wasn't sure if she believed her.

"Well, you were right about which man was killed. How did you know that?" Lucy pressed. "Did you hear something?"

Tilly shook her head. "No, I figured it out. He was the only gent I didn't see later. You know, when we were all mad to get out when the church bells started ringing fire." For a moment her face took on that same dull glazed look common to those who'd suffered through the blaze. "Dreadful that was. I lost everything, except for a few meager belongings I could carry on my back."

"Did you know any of the other men at the table?" Lucy persisted. She had the feeling that Tilly knew more than she was saying, although she could not tell if the barmaid was withholding information on purpose or not. "Were they all strangers?"

"Just Jack. I know him a bit." Seeing Duncan's waiting expression, she went on reluctantly. "He's just an old card sharp. He's the one who set up the game. The barkeep, Fisher, he wasn't there. I had to do all the fetching and serving, didn't I just? All for a meager bit of shillings. How fair is that, I ask you?" She looked under her eyelashes up at the constable.

"Where is Fisher, do you know?" the constable asked.

"Nah. Last I heard, he beat if off to a dock and jumped a ship there. Haven't heard nothing more. Headed to the New World, for all I know. Would be like him, wouldn't it just?"

"What about the others?" Lucy asked, refusing to let Tilly lead them off their line of questioning.

"The others, I didn't know. We used to get all sorts at the Cheese."

Tilly pursed her lips, a coy look on her face. Duncan raised an eyebrow. "Is there anything else you can tell us, Tilly? About Jack?"

"For a few coins?" the barmaid asked, looking hopeful. "Help get me back on my feet?"

Duncan gave her a stern look. "Maybe I won't have my bellman lock you up. Or shall I let you rot alongside all the other murderers and cutthroats?"

"Hey!" Tilly cried, her shrill tone grating on Lucy's ears. "Hey now. I'm willing to cooperate, ain't I?"

Duncan leaned in toward her. "I'd be ever so grateful for your help, Tilly," he said, smoothly changing his tack. He moved his hand near Tilly's where it rested on the wooden table.

Under the constable's attention, Tilly's tongue loosened. "The other gent was beside himself when Jack won the poem, and read it out loud. Said it was not meant for public ears. That leather pouch was the last thing he had to his name, he said. Especially since none of them would let him put in his shirt or coat." She touched Duncan's sleeve. "Jack said we could all use a bit of love in our souls, and that's why he read it as payment. The foreign gent was quite upset, I tell you."

"Do you think this man, Jack, killed him?" Duncan asked, edging ever so slightly away. Tilly did not seem to notice.

"Oh no! Jack is a cad, and a bit of rogue, but is not the likes to kill! Plus, why would he? He was the one winning everything!"

"Then how did the bag end up with the dead body? He must have been the last to see the man alive!" Lucy pointed out.

"No, no! It wasn't Jack!" Tilly exclaimed again.

Lucy and the constable exchanged a glance, hearing the real feeling in her voice. "Sounds like you know Jack pretty well after all," he commented blandly. "Do you, perchance, know his surname?"

"His last name?" Tilly frowned, scratching at the inside of her bodice. "Durand."

Lucy leaned forward. "What about the other men? What did they look like?"

"I don't know," Tilly said, shifting her weight from side to side. "Truly. I don't remember anymore. My ma taught me a long time ago not to look too much at faces. 'The devil don't like to be looked at, Tilly,' she used to say, and I reckon she was right." She knocked her knuckles on the wood table impatiently. "Good Lord, there's little else I can tell you. The game went on for some time. A few hands passed. The stakes got higher. The men were digging through their pockets, for anything they had. All desperate to win." A funny look crossed the barmaid's face. Fear? Anger? Lucy couldn't tell. Tilly looked at the constable. "Looky here. I made a mistake, all right? No harm done. Why don't you just forget I came by? The leather bag wasn't mine, was it now? And I don't know who killed that fool. You can't hold me, I've done my duty."

With that, Tilly ran from the room, knocking a stool over in her haste.

"That was strange," Lucy said, righting the felled stool.

"Did you believe her?" the constable asked.

"Yes. At least I mostly believed her," Lucy replied. "I do think she was genuinely surprised to find out that the bag had been found in the barrel with Darius. I don't think she had anything to do with the murder herself. Even she couldn't be so foolish to visit a constable if she'd played a part in Darius's murder. She came here for the trifles, to be sure."

"Agreed," Duncan said, moving his arms briskly. Being in the cramped space seemed to wear on him. "That doesn't mean, of course, that she doesn't know what happened. Certainly, we know a little more than we did before."

He sat back down and gazed at his hastily scratched notes.

"I'm more interested in what the contents can tell us about who was in the tavern when Darius was killed. Who was at that last hand of cards? Did he have an enemy prior to the game, or did he make an enemy there? Was this a gambling game gone bad? One man kills the other?"

"Over a game?" Lucy asked. "A man would murder over cards?"

The look Duncan gave Lucy was pitying. "I'm afraid so." He continued to muse out loud. "Why, then, did the killer leave the winnings? Why leave them with the body? Why not take them?"

"Besides, Tilly said Jack was the one with the winning hand," Lucy pointed out. "You'd think Jack would have been the one who was murdered, not Darius." She frowned. "Do we know for sure the body wasn't Jack Durand's?"

"One, Dr. Larimer did think the man had Eastern skin and features," he said, using his fingers to count off his points. "Two, this would fit with your Miss Rivers's assumption that the murdered man was someone she knew from Persia. Three, Tilly had assumed, without us telling her, that it had been Darius—the 'foreign gent'—who'd been murdered. Remember she said she'd seen the other men when the church bells started warning about the fire. Perhaps she's even seen Durand since; I got the feeling they were friendlier than she cared to admit. I think it's safe to assume that the murdered man is Darius, and not Durand."

"So Darius was the victim then." She thrust aside an image of Miss Rivers, grieving at the Golden Lion. Lucy scratched her elbow. "Hmmm. I still got the feeling Tilly was lying about something. I can't explain it."

"Let's think about this again." He pulled the bag out from

under the table. Carefully dumping everything out on an over-turned wooden barrel, Duncan started to divide the contents into four piles.

"The bag may have been Jack's. If he won the stakes, he prob-ably scooped everything into it. The cards, then, were probably his. We know the poem had belonged to Darius."

"The money could have belonged to anyone," Lucy added, feeling unhelpful. "Perhaps the French coins belonged to Darius? Picked them up on his travels from Persia."

"Yes, that could be."

"The chess piece could have belonged to Jack?" Lucy ventured again, feeling like she was picking through jackstraws. "Do you think a gambler would carry a game piece with him?"

"Perhaps. Though I don't think of chess as a gambler's game." He stopped.

Lucy glanced at Duncan. Their conversation seemed to be over. He was studying the signet ring again, flipping the coat of arms and the hunting scene. "A valuable piece?" she asked. Again he didn't respond. She turned to go, feeling inexplicably piqued.

At the door, he called to her. "Lucy, wait. It's just occurred to me."

"What?"

"Well, it's just this. Clearly, Tilly knows that the bag survived the Fire, and Miss Rivers knew you had found the poem. Indeed, Miss Rivers knew to approach you directly."

"So?" She could see he suddenly looked agitated. "They fig-ured it out."

"This means that others, including the murderer, might figure out the same." His voice grew taut. "Let me know immediately if anyone else inquires into the contents. Will you do that for me, Lucy?"

His sudden fervor startled her. She had been about to respond in a flippant way, but instead she simply meekly nodded. "Yes, I will," she promised. She paused as she reached the door, noticing that the tallow chandler who used to own the dwelling had carved his sign—a taper and flame—into the wood.

"Odd, isn't it?" Duncan said from behind her. "The candle-maker's shop being one of the few establishments around here to survive the Great Fire. There by the grace of God."

Shivering, Lucy could not keep her hand from knocking on the wooden doorframe as she passed through it. A futile gesture to be sure, but one she still hoped would keep bad happenings at bay.

·5·

Later, Lucy stood in front of the magistrate's house. She could see light inside only from the kitchen, where Cook was preparing supper. John was probably stoking the fire or polishing silver, and Annie was no doubt stirring pots or chopping up carrots. Doing the tasks that Lucy used to do. The rest of the house was still dark, suggesting that the magistrate was not at home. Adam, she knew, had taken up temporary residence with the other surveyors. She wasn't sure, but she thought he was supposed to return for the Sabbath in a few days' time.

An unexpected lump rose in her throat. Other than the magistrate, she had not told the others yet she was leaving. Lucy shook herself. "No melancholy for you, Lucy girl," as her mother used to say. "The sun's still likely to come up tomorrow, just the same."

Inside, Lucy found Cook finishing up a warming stew, a bit of lamb, a bit of beef, all thrown together with some barley, potatoes, and onions. The September nights were growing chilly, so she gratefully held the steaming wooden bowl by her nose. As they ate together, Lucy looked around at her little family—John and Cook who'd been like parents to her, and Annie, who'd been as sweet and dear as her own true sister.

Hearing her sigh, Cook stopped her fork midway to her mouth. "All right, lass. Out with it. You've been sighing since you got home."

Lucy could not put off telling them about her apprenticeship any longer. She took a deep breath. "I've apprenticed myself to Master Aubrey." She focused on scraping the last bits of stew off the sides of her bowl. Without looking up, she added in a low tone, "I'm aiming to keep house for Will. He needs someone to look after him. I'll be leaving in the morn."

At the last, Annie let out a soft wail. Cook and John stopped chewing for a moment, exchanging a glance. Neither seemed particularly surprised. Like Lucy, they had known for some time that she had no place in the household, since she was neither servant nor family. A friend she was, to be sure, but London's community would not think much of a friendship between a magistrate and his former chambermaid. Especially one now apprenticed, un-woman-like, to a master printer. No one liked it, but that was the way of it.

"You'll still come around for pie," Cook predicted, causing Lucy to smile.

"Of course," she replied, blinking away a tear.

"Fare thee well, child," John said softly. Lucy warmed to the intimate address used among family. She tried to avoid looking at Annie sulking in the corner.

No one spoke much after that. They were nearly finished eating when the magistrate returned home. Like John, Lucy rose to greet her former master, fetching him a bowl of the piping hot stew and a mug of ale. Ever since his wife had died and his daughter had become a wandering Quaker, Master Hargrave seemed to draw comfort from his servants even if, as before, he rarely supped with them in the kitchen.

Tonight, though, he surprised them by sliding his long legs onto the long bench across from Cook and John. "I'll have my supper here. It's been a long day. I should enjoy a bit of company. No, no girls, don't move off." He patted the bench next to him, and smiled when Lucy and Annie sat back down. A quiet smile lit his eyes. "It may be a long time where we will all break bread together. I take it, Lucy, you've told them about your change in employment?"

Lucy nodded, her throat suddenly tight again. She wondered if he had noticed their downcast state. She was grateful when the magistrate continued. "I'm pleased that Lucy has found work with my good friend. We'll miss her to be sure, but she'll come around. Right, Lucy?" She nodded again, pleased that Annie looked a little more mollified. "Now, tell me. What have you been doing at good Master Aubrey's? Has my old friend treated you well today?"

"Yes, sir. Indeed he has," Lucy replied. "And how have you fared, sir? The sessions must be more full than usual?"

"I have observed what I can only describe as a universal resignation. Complaints to be sure, but an odd lack of repining among sufferers. It is almost as if they expected this calamity."

Cook nodded at Annie to stack the dirty dishes by the

washbasin. "I heard tell," she said, "that a flock of sheep had been found butchered outside Warwick. Before the Fire."

"What are you on about?" John asked his wife. "What difference does that make?"

"Ah, but the only thing taken from each carcass was hard fat," Cook responded. "Tallow."

Annie nodded. "That makes sense," she said. "*I* heard the Fire came from a fireball." She pronounced this with the grave authority of the young. "'Twas likely Robert Hubert."

Lucy kicked Annie under the table. Master Hargrave did not like when people accused poor Robert Hubert of setting the Fire. It made no matter that the watchmaker claimed to have thrown a candle through the open window of the Fariners' bakery, starting the Great Fire. "Annie," the magistrate said, in his gentle firm way. "The man's wits were addled. He scarcely knew to what he was confessing." Seeing Annie's chastened look, he patted her hand. "That reminds me," he said, laying a copy of the *London Miscellany* on the table. "Lucy, is this the piece you were out selling today?"

Annie beamed at Lucy. "I told him we were the ones who found the body." Clearly, the truth was of little concern to her. Under Lucy's steady gaze, her smile turned a bit sheepish. "I mean, we were there when the body was found."

Lucy turned her attention back to the magistrate, trying to read the set to his face. In the past, she'd heard him disdain some of the penny accounts. "Yes, I wrote it," she admitted reluctantly.

Master Hargrave smiled. "I thought as much. There's a womanly sensibility to the piece that I fear is much lacking in old Horace Aubrey. I think you may indeed have found your calling."

Warming under his pride, she could not help but brag a little. "I learned something interesting about this poem," she said. "When I was out selling."

"Oh?" The magistrate said, clearly happy to indulge her. "Do tell."

Quickly, she recounted her conversation with Miss Rivers.

His eyebrows raised. "You actually met the woman for whom this poem was intended? What a remarkable occurrence!"

"Yes. I realize now she'd been outside Master Aubrey's shop. She must have heard him tell me to go to the Golden Lion, and that's when she told me—"

The magistrate's smile faded slightly. "You mean this woman followed you?"

Hearing the concern in his voice, Lucy hastened to ease his worry. "No, no. I think it was all right. She was just upset, you see, and for good reason. I reckon she just wanted a bit of privacy." Lucy began to speak even more quickly, hoping to distract him. The last thing she wanted was for the magistrate to tell her he didn't want her peddling pamphlets out in the streets. She was no longer in his employ to be sure, but she did not want to jeopardize his good opinion of her. "See, it's an acrostic." Proudly, she pointed to the column of descending letters. " 'Nasrin I'm Here' it reads. Her name isn't actually Nasrin, you see. The Persian name for rose is Nasrin, while the Welsh name is Rhonda."

"How fantastic!" the magistrate exclaimed.

"There's more. See, the person who wrote this poem was Miss Rivers's—" She paused, searching for the word. Lover? She couldn't use that word with the magistrate. Friend? The word seemed too benign, given Miss Rivers's display of emotion. "Sweetheart," she decided upon. "This sweetheart wrote this letter—or is it a poem?—to let her know he was coming to see her."

A gleam appeared in the magistrate's eye. Though he had seemed tired a few moments before, the idea of a puzzle had perked him up. She'd seen him the same way when tackling a Greek translation or pondering a particularly elusive passage from More's *Utopia*. "You know, Lucy, monks used to create acrostics to send messages to each other. Until Henry the Eighth dissolved the monasteries, I've heard tell this is how they would keep tabs on each other, and of course, the archbishops."

"I think acrostics have become more common now," Lucy ventured. "Master Aubrey showed me several of the Fire acrostics. Roger L'Estrange seems to quite enjoy them. He's the licenser to the Stationer's Company, you know. I don't think Master Aubrey likes him so well."

"That's probably because L'Estrange was appointed by the King to censor what Master Aubrey publishes. 'Tis not surprising my friend doesn't take to him."

"I see," Lucy said, temporarily diverted by this information. Then she remembered the other thing she had learned from Miss Rivers. "The other part is a passage from another poet. Someone named Rumi."

The magistrate glanced at the words, a frown furrowing his brow. "Fascinating!" Then he murmured something under his breath that Lucy did not quite catch.

"Pardon, sir?" she asked.

"Come with me, Lucy," he said. Without another word, Master Hargrave left the room. They heard him open the door to his study.

Lucy glanced at Cook, who shrugged. "Go ahead. Annie can sweep up the crumbs."

Master Hargrave had left the door to his study open. Lucy stood for a moment at the threshold not wanting to step on the new red carpet. It was one of the few luxuries he'd purchased for his home since they had moved in. She watched him pull some sheets of fine white paper out of a desk drawer and dip his quill in his pot of ink.

Seeing her, he rubbed his hands gleefully. For all the world, he looked like a young boy who had just received a great gift. "Come in, Lucy. Come sit down!" He picked up the *Miscellany* again. "Yes, it's an acrostic," he said. "And yet, I think there's more to it. Let's look at this verse, line by line."

"What do you mean?" Lucy asked, feeling her own excitement grow in the light of his.

"Well, several lines are from Rumi's poem, yes?" the magistrate asked.

Lucy marveled at Master Hargrave's vast knowledge. "You know this poet?"

"Know of him, yes. He's been long dead. Some four centuries now, I would say."

"Miss Rivers said that this passage was one of her favorite poems by Rumi, except that Darius had added the word 'remember,'" Lucy explained. "She thought Darius must have added the other lines to make the acrostic happen. To spell out Nasrin's name."

"Her given name is Rhonda," he mused, scratching idly on the paper. The next moment he sat up straight.

"Aha! Look at this! It's an anagram!" He exclaimed. "Another puzzle, hidden inside the first."

"Oh! Like L'Estrange's London poem?" Lucy peered at the poem, trying to see the other puzzle.

"Read this first line," commanded the magistrate.

Dutifully, Lucy read what he had copied onto a sheet of paper. " 'Now, Dear Hart—' "

Master Hargrave stopped her. "If you look carefully, you can see the name "Rhonda" spelled out in here. Do you imagine that's a coincidence?" Without waiting for her to answer, he began to strike out letters. "Let's see what happens when we remove the letters of her name. 'R-H-O-N-D-A.' That leaves us with "W-E-A-R-T." The magistrate looked at her expectantly. "What could that spell?"

"We art?" Lucy read. " 'We art Rhonda.' " She put down the paper. "I don't understand, sir."

"I agree, there's no sense to it. How about 'A Trew Rhonda'?" The magistrate shook his head. "Possibly. Not much sense though, does it?"

Lucy shook her head, still peering at the puzzle. "How about 'Water'? I can see that word," Lucy said. "Does that make sense? Does she remind him of water?" She paused. "Could 'Water' be her last name? Rhonda Water?" She rapped her knuckles on her table. "She did give her last name as 'Rivers.' Rivers, Water. That makes sense, doesn't it?"

"Perhaps," the magistrate replied. "Perhaps not."

They both studied the poem for another moment. Lucy sighed. "Can we ever find the answers here?"

The magistrate looked at her, a keen expression on his face. "Why does it matter to you? To solve this riddle?"

"I'd like to find Miss Rivers again. Miss Water. Rhonda.

Whoever she is! I'd just like to speak to her again. She was so sad today at the Golden Lion. I wonder if the constable would be able to give the items back to her, if this message could truly prove the poem was intended for her."

"There's no way to know that they did belong to her sweetheart. You know that, Lucy. The constable can't return those items to her, I should think."

"I suppose I just would like to help her discover his last words to her," Lucy said slowly, pondering her own motivations. "I find it quite tragic to think they were parted by the Fire, never to be reunited." Unexpectedly, she found herself almost near tears, as inexplicably she thought of Adam. They hadn't been parted by the Fire, had they?

"Ah, I see." From his tone, it seemed the magistrate did see, more than she wanted him to. "My son has been—" he began, but broke off when she looked away. She did not want him to speak of Adam. "Lucy, I do not wish to distress you further. Certainly, you've been as a daughter to me, a solace especially now that my own dear Sarah has taken up with the Quakers. As I told you last night, please don't let anything keep you from visiting here." Did he have tears in his voice? She wondered, even as he continued. "You should get some sleep. You have a big day ahead." As she stood up, he modified his words. "No, not a big day. A big life ahead! And I, for one, am eager to see what you make of it."

Lucy hadn't realized until this moment how much she needed the magistrate to be pleased with her plan. A great weight lifted from her chest. Impulsively she dropped a kiss on the magistrate's forehead, something she'd never dared do before. "I'll always come back," she said, "I promise!"

"To bed, my child," he said gruffly.

She tiptoed up to the tiny room on the top floor that she'd been sharing with Annie these last few weeks. There she found Annie asleep, tired out from her long day's labors. For a moment she gazed around the darkened room. Her own little respite, her place of solace and girlish dreams. The moon gleamed through the window, giving her enough light to begin to pack her worn valise. She moved quietly, not wanting to wake Annie.

She didn't own much. Two work dresses, a good dress for church, a few petticoats, a second cap and apron. Her old shoes. Some wooden animals, carved by her father before he died. A jar once full of lavender scent, given to her by a friend whose time had come too soon. Ribbons and baubles from Sarah. A packet of pamphlets and her own scribblings. A few books given to her by the magistrate, and of course, the Bible her mother had long ago pressed into her hands when she had first entered the magistrate's employ.

Leaving the valise by the door, she sat down beside her friend's sleeping form. "I'll miss you, Annie," she whispered.

"I'll miss you too, Lucy," Annie murmured, still half asleep. "But I understand you have to go." She stretched out her hand. Lucy climbed in beside her for the last time, and soon they fell asleep, their fingers intertwined.

·6·

When she arrived at the printer's shop the next morning, Lucy stood uncertainly by the open door with her small valise. The presses weren't running yet, and the fires hadn't even been lit. Indeed, the place seemed a bit of a mess—papers were strewn all about. "Good day?" she called. "Master Aubrey?"

The master printer came from the back room, his face looking more red than usual. "We had a thief here last night," he said. "I heard him, a few hours ago, poking around a bit down here. Nothing seems to have been taken though. As you can see, I haven't had a chance to pick up the place yet."

"Oh!" Lucy exclaimed. "I wonder what he was looking for."

"It may have been one of those hacks, Hanson or Ellsbreth," he said, referring to two rival printers. "They both lost their printing shops in the Fire. They might be looking to start up again. Take some typeset, or a bit of my press. Not much here that would

interest anyone else. The man fled when I came down the stairs."
He looked around at the mess. "Help me pick these papers up,
will you? We've must get this batch ready."

After she and Lach straightened up the shop, Master Aubrey
watched her set the movable type into the press. "An apprentice
who is topsy-turvy with his letters is not too useful to me," he
told her.

Even though she knew what to do, setting the type was hard
work. Within minutes her fingers felt a bit numb from pulling
the letters from the typecase and setting them in place. Remembering Master Aubrey's speed, and even how quickly Lach had
moved, she was determined to train her fingers to fly too. Still, there
was much to remember. As it turned out, many parts of the press
were named for different parts of the human body. There were
heads, cheeks, faces, mouths, and even toes, in addition to the body
of type such as roman, italic, and gothic.

Lach came over once or twice to laugh at her. "Can't you keep
it straight?" he said, adding with a leer. "This is the male-block,
and this is its tongue. The tongue fits into the groove of the female-
block. Like so." And then he proceeded to cast the letters for type.
"See, the stick of letters is transferred to the male-block, so that
the face may rest upon the tongue of the female block . . ."

Blushing, Lucy interrupted him. "Yes, yes. I see. Thank you."

"Do you?" Lach said, running his tongue over his own teeth.
"Do you indeed?"

She rolled her eyes at him. She soon learned too that Master
Aubrey and Lach regarded the two presses almost like children to
be tended to. "They eat, they sweat, they grow weary, they stop
working, and when they do," Lach kicked the machine when he

thought Master Aubrey wasn't looking, "we punish them." Seeing her giggle, he held up his hand. "Don't laugh," he said. "You'll see. They even piss blood after we add the dye!"

Lucy found her fingers grew clumsier as the morning passed. Master Aubrey worked his apprentices hard, but he was not unkind, letting them take quick breaks to dip their cups into the water pail, or relieve themselves in the pot out by the woodpile. He also left them some bread and cheese to have for their noonday meal. For his part, the printer spent most of his time up front, hawking different woodcuts and ballads, and Lach helped him do this. She began to see that the master had a system, rotating true accounts of murders and monstrous births, with bawdy jokes and scenes. Jack and Jill stories about cuckolded husbands and the scolds who boxed their ears seemed to go over well.

Lucy was working on a piece about three witches hanged in Dorset when Duncan called to her. She had not even heard the constable enter the noisy shop.

"Lucy," he said. "I was thinking about the signet ring we found. It occurs to me we might be able to trace the owner through the coat of arms."

"Yes, that makes sense," Lucy said, wiping her brow. She thought about reminding him how she'd suggested as much the other day, but refrained. Her mother had told her many times that men liked to believe they had come up with ideas for themselves. "I'm sure Master Hargrave would know. He knows many noble families. He might recognize the family insignia."

"That's what I was thinking," Duncan agreed.

"I have news too," Lucy said. "I also talked to the magistrate last night about the poem. He thinks that there is an anagram hidden within the acrostic." Lucy picked up a copy and pointed to the line in the poem, showing him how the letters could be rearranged. "See, it spells Rhonda Water. That could be the name of the woman I met at the Golden Lion."

"I thought you said she was Miss Rivers?" he said, confused.

"I also said that I didn't think that Rivers was truly her last name. Water makes sense," she insisted. Something made her add mischievously, "You know? The magistrate agreed with me."

The constable raised his eyebrows. "I'll look into it," Duncan said. He moved to the front door and Lucy followed. "See if I can find anyone named Water. Or Rivers. I might be able to discover if they have a relative named Rhonda. In the meantime, here is the ring. Pray do not lose it!"

He pulled it out of his pocket and placed it into her hand. For a moment, his hand closed around hers but then let go, even as she pulled away. A momentary awkwardness came over her, and she looked down at the signet ring. She was flipping the ring's movable face again, twisting it between the coat of arms and the tiny hunting scene, when a familiar voice said her name.

"Adam!" Lucy exclaimed, hardly noticing when Duncan stepped away. "What are you doing here?"

"Good morning, Constable," Adam said, still standing outside the door, stiff-backed in his fine embroidered coat. His handsome features were taut, unsmiling. He seemed to be studying the constable. "What brings you here?" His voice, always a bit noble-sounding, seemed chilly to Lucy's ears. When he glanced at her, his gaze softened slightly, and he reminded her of how they had been when they had first met.

"The constable wanted me to ask your father about the coat of arms on this ring," Lucy said eagerly. "Did you know it was found on a body that—"

"I know all about it, Lucy. *Father* told me."

"I would have told you myself," her voice trailed off. He seemed angry. "Is something wrong?"

"So you don't know anyone else but my father who might be acquainted with heraldry?" Adam asked, turning to Duncan. He squared his shoulders. "So, you needed Lucy to do this for you?"

"I suppose I don't travel in those circles, *sir*," Duncan replied, his own voice tight. "Yes, I thought Lucy might be able to take on this small inquiry faster than me."

Lucy stared at them, a bit bewildered by the exchange. Why Adam was angry, she could not understand. A year ago she'd been quite angry at Duncan herself, for hauling her brother off to Newgate, but she'd long since forgiven the constable.

"I'll be off, Lucy," Duncan said, turning to go.

"Wait a moment, Constable," Adam said. He sounded reluctant. "Father informed me that he did indeed recall a tutor of the Near East, a Persian scholar over at Oxford. The man goes by the name of Water. He was not sure which college he was in, but thought perhaps Merton. I was going to stop by the jail to tell you this, Duncan. I didn't know that I'd so conveniently encounter you here, with Lucy."

"Oh, I knew it!" Lucy squealed, clapping her hands. "Didn't I just? I'd wager you anything that he is Rhonda's father! You should be able to find him straightaway."

"Thank you, sir," Duncan said, looking more annoyed than pleased. "I am in your debt."

"Constable," Adam said, suddenly seeming uncomfortable. "You will not be able to approach him directly. He will not see you. Oxford's out of your purview."

"Thank you. I assumed as much. Nobles aren't too keen on thief trackers, now are they?" Duncan grinned, but did not look particularly friendly. "Too good, aren't they, for the likes of me?"

Lucy looked from one to the other. There was clearly something unspoken going on here. She cast about for a different tack. "Well, perhaps I could just see Rhonda whatever-her-last-name-is myself. No one needs to talk to Master Water at all."

"This is not your business, Lucy," Adam frowned. "Why are you getting involved here?"

"She wants to help," Duncan said. "I, for one, am not trying to stop her. I've got a dead man to identify, and I'll take any help I can get. If you'll excuse me, I need to return to work. Lucy, if you'll let me know what you learn about the ring, please come to the jail or send me a note."

Lucy nodded and the constable took his leave.

"He seems very familiar with you, Lucy," Adam said, carefully. "I do not think he harbors ill intentions toward you," he added hastily, seeing her frown. "It's just that," he paused, "everything is so different." He paused again. "*You're* different. I thought—" he broke off, running his hand through his dark hair. Unlike many other men of his station, he did not wear the extensive curled wigs made popular by the king. He had told her once that though he was no Puritan, he had no wish to be adorned with such frippery.

Lucy waited, but Adam didn't complete the thought. Instead, he looked around the room, taking in every detail. "Father said you left his service. This morning! Why ever didn't you tell me?"

"Forgive me. I don't know. I suppose it just all came about so quickly. Finding the body, coming across Master Aubrey . . . I suppose the idea to be his apprentice just came to me. And," she added gently, "I've no real place in your father's home. I've told you that." Seeing the flash of hurt in his eyes, she touched his arm, wanting him to understand. "Will and I have taken rooms above. I'm to keep the shop tidy and Master Aubrey said he'd teach me the trade. Let me help out with the bookselling and the printing."

He looked around the room again. "Do you think you'll be content here?" he asked. "Truly, Lucy? You're not just here because," he said, still turned slightly away, "because you were no longer happy in my father's employ?"

"Oh, Adam!" she exclaimed. "Leaving his home was the hardest thing I've ever done. But I love this work already. To create books! It's hard work, but I'm used to that!"

Adam turned back to her, studying her face. He smiled slightly. "You're glowing," he said. With that, the tension between them faded as quickly as it had arisen. He reached over to tuck an errant brown strand back behind her ear. His mood growing lighter still, he added, "An apprentice! Who'd have thought?"

"Not officially. I won't be here for seven years."

"Glad to hear it!" Adam grinned. "I don't think I could take that."

"But I will be a petticoat author," Lucy said, smiling in return, feeling like a weight had been lifted from her heart. She hadn't quite realized how much she had needed to share this news with Adam. How much she needed him to approve of what she was doing. "My first piece has already caused quite a stir."

"Yes, I can see that." Hearing the bellman call the noon hour, he sighed. "I must get back to the survey. I just wanted to stop by, give you that information from my father."

As he took his leave of her, Lucy smiled inwardly. Although they were far from what they had been just a few weeks before, "stopping by" meant he had walked several miles out of his way to come see her.

Later, Lucy watched Master Aubrey bringing up bottles of wine that he had buried in the dirt floor of the cellar. "Whatever are you doing?" she asked.

"Thought to protect my wine from the Fire," the printer grunted. "For the Rhenish wine alone, I thank the good Lord for stopping the Fire from advancing these six more dwellings down Fleet Street."

Lucy shook her head at him playfully. "Now, now, Master Aubrey," she warned. "The Lord giveth, and the Lord taketh." She wiped one of the bottles clean with a towel. She struck a casual tone. "I can see from your imprint that you sometimes sell chapbooks and the like as far away as Oxford. However do you manage it? Do you go yourself, or do you send someone?" She handed him the bottle.

Taking it, he said, "I've a merchant, Ivan, who takes a pack to Oxford. He's got a fishwife there who'll hawk them proper." He popped off the cork. "Care for a swish? A bit of welcome-me-home for you? Hey, when's that brother of yours coming? Can't have unescorted women living here. Can't say I'd like gossips wagging on about me starting a nunnery."

Lucy smiled at the reference. By nunnery, Master Aubrey did not mean a papist haven, but a den of women of the much more naughty sort. "I should think not. Don't worry. My brother will settle in soon enough," she said, holding out her little pewter cup. Not for the first time, she wondered why everyone seemed so fearful of women living on their own. Women were to be chaste, silent, and obedient. She'd heard those virtues extolled often enough in the pews, from ministers quoting St. Paul. Well, not to be bothered about it now. She laid the coins on the table. "Today's take."

His eyes gleaming, Aubrey swept the coins into his hand. "Good job, lass."

Will arrived then, a great cloth bag under each arm, and after Lucy quickly introduced him to Master Aubrey, she took her brother up to show off their new rooms. There were truly three rooms all told. They each had a tiny chamber, and there was a third room which they shared, consisting of a stone hearth and pot, a table and three stools, shelves for storing some dishes, as well as roots and vegetables, and even a tiny larder for hanging meat or mallards, should they be lucky enough to get such luxuries.

Will looked around in satisfaction. His lean muscular frame seemed to fill the room. All the weight and muscle he'd lost during last year's ordeal had returned, making him seem far more hale and hearty than she'd ever seen him. He answered her smile with his own lopsided grin. "Well done, sister. Maybe no Hargrave manse, but quite nice nevertheless. Now, tell me about what you've been doing. Petticoat author."

"Alas, more typesetter and stoker of fires, I'm afraid. Although I did get to hawk my piece," Lucy said, setting a cup in front of her brother. "Something interesting has arisen." She proceeded then to tell Will about everything that happened in the last few days. When she got to her encounter with Rhonda, Will whistled.

"That's some tale, sis," Will said. "You sure know how to tell 'em."

Lucy stared at him. "You don't believe me?"

"You're serious? A body, a puzzle, and some sort of desperate love affair. Surely you're having a bit of fun."

"Look at this." Lucy pulled the signet ring from the second pocket she kept hidden deep within her skirts. "Do you think someone would be willing to kill for this? I wonder if this is what got poor Darius killed." She paused. "We need more answers."

"We do?" Will asked, raising his eyebrows.

"Yes," she said firmly. Idly, she flipped the signet ring over, staring at the family insignia. "Perhaps you will be the key."

The fires stoked, the type set, and the printer ready for pressing, Lucy beamed at Master Aubrey and Lach the next morning, when they came stumbling down the steep stairwell, a bit worse for wear for tippling the night before.

"The presses are ready to go, sir," Lucy said, not minding the redheaded apprentice's scowl, or the gesture he made at her when Master Aubrey wasn't looking.

She had particular reason for Master Aubrey to think well of her, and she wasn't going to let this pimply lad ruin her plan.

Aubrey merely grunted, grimacing when he opened the shop's shutters, letting in the sun just breaking through the ever-present London fog. He and Lach began to place the sheets across the typeface. Lucy would have done that too, but it was truly a two-man job. In a few moments, they had gotten the press started, and had to shout to be heard above the din. Master Aubrey would bark orders, and Lucy and Lach would only speak as necessary. They got into a ready rhythm, even as Lucy's shoulders burned and her fingers increasingly blistered from moving the great lever back and forth.

She needed to wait until Master Aubrey was in a good mood before speaking to him. Finally he called for a break. Lachlin disappeared out back, to "check on the woodpile" as he explained in his fast trot out of the shop. It was clear from his uncomfortable bouncing that he'd needed to relieve himself for an hour or more, but he had been too afraid of Master Aubrey to say so. From his grin, the printer was well aware of the distress he was causing his hapless devil.

Lucy grabbed two apples from the bin and sat down on a low bench, after handing one to the printer. "Master Aubrey," she began, then stopped. She wasn't exactly sure how to make the request she was about to make.

"Out with it, girl!" the printer bellowed. "Time's a-wasting!"

Lucy smiled brightly, deciding to plunge right in. "Master Aubrey, sir. I was hoping that I might go to church with Master Hargrave and his family tomorrow. Perhaps eat Sunday supper with them too." Seeing the printer frown, she hurried on. "I know you would expect me to go to church with you, and that I shouldn't expect any Sundays off just yet. But I thought I could get up extra early, leave you a bit of stew to warm up when you got back from St. Michael's. It being Sunday and all." She hesitated again, wondering if tears would be too much. She decided against them, just adding simply, "I miss them. I would like to see them. Please."

Master Aubrey mopped his balding head. He looked more puzzled than angry. She could almost read his thoughts. Apprentices weren't supposed to ask for more time off than the guild regulations stated. Clearly, Lach had not made such requests, and he wasn't quite sure what to say.

Seeing him waver, she added one more thing that she thought would turn him completely. "I know you would want to ask me about the sermon, as is your obligation as my master," she said innocently, "but I could talk it over with the magistrate instead. He always wanted that his servants understood the minister's words."

There, that ought to do it. She smiled inwardly. There was no way the printer would want to sit through a long church sermon and then have to listen to another sermon from his servant on top of it. Lach had already told her that the master printer was a reluctant church-goer. Before he could find his voice, she sweetened her offer a little more. "I'll bring you back a piece of gingerbread, if you like. Everyone says Cook's gingerbread is a delight."

"Alright, lass! Enough! No more of your cozening ways," he said, looking exasperated. "Just this once, mind you. I can't be taken as a master of shiftless servants." Under his breath, he added, "Such a little minx."

·7·

The next morning, Lucy and Will walked toward the Temple Church, the church now attended by the Hargraves. Another great structure to have survived the Fire, the church was located just at the end of Fleet Street, by the Inner and Middle Temples of the Inns of Court. As at all the surviving churches, homeless people still milled around the pillars, touching the walls, clearly hoping that touching sacred stone would bless them and reverse their fortunes. Thankfully, this number was starting to decrease, as these confused citizens, numbly coping with their losses, found their way to new homes in other areas of Westminster or London, or beyond the region altogether.

As they approached the stone steps of the church, Lucy noticed a middle-aged woman rocking back and forth by a small tree, and humming a little song. Clad only in a tattered night-dress and wearing her hair in a single tussled braid down her back, the woman looked as she must have when first aroused from sleep by news of the Great Fire. Having caught Lucy's eye, the woman jumped up and moved toward them.

Instinctively, Will stepped in front of Lucy. "Back off," her brother growled.

"Have you seen Charlie?" she asked Lucy in a hoarse voice. "I don't know where he got to. Have you seen him?"

Mutely, Lucy shook her head. She didn't want to ask who Charlie was. The woman's eyes were wild. She allowed her brother to lead her away. When she glanced back, she saw that the woman had sat back under her tree, and had resumed swaying. So many people had been lost after the Fire. Saying a swift prayer for the woman, Lucy mounted the steps to the church and went in, holding on to her brother's elbow.

The church was already quite full. Now that she was no longer in their employ, Lucy could not stand beside the family, as was the custom for servants when there were no pews available. She and Will took their place in the back of the church, with the other unconnected servants. If she had attended Master Aubrey's church, as he had kindly invited them to do, she might have had a seat far closer to the nave. From her vantage point, she spotted Master Hargrave almost immediately, accompanied by John, Cook, and Annie. Adam was nowhere to be seen.

After the service, Lucy followed Master Hargrave out of the church, pulling Will by the elbow. A moment later, she greeted them, feeling shyer than she expected.

"Ah, Lucy, Will," Master Hargrave said warmly. "It's very nice of you to join us. You know, my dear, that I no longer need for you to recount what you learned from the sermon? That is Master Aubrey's job now."

At that, Lucy felt a slight pang. "I know, sir," she said. "I was hoping to get your opinion on something else."

"Oh?" The magistrate raised an eyebrow. "Pray tell."

As they strolled along the street, she told the magistrate about the ring. Once inside the house, Annie followed Cook and John into the kitchen to put together their Sunday dinner. Will wandered in after them, eagerly sniffing the air.

"Bring me the ring," the magistrate said to Lucy. "I'll be in my study."

After discreetly pulling the ring from beneath her skirts, Lucy followed the magistrate to the study. He was already sitting at his desk, a stack of papers in front of him.

"This ring is quite a fine piece," she said, holding it out to him. "You can see by the wax, it's been used as a seal. Constable Duncan thinks it belongs to a nobleman, and we were hoping you might know the coat of arms."

The magistrate took the signet ring, turning it this way and that. "I agree. This ring was made for a man of means. However, it's no family coat of arms I recognize," he added. "Let us consult the book of heraldry."

He moved over to his bookcase. Though he was nearly as tall as Adam, he still had to stand on his tiptoes to reach a book from the top shelf. He laid the book, a huge leather-bound tome with elaborate stitching, on his desk. "Not a book I look at very often," he commented, blowing a bit of dust off the cover. Annie clearly was not cleaning as she ought. "Let's look at that ring again."

He swiveled the signet ring so that the family insignia was showing, and started paging through the volume.

"This is Latin, isn't it?" Lucy asked, pointing to the words in the middle of the insignia. "I can't even pronounce it."

"*Semper Paratus.* 'Always ready,' " he explained. "Not all that helpful, though. Many families have mottos along those lines."

"Do the Hargraves?" Lucy asked. "Have a family motto, I mean."

"Oh, to be sure. Our motto is *Vincit Amor Patria.* Which means 'My beloved country will conquer.' Here, I'll show it to you." He opened the book to the Hargraves' coat of arms. It looked quite impressive, depicting a knight's helmet above a blue shield. The shield held three deer, with two of the deer above a lattice of red lines and the third deer just below it.

"I like the deer. They're sweet," Lucy said. "Do they mean something?"

"Yes, indeed. Every element of a coat of arms conveys a different virtue. From what I understand, the deer on the shield are meant to convey that my family will not take to arms unless provoked. I always assumed we had quite a cowardly ancestor to have earned that title." He chuckled. "It doesn't help that Hargrave comes from an old town in Cheshire, and means 'Grove full of rabbits.' I suppose I should be glad that our heraldry is not festooned with the noble rabbit." He pointed to the red lattice intersecting the shield. "These crossed lines here are called 'frets.' They are meant to convey persuasion. The blue background of the shield, and here on the wreath and mantle, means truth and loyalty, while the gold means elevation of the mind. The helmet on top—a standard feature on most coat of arms—conveys protection and defense."

"Maybe your ancestors were magistrates too," Lucy said. "Protectors of truth, doing battle with words, not arms." She savored the words. " 'Elevation of the mind.' "

"You know, Lucy," Master Hargrave said, flipping the pages of the book toward the front. "The Campions are a noble family too. They came over from Normandy after the Battle of Hastings, over five centuries ago. You descend from Norman champions." Chuckling, he showed her the Campion family coat of arms.

"I never knew my family had a coat of arms," she said, examining the image. The Campion family emblem depicted a dog's head above a knight's helmet. Below was a shield with three dogs' heads, similarly looking to the left, two thick black lines intersecting them. In the background, there was a great deal of red foliage. "Do you know what the dogs mean?"

"It's been a long time since my tutor insisted that I learn these symbols, but I'll see what I can recall. The dog, placed as it is above the helmet, is your family's crest. Dogs usually convey courage, vigilance, and loyalty." He tapped the helmet. "The presence of the helmet here means your ancestors were also protectors. This is further conveyed by the chevron." He pointed to the thick black lines. "The chevron indicates protection. Usually it indicates builders, or those who have accomplished some work of faithful service." He glanced at her. "Your ancestors must have been loyal and faithful servants too. Maybe they helped build castles or bridges."

For some reason, knowing that her family had a place in the magistrate's book of heraldry made her feel proud. Even if her parents hadn't descended from any gentry that she knew about, perhaps her own ancestors had been friends with the Hargraves. She said as much to the magistrate.

For a moment the lines on the magistrate's face softened. "Yes, I would like to think that our families were comrades. Today, as you know, these coats of arms still mean a lot. They serve to legitimize claims and prove a person's place in society." He gave his customary chuckle. "Now let us try to determine which family has lost this most fascinating ring."

"Try the 'Water' family," Lucy suggested.

The magistrate nodded, but the coat of arms did not match that family name. "Too bad," he said, pulling out his timepiece, one of the rare indicators of wealth that he carried about with him. "I'm afraid, Lucy, I must read over some documents before court tomorrow. Why don't you look through the book of heraldry yourself and see if you can find the coat of arms that appears on the ring?"

For the next hour, Lucy sat in the chair by the magistrate's unlit fire, patiently looking at each coat of arms, painstakingly comparing the ring to the image on the page. Some insignia were close, bearing a similar blue-and-gold-checkered pattern, which she now knew was called "chequy." Most displayed the helmet. Some had blue and gold wreaths and mantles. Very few had the red griffin on top. She did laugh once, softly so as not to disturb the magistrate, when she saw the chamber pot with the Chamberley name. "That well could have been my name," she murmured, "should they be still giving out names now."

After a while, her eyes began to blur, and several times she nearly rested her head on the table. To wake herself up, she began to flip back and forth through the book, no longer reviewing them systematically. As she turned the page, about to give up, she noticed that a few pages toward the front of the book had stuck together. Excitedly, she compared point by point. Chequy, red griffin, blue and gold flourishes—all exactly the same. "Sir!" she called to the magistrate. "I think I found it!"

Master Hargrave came up and peered at the book of heraldry. "The Clifford coat of arms. Interesting. This would suggest this ring belongs to the family of the Earl of Cumberland," he mused.

Lucy peered at the coat of arms. She didn't see anything about Cumberland. "I'm not sure I understand, sir."

"The surname of the Earl of Cumberland is Clifford. If we think this ring belongs to a noble, which I believe it does, it stands to reason it would come from that branch." He stroked his chin. "To my knowledge, the title hasn't been used in a while. I seem to recall, though, an issue about someone trying to claim the Earl's seat in the House of Lords."

Lucy wasn't truly listening. "Do you think an earl was playing cards in the tavern?" Her thoughts flashed to Sid. "More likely someone filched the ring and wagered it during the card game."

"Hmmm. Men can be desperate." He paused. "There was something else too. About his son. I don't quite remember—" He dropped off. Lucy waited, but she knew he would not be inclined to give in to gossip. He surprised her though. "I'll see what I can find out."

Lucy had no reason to think about Rhonda or the puzzle over the next few days. September was passing quickly now, with so much to do. Each morning, Master Aubrey had her first boiling pulp to make into a lamentably cheap paper. She came to learn that a finer grade was made elsewhere. The lesser grade that was made in the shop was far more flimsy and often did not make it through the press intact. Master Aubrey used it only when he wanted a bigger batch of the more popular pieces. "Gives us a chance to make more coins on each printing," he had explained, rubbing his hands together. When the printer's back was turned, Lach had turned to Lucy and whispered fiercely, "Can't wait to see *you* try."

On Thursday afternoon, Master Aubrey sent her out to hawk a few sheets, including the broadside about the Dorset witches. After several hours of plying her pamphlets and tracts, she glanced at the sky. Nearly dark. The curfew was still in effect, so she began to wend her way back to Fleet Street. As she passed by the remains of the Cheshire Cheese, she could see Duncan digging through some of the rubble.

"Find anything interesting?" she called, tugging at her green cloak. The wind had picked up a bit.

"Not much," he said. He brightened when he saw her pail. "You weren't coming by with my supper, by any chance? I haven't had any time to eat all day."

"Sorry, this is empty." Lucy looked at the darkening sky. "You won't get much more done tonight, will you? The sun is nearly down. I don't think the Lord Mayor would care for you walking about with lit torches, do you think?"

Duncan scratched his head. "I'm sure you're right. They want this rubble cleared now! It's all I can do to keep them from carting everything away."

"Do you expect to find anything else? Something that will help you?"

His face said it all. He looked so tired, defeated, and just disappointed, Lucy was sorry she had asked him. Without stopping to think, she blurted out, "Would you like to sup with us? I'm just above Master Aubrey's shop."

Duncan was silent for a moment. Lucy felt uncomfortable. "I mean, we haven't much. It's just me and Will. And of course your wife must be waiting—"

"Yes, thank you. I shall be glad for a bite to eat."

They walked back to the shop, neither talking much. For her part, Lucy was frantically reviewing the contents of their stores, hoping she could at least make a bit of stew. When they arrived, Master Aubrey was not around and Lach was just shuttering the windows.

She was grateful that Duncan was angled away from Lach, who was making mocking faces at him behind his back.

"Lachlin, this is *Constable* Duncan," she said meaningfully. "He's joining *Will* and me for supper. Constable, this is Master Aubrey's other, less quick, apprentice."

"Constable? You don't say. You know we were burgled last week?" Seeing Duncan's raised eyebrow, he added, "Oh, you mean Lucy didn't tell you about it?"

Duncan cocked his head at Lucy. The gesture contained both a question and a command to explain.

"It happened the night before I moved my belongings from the Hargraves' household. Master Aubrey said nothing was taken. He thought it might have been a rival printer seeking to rebuild his shop." She turned back to Lach. "Has Will come home yet?"

"No, not yet."

Not to be deterred, Duncan pulled out a piece of paper from his pocket already stuffed with papers. "Any names of these 'rival printers'?"

"I don't think we need worry about it," Lucy said hastily. "Master Aubrey wasn't concerned."

"As you wish." His suspicious look remained, although he followed her up the stairs without another word.

When they reached the rooms that she shared with Will, she seated Duncan on one of the low stools and put a pot to boiling. Dumping in the last of the stew and some rabbit she'd picked up at the market, she told him about the Clifford family crest.

"Thank you, Lucy," he said, watching her. He voiced the question in his eyes. "Why are you so keen on helping me? Don't get me wrong, I appreciate your help."

She shrugged, turning back to the boiling pot. Hearing her brother's step on the stairs, she added, "Hand me those bowls, will you?"

Will entered the room then, stopping short when he saw the constable, the wooden bowls in his hand. Lucy hastened to break the silence. "Will, you remember the constable. Duncan, I'm sure you remember my brother, Will Campion."

For a moment, the two men stared at each other. The last time they had faced each other was at the Old Bailey when Will was on trial for murder, and Duncan had been the one who had put him there.

"I take it I'm not under arrest?" Will said stiffly.

Duncan clenched his jaw. "I take it you haven't murdered anyone?"

Lucy rolled her eyes. "Of course he hasn't. Now sit down, both of you. Duncan was working pretty late, so I invited him to break bread with us."

The tension broken, they squeezed in at the small wooden table. Over their simple meal, which Duncan ate heartily, they discussed the murder.

Will mostly listened, but asked questions here and there about the different items they had discovered. "You know, if I were you, I'd try to talk to the barmaid again."

"Tilly Baker?" Lucy asked.

"Yes. She probably knows more than she lets on. Barmaids always do."

"You would know, wouldn't you?" Lucy nudged her brother gently.

"She shut down when I tried speaking with her before," Duncan said. "I'm not sure what more I can get out of her."

Lucy darted a glance a Will. "Maybe *we* could talk to her. She said she's working at a tavern in Smithfield. What was it called again?" She snapped her fingers. "Oh, right. The Fox and Duck. What do you say, Will?"

Will set down his cup. "What?"

"*You* could talk to her," Lucy said. Duncan looked startled, but then more contemplative as he considered Lucy's comment.

Seeing Duncan nod in agreement, Will scowled. "Me? Why me? Why should I talk to Tilly? I'm no thief-taker."

"You'd be able to put your charm with the ladies to good use for once," Lucy pointed out, her smile a bit wicked. Then turning serious, she added, "We need to find out more about that card game. Someone at that game murdered Darius, I just know it."

Will scowled. "I thought that was *his* job to figure it out," he muttered, jerking his head toward Duncan. His hostile look returned. "Why do we need to get involved?"

"Because," Lucy said simply, "that poor murdered man deserves better. It is the right thing to do."

Both men glanced at her, taking in her set jaw. "Alright," Will said grumpily. "I'll do it."

·8·

Around noon the next day, Lucy stood on Cock Lane in Smith-field, staring across the street at the Fox and Duck. She'd been waiting for Will about ten minutes already, and was starting to feel a bit anxious. Though he'd agreed to speak with Tilly Baker, she couldn't help but wonder if he had changed his mind. When she'd awoken that morning, she found that he had already left, forgoing his usual hot pottage.

She opened her peddler's pack. At least I could be making some coins, she thought. "Oh! Where are you, Will?!" As she waited she looked around. She hadn't been in Smithfield since well before the Fire. Yet, to her eyes, it looked remarkably as it always had, since it had stretched beyond the Fire's mighty reach. Cock Lane ran between the livestock market and the open grassy area that once a year held Bartholomew's Fair, a wonderful fort-night of fortune-tellers, flamethrowers, games, and dancing.

Before the plague, two years earlier, the magistrate had let Lucy and the other servants accompany his daughter Sarah to the Fair. Even Adam had accompanied them on one of his rare visits home from the Inns of Court. Such wonderful times they had had! For a moment, Lucy felt the happy memories absorb her. How young and carefree she'd been then. So much had changed now. Not for the first time, she felt a little shadow pass through her heart.

A familiar voice roused her from her dark reverie. "Lucy!" her brother called to her as he strode up. "Why ever are you waiting over here?"

Lucy smiled brightly at Will. Why had she doubted him? She followed him into the Fox and Duck, trying to keep her gaze averted so she would not catch Tilly's eye.

"Let's sit here," Will said, pulling out two chairs from a corner table. He positioned them so they could both see the ale-house. When she sat down, she rested her cheek on her hand to better obscure her face.

Will nodded toward a comely tavern maid as she passed near their table. "Is that her?" he murmured to Lucy, rolling up the sleeves of his gray woolen shirt.

Lucy glanced over. The woman was at least ten years younger than Tilly, and with far fewer wrinkles. Like Tilly, though, her dress was low-cut, designed to display her bosom to full advantage. "I'm afraid not," she answered. Then, spying a familiar face at the other end of the tavern, she nudged her brother. "I see her."

"Where?" Will asked. He cracked his knuckles.

"Just there," Lucy said, crooking her finger slightly, so no one would see the gesture. "However shall we get her over here?"

"Leave that to me," Will said.

Rather than approaching Tilly as Lucy had expected, Will instead stopped the other, decidedly more comely, tavern miss as she walked by their table. About to shake him off as she would any drunken lout, the woman grew coy as she took in Will's handsome countenance, her expression losing its jaded, guarded quality.

"Yes, love?" she winked, darting a look at Lucy. "Pints for you and your—?"

"Sister. Yes, thank you. We'll each take a pint." Will pressed a coin into her hand. "Why don't you join us for a spell, if you've time for a break?"

"I'll get them straightaway," she said, simpering. Over her shoulder, she added, "I'm Jeannie."

"What are you doing?" Lucy hissed at her brother, as Jeannie walked away, a new sway to her hips. "Duncan gave us those coins to get information, not to cozen every hussy in the tavern."

"Just wait," Will said.

A few minutes later, Jeannie had joined them, and she and Will were soon carrying on as old acquaintances. Tilly looked over once or twice, clearly annoyed that she'd been left to tend the tables on her own, although there were only a few people there.

Will nuzzled Jeannie's arm. "You know, your friend looks a bit peaked. Why don't we invite her to join us for a spell? I had a bit of good luck recently, and I don't mind sharing my coins."

Squealing, Jeannie called Tilly over, making introductions. Tilly barely glanced at Lucy, her eyes only on Will. Lucy didn't speak much, watching her brother jest with the two giggling barmaids. Skillfully, he navigated the conversation to the Fire, a topic so easy to get everyone started on these days. Where were you when the bells started tolling? That's what everyone asked, and the tavern misses were no different. Jeannie and Tilly had both been at other taverns that had since burned down.

"That's when you started working here, is it?" Will asked Tilly, leaning toward her a bit. "What was it like at the Cheshire Cheese?"

"Oh, good enough, I suppose. We had all sorts though. Some rough ones, if you know what I mean," Tilly said, with a meaningful look at Jeannie, who nodded in return. "Excepting, the very last night, some blunderbuss got himself crashed, he did. Before the Cheese burnt down. Found the body in a barrel, they did."

"Coo! A murder!" Jeannie exclaimed.

Will pushed Tilly's arm. "Get on with you!"

Unexpectedly, Jeannie proved to be quite valuable, helping ply Tilly with questions. Who had been murdered? When did it happen? Had she seen it happen? Tilly, enjoying the attention and the free pint, spoke freely, adding considerable detail to what she had originally told Duncan.

The men had been playing with some of "Jack's fancy cards." "We got some nobility here, lads," Jack had said, "best we play with something honorable." Tilly pulled out a playing card from her pocket, and put it on the table. "See, I have one of Jack's fancy cards here. He gave it to me. It's a 'Jack,' same as his name."

Again, Jeannie unintentionally helped their cause. "Who was the noble?" she asked. "One of the players?"

"Yeah, I think so," Tilly said. "He was dressed regular-like, but he was wearing mighty smart boots. Nice leather, didn't he? Treated me like a trollop, he did. Which I ain't." She glanced at

Will, who murmured something and patted her hand. Satisfied, she went on. "A currish fellow he was, off his Lady's leash." She shared another glance at Jeannie who nodded. Clearly they were both used to noblemen who didn't behave very nobly. "I think he had some manservants," Tilly continued. "They weren't sitting with him, but I think they were protecting him. Like guards, you know?"

"Do you know who he was?" Will asked. "Someone important, I ken."

"Nah, I never saw him before. Jack sometimes would bring in bleaters, try to make a bit of coin off their foolishness. This swell, though, he was good. As good as Jack, even. He was winning for a while."

Swatting away a fly that kept trying to land on her ale, Tilly added, "It was an odd game."

Will and Lucy exchanged a glance. "How so?" her brother asked.

"Can't rightfully say. I don't think the men knew each other, for one thing. Jack invited the swell to play, but the other two seem to have just found the game. One of them had the gambling sickness. Another one seemed moody-like, sometimes angry, sometimes sad. I think he was a soldier."

"Was anyone else there?" Will asked.

Tilly thought for a moment. "Yeah. Now that you mention it. Another gent sat in the corner, drinking his ale, slow. He was watching the game, but never joined in. Not for lack of money though; he looked rich enough. Some gents, you know, don't know the game. And Jack had his hands full with the others, or he'd have dealt him in for sure. A fool and his money are soon parted, that's his thinking."

"So four men played cards. Two other men were keeping tabs on the noble, and a third man sat nearby, watching the game," Will recounted. "Seven altogether."

"And Fisher in the corner," Lucy added. "Ow!" she exclaimed, when Will kicked her under the table. With a grimace, she remembered that she wasn't supposed to know about the innkeeper. That information had come out during their interview with Tilly in the constable's jail.

"Mmmm," Tilly murmured, not seeming to have caught the exchange. She seemed completely lost in the memory now. "There was something going on at the game. I thought some ale would do the trick—it usually does—but not this time."

"That does seem odd," Lucy murmured.

"I don't know what Jack was on about it. He seemed to be egging them on. I couldn't make heads or tails. Usually, he could charm frogs from a snake's mouth; I truly didn't know what he was doing."

"You said the noble, that 'swell,' was winning," Will said. "Did you see what the others had put up for stakes?"

Now it was Lucy's turn to kick her brother's leg under the table. Truly, Will needed to be a little more subtle. Luckily, Jeannie had gotten up just then to fetch an ale for a customer, causing Tilly to smile broadly at Will, and lean a bit closer.

"As a matter of fact, I did notice. I know because Jack had been winning for a while, and I like to keep an eye on what he brings in. The man with sad eyes put in the brooch. It was a pretty little thing. If Jack had kept the stakes, he might have given it to me for safekeeping."

"Safekeeping!" Will hooted. "That's rich. I guess you see this Jack-fellow regular, hey?"

"Sometimes he gives me trinkets," Tilly smirked, her insinuation evident. Clearly, she exchanged her considerable favors for baubles. This also meant she knew Jack far better than she had let on in her earlier conversation with the constable. Not wanting to nix her chances with Will though, the barmaid hastened to add, "I haven't seen Jack since the Fire. Just as well, everyone's gunning for the papists these days. Jack, he's a nifty one, but he's probably back in France. A mob's likely to kill him." For a moment, Tilly looked ever so slightly worried about the fate of her lover. Then, she continued her tale. "Jack had the stakes toward the end. That's when he read the verse. Out loud, you know."

"Oh, yeah?" Will prompted with a grin, letting his eyes crinkle a bit at the corners. Tilly giggled. Lucy hid a smirk, always amazed at how silly women became around her brother.

"That foreign guy had wagered the leather bag, promising something valuable was inside. He expected to win, I guess, but it was Jack who won the hand."

Tilly sucked in her cheeks, recalling the scene. "I can tell you, when Jack opened the bag, he wasn't too happy that it only contained a poem! Expecting a treasure, wasn't he? Even though the man begged him not to read it out loud, Jack did anyway. I think to taunt him. The foreign gent started shouting at him. That's when they both stood up, and the scuffle started."

"Who? Jack and the foreign gent?" Will asked.

"That's right. He came swinging at Jack, and Jack ran outside, through the back door. Next thing I knew, we heard the alarm bells clanging, and I took off too, out the front door. Church bells ringing at such an hour is never a good sign, is it?"

"Did you see what happened to the 'foreign gent'?" Lucy asked, without thinking.

Tilly stopped then, the spell broken. "Wait a minute," she said, looking at Lucy's face for the first time. "I know you. You asked me that before. With that constable!" She squinted. "You were selling the poem, weren't you? I saw you!"

Will shook his head at Lucy. "Better drink up, sister. I think we're about to be tossed out on our ears."

Amid Tilly's screeching, they downed their pints and made their way out of the Fox and Duck. Wiping his mouth, Will waved to Jeannie, who blew him a kiss in return.

"I do have a way with the ladies," Will conceded, as they began their walk home. "Looky here." He pulled Tilly's playing card from his pocket. "At least I have this."

They looked at each other and began to laugh.

After she helped Master Aubrey and Lach close up the printer's shop later that evening, Lucy looked closely at the playing card Will had lifted from Tilly. The image was red, and depicted a man clad in royal garb. It was exactly like the others that had been found in the leather bag. Will had told her that it was called the Jack of Hearts. The card clearly had been well handled, but she could make out the faint presence of a printer's mark. She asked Master Aubrey about it, as he was about to make his way up to his rooms.

Examining the card, Master Aubrey scratched his beard. "This is quite interesting, Lucy. This is a special card, licensed by the Worshipful Company of the Makers of Players Cards. See?" He turned it over. "Made during King Charles I's time—1635. Only members of the Company could produce these." He smiled slightly. "Truly, 'tis a wonder the cards survived Cromwell and his godly men. How did you come by it?"

"My mum says it's a wonder any of us survived the Puritan's lack of merriment," Lucy commented, sidestepping his question. Fortunately, the printer was not really listening to her, as he was still scrutinizing the card. "Do you see something else?" she asked.

Master Aubrey moved over to the unshuttered window and held the card up to the fading light. "I can just make out some initials, by the printer's mark. Unusual, even for a member of the royal cardmaking company."

"Why is that unusual?" Lucy asked.

"I don't know too much about this guild, but I don't think most used their own initials. To be sure, this printer had pride in his work." He squinted some more. "Ah, I can just make out the letters. J. D."

"J. D.," Lucy repeated. "Jack Durand? Could that be?" Seeing the printer shrug, she added, "Is there a way to find out whose initials they were?"

The printer shrugged. "I don't rightly know. Guild and company records have always been kept at Guildhall, which was—"

"Destroyed by the Fire," Lucy interrupted, feeling a sharp twinge of disappointment. That was the common sorry state of things at the moment.

"Yes, but only partially destroyed, as I heard tell. Commoners, especially women, cannot simply walk in and search the records," Master Aubrey said as he reached up to shutter the windows. "They are sealed from public view, I'm afraid."

"I imagine, though, that royal companies shall want to discover the extent of any damage that may have been done to their important documents, shouldn't you think?" Lucy asked.

"What are you getting at, Lucy?" Master Aubrey asked. He looked down at her suspiciously.

"I just thought you might want to check on the records of the Royal Stationers."

"And while I'm there, I might find myself inclined to check on the records for the Royal Company of Playing Cards? Maybe they have some lists." He paused. "I'm starting to see your pretty little ways," Master Aubrey said, wagging his finger at her. "You have some news, Lucy, don't you? About that murder?"

Lucy smiled. "How about I write a True Account for you. 'A True Plot sealed in a brewer's barrel, of a most monstrous act.'"

Master Aubrey rubbed his hands together. "That's catchy! I like it. Let's say to the tune of 'Three Merry Maids at the Fair.'"

"First, though," Lucy said, dashing her master's hopes a bit, "we must locate this Jack Durand. Hopefully, then we can find some answers about what happened the night of the murder."

·9·

As it turned out, it was not so hard to locate Jack Durand after all. The next morning, Lucy was alone in the shop, setting the text of a ballad *A Merry Juggler Juggles Two Wives*, when a man walked into the shop. Master Aubrey was hawking down by London Bridge, and as it was a Saturday, Lach had been sent to the paper mill to fetch a new supply of the paper used for woodcuts and broadsides.

Glancing at the stranger, Lucy guessed he was probably in his late forties, or even his early fifties. His hair was rich and full, but streaked with gray, and his once handsome face was soft and full of wrinkles. He was slim and nattily dressed, however, moving with the lithe grace of a dancer as he slipped among the great rolls of paper, the stacks of penny pieces, and the two printing presses. "You were asking about me?" he asked, with a trace of an accent.

Lucy shook her head. "Do I know you?"

"I am Jacques Durand."

"What?" Lucy said, taking a half step back. She could feel her heart begin to pound. "What are you doing here?"

The man put up his hands, palms toward her. "I'm not here to hurt you," he said, in a soft careful way. "Tilly said you were asking about me. I must know why."

"How did you know I was here?" Lucy asked. Pulling out the Miscellany, he pointed to the bottom. "Sold by Master Aubrey, master printer," he read. "Easy enough to find you."

A long moment passed as she studied him. He did not seem to mean her harm. She could feel the rapid pace of her heart subsiding. "You are a member of the Royal Company of Playing Cards?" she asked.

His eyes flickered slightly. If he was surprised by her question, years of card-playing had taught him to bluff well. For a second, she thought he wouldn't answer. "Yes," he responded, regarding her steadily. "I was invited to join the guild as a very young man, even though I was not," he paused, "English." He looked at her intently.

She thought about how he pronounced his name. *Jacques,* not *Jack.* "You are French," she said.

"Back then, it did not matter!" he said. "Not like now." It was now his turn to look at her appraisingly. He took a step back toward the door, as if he were ready to flee. "We were not so harassed, so ridiculed, as we are now!"

"I know you are French," she said, glancing quickly around, "and what it costs to admit that. But I am not one of those silly sorts who would hold such a thing against a man."

Hearing the sincerity in her voice, Mister Durand relaxed and went on. "I was one of the very few allowed to make cards. As you can imagine, I was quite welcome at court. Then Cromwell came along and changed everything." He rubbed his hands together. "The guild's since been reestablished, of course, but the restrictions also changed, and I was not allowed back in. However, I've no need now to make a name for myself as I once did." He took a step closer. "Now tell me why you were really looking for me. I know it isn't to learn about my trade."

Since he'd been forthright so far, Lucy thought she could be honest. "The constable is simply trying to discover who murdered the man at the Cheshire Cheese," she said. "He knows you were there that night, playing cards."

"That does not explain why *you* were asking about me. Why are you doing the constable's work?"

Lucy paused. Images flashed through her mind. Duncan's pleased countenance at her assistance. Rhonda, bewailing the loss of her sweetheart. Finally, the body tumbling from the barrel. Darius. "I was there when the man's body was found. No one deserves to die like that."

Unexpectedly, Jacques moved toward her. Before she could stop him, he had gently taken his hand in hers. *"Mon ami!* I cannot agree with you more. I think the same thing myself." He smiled at her then. It was clear he'd been a great charmer in his youth. She almost returned his smile. "That's why I came to see you. I should not like to speak to the constable myself, *comprenez-vous.* He might not like my entertainment." He winked. This time, Lucy could not help but smile in return. Card playing and gambling were no longer banned in England, of course, although the

law did not look kindly on those who promoted licentious be-
havior.

Hearing the bellman call the hour, Lucy knew Lach might
return soon. She did not want to lose the opportunity to speak to
the sharp. "You arranged for the card game?" she asked.

Jacques nodded. "*Oui.* I can tell you no names, you understand. One man, a noble, I invited. I will say no more about him."
He looked toward the ceiling, trying to remember the scene.
"There were five others at the Cheese already. One was spoiling
for a game. I've seen his type before. They get the gambling in
their blood, and they will not be soothed until they have card and
coin in their hands."

Lucy nodded. This fit with Tilly's description of the man with
the gambling sickness. "What about the other men at the tavern?" she asked. "Did they not join the game?"

Jacques furrowed his brow. "I invited the others to play. Two
men—oafish sorts, vagabonds really—just drank and flirted with
my Tilly. One said he did not play cards, which was a shame because I could see his clothes were a finer cut. He took a keen interest in the game though."

"Another noble?" Lucy asked hopefully.

"I don't think so. Gentry, though, to be sure."

"What about the last man?"

"Ah, the last man." Jacques furrowed his brow. "Him, I could
not place. Thick accent from the north. Soldier, I could tell, but that
was all. He did join the game. Within a few minutes, though, it was
clear that he did not play cards. He lost all that was in his pockets
very quickly. He had, as you English say, not a rag in his sock."

"Why do you think he joined the game then? For the pleasure?"

Jacques shook his head. "No. He was a man who knew no pleasure. He was, how do you say, *très désolée*. A deeply unhappy man. His unhappiness made him bitter."

"What did he lose?"

"Some coins right away. By the second hand, he had lost a brooch. A very fine one, at that. Three flowers intertwined around a heart. I've rarely seen the like. He kissed it for luck, for all the good that kiss did him. He went out the same hand."

"Did he leave then?"

"No, he moved off to the corner. Very out of sorts. Nursing his ale, drinking in tiny sips. He would've had to leave, you see. Innkeepers don't let penniless sorts take up a table."

"Who put in the verse?" Lucy asked. "Tilly said you read the poem out loud."

Durand sighed. "The man with the sickness—the one who was killed—put it in."

Lucy nodded. This confirmed what they already knew, that Darius had put the poem into the pot. "Why did you let him put in the poem?"

"We didn't know. He made much show of the value of that little oilskin package. Told us there was something valuable hidden inside. It was clear that he did not wish to put it in the pot." He shook his head. "He was full of drink, full of passion. We believed him. We *wanted* to believe him. I should have known. Men with the gambling sickness lie about everything when they want to play in the game. He'd parted with all his coin, everything he'd carried in his pockets." Durand made a regretful sound. Lucy couldn't tell if he was regretting having been conned, or that a man would be so besotted by gambling he'd risk everything. He continued. "Then he lost the hand. I won it."

"Then you read the poem?" Lucy asked.

"I was curious. I wanted to know what I had won. When I opened it up, to find that . . . that . . . paper!" A shadow passed across his face. To her surprise, Jacques wiped his eyes. "Blessed Mary, I wish I had not taunted the man as I did. I was angry, *comprenez-vous*? The man had led us to believe there was something of extraordinary value inside. He had already put the jade elephant in, so we all assumed he must have some jewel or some such thing.

"I should have known better. He was too feverish in play. I've seen men wager their shoes, their wigs, even their undergarments, just for the thrill of the game. They all end up losing everything. So I was angry," Jacques said wearily. "To deceive me! *Moi,* Jacques Durand! After I put my winnings back in the bag—it was clear I'd taken nearly everything I could from these men—I read the poem aloud. I did not stop, even though the man begged— begged!—for my silence. I did not care you see. If I knew what would happen, well—" He paused.

Lucy waited for him to continue.

"After I read the poem, he came at me!" Jacques frowned at the memory. "I had no choice but to scoop up my winnings and flee. I ran out the back door, only to find this man was hot on my heels. He backed me up against the empty malt barrels and stole the bag back from me! I would have"—here he made a fist—

"taught him a lesson in losing with honor, but alas, I did not get the chance."

"Why not?" Lucy asked.

Jacques looked away, perhaps in shame. "The two other men, the ones who'd been flirting with Tilly, followed us out of the tavern." His voice dropped. "Completely worse for drink, they were. They set upon him, calling him all sorts of names, striking and kicking him until he dropped. One of them told me I'd get a beating too, if I stayed. I assure you, I did not need to be told twice." He sighed. "By then, the bells were ringing with such force. I knew something dreadful had happened."

For a moment the card sharp seemed overwhelmed. "Even before the Fire, I have often hid that I was born a Frenchman. I've no wish to be pulled apart by angry mobs, as some of my comrades were. Just for being French!" He gave a very un-Gallic snort. "I fear now that he was set upon—and killed—for being a foreigner," Jacques sighed. "But so many are out for blood." Jacques looked straight at Lucy, the twinkle gone from his eyes. "Those two men were just drifters, vagabonds—up to no good. It is quite tragic that this harmless man was killed, but I have no doubt his killers have long moved on. They will find their justice before the mighty sword of the Lord, of that I have no doubt. You can pass that on to your constable." Impulsively, Jacques reached over and drew the back of her hand to his lips.

Before he could release her hand, Lucy instead clasped his hand between her own. She was not completely sure he was telling the truth. Besides, he seemed to have left a few details out. "Were those men traveling with the nobleman you invited?" Drifters and vagabonds indeed! That did not fit with how Tilly had described the men.

This time, Jacques could not quite hide the slight widening of his eyes. He wagged a free finger at her. "Tut tut, *mon cherie,*" he said. "I cannot tell you."

"Did you learn anything about the man who was killed?" she persisted.

"Nothing more than what I have already told you. A stranger, from a far-off land, bearing an important message to his sweetheart. I know nothing else." He glanced down at her hand, which was still holding his tightly. "My dear, *s'il vous plaît.*"

"Was the nobleman you invited by any chance related to the Clifford family?" she asked, desperately. "Lord Cumberland, perchance?"

To her disappointment, Jacques's noncommittal masque slipped back over his features. "I do not know the man of whom you speak," Jacques said, "or how that guess may have come about." Pulling his hand from her grasp, he added quietly, "I would suggest that you do as I have done—accept that there is nothing more to be learned about this poor foreigner's death and convince the constable to put the matter to rest. With that, my dear, I bid you farewell."

"That's all he had to say?" Duncan asked, disgusted, a short while later. "That divine providence would be sufficient to bring the man to justice? He wouldn't share any names? No descriptions? I mean, does he even know with certainty whether those two men were the ones who killed Darius? Or was he just speculating?

'Vagabonds,' he called them?" The constable broke into a bad French accent. 'They killed him because he was French!' " In his regular speech, he added, "What am I supposed to do with that?! Truly, Lucy, I fear you do not ask enough questions."

They were walking through Covent Garden, accompanied by Annie. After her conversation with Jacques, Lucy had sent Duncan a note to meet her at the marketplace, not wanting to miss a minute of her afternoon off with Annie. If he wanted to hear about what Jacques had told her, the constable would have to meet her on her own terms. After all the markets in the eastern half of London had been destroyed by the Fire, Covent Garden had quadrupled in size. Even in September, there was an abundance of fruit, vegetables, and flowers spilling over the stalls, as ships bringing goods from the continent and the New World were finally able to dock along the Thames and unload their wares.

"Well, we learned who was there, even if we don't know all their names." Lucy ticked them off with her fingers. "I count eight who were at the Cheshire Cheese that night. Darius, of course. Tilly. Jacques Durand. The Earl and his two companions. A man 'with sad eyes,' who put the brooch in. The gentleman who didn't play but who watched the game. We know only four played." She stopped at the herbalist's stall, and picked up a piece of dried thyme.

After rubbing the dried leaves between her thumb and forefinger, she raised her fingers to her nose and sniffed. Satisfied, she counted her pennies to pay for the thyme as well as a bit of sage, bedstraw, and wood betony. She wanted to stock up on all the herbs Nicholas Culpeper, that esteemed physician, had recommended in the *Complete Herbal*. "Besides, is it for me to ask questions?"

"Of course it is," Duncan stated. "I don't hold that women are supposed to be silent. In my experience, none of them are anyway." He grinned at her.

"Didn't you tell me the very same thing, after my dear friend was murdered two years ago?" Lucy asked, carefully placing the herbs in her basket, for fear they would be crushed. "That Divine Providence would take its due course." Seeing that Annie had moved on ahead to pick out some vegetables for Cook, Lucy continued, "I despised when people would say that to me. In this case, though, I wonder if they're right. We didn't know the victim and—"

"I can't let it go, Lucy. I'm surprised that you of all people would even ask that." Lucy looked up at him. Duncan seemed uncharacteristically vehement. "You said that his sweetheart—Rhonda?—was quite distraught."

"She asked me to let it go. She thinks there's nothing that can be done." Lucy looked up at him. "Duncan, why are you angry?"

Duncan glanced down at her, then looked away, fingering a brightly colored woolen scarf hanging at a stall. "I'm not angry at you. I didn't listen to you, and I should have."

"Whatever do you mean?" Lucy asked, stopping. "When didn't you listen to me?"

"Your brother. Will. He could have died at Newgate. He could have been hanged. He would have been too, had your Master Adam not stepped in. Helped him at the trial."

Although it pained her deeply to think of that time, Lucy put her hand on his arm. "Duncan, you were doing your job."

He shook his head. "I've got to finish this investigation. I must discover who Darius was. I must find out the truth." He pulled out a second scarf. "To do this, I must speak to Rhonda Rivers or Water or whatever her bloody name is!"

Lucy did not feel very optimistic. "Duncan, I don't know. She said to let it go—"

Duncan waved off the weaver who owned the stall. "I'm not buying," he told her. The woman sat down, clearly disappointed. To Lucy, Duncan said, "Interested in taking a little journey?"

"Where?" she asked, suspiciously. Duncan suddenly seemed in a very merry mood.

"We could find Miss Water. In Oxford."

"What?" Lucy stared at him. "You're jesting."

"No, I'm quite serious. We can lay this matter to rest once and for all," he said. "I need you to come with me. Today."

"I couldn't possibly—" she began to protest.

"Please," he interrupted her. "I have no idea what Miss Water looks like. Even if I did, I can scarcely think her father would allow her to speak to a constable, especially one from outside Oxford. I need you to help me. You must speak with her. You know that I can't."

Lucy admitted to herself this was true. Daughters of gentry were highly protected, their male acquaintances kept to a tightly confined circle, or so their fathers and brothers liked to believe. Lucy had seen enough of gentry households to know that young women managed to navigate within social strictures when they wanted to. Still, Duncan had little chance of engaging with Rhonda outright. She did not know, though, if she could get any closer. Rhonda had made it clear that she was uninterested in pursuing the inquiry, so Lucy did not know how she would react upon seeing her again.

Still, Lucy had summoned other objections. "Oxford is a half day's journey from here. Are you proposing we walk?"

Duncan smiled. "Ah! I've thought of that. As it happens, I know Master Aubrey's man, Ivan, will be making deliveries to Oxford. Let's see, what else?" He proceeded to check off more points. "The roads should be well enough, since we've had no great rains recently. You're allowed some Sundays off, right? You could do some selling in Oxford. Aubrey's a man of sense—he'll agree to that."

Lucy nodded. That might be the case, although she knew she might not be allowed to sell on a Sunday. Even travelling on a Sunday was frowned upon, but Lucy knew that the king's men would likely let harmless travelers like themselves pass easily, particularly if they carried a letter from her master. Still, she had another objection. "I don't think it's quite proper for me to travel with you, alone. Ivan cannot exactly serve as a"—she winced slightly—"a chaperone." She felt silly even saying the word, since usually servants and apprentices could not avail themselves of chaperones. She still needed to preserve her reputation, though.

Duncan's grin widened. "You can travel as my wife. No shame upon you."

Lucy gulped, not knowing what to say.

Seeing her discomfort, he snorted. "Nay, I'm just teasing. We'll bring Annie along—you want to come, right, Annie? We can all be cousins." He said to Annie then, who had stepped away to examine some ribbons. "Annie, want to come to Oxford with us?'

"Of course," she answered, looking trustingly at Lucy.

Despite some misgivings, the journey was easily settled. As Duncan had assumed, Master Aubrey had, with a surprising alacrity, even gave them the name of a fishwife he knew in Oxford. "Just give Mrs. Danforth my name. She'll set you up nice," he had told them, his eyes twinkling a bit. He's expecting a good tale out of this, to be sure, Lucy thought.

Lucy had hastily scrawled a note for Will, and Master Hargrave had given his permission for Annie to accompany Lucy. "If you think this will help the constable find justice, then I am glad to spare Annie for a day or so." Uncomfortably, she tried to forget the way his thoughtful eyes had turned upon her. "I just hope, my dear, that you think carefully about what you are doing. I trust Annie in your care, and in the care of the constable." The weight of the magistrate's trust in her was great, and she was worried about letting him down, about leading Annie astray. What if they arrived at Oxford after dark? What if they couldn't find Mrs. Danforth? At this point, she was far less concerned about finding Miss Water as she was that she keep Annie and herself safe.

·10·

A short time later that same afternoon, Lucy found herself traveling to Oxford, tossing about in Ivan's rickety wagon, clinging to the ropes that held his deliveries. Seated across from her, Annie was doing the same. Every time the wagon hit a rut or bump, Lucy felt sure they'd get pitched out on the muddy dirt road. Ivan's wagon, little more than a cart, was nothing like the fine hackney coaches the magistrate would hire for long journeys back and forth to the family's summer seat in Warwickshire. At least Ivan's horses—Clancy and Paddy—had seemed strong enough and kept up a brisk enough pace for this first part of the journey.

Slapping away flies that buzzed about a barrel of salted fish, Lucy scowled at Duncan's back. The constable had claimed that he thought the girls would be safer riding in the cart, but right now he looked plenty comfortable sitting up with Ivan. Instead of his characteristic red coat, he had changed to a dark wool coat that

Lucy had never before seen. Even his soldier's ramrod straight bearing seemed to have relaxed somewhat. He could have been a tradesman making his way to market.

Lucy clenched the side of the wagon tightly, watching her knuckles whiten. "Little journey," she muttered to herself, remembering the words he had used. They were just fortunate that the roads were tolerable. There had been little enough rain, so the wheels did not get caught in muddy ruts. Except for a quick stop to relieve themselves and exchange horses at a coaching-inn in High Wycombe, they had barely rested. She was starting to feel a bit overwrought.

At that moment, they crossed a particularly big dip in the road. "Whoa!" Annie squealed.

Duncan turned to look down at them. "Alright?" he asked. He looked like he was about to laugh.

Judging from Annie's disheveled appearance, she knew she could not look much better. "We're fine," she said, hoping he couldn't hear her stomach growl. She peered anxiously at the setting sun.

Duncan's grin faded. He watched her reposition herself on a sack of grains. "We're almost there."

"I hope so," Lucy said. "It's nearly nightfall."

Not for the first time she wondered what had possessed her to agree to the constable's madcap plan.

"Look, Lucy!" Annie called, interrupting her thoughts. "Oxford! I see it."

Lucy craned her head beyond the cart, feeling excited in spite of herself. Set against the rosy sky, Oxford's spires came into view. They were as beautiful as she'd heard tell. Maybe they'd get to see the university too. Ivan turned the wagon down High Street. Having arrived just before dusk, the sellers in the main market were starting to close up their stalls, no doubt heading to their homes for supper. Now she couldn't help but wonder what they'd do for their evening meal. Her stomach had been complaining for hours.

As if he'd heard her rebellious stomach, Ivan whistled to the horses and pulled the wagon to a stop in front of a bustling inn. From the looks of the place, the inn must have been around for at least a hundred years. The cracked sign above the door was weather worn and difficult to read. Straining her eyes, Lucy was just able to make out the words. "The Scholar's Head," she read out loud.

"Named for Thomas More," Duncan said, having overheard her. "Got himself beheaded, he did."

Lucy nodded, remembering Master Hargrave conversing with Adam about the man. A cleric and a scholar, Thomas More had been beheaded by Henry VIII the previous century for refusing to accept the monarch as the head of the Church of England, and perhaps, even worse, for not sanctioning the King's nuptials to his second wife, the ill-fated Anne Boleyn.

Unfastening the little door at the back of the cart, Duncan looked at them. "Fancy a bite to eat?" he asked.

Lucy felt her pocket, hidden beneath her petticoats, a bit doubtfully. The Scholar's Head did not look too fine a place. Still, she didn't have too many coins to spare, and she wasn't sure how much she'd have to give to Mrs. Danforth.

Interpreting the gesture correctly, Duncan said, "Don't trouble yourself. 'Tis my pleasure to treat you both." He extended his hand to her.

The graciousness of the gesture confused her. Standing up,

Lucy leapt neatly from the edge of the wagon, not touching his outstretched hand. She'd underestimated though, how cramped her legs had been. When she landed, she yelped softly in pain. Duncan looked at her curiously. She mustered a small smile, her face flaming. Her flush deepened when she saw him turn to Annie, who allowed him to grasp both her hands and pull her, giggling, out of the wagon.

"Shall we go in?" Lucy said blandly.

Not too long later, Lucy and Annie dug into their suet pudding. Duncan sat across from them, eating from a platter of meats and cheeses. Ivan was nowhere to be seen.

Her hunger abating, Lucy took a long sip from her draught. "Where did Ivan go?" Lucy asked, craning her head around the crowded inn. "I thought he would join us."

Duncan shrugged. "Ivan gave me Mrs. Danforth's address. We'll walk to her home when we're done here. He knows to meet us in the morning."

Lucy put her hand to her mouth, trying to hide her sudden feeling of dismay. Oxford was much more crowded than she had expected. For some reason, she'd thought since Oxford was nowhere near the size of London, that it would just be a quiet town, full of men like the magistrate pouring over great tomes, speaking quietly to one another. She'd not expected this great jumble of people. Even though many of the men seated in the tavern were wearing scholars' robes, they were as boisterous and merry as any men in any tavern back in London. Somehow, when they had been standing back in Covent Garden, it had seemed so easy.

"Constable Duncan, how do you propose we find Miss Water?" Lucy asked, setting down her fork. "Master Hargrave had said Merton College. Should we start there? He had thought a Persian scholar might live there. I know Oxford has quite a few colleges though."

"You know, my first name is Jeb," the constable said, taking a swig of ale from his mug. Annie glanced up at him, and then at Lucy, before sucking some marrow from a chicken bone. "You should probably know that. We're cousins, after all." When Lucy didn't answer, Duncan continued more briskly, more like the soldier he was when she first met him. "We will not be allowed inside the College, not unsolicited and without a letter of reference. I think young Master Hargrave made that abundantly clear that we are unlikely to be admitted directly into Master Water's home."

Lucy flushed slightly, hearing the tautness in the constable's voice when he spoke of Adam. He went on. "Besides, we don't want to run the risk of meeting her father there, assuming what she told you of her unhappy love affair is true. We'll have a better chance if we can catch her in a more public place."

Duncan went on, laying out the details. "There are six churches in Oxford. Ivan assures me, however, that there is only one attended by the university scholars. 'Dandyprats,' he calls them. St. Mary's. We'll start there."

"Unless the Waters have taken up with the Quakers," Lucy pointed out. "You'll never find her then." Everyone knew that Oxford was full of nonconventicle sects, dissenters from the King's Church of England. King Charles had promised them religious freedom, but they still encountered much strife and animosity. Having witnessed Quaker secret meetings, she knew they rarely met in the same place twice, largely to avoid trouble with the local God-fearing community who despised them.

"Do you think the Waters are Quakers?" Duncan asked, a bit deflated. Clearly that thought had never occurred to him.

Lucy thought back to her conversation with Miss Water. "No," she said honestly. "She did not speak in *thees* and *thous*. You know that's how the Quakers speak." She reflected a bit more on what she knew of the woman. "Moreover, I believe her dress was too fine for ones such as they."

"Alright then. We'll find her at the church, get her away from her father, and convince her to tell us Darius's last name, to bring peace to his family."

"Sounds easy enough," Lucy murmured, thinking the exact opposite.

Duncan shrugged. "We've come this far."

During this whole exchange, Annie had been quiet, content to gnaw on a bit of lamb that the constable had left. For the first time in the entire journey did she display any curiosity. "Who's Miss Water anyway? And why are we looking for her?"

Early the next morning, Lucy rolled off the rush matting in the cellar of Mrs. Danforth's dwelling, being careful not to wake Annie. The poor girl needed as much sleep as she could get.

The night had not passed easily for Lucy. She'd spent many hours tossing and turning on the rush matting, while Annie snored blissfully beside her. Truth be told, it wasn't just the hard conditions of the fishwife's accommodations that had kept Lucy awake. Thinking about finding Miss Water, worrying about keeping herself and Annie safe, all weighed heavily on her heart. That wasn't to say she didn't trust the constable completely. "Maybe I trust him too much," she muttered to herself. "Look how I've done everything he's asked of me." She wondered what Adam would think about her taking this wild trip over to Oxford. Funny enough, being with the constable reminded her a bit of being with Adam, even though the two men were so different. She wasn't sure if she enjoyed her time with the constable exactly, but in the excitement of the journey she'd barely thought about the magistrate's son at all.

Feeling a little prick to her leg, Lucy glanced down to see a long straw poking through her petticoat. Sighing, she brushed the straw away before pulling her Sunday dress over her head. They had contemplated not bringing their Sunday clothes with them, but Lucy thought the magistrate would expect them to look nice for church. Not that the magistrate would see them of course— and not that Lucy could not dress as she pleased, now that she was no longer in his employ—but she would always value his good opinion.

Lucy eased her way to Mrs. Danforth's kitchen and set the pot to boiling. They had found the fishwife to be a decent sort, if a bit loud and hard of hearing from her forty years of hawking fish on the noisy streets of Oxford. She was kind enough, and they had found it reasonable when she requested that they do a bit of cleaning and scouring pots to earn their night's keep.

Mrs. Danforth was certainly pleased when she entered the kitchen a little while later, finding Lucy hard at work preparing a bit of porridge and salted potatoes she'd found in the stores. "A blessing you are, my dears," she'd said, inspecting the pots Lucy and Annie had scrubbed the night before. "Tell Horace Aubrey he can send you to me anytime. Why don't you just finish up these dishes, and help me get supper on. Lord knows I could use a good supper on His day."

An hour later, at seven, Annie and Lucy were just finishing up in Mrs. Danforth's kitchen when the constable knocked briskly at the door. He'd obviously found comfortable accommodations elsewhere, since he was whistling a bit and looked clean-shaven. He was wearing the same dark suit as yesterday. "Ready?" he asked, looking at her apron quizzically. "I hope you don't mind walking. I asked Ivan to meet us with the wagon later."

"Of course not," Lucy quickly untied her apron and handed it to Mrs. Danforth. "Let me just tidy my hair."

She was conscious of him studying her appearance, taking in her Sunday dress. For a moment she thought he would pay her a compliment, but he didn't. "I'll wait for you outside."

"He's a handsome one, ain't he?" Mrs. Danforth said, reaching up to straighten Lucy's cap.

"I suppose," Lucy said. She hoped the constable was out of earshot. He was waiting a few paces away.

"Got your hooks in him, eh, honey?" The woman elbowed Lucy in a friendly way. "I can tell."

"Oh no, Mistress Danforth," Lucy said, floundering a bit. She started toward the door. "You've got it all wrong." She threw a mute plea to Annie, who had heard every bit of the exchange.

"Lucy's betrothed already," Annie said loyally. "To my master's son. Her sweetheart's a barrister."

"Is that so?" the fishwife said, chuckling. "So, banns been read?"

"No," Lucy said, suddenly feeling miserable. "It's hard to ex- plain—"

"No need to explain at all," the fishwife said, waving at Duncan. To Lucy's deep chagrin, she called out loudly, "She ain't betrothed to that barrister, you know that?"

"I know that!" Duncan said, glancing at Lucy. What he made of the fishwife's comments or her own mortified expression, she couldn't tell. Thankfully, he didn't say anything else. "Ready for church, then?"

When they reached the south entrance of St. Mary's church a few moments later, Lucy touched the swirling columns that framed the door and porch. She'd never seen anything like them. The churches she'd been to in London only had straight Roman-style columns, and of course the one she grew up attending in Lambeth had no columns at all. The columns of St. Mary's twisted, drawing her eyes upward. There she could see the majestic image of the Virgin Mary holding the baby Jesus in one arm, standing in a scalloped throne, looking out at Oxford. Jesus was crooking his finger in eternal blessing to all those who passed within the church. It was a blessing Cromwell hadn't destroyed the church in his effort to rid England of all papist influences. She whispered as much to Annie.

"Ah, but see these holes there?" Duncan asked, having overheard her remark. He pointed to a pattern of gouges in the side of the church. "Cromwell's men turned their guns on the church during the war." He sounded disgusted. Once again, Lucy wondered what his experience in the army had been like. Now was not the time to ask.

As they passed into the church, Lucy let out an audible sigh. St. Mary's was magnificent indeed. Immense stained-glass windows lined the walls and great arches gracefully framed the painted ceiling. The vicar had not yet climbed the small winding stairs to his pulpit. Instead, he was speaking to a small group of parishioners clustered around him.

"Let's sit toward the back," Duncan said, resting his hand lightly on her waist to guide her.

Stiffly, Lucy took Annie's arm and moved the younger girl to a pew at the back of the church. Duncan followed, sliding in beside Lucy. The church was growing crowded, and latecomers had to position themselves against the walls in preparation for standing through the long service.

Glancing around, Lucy could see that Ivan had probably directed them toward the right church. She could see that St. Mary's was full of scholars from the university, attending the service with their families. Unmarried Fellows might have attended the smaller private services connected with the different Oxford colleges. Like Merton College, Lucy sighed to herself.

The church grew quiet then as the vicar mounted the pulpit and called them into prayer. When he began his sermon, Duncan put his head close to hers. "Is that her?" he whispered, pointing his finger ever so slightly toward a young woman a few pews ahead of him. She was seated beside an elderly man dressed in faded gray breeches and shirt.

Lucy shook her head. "No, Miss Water's hair is darker."

Hearing them, a man seated in front of them turned around, giving them a warning glance.

"Pardon," Lucy mouthed. The man turned back around.

"What about her?" Duncan whispered again. Lucy shook her head.

They did this several times. "This isn't working," Lucy

whispered. Catching the eye of an elderly woman leaning against the wall, she stood up and gestured to the woman to take her seat. Gratefully the woman slid into the pew that she and Duncan had vacated. Annie didn't even seem to realize that they had left her.

She and Duncan made their way down the side aisle, trying to bring as little attention to their movements as they could. Fortunately, the vicar had just called everyone to stand, and they were able to walk hastily toward the front of the church, stepping carefully among the parishioners who lined the walls. She kept her face down, hoping if Miss Water were there she wouldn't see Lucy first. Duncan stood slightly behind her, so that the back of her shoulder was touching his arm.

Peeking out through her lashes, Lucy could tell that she had a far better vantage point to see the congregation than before. She let her eyes sweep over the church, especially toward the front where the most important families usually sat in their inherited pews. She studied each brunette female in turn. Some noblewomen, some servants, a few gentry. One or two looked enthralled by the vicar's sermon, but most wore the same slightly bored expression that she was used to seeing on the faces of churchgoers at home.

A woman delicately blowing her nose into a bit of red silk caught her attention. Lucy caught her breath, and she craned closer. The woman was seated next to an older man who was nodding his head at the vicar's words. Could it be—? Yes. It was the woman who called herself Rhonda Rivers. The woman whom Lucy believed was Rhonda Water.

Reaching slightly backward, Lucy tugged on Duncan's sleeve. He leaned in. "Do you see her?" His breath tickled her cheek.

She nodded, not wanting to lose sight of Miss Water. Eventually, when the vicar bestowed his final blessing on the congregation, Lucy and Duncan began to move their way to the back, keeping their eyes on Miss Water, so that they would not get caught in the crush of the congregation leaving the church. As people passed them by, eager to get home to their Sunday suppers, Lucy could see that Miss Water was still standing beside the older man, who she could see now was dressed as an Oxford fellow. She assumed he was Rhonda's father, Master Water. He had become engaged in a conversation with some other men. As Lucy watched, Rhonda said something to the man and left his side, making her way out of the church. Lucy followed, hoping Duncan would look after Annie.

Miss Water moved out onto High Street, turning toward the church graveyard. It was there that Lucy caught up with her.

"Miss Water?" Lucy said. "May I have a word?"

Miss Water stared at her. "You!" she exclaimed. "Whatever are you doing here?" She looked anxiously around. "How did you know my name."

"I came to find you."

"However did you discover where I live?" the woman looked about anxiously. "I know I never told you."

Lucy pulled out her crumpled copy of the *London Miscellany*. "It's here, in the first line. See, Darius wrote an anagram for you, within the acrostic. Rhonda Water. That's how I knew your full name."

Miss Water's eyes misted over. "He loved puzzles, Darius did."

"You had told me your father taught at Oxford," Lucy went on, feeling her stomach churn a bit. She did not want to cause the woman any more distress. "From there, it was not too hard to discover a scholar of the mystic East who had a daughter named

Rhonda. It wasn't too hard to learn that he was at Merton College. We knew you would attend church. And the rest"—Lucy
waved her hand—"well, here we are."

Miss Water pulled out her own much handled copy from her
pocket. "How many times have I read these words, without realizing he had anything more to say to me. How could I have
missed it?"

"You were grieving," Lucy said softly.

The woman continued to stare at the poem. "Was that all he
said? Did you find . . . anything else?"

"Not in the poem. If there is anything else hidden in there,
we could not find it."

"We?"

"Constable Duncan and myself."

Miss Water turned away. "Oh, Lucy!" she cried. "I asked you
not to involve the constable! My poor Darius is gone, there's nothing we can do for him now."

"Except inform his family of his death," Lucy said. "Don't they
deserve to know the truth?"

"Yes, I suppose." She rubbed her hands against her skirt. "You
must think mighty poorly of me."

"Why ever would you say that?" Lucy asked, noticing for the
first time how mud had splattered across her own skirts. Standing
beside Miss Water, in her beautiful, tailored clothes, Lucy felt like
an absolute peasant. Her mother would not have been pleased, had
she been able to view them right now.

Miss Water sighed, and sat down on a small stone bench. Instead of answering, she pointed to a white gravestone with a beau-

tifully carved angel a few feet away. "That's my mother's grave," she said.

Lucy knew the pain of losing a parent. "I'm sorry," she said, even as she wondered what that sad fact had to do with anything.

Hearing the question in Lucy's voice, Miss Water continued, "My mother died a year ago. Distemper, I think, although Father said otherwise. We were living in London at the time."

Lucy nodded. A year ago the plague was just starting to hit London, although in the beginning no one wanted to admit it. Many people hid when members of their families had taken ill, even as their sons and sisters lay dying, or else the King's army or the London authority would be likely to quarantine them all in their houses, imprisoned until they all succumbed to the inevitable.

"After she died, Father had to get away. Get away from London. He took me away to the furthest place he could think of. A place he had long studied from afar."

"Persia," Lucy stated. "Where you met Darius." She had a quick image of a woman standing in robes, amid the fragrant flowers of a beautiful hanging garden, waiting for her beloved to appear. *Come to the garden in spring. There's wine and sweethearts in the pomegranate blossoms.*

"Yes," Miss Water said, interrupting her momentary reverie. "I never knew his last name. He was just Darius to me, beautiful, lovely Darius." Then angrily she added, "I don't know what he was doing in a place like the old Cheshire Cheese. He didn't drink much, and he never gambled. What was he doing playing cards?"

The whole journey to Oxford was for naught, Lucy thought.

"Perhaps you'd like to claim some of the other items that he had with him?"

"What kinds of things?" Miss Water asked, a slight catch to her voice.

"Well, a small ivory brooch. That might have belonged to another man, though."

"A brooch? That would seem strange to take if it belonged to someone else."

"A signet ring," Lucy said. "With a coat of arms on one side, and a hunting scene on the other.

Miss Water shook her head. "Darius had no such thing. What else?"

"A green elephant. Made of jade, I think. Duncan said it was a rook, from a chess set. Wait, what's wrong?"

Miss Water had paled, and looked like she was about to faint. Tears had sprung to her eyes. She was trying to speak, but seemed quite overcome, half crying, and, inexplicably, half laughing. Truly, she looked quite hysterical.

Lucy looked about anxiously. She saw the well she had taken a drink from earlier, and brought Miss Water a dipper full of water. She watched Miss Water drink, waiting impatiently for her to speak.

Finally, she did. "The murdered man!" Miss Water uttered, her voice oddly strangled.

"Yes?" Lucy asked. "What about Darius?"

"No!" Miss Water said. Inexplicably she began to giggle. "Don't you see? Oh, how you can see? It wasn't Darius. The murdered man was someone else! Darius must be alive!"

Lucy stared at Miss Water. "Whatever do you mean?" Perhaps the shock over Darius's death had finally touched her wits.

The woman swayed back and forth. For a moment, she was quite overcome. Finally, she spoke. "Tahmin. It must have been Tahmin. Oh, poor Tahmin."

"Tahmin?" Lucy asked. "Who's Tahmin?"

Wiping the tears from her face, Miss Water stumbled to explain. "Tahmin was Darius's friend. Or even his manservant. He was so protective of Darius, he sometimes seemed like his bodyguard. But Darius was just a translator, why would he need a bodyguard?"

"I don't know," Lucy said, trying to follow Miss Water's wild speech. "Tell me why you no longer believe the murdered man was Darius? You were so sure, when we first met at the Golden Lion. I told the constable."

"You should not have done that," Miss Water said, frowning. "How can it possibly matter now?"

"The constable's job is to restore order. Find justice." Lucy cocked her head sidewise. "How do you know it was—Tahmin, did you say? Not Darius."

Miss Water waved her hand. " 'Twas the rook, you see. Tahmin never let it out of his sight. I think it was his good-luck charm. Darius used to josh him about it. It makes sense. Tahmin was the card player, the gambler. Not Darius."

Lucy thought back to Jacques's description. "Sickened by cards," he had said. From the way that Miss Water had described the two men, she was beginning to agree that it was indeed Tahmin, not Darius, who had been murdered in the tavern. "What's the matter?" Lucy asked. Miss Water had gripped her arm.

"Father is coming. Please leave me. There is nothing more I can tell you."

"Tell me who Tahmin was," Lucy said. "Please! His last name! He's been buried in an unmarked grave in Houndsditch. Carted away by the raker! Don't you think his family, his parents, deserve to know what happened to him?"

Miss Water quivered, her eyes filling with tears. "I am heartfelt sorry. Truly, I am. I would send a letter if I could, but I have no idea where to send it. Oh!" she suddenly sounded a bit scared. "Here's Father!" she whispered. In a louder voice, "I've nothing else for you!"

Lucy gave a quick bob as she passed Master Water on her way out of the graveyard, but did not speak to the man. He looked annoyed.

"Who was that?" she heard him ask his daughter. "Did you know that young woman?"

"No, Father! She was just seeking a bit of silver, for which I did not oblige."

"Good girl, Rhonda," Lucy heard him reply. "The Fire's brought too many beggars to Oxford. We must not indulge them, or we'll never be rid of them."

Lucy's cheeks were still flaming as she marched up to Duncan where he stood with Annie by the church's great stone entrance. Beggar indeed!

"Hey, slow down!" the constable said. "What did you find out about Darius?"

"He's not Darius, for one thing," Lucy said, without slowing down.

"What?" Duncan said, scrambling after her. "What did she say?"

"Lucy!" Annie called. "Wait for us!"

Striding down High Street, back toward the Scholar's Head, Lucy could not help but think about Miss Water's pale, tear-stained face. "She seemed so scared of her father," Lucy said, finally slowing down. "He did not approve of his daughter's love."

Lucy kicked a rock on the road, watching it ricochet into the carcass of a dead rabbit, before sinking into the decaying pulp of flesh and fur. She looked away in disgust. "A wasted trip, I'm afraid. We're no closer to bringing a murderer to justice." She looked at Duncan, daring him to disagree.

"Why do you say that, Lucy?" he asked patiently. "I've not understood a single thing you've said, this whole way back from the church."

Beside him, Annie nodded her head emphatically in agreement. "Yes, Lucy, what did she tell you?"

Having reached Ivan and the cart, Lucy stopped. She looked squarely back at Duncan. "I had told her she could have the contents of the bag back and—what?" she broke off, seeing Duncan's face tighten.

"You told her what?" he roared.

Annie gaped at him a moment before climbing back into the cart. Ivan continued to placidly brush his horses, in preparation for their long journey back to London.

"I thought she should have the contents of the bag back,"

Lucy said, defiantly. The constable's reaction was not what she had expected.

"You had no right to tell her that!" Duncan exclaimed. "We don't even know those items rightfully belong to her anyway! Especially since you said the dead man wasn't Darius at all." Something flickered in his face just then. "How did you know that?" he asked, a bit reluctantly. "What did she say?"

She told him quickly about the rook, and Miss Water's conviction that the man could only have been Darius's faithful friend Tahmin.

After that, Duncan didn't say anything, but started untying the horses from the post. His disappointed silence suddenly made Lucy angry.

"If it were not for me, I dare say you wouldn't have known anything about this crime! You wouldn't have known about Darius, or Miss Water, or Tahmin, or Jacques Durand! Not anything!" She couldn't stop the words from spilling out of her mouth. "I gave up two days to go on this ridiculous journey. Everyone's questioned why I've been helping you so much, and I have to say, I don't know!"

The constable seemed at a loss for words then. She glared at him, before turning away.

Lucy spent the next three hours gazing stonily at the passing scenery along the London road. She wouldn't even look in Duncan's direction in case he turned around. Consequently she developed an ache in her neck from her strained position.

Only when they finally stopped at a coaching inn to exchange horses did Duncan try to make stilted amends for his harsh words. "I'm sorry, Lucy," he had said, watching her rub the crick in her neck. "I was angry because I thought you told Miss Water about the items because you didn't think we'd catch Darius's—well, Tahmin's—killer."

"I would never think that way."

"I know." Duncan ran his hand through his dark hair. "My superiors want me to drop my pursuit of this murderer, to turn my attention to other matters. I can't rest easy until I do. Every day that passes, the murderer will be harder to catch."

Lucy nodded, the bitterness somewhat lessened between them. She climbed back into the cart. As she settled in, Duncan stood beside her. "I appreciate your help, Lucy. I do. You've got a keen mind. I'm utterly capable of admitting that you've helped me think through this crime. You've discovered some helpful information." He paused. He glanced at Annie, who seemed to have been rocked to sleep by the steady clip-clopping of the horses. "I know, too, that not everyone in your acquaintance is happy that you're helping me."

Adam's face flashed through her mind and she looked away.

"I certainly don't want to cause you any problems. Nor do I want any strife between us." Duncan touched her arm where it rested on the wagon. "I hope you will accept my apology." He moved away then, to reclaim his seat next to Ivan.

Annie opened her eyes. "You'll forgive him, right?"

Lucy swatted at her. "Wretched girl. Were you awake the whole time?"

Annie smiled. "The constable needs us. We can't let him down."

· 11 ·

The next morning, back in London, Lucy finished inking a new piece called *A True Account of Joan Little, Moll Cut-Purse*. Even though she was not supposed to run the press by herself, she laid one of the pieces of paper carefully on top.

"Master Aubrey will be so surprised when he returns, and Lach too!" she said, smiling to think of the looks on their faces. Using the long lever she pressed with all her might, bringing the great lid on top of the paper and type.

To Lucy's dismay, she heard a sickening crunching sound from within the press. Quickly raising the cover back up, she tore off the paper and looked at the typeface in consternation. The wood-cut she had used, the one Master Aubrey preferred for pieces that portrayed an ill-bred woman, had completely shattered.

Swearing, Lucy began to extract the delicate slivers of a wood-cut from the press. "Must have tightened it too much so that it

popped out a bit!" she muttered. "Dolt!" she berated herself.
Thank goodness neither Master Aubrey or Lach were around. She
could only imagine what the printer would say when he saw the
broken woodcut. Deduct the cost from her wages, that was certain. Even worse, how Lach would smirk. She grimaced even
thinking about how the apprentice would mock her.

Her mood didn't improve when Sid walked into the shop. Lucy
groaned. "Truly, Sid, I have no time for your nonsense right now."

"Is that a kind way to speak?" Sid asked. "Here I come with a
note for you from the magistrate, with nary a thought for myself,
and you only have harsh words for me."

"A note? From the magistrate?" Lucy stood up, wiping her
hands on her apron. Annie had mentioned that Sid was still hanging about the magistrate's household, doing odd jobs here and
there. It seemed that the magistrate had begun to trust the former pickpocket with more personal duties. "What's it say?"

"Dunno," Sid said, shuffling his feet. "I never went to no Dame's
school."

"Oh, Sid, you must learn to read." Lucy said, taking the note
gingerly, careful that her ink-stained hands not mar the letter.
She had never received a note from the magistrate before.

"Dear Lucy," the magistrate had written in his eloquent script.
"I hope this letter finds you well. Annie told me a bit of what you learned
in Oxford, and I am sorry that your inquiry is at a standstill. I have
taken it upon myself to invite Lord Cumberland to my home for supper
this evening, as well as the physician Larimer, and their wives. Lucy
smiled. Trust the magistrate to figure out the next step. She continued reading, "I had heard he was in London for a spell, checking on
his rents. I just received word that he is pleased to join me. Annie is a

delightful child, but has nowhere near the experience you have with waiting upon nobility. I hope you would not take it amiss if I asked you to help us serve this evening at six o'clock. Pray forgive the short notice. I shall be quite beholden to you. Yours in haste, Thomas Hargrave."

Lucy smiled as she turned the note over. Carefully, she wrote. "*Dear Sir, I would be happy to oblige. Yours faithfully, Lucy Campion.*" She handed the note to Sid. "No dawdling now, Sid. You must return to Master Hargrave straightaway, you understand me?"

After Sid left with his customary swaggering step, Lucy returned to her struggle with the broadside. As she pulled out the tray of woodcuts, hoping to find one that would similarly depict a vixen or hoyden, she picked up a piece about two inches wide all around with the image of a princess. Sometimes they used this woodcut with ballads or pamphlets that jeered the French royals. She was about to set it aside when she looked at the piece more closely. The woman was wearing a fanciful French hat, a great necklace, and rings on every finger. "I wonder what princesses truly look like," she wondered. "Do they really have fingers dripping with jewels?"

As she set the woodcut aside, she began to think of beautiful jewelry she'd seen, and her mind flashed to the brooch that had been found with Tahmin's body. Not too many people owned ivory jewelry, she thought. "If only we could take it to the comb-seller," she said out loud. "I bet he'd know who had crafted the piece." Too bad his shop had burned down in the fire. She'd spent some time looking for it the other day.

Who else would know about ivory, she wondered. As she continued to reset the type, her mind turned to supper that night.

Maybe she could show the ivory brooch to Sir Larimer, she thought, since he would be dining with Master Hargrave that night. She'd overheard enough conversations with the physician to know that he fancied himself a man of the world, knowledgeable in many things, in the manner of that long-dead Italian fellow, Da Vinci. He was also a lover of luxurious things, and might be familiar with the artisan who had crafted the brooch. At the very least, he might know who traded in such luxury items. Perhaps that would give the constable a lead on who had owned the brooch.

Lach returned then, and helped her finish the run. He didn't notice that she had switched the woodcuts, and she was certainly not going to tell him. Not straightaway at least.

"Master Aubrey said you're to sell at Tyburn today," he said to her, lifting his eyebrow. He knew her brother had almost been sentenced to be hanged at the infamous gallows. Or the "Tyburn tree," as Londoners affectionately called the grisly site. "You haven't hawked the murder ballads there yet. They've rebuilt them you know."

"I know," Lucy muttered. She'd been dreading having to sell at Tyburn. Even though Newgate and the Fleet had been destroyed during the Great Fire, the executions had not been ceased for long. It made sense, though, to sell there. The crowds that gathered to see the day's hangings would have a hankering to buy the most sensational and gory pieces they had in stock.

Thoughtfully, Lucy put together her pack. Last April's hanging of Jack Parr and his wife for cozening their master out of a good deal of money. A recent poisoning. A few last dying speeches and the "True Confession" of Robert Hubert, the watchmaker who'd confessed to setting Fariner's bakery—and London—on fire.

———

Before walking over to Tyburn, Lucy first stopped at Duncan's jail to ask him about the brooch. The whole way over she'd argued with herself whether she should continue to help the constable or not, especially after their words the day before. "I want justice to prevail," she told herself firmly. "I'm not doing this for the constable. After this, I won't help him anymore. Or go see him."

When she'd entered the jail, she tried not to notice how the constable's face brightened when he saw her. "Lucy!" he said. "I didn't expect to see you."

Again? Or so soon? Lucy couldn't help wonder. She plunged right in to the purpose of her visit. "I was just thinking about the brooch. When my acquaintance saw it, you know, that first night we looked at it, he said it didn't come from oak, cherry, or ash. I think it's ivory. I'd say take it to the comb-seller, but his shop burnt down. So, I thought that perhaps Dr. Larimer could look at the brooch. It may be from Persia, of course, but I thought he might know something about the craftsman or the guild. Or, maybe he would know someone who trades and sells in ivory." She looked at Duncan expectantly.

"Oh?" Duncan said. "Dr. Larimer knows that sort of thing, does he? That's a good idea. I'll send my bellman around to Larimer with a note." He looked at her expectantly. "Is there something else?"

Lucy twisted her hands. "Actually, I'll be seeing the physician. Tonight. I'll be at Master Hargrave's. I could ask him about it, if you like."

"I see." He didn't say anything else for a long moment. As he pulled out the brooch from the little bag, he asked, "You've decided to keep helping me?" Was his tone hopeful? Rueful? Lucy couldn't tell.

"I want to help see justice done." Hearing the bellman call the hour, she added. "It's late. I'm off to the Tyburn tree." She gestured to her pack. "I'm to sell a few horrid pieces there."

"At a very horrid site." He hesitated before handing her the brooch. He looked at her closely. "Will you be alright?"

"Of course," she said hastily, taking the brooch. His concern made her uneasy. "I'll let you know if Dr. Larimer can tell us anything about the brooch."

After she left the jail, the rose brooch carefully hidden beneath her skirts, Lucy began to make her way slowly over to Tyburn. Before the Fire the walk would not have taken long at all, but now she had to cross through much of the area ravaged by the inferno. While a great deal of the rubble had been cleared, new dwellings were being constructed everywhere, which made navigating the streets quickly a challenge. At least the buildings were all going to be made of stone and brick now. That was one of the first recommendations that Christopher Wren had put forth to the King after the Fire.

Despite how slowly she'd walked, she finally made it to Tyburn. A quick peek at the gallows revealed no one was on the scaffold—neither criminals to be hanged nor the executioner with his notable black hood. However, though the afternoon was growing late, Londoners were still making merry, passing about their

jugs of wine and ale. This meant she hadn't missed the last hangings of the day.

Her throat was already a bit parched and sore from the slight
smoke that still hovered in the air in this area. She knew from
experience that if she didn't have water on hand she could easily
have a coughing fit in the middle of a song, or worse, go hoarse
entirely. She didn't want to lose her voice—Master Aubrey had
impressed that on her enough. Looking around, she spied a well
from which she could fill her little tin cup.

Peering into the dark well, she could just see the glimmer of
water far within its depths. She lowered the bucket down, and
when it felt full, she began to pull it up. "Please let the water be
clean," she uttered softly. One time she'd drawn some water from
a well, only to find some dead bats inside the bucket, tainting the
water in the well. When the bucket came into view, she gave a
small prayer of thanks. The water looked sparkling and clear. She
drank a cup eagerly, and carefully filled a second cupful while she
sought a good place to sell her pieces.

She spied a stump of an old oak tree nearby. "That should
work," she said to herself. Before climbing atop the stump, she ran
her hands across the burnt surface. She could tell the tree had been
chopped down well before the Fire, probably because the branches
had obscured the spectators' view of the spectacle on the scaffold.
Now the stump, about thirty yards from the gallows, was perfectly
situated to offer a fine prospect of the gallows. How many people,
she wondered for a moment, had clambered up, just as she had, to
watch the condemned men and women swing?

"Enough of your fancies, Lucy," she scolded herself. "Time to
work." She began her customary singsong, calling the stories she'd

brought along. Sometimes it was hard to start, but today she just dove in, hoping to sell all her pieces quickly. Over the last few weeks she'd begun to perfect her call, starting with a gripping first line that got the crowd to gather. She had to get over the uncomfortable feeling that she was being watched—today the feeling seemed particularly strong. "Of course they're watching you, little twit," she said to herself, surveying the crowd as she began.

She was beginning to understand how to read the crowds as well. This crowd, as she had expected, was particularly interested in Hubert's confession and news of his upcoming trial. "He'll be doing the Tyburn jig soon enough!" one man called, to the great approval of others who had gathered about.

Within thirty minutes, Lucy had almost sold everything in her pack. She hoped to finish before the last of the condemned would be carted into Tyburn. That hope died a quick death, however, when she heard a great shout behind her. The criminals had arrived.

Around her, everyone scrambled to their feet. From her vantage point on the stump, she could see a cart bearing two tied-up prisoners, moving slowly toward them. A great procession of followers were shouting and chanting alongside the cart. Lucy counted five soldiers walking beside the cart as well, a pike held stiffly in each man's right hand.

As they passed, Lucy could see the faces of the two criminals. One man looked like he had been weeping, but his eyes were closed, and in his free hand he clutched a Bible to his heart. His mouth was moving in silent prayer. The other man, a young handsome sort, was laughing loudly, exchanging taunts with the crowd. He looked for all the world like he was drunk, but Lucy doubted that he was. She knew that, traditionally, prisoners were entitled to one last drink at a pub along the road. He was putting on a brave front, even as the gallows loomed. She didn't know his crime, for all she knew he was the most horrible cutthroat there ever was. In the moment, however, she admired his bravery in the face of upcoming death. He cut a fine enough figure in his church-going suit, to be certain.

Perhaps her face betrayed her admiration; perhaps because she was hands and shoulders above most of the crowd, she caught the handsome criminal's eye. To her shock, he grinned at her. Without a second thought, she crooked her finger, calling down an ancient blessing to ease his soul.

Seeing the gesture, he winked and blew her a kiss. "Thanks for the thought, sweetheart, but I don't need your pity," he called to her. "A kiss, though, I'll take. I'd kiss you myself, but alas"—he gestured to his left hand tied to the cart—"I've got some business that keeps me tethered. Come here! Give poor Rhys Whittier a kiss!"

The crowd laughed. They turned to Lucy expectantly.

"Alas!" Lucy called back, getting into the morbid humor of it all. "I cannot kiss you—I fear your business will always come first in your life. You'd take my kiss and leave me—I have no doubt!"

"Ah, but I promise to love you as long as I live!" Seeing Lucy shake her head, he added, "You're probably right. I think our love is doomed to fail." He outstretched his free hand in mockery of a court suitor.

Lucy couldn't help but smile at the young man's bravado. She blew Whittier a kiss then and he put his hand to his heart. A moment later the cart stopped, and the executioner stepped forward.

She saw Whittier gulp, his cocky grin fading. The other criminal opened his eyes and began to sob openly, begging for forgiveness.

She turned away then and stepped blindly off the stump. She couldn't bear to see the gallant young criminal go to his death. She began to edge away from the crowd. All about her, the mob was surging forward, and she could sense a changing mood among the spectators. Less friendly, more animal-like. They weren't quite salivating, yet there was something lustful appearing on the faces of the old and young alike.

Lucy began to feel queasy. She could feel her knees begin to buckle.

As she was starting to pitch forward, someone grabbed her arm. "Let me help you," a man murmured. "You can rest up here."

"T-thank you," she said, gratefully letting the stranger direct her toward a small copse of shady trees away from the screaming crowds. "I'll be fine now."

When they reached the copse, she began to pull away, but to her surprise the stranger still held her arm tightly. "Let go of me!" she said fiercely. "I said I'm fine!"

Instead of letting her go, the man tightened his hold and then, in a single fluid motion, clapped his hand firmly over her mouth.

Lucy immediately started to struggle against her captor. The strong filthy hand, clamped against her mouth, muffled her shouts. Making matters worse, her struggles made her even more entangled in her own pack, effectively binding her arms against her sides. She began to try to bite the man's hand, her fear overcoming her revulsion at the sweaty taste of his skin.

"Give 'em to me!" the man's hoarse voice whispered in her ear.

Lucy began to struggle harder. The thought of Master Aubrey

selling a broadside about her murder, or worse, her ruin, caused her to flail about as hard as she could. Did no one see her plight? Unfortunately, a great roar from the crowd just then indicated that the hanging was getting under way. No one was likely looking to see what was going on in the patch of trees. *I have to get free,* she thought wildly to herself.

With all her might, Lucy drove her head back, ramming the man's jaw with her own skull. Hearing her attacker groan, Lucy renewed her struggles. With some effort, she managed a backward kick as she'd seen young colts do. The man cried out in anguish again and let her go, collapsing to the muddy ground while holding his shin. She backed off, keeping a safe distance between them.

She glared at him, warily taking in his appearance. Her attacker was in his mid- to late forties and had the short-trimmed hair of a soldier, although his rugged wool clothes could have belonged to any tradesman. Still doubled over in pain, he looked a bit pitiful, but Lucy's heart was hardened against him. "Serves you right," she said, stepping backward. Even though he was still on the ground clutching his leg, she was taking no chances.

"Ach," the man said. He had a funny way of speaking, but Lucy couldn't place the region. "I just wanted the ring back. The brooch, too. I know you have them!" The man's eyes narrowed. "You know they don't belong to you!"

Lucy froze, even as her heart and brain continued to race. The man knew who she was; he must have been following her. "I don't have them," she said, eyeing a branch that had broken off a nearby tree. "I gave them to the constable." She stretched her fingers.

"You're lying. I saw him pass them to you. Yes, when you were at the jail. Saw you put them in your pocket, under your skirts too!" Seeing her flinch, he added, "Look, I don't want to hurt you," the man said. "But I will." He leapt up, his hands reaching for her.

Having anticipated his leap, Lucy grabbed the branch and swung blindly. With a terrible crack, she heard the wood strike his crown. The man yelped, before slumping down, knocked senseless.

For a single shocked moment, Lucy stared at the man, the bloodied stick still quivering in her hand. Dropping the stick like it was a hot iron, Lucy grabbed her pack, stumbling away. She could not bring herself to see if the man was still breathing. "Wretched footpad!" she muttered. He'd brought it on himself!

Keeping her head down, Lucy walked away stiffly, before breaking into a run once she was away from the Tyburn crowds. When she reached an open grass field, she dropped to her knees, then flopped full into the tall grasses. The birds about her chirped brightly against the blue sky. She could not rid her mind of the image of striking the man, hearing the crunch as she connected with his skull, the blood at his temple. She groaned again. "Please, Lord. Don't let me have killed him."

For a moment she couldn't decide where to go. Her mind cast through the possibilities. She was fairly near Aubrey's shop, but Will was unlikely to be there at this hour and she was afraid now to be alone. The constable? No, she couldn't go see him again. There was really only one place left to go, the sanctity closest to her heart. The magistrate's home.

·12·

A long stumbling run later, Lucy was still panting heavily when she opened the door to the kitchen, trying to put the attack out of her mind. The normalcy of the scene made her blink a bit. Cook was dipping a ladle into the bubbling pot, just raising it to her lips for a taste. Annie was slicing potatoes, and John as always was polishing something, this time the master's leather shoes.

Cook smiled when she saw her. "Nice and early," she remarked with satisfaction. "I knew I could rely on you, Lucy." She looked Lucy over. "You look a bit peaked, dear. Are you well?"

Despite the fright she had just experienced, Lucy smiled wanly at her friends. "I'm fine. I ran all the way here. Let me just sit a spell."

"Oh, you do that, dear. Annie, get Lucy some tea, will you?" As Lucy sank gratefully down onto the magistrate's familiar kitchen bench, Cook continued in her breezy bustling way. "I truly don't know what the good master was thinking."

Hearing Cook prattle on was immensely comforting to Lucy. Her frightening confrontation already seemed more distant, as if it had happened to someone else. Except it hadn't. Once again she patted her skirts, feeling the outline of her pocket containing the brooch.

"Can you imagine?" Cook went on, unaware of her distress. "He invited the Earl to dine this evening, without first discussing what we had in our stores."

Cook wasn't fooling anyone. Lucy knew she secretly enjoyed it when the master brought important people to dine at their table. Her standing among the local gossips rose considerably whenever she could drop a name or two. Now she bustled about. "Certainly the magistrate hasn't entertained much since the mistress, bless her dear heart, passed away, and Sarah ran off with those Conventiclers."

"Quakers," Lucy gently corrected, knowing how dear Sarah was to Cook. The normalcy of their conversation was gradually steadying her. "They're called Quakers."

Cook sniffed. "Nothing wrong with the Church of England, I should think."

Lucy let the comment pass. The decision by the magistrate's daughter to take up with Quakers and leave England was something Cook could never understand. Mostly because she just missed Sarah, who had been a bright and merry presence in the household.

"Let me help shine the silver," Lucy said, taking up one of the candleholders that would go on the dining room mantel. Having caught her breath and feeling able to stand, she moved into the dining room to lay the table for supper. She was just smoothing the Holland lace tablecloth when Adam strode into the dining room.

"Lucy!" he said, stopping short when he saw her. "Whatever are you doing here?"

Lucy thought for a moment he was going to embrace her, but he didn't. "Your father asked me to help prepare supper. I gather you know he invited Lord Cumberland to dine."

"Yes, that's why I'm here. He asked me specially to make sure I was in this evening." Adam rubbed his chin. As always, he had light brown stubble by this point in the day. "I don't like you acting as a servant here. I wish Father had not asked you do this."

"I don't mind helping your father, Adam," Lucy said quietly.

"This is all so sudden," Adam said, pacing about. He glared at the oil portrait of his grandfather, poised above his many vellum-bound law books. "We do not even know this Earl. In fact, his reputation is a bit sodden at the moment. I'm quite surprised Father would have him here."

"Why is that?" Lucy asked. "What is being said of the Earl?"

"Why are you interested?" Adam asked, suspiciously. "It's not like you to pursue empty gossip."

Lucy let that comment pass. Little did Adam know that gossip, empty it may be, was often a valuable way of getting information.

"Oh, what a dunce I've been!" Adam said, slapping his head. "Cumberland! The family coat of arms on that damned signet ring. Father told me all about it." His jaw tightened. "I don't appreciate that you've asked my father to do the constable's work now."

"Your father wants to see justice done as much as we do," she said quietly.

A knock at the front door saved them from further conversation. Dr. Larimer had arrived with his wife, who immediately went upstairs to use the necessity. Adam left to fetch his father, a grim set to his features. As John easily could have summoned the magistrate, Lucy knew he did not wish to stay in the same room as her.

Thankfully, Dr. Larimer did not seem to notice, or didn't care, being more interested in the Rhenish wine Lucy was pouring into his goblet. "Lovely, Lucy," he said. "Thank you." He took a sip. "Trust Thomas to always have something fine in his stock."

"Yes, sir," Lucy said, twisting the brooch in her hand. She took a deep breath and jumped right in. "Sir, could you please tell me where this ivory brooch might have come from? Who may have made it? Or at least, who might trade such a thing?" She paused. "Maybe it's from outside England?" Hoping she wasn't going too far, she added, "As a man of the world, I thought you might know."

Reaching for the brooch, Dr. Larimer gave her a keen look. "Hoping to build your dowry a bit, hey?" He turned the brooch this way and that. "Quite ornate," he mused. "Real workmanship." He paused, a quick look of disgust passing over his features. He did not finish the thought. "Where did you get this?" he asked instead. "Did someone give it to you?"

"I found it," Lucy responded, wondering at his tone. "Why?"

Instead of answering her, the physician walked over to one of the candles. "I need to inspect this brooch more closely," he muttered more to himself than to her, opening up the bag of medical instruments he always carried with him. As Lucy watched, the physician took out a small horn case about the size of his palm. Opening it, he took out a circular piece of glass, which he positioned a few inches away from the brooch.

"What's that?" Lucy could not help but ask.

"This is a flea-glass," he answered, still studying the brooch. "It magnifies what I look at. Other fellows use it to look at fleas and flies. I find it useful to discern details that the naked eye cannot readily see." Now he took a long thin needle from his bag. To her surprise, he held the needle's point in the candle flame for a moment, then touched the tip to the back of the brooch. Leaning down, he sniffed deeply.

Lucy sniffed too, an unpleasant smell wafting along her nostrils. "What's that smell?" she asked.

"Ever been to a tooth-puller? Or a sawbones?" the physician said, still looking closely at the brooch. The needle had left a small scorching mark on the surface of the brooch. When Lucy shook her head, having never had a tooth or limb removed, he went on. "A fortunate thing that. Wretched occupations. That's the smell of burning bone."

"Ivory is bone?" Lucy asked, curious. She'd never thought about where ivory came from. "Oh, that's why the comb-seller had a picture of an elephant."

"In a manner of speaking. But ivory comes from the tusks of the elephant, which are on the outside of the animal. No blood flows through those tusks. Moreover, with ivory there is generally some color variation, from the tusks having been exposed for so long to the elements. But this piece—" He frowned at the brooch.

"There's very little variation in color, which suggests that it was internally located, not external. I was able to burn it just now, and it's my understanding that ivory does not burn. The brooch is smooth, presumably, because the artisan polished it. However, if you use the flea-glass, look at those tiny spaces between the heart and roses. There are tiny ridges that the artisan could not smooth."

She looked, but did not know what to make of what she saw. She said as much to the physician, who was looking at her expectantly.

"Lucy, unless I'm not mistaken, which, quite frankly, I'm not, this brooch was carved from human bone, not from the tusks of an animal."

"Human bone?" Lucy repeated, feeling sick. Instinctively she stepped away from the table where the brooch rested.

"Indeed. If I had to guess," the physician continued, "I would suggest that this was made from a recently deceased person. Not some old papist relic, made from the finger of a long-gone saint. More malleable, you see." He bent the brooch slightly. "Old bone is far more dry and brittle." Grimacing, he added. "Probably from a woman."

"What makes you say that?"

"I'm just guessing, you understand. If it were a part of the pelvis, I'd know for sure." He turned it over in his hand. "I've just seen this kind of brooch before, and it's always from the bones of a woman."

"Who would do such a thing?" Lucy asked, slightly ill.

"Someone deeply distraught, I'd imagine."

"The Church wouldn't approve of that," Lucy said. "Would it? I mean, bodies are supposed to be buried, not—" she cast about for the word, "defiled."

"You're quite right," Dr. Larimer said. "If I were to guess, the Church didn't want to bury this woman in sacred ground. A fallen woman. Without being able to mark her death properly, I imagine the family wanted to remember her in a different way. A scandalous practice, to my mind." He held it out to her. "Not a nice piece for your collection, I'm afraid."

Lucy was just pocketing the brooch when Adam led the Earl and his wife into the room. As she rushed to take wraps and fill goblets, she tried not to feel repulsed by the object under her skirts. The Earl had affected one of his sheepskin wigs, dyed black as favored by King Charles, although he looked neither foppish nor effete. While in his early fifties, indeed, he looked vigorous and strong, seeming more like a medieval chieftain than a member of the House of Lords. He reminded Lucy a bit of pictures she'd seen of Henry VIII in the handsome days of his youth, not the dissolute figure he became in his final years. Lady Cumberland, a sallow, refined creature dressed in a fluff of lace and taffeta, looked about the room, a speculative expression on her face.

The magistrate had spared little expense on supper. The six dined on Cornish game hens and treacle tart, washing their meal down with Rhenish wine and claret. Cook had even procured a bit of chocolate, to the delight of the ladies.

Throughout, Lucy hovered nearby, refilling wineglasses and clearing chargers, trying to ignore Adam's gaze. As she expected, though, the conversation at supper remained mainly at the cordial acquaintance stage. As a rule, the men avoided politics, although Christopher Wren's plan to rebuild London came up. Discussion of the Fire led naturally to Robert Hubert's confession.

"The man, it's been proved irrefutably," Adam said, "was not even in London at the time of the Fire."

"Yet the watchmaker confessed?" Lady Cumberland asked. "Why ever would he do such a thing? He'll be hanged for sure."

"If not torn apart by a mob," Master Hargrave said, his voice grim.

"The man's wits are surely addled," Dr. Larimer added. "There's little hope for him if he keeps up with this 'confession.'"

"The whole confession is riddled with holes," Master Hargrave commented, his tone brittle. "'Tis a shame that everyone is so quick to believe."

"I have not read the confession," Lady Cumberland commented, taking a delicate nibble of sweetbread.

"I would have Lucy run and fetch her pack," Mistress Larimer commented, "if I thought it was of interest."

Lady Cumberland raised an eyebrow. Her eyes flicked toward Lucy, but then looked away as though she'd seen something distasteful. "Her pack?"

The magistrate hastened to explain. "Lucy works for Master Aubrey now, selling books," he beamed at her. "I just borrowed her back for the evening, since she was our very best maid at one time. I should not think, however, she need fetch the tract. She's got quite a gift though. Wrote one about a poem found in the Fire." Catching sight of their dismissive expressions, the magistrate tightened his jaw. "Lucy's very dear to us. A member of the family still."

The Earl scrutinized her for a moment. Seeing his wife sniff, the Earl said, "Indeed. How interesting. Publishing is a lowly occupation, but a necessary one." He poured some more wine into his goblet. He turned back to the magistrate. "What news have you from the Court?"

Stinging a little from the noble's rebuke, Lucy stepped back into the shadows. Adam's face was inscrutable, although for a moment she thought she saw something pass across his features. Disgust? Unease? Worry? She couldn't tell. For the first time, she wondered about the profession into which she had blindly apprenticed herself.

Not until the group had retired to the drawing room, to sit before the carefully gated fire, did the conversation grow interesting. As Lucy filled the men's pipes with New World tobacco, Master Hargrave turned to the Earl's wife. "How is your son faring?" he asked, his voice low.

"He is well," Lady Cumberland responded, darting a quick glance at her husband.

Dr. Larimer, hearing the exchange, asked, "Was your son ill?" His inquiry sounded more out of politeness than true professional curiosity. Lucy could understand. These days, everyone was suffering from some malady or other.

"I should say so!" the Earl exclaimed. "He was poisoned a few months ago!"

"Poisoned! Oh my!" Mistress Larimer said, gulping down a bit of her wine. Lucy could almost read her thoughts. One might gossip about murder and intrigue when one's husband was a royally appointed physician, but it was quite another thing to speak with intimacy of such a sordid thing. And for an Earl! Still, such details must be known. "Who could have done such a terrible thing to your son?" the physician's wife pressed.

Again, the Earl and his wife exchanged a glance. "I'm afraid," the Earl said slowly, "our family's been targeted by lunatics."

Lucy almost spluttered into speech, but remembered to keep silent just in time. Servants do not speak to, let alone question, earls. Master Hargrave gave her a meaningful glance. Taking the hint, she began to refill goblets. This little act gave her the chance to remain in the room without drawing attention to herself.

Luckily, Dr. Larimer asked the question burning on Lucy's tongue. "Whatever could you mean? Sir, I beg you to explain such a surprising statement!"

Taking a deep swallow of wine, the Earl continued. "First, a young woman in our employ thieved from us and then attempted to poison our son. Fortunately, the dose was ill-prepared and we were able to provide a remedy in time."

"Indeed!" the magistrate murmured. "Do tell."

"Then, a month or so before the Fire, a man plundered by his own bad luck made several attempts on my life. These occurred at our family seat." The Earl looked around. Everyone had leaned forward. Satisfied, he continued his story. "Once, the reins on my horses were suspiciously worn, where no such wear had previously occurred. On another occasion, a shot from a flintlock pistol came bracingly near my head, and no hunt was in progress."

"A flintlock pistol is hardly used for hunting," Larimer commented, having gone on many hunts himself.

"Precisely," the Earl agreed. "We felt compelled to leave, and return to London. Yet, this very afternoon, some rocks were lobbed at me as I was walking. The madman must have followed me here."

"Why do you suppose it was the same man?" Adam asked, without looking at Lucy. She appreciated him asking the question she wished to pose, but wished he did not sound so resentful. "Unfortunately, despite His Majesty's best efforts, London seems a bit lawless at the moment."

"I have seen him. 'Tis the same man, I assure you. Thrice he has accosted me, each time making wild claims that I had stolen something of his."

"Oh? He claims *you* have something of *his*?" Adam asked. "That hardly seems possible."

The Earl laughed, a low angry noise that sounded like a growl. "A ring. One that has been in my family for generations. Crafted for my own great grandfather. The First Earl of Cumberland."

His wife sat mutely beside him, her hands clenched tightly. "Can you imagine? Trying to claim the symbol of an earl's birthright. Makes no sense, does it?" He took another long draught from his goblet. "Indeed, I believe he's behind the current rumors being spread about in Parliament that I've not a legitimate claim to my seat in the House of Lords." He set the cup down with a bang, so that a few drops spilled out. "Poppycock all."

"I must agree. Dashed odd," the magistrate said. His tone was dry, unreadable. "Simply owning such a ring would not make one an earl, after all. Although, I suppose in your case, it may help clarify your claim. Since you're rather new to us." Master Hargrave poured some more wine into the Earl's goblet. "I understand that you grew up with a distant family member. The title was dormant for a while, was it not? It hadn't been held in a few generations." The magistrate's voice was deceptively bland, inviting confidences in his quiet way.

"That's correct. The last Earl only had a daughter, so it passed through to his nephew, my grandfather. Under Cromwell, my family couldn't very well lay claim to the title. Fortunately, a few years ago, some papers were unearthed that proved I was who I said I was. That I was the rightful heir." The Earl reached over and topped off his glass of wine. A gauche gesture to be sure. "Of course, by then my guardians, who were supposed to have watched over my inheritance, had squandered a bit of it. Fortunately, my wife had a tidy sum. Her father was in—" he stopped abruptly when his wife coughed into her handkerchief. It was ill-bred to speak of one's fortune in social circumstances. Lady Cumberland flushed, realizing her husband's faux pas.

Smoothly, the magistrate handed him the tray of sweets. "Do you still have the ring?" he asked.

"Why no, I don't, in fact," the Earl said. "I think the dastardly fellow stole it from me."

Lucy caught the magistrate's eye, puzzled. Jacques Durand had said the ring had been put in the stakes during that ill-fated game of cards. Perhaps by the Earl himself. The magistrate seemed to understand exactly what Lucy was thinking. Ever so slightly, he shook his head. "When did the theft happen?" he asked the Earl, taking a last bite of pie.

"A few weeks ago," the Earl said, vaguely. "I bloody well want that ring back! Excuse me, ladies, this fine wine is helping my tongue run a little free."

"Yet the attacks continue on you," Adam murmured. "Even

though he has already taken the ring from you. Have you any thought as to why he would do such a thing? Why he would assert such an outrageous claim?"

"Madman," the Earl shrugged. "Just a madman."

Thinking of the man who had set upon her earlier, Lucy could not help but agree. Clearly, he was mad. She frowned. Yet why would he have wanted the ring back? She shook her head. Perhaps the man who had attacked the Earl was not the same man who had attacked her earlier.

Mistress Larimer passed the silver salver of chocolates to Lady Cumberland. "You say that your son is recovering? Thanks be to God! Is he at your family seat then, in Westmoreland?"

The Earl and his wife exchanged another quick glance. "No, he has come to London." The Earl took a bite of his biscuit. "We thought it best that he recover elsewhere."

"Why, then, have you not had this man arrested?" Master Hargrave asked sternly. For a moment, they could have all been in an assize session. "Attempted murder! This is a serious accusation."

Hearing the magistrate's tone, the Earl set down the morsel. "I should like to bring him to justice, certainly, but we have no interest in creating a scandal." He seemed to be about to say something else, but thought better of it.

"What do you do for protection, then?" Adam asked. "Surely, you would like to be able to move freely about without fear of being set upon."

"I have some men who work for me. They accompany me when I need them."

Sensing an uncomfortable mood shift, Mistress Larimer took

it upon herself to change a distasteful conversation, as any well-bred lady would. "Have you heard the latest of Lady Castlemaine?" she asked, before launching into yet another story of King Charles's current mistress, and her extravagant actions at Court.

After Master Hargrave's guests finally took their leave of the household, Lucy set down the tray of dirtied dishes and turned toward the magistrate. "I think the Earl was lying," she said. "I think he lost the ring in a hand of cards. I don't think the man stole it. Why else would he be looking for it now?"

"Lucy, the Earl does not seem to know that the ring was recovered from the Fire. This would suggest he does not realize we know anything about the game," the magistrate said, carefully blowing out each taper. "We don't even know how the ring ended up in the stakes. For all we know, the man still thinks the Earl has the ring, although why he has laid claim to it is anyone's guess. Especially if he's truly a madman—his wits may not be about him."

"The madman, if he is the one, knows the Earl does not have the ring," Lucy said, slowly. "He told me so today."

"What?!" Both Adam and his father exclaimed at once. Reluctantly, Lucy described her encounter at Tyburn with the man. She did leave out her deepest worry—that she might have struck the man dead. To voice such a thought aloud! She shook her head.

"This has gone quite far enough, Lucy," Adam said, glowering at her. "You must stop trying to help the constable. You are going to get hurt."

"I have done nothing wrong!" Lucy cried. "That man set upon

me because he thought I knew about the items that were found with the poem. I wasn't trying to help the constable, with this—" She stopped abruptly, checking her words.

Adam glared at her. "You should not be out and about this way." Seeing his father cough slightly, he said, "No, Father, it's true! Lucy must stop this bookselling. Who knows where Aubrey will send you next!"

"I won't!" She glared back. "I can take care of myself."

"I'm not so sure you can!" He took a deep breath. "I must clear my head. Father, do not wait up for me." With that, he stalked out of the house without bidding her farewell.

Lucy felt stunned. The magistrate touched her elbow. "You must do what is right. That is who you are. Adam will understand that." But his voice carried little conviction.

"I suppose," Lucy said. "I truly don't know."

·13·

Lucy slipped out of the magistrate's household early the next morning, just as dawn was breaking. She wanted to run back to Master Aubrey's and get the fires stoked and ready for the day. Along the way, she kept darting quick glances around her, praying that no one would jump out at her. Although the air was chilly, she was sweating from the strain.

As she ran lightly through the muddy cart paths, Lucy tried to keep the memory of Adam's angry countenance from her thoughts. "I must speak with him soon," she whispered to herself. She could certainly stop helping the constable. Yet if Adam didn't like that she was selling books, well, that was something she didn't want to think about.

Heading down Fleet Street, she could hear small sounds of life inside the shops, as apprentices and chambermaids rose groggily from their rush matting and root cellars to start the day for their mistresses. Arriving at Master Aubrey's shop, she could see the windows were still shuttered and she couldn't see any candlelight coming from within. "Ah, Lach, you're not up yet. Tut, tut!"

The next instant, she stopped short. A shadowy figure was lying on the cobblestones in front of Master Aubrey's door. Her attack the other day fresh on her mind, she approached the figure warily. He was effectively blocking anyone from going in or out of Master Aubrey's. The ever-present fog swirled about, adding to the figure's mystery.

"Good day!" she called. Probably a poor chap who'd been too merry at the George the night before. Still, best to be cautious. "What cheer?"

The next moment, the figure sat up, a cloak obscuring its face. Lucy stumbled a bit back, trying to suppress a natural little shriek. "What do you want?" Lucy said, shivering. "You'd best get along now! Master Aubrey won't be pleased to find you on his stoop!"

"Lucy? Are you angry with me?"

With a start, Lucy kneeled down beside the crouched figure. "Avery!" Lucy cried, looking with delight on her friend. "Whatever are you doing here?"

"Avery came to see you." His eyes were bloodshot and troubled. "Yesterday, I think."

Lucy smiled at him, trying not to show the pity she felt. She'd known Avery a few years now. From his fragmented words and stories, she'd pieced together snippets of his life. A big man, he'd been a soldier who seemed to have received a head wound during the bloody wars between King Charles II and Cromwell. He'd also lost several fingers, no doubt from a musket injury. The last she'd heard, he'd been living at a local parish. He was not quick-witted to be sure, but he'd been quick enough when her life was in danger a few weeks ago.

"How do you fare?" she asked, as if he were a fine visitor coming to dine, rather than the bedraggled sort he looked. His brown hair curled damply over his face. He looked like he hadn't bathed for a while. His eyes, usually shining with innocence, today looked troubled. "Why don't you come in for a moment, get warm?"

Lucy unlatched the shuttered window, and climbed inside the printer's shop. Like most of the shops on the street, it could only be locked from within, although a child or a lad slim like herself could climb inside and unbar the door. A moment later, she had opened the door and thrown the wooden shutters wide open. "Pray, come in, Avery."

The ex-soldier came in, looking about. He did not spend a lot of time inside people's homes, and with little coin in his pocket, he spent even less time within stores and shops. Lucy seated him on a low wooden stool as she stoked the banked embers. In a few minutes, she had set to brewing a warm drink for him.

"How are your mousers?" she asked. Avery took care of a number of cats, but none were as dear to him as the dainty white one with blue eyes that he had saved from being killed by some vicious boys a few years before. He did not talk, simply stared at her with round, troubled eyes. "Avery," she asked, gently, "why do you stare at me so? Is something wrong?"

"Avery was afraid Lucy was hurt. In danger."

"Why did you think I was hurt?" Lucy asked, placing a steaming cup of wormwood in front of him, hoping to dispel the morning chill. Avery didn't answer; instead he rocked back and forth, looking away from her. "Avery," Lucy pressed, a bit more firmly now, "please look at me." When the man did, she asked him again why he had thought she was in danger.

"Avery came here. Last night. Lucy wasn't here." He blew on the steaming liquid before venturing a sip.

"No, Master Hargrave asked me to help him. He had a special visitor come to dine. I was with the magistrate." She paused. "Don't tell me you were here all last night?" At Avery's nod, Lucy sighed. "Oh, Avery, I'm fine. Just because I'm sometimes away, doesn't mean anyone has hurt me." She began to lay out the paper for pushing through the printer's press.

"Avery saw the man follow Lucy."

Lucy stiffened. "Yesterday? Were you at Tyburn then?"

"Avery wanted to say good day. Avery saw you walking to the hanging place. He saw that man following you. Watched from behind."

"So you saw someone following me. Why didn't you say anything?" Lucy asked, trying to hide her annoyance. The next moment she was glad she had held her tone in check.

"Lucy went up to Tyburn." Avery gulped, looking like he was going to cry. "Avery sad. Avery don't like dead men. Hid behind tree. Then Lucy was gone."

Lucy was starting to put it together now. Avery must have noticed the man follow her from the market, and was worried enough to follow her, even though he was afraid of the hangings. He must not have seen the man attack her. Like her, the wounded ex-soldier must have averted his eyes from the dreadful site of a man being hanged.

"Man walked away, but Avery came here. Must find Lucy."

Lucy felt a wave of relief wash over her. The man walked

away! She had not killed him with the stick. "Are you sure?" Lucy asked. "Are you sure he walked away?"

Avery nodded. "Avery thought man coming here. Had to take care of Lucy."

She tapped her foot on the cold cobblestones. Hardly a comfortable bed. She felt a rush of affection for the scarred man. "Did he?" Lucy asked. "Come here?"

Avery shook his head.

"Thank God," Lucy said. She would have hated to see anyone get hurt. She felt sick thinking about the man attacking Master Aubrey or Lach, or herself, of course. She looked at Avery. "Would you know this man again? Should you come across him?" she asked, not feeling optimistic about the prospect.

"Dunno," he said, rubbing his head.

Lucy sighed. That would have been too much to ask. She'd seen the man herself and would have no idea how to locate him again.

"Sid would though," Avery said. "I think."

Lucy stared at him. "Whatever do you mean?" she asked. "How do you know Sid?"

"Seen him with Annie."

Lucy didn't like the sound of that. I need a talking-to with Annie, she thought. Why ever had she taken up with Sid? She couldn't be concerned with this right now. "So Sid was at the hangings? I never saw him." She wasn't really surprised though. Of course Sid liked being near crowds, especially those where people would be too busy watching a spectacle to pay attention to their pockets.

Avery beamed, making Lucy grin widely in return. He truly

did have the sweetest smile. "Avery asked Sid to follow the scary man, and he did. Avery said he'd wait here."

"Let me get this straight. You asked Sid to follow the man who attacked me?" When he nodded, Lucy hugged him then, not caring about his layer of grime. Her hands still on his shoulders she said, "Now we just have to find Sid."

"Oh, he told Avery. A few hours ago. Said the man was sleeping at St. Martin-in-the-Fields."

By the time Master Aubrey descended the wooden stairs fifteen minutes later, Lucy had already hastened Avery off. She didn't think Master Aubrey would take too kindly to her letting a strange man in his shop before it had been opened for the day. Now Lucy just had to convince Master Aubrey that he needed her to peddle some penny pieces at St. Martin-in-the-Fields. "Good morning, sir," she said, smiling, and handed him a cup of warmed ale and a bowl of porridge. "I'm ready to do some selling!"

Lach wandered in then, slightly bleary-eyed. "Chipper today, are you?" The apprentice said, then lowered his voice. "Eager to be off, are you? Wanna leave me with all the work again, do you? Well, we'll see about that!"

"Oh no, Lach, don't," Lucy said, alarmed.

"I see some dirt about," Lach commented loudly, ladling a bit of porridge into his bowl.

"Hrrumph." Master Aubrey sat heavily down, so that the bench groaned a bit under his weight. He looked around, scratching his whiskers. "Floors not swept, lass?"

Lucy groaned inwardly. How could she have forgotten? For the last two weeks, Master Aubrey had been reminding her again and again that the shop must be as free of dirt, leaves, and feathers as possible, lest they get caught in the press and muck up the works.

"Here you go, Lucy," the apprentice said, handing her a straw broom. "I see some piles of dirt there, and there. Oh, and over there."

"Thanks so much," Lucy said sweetly, before sticking her tongue out at him. She took the broom and began sweeping vigorously.

"Easy lass! Easy!" Master Aubrey spluttered. "We've no important printing today. No need for such speed. You're raising more dust than your settling."

Gritting her teeth a bit, Lucy went a little slower with the broom. In the meantime, Master Aubrey set Lach to laying type. Another of Nicholas Culpeper's apocryphal remedies. "I was thinking, sir," Lucy said, "that we haven't sold by St. Martin-in-the Fields."

Lach raised his eyebrows. "Is that where you want to head to?" he whispered. "Why? Are you meeting your Master Hargrave there? Or is it the constable you seek?" He wagged his finger at her. "Naughty lass."

"Stop talking, you silly boy!" Lucy hissed back. Truly, the lad was just impossible sometimes.

"All beggars and the sickly, seeking miracles and cures," Lach said, with a mischievous glance at Lucy. "No one with any coin to spare. Better to peddle at Covent Garden again."

Master Aubrey turned around. "St. Martin-in-the-Fields?" he asked. He seemed to be thinking. "You know, that may be quite a good place to sell."

"But you've always said—" Lach began, before being cut off by the printer.

"Normally, I would agree with you, Lach. But since the Fire, many people have set up camp there. Not just vagrants. People with money. 'Sides, they might like a fair story. Raise their spirits." Master Aubrey looked doubtfully at Lucy. "You think you can handle it, lass? At the first sign of trouble, run. I can't have my apprentices torn to shreds by an angry mob. Besides, Master Hargrave might be a bit put out should I let anything happen to you."

Lucy shivered, thinking again of the man who had attacked her. Not for the first time, she wondered what she was getting herself into. Yet she felt determined to see this through. "I'll be fine," she said, mustering a bravery she did not feel.

On the way out, Lucy waved airily to Lach, as he painstakingly began to set the type for Culpeper's herbals.

As she approached St. Martin-in-the-Fields, Lucy felt her earlier confidence begin to fade. Along the way, she'd passed the bellman and handed him a note that she'd hastily scrawled to the constable. She hoped the man would take it to Duncan in a timely way. "Can you meet me at St. Martin-in-the-Fields? L.C." She hadn't wanted to write much more. She squirmed under the bellman's cheerful scrutiny. Nice young ladies do not send notes to constables. Nice young ladies do not walk around unaccompanied.

For that matter, nice young ladies don't involve themselves in murder investigations.

At St. Martin-in-the-Fields there were people everywhere, many in makeshift camps, many looking a bit helpless and sick. They reminded Lucy of the gypsies she'd known, yet without the gypsies' cheer or organization. Before long, she spotted Avery, standing helpfully by the pillars of the great stone church. His eyes brightened when he saw her.

"I've got to do a bit of selling first," she explained, indicating her bulging pack of penny pieces. "Did you find Sid?"

Avery nodded, and pointed to a crowd that had gathered. Sid, it appeared, had picked up a new skill, doing conjuring tricks for a rapt audience. "Is the man who attacked me still around?"

Avery nodded. "He's on the other side of the church. Sid can see him."

Lucy climbed up on the stone steps so that she could easily be seen. She glanced through the titles that Master Aubrey had packed for her. A few murders—she'd save those for last. Another broadside caught her eye. "Gentle ladies, gentlemen, I give you the ballad of the good maid Marian, and that stouthearted highwayman, Robin Hood of Locksley." Taking a deep breath, Lucy began to sing. "A bonny fine maid of a noble degree, with a hey down down a down down."

A little crowd began to gather, and Lucy continued the ballad, describing how the Earl of Huntington and Marian fell in love, until "separated by fortune." When she got to the part where the two met again, the maid "strangely attired," and Robin Hood "himself disguised," and they fell to blows because they did not recognize each other, Lucy had the crowd leaning on every word.

"They lived by their hands, without any lands, And so they did many a day, day." She stumbled over the last lines, having looked up to see Duncan watching her from the back of the crowd. She was pleased he'd come, but she could not discern the constable's expression.

Lucy spent the next few moments passing out sheets, and collecting pence. As Master Aubrey had assumed, this was a good place to sell. When she was done, she ducked behind the stone wall and tucked the coins inside her inner pocket, hidden beneath her skirts.

"Ho there, Lucy," Avery said, saying her name in that special way of his, as if they had not just been speaking together a little while before. "Avery found the constable."

"What is going on, Lucy?" Duncan asked, keeping his body partially turned so that he could keep an eye on the crowd. "I got your note. I can't say I understood it."

"Well, it's a queer thing, actually," Lucy said, flicking a bit of mud from her sleeve. "Yesterday, Avery saw a man following me when I was selling broadsides at Tyburn. He didn't see the man attack me but, thanks be to God, he sent Sid after him." She finished in a rush. "So Sid knows where the man went. We just need to find Sid." She hesitated. "Duncan?"

Duncan was staring at her, his attention no longer divided. "Wait a minute. Slow down. Tell me from the beginning, and don't skip anything important."

Lucy related the story again. When she told him about the man setting upon her, she could see his jaw tighten. "I conked him over the head though," Lucy added hastily. She thought it best to omit the detail where she thought she'd killed the man. The constable might not take that fact well.

"So he told you he wanted the ring and the brooch back, because they belonged to him?"

Lucy nodded. She then proceeded to fill him in on what she had learned from Lord Cumberland the night before. "I think this man may also have set upon the Earl." Out of the corner of her eye she could see Sid gesturing impatiently to her. "Uh, I think Sid wants to talk to *me*." She stressed the word "me" ever so slightly, hoping he would get the hint.

He did. "I suppose he doesn't want to talk to a constable." He clipped his feet together, military style. "I'll wait over here. And Lucy—"

"Yes?"

"Make sure Mister Petry doesn't do any picking while I'm watching, alright?"

"I'll do what I can," she said, walking over to Sid, who was now talking to a perfume-seller. The woman's pocket was hanging a bit heavy at her side, not tucked away as it should have been. An easy mark.

"Hey there, Sid," she said. "Planning on buying some perfumes?"

He grinned, not looking at all chagrined. "Lucy!" he said, moving away from the perfume stall. Only a quick flick of his eyes toward the woman's purse betrayed his thoughts. "No one after you today?"

"It seems not," she said. "Listen. Where's the man who followed me yesterday? We need to ask him some questions."

" 'We?' Is Annie here?" Sid rubbed his light brown whiskers. "Oh. You meant the constable." He looked disappointed.

"Sid," Lucy said firmly, drawing his arm in hers. She started to walk him toward the constable. "Constable Duncan isn't concerned—at this moment—about your goings-on. I need you to tell him everything about that man you followed yesterday."

"I'll point him out." Sid grimaced. "You know, he's a funny sort."

"How do you mean?"

"He didn't come here straightaway," Sid explained. "I followed him to The Sparrow. You know, the inn down by the docks."

Lucy shrugged. She'd not spent too much time in that area along the Thames, as she'd heard that sailors were a rough-and-tumble lot. "Do you think he's staying there?"

"I thought so. He didn't go in though."

"No?" Lucy asked. "What did he do?" She waited for Sid to respond, but his eyes had slid over a buxom young woman carrying a large straw basket on her head. She pinched his forearm to reclaim his attention.

"Ow!" he cried, rubbing his arm. "That hurt!"

"Where did the man go?"

"That's the odd part. First, he hid behind a bush. Which meant I had to hide too, so *he* wouldn't see *me* watching him."

"That is odd," Lucy said, trying to imagine the scene. "Then what happened?"

"He was watching the door of the inn, as far as I could tell. I was about to leave when a man came out of the inn. Gentry, you know? So our man followed the chap." Sid pushed his gray cap back. "He followed him straight to the magistrate's house, if you can believe *that*!"

"To the magistrate's house?" Lucy exchanged a glance with Duncan, who'd been listening intently. "Was the gentleman the Earl of Cumberland?"

"Dunno," Sid grinned. "Don't know no earls."

After Lucy quickly described the Earl, Sid shrugged his shoulders. "Yeah. That sounds like him. I saw a woman waiting for him a few houses down the way. Fancy-like, but not gentry, you know what I mean? She looked like she knew the Earl quite well. Plopped a kiss right on his cheek. Earl's ladybird, if I had to guess."

"No, I think that was the Earl's wife, Lady Cumberland," Lucy said slowly. It surprised her that the pair had arrived to the magistrate's home separately, and that neither had arrived in a carriage.

"You don't say?" Sid smirked. "She smelled of trade, that one did. I can always spot one of our own. They did go in together, that's true enough."

Duncan interrupted them then. "Did the man say anything to the Earl, before he went inside?"

"As a matter of fact, he did." Sid looked at them expectantly. "I'll tell you, for a small price."

Seeing the constable's jaw clench, Lucy jumped in. "The constable's not going to pay you for your information, Sid," she said. "You need to tell him everything."

Sid frowned. "The man started shouting at the Earl. He said, 'Get them back for me!' Then he pitched a few rocks at them before they made it inside."

"'Get them back for me'?" Lucy repeated. "You're sure that's what the man said?" At Sid's nod, she asked, "Well, what happened next?"

"Our fellow stayed outside, watching the magistrate's door." Sid put his fist in his other hand. "I didn't like him hanging about, no siree. I thought he might have scared Annie. So I tore into him. Made like someone escaped from Bedlam, I did. Came at him, mad-like." Sid smacked his lips. "Then, I followed him here."

"And he's still here?" Lucy asked, looking at the sprawl of humanity made homeless by the Fire. "He didn't leave?"

"Naw, he's still here. Last night, I could tell he was settling down, like everyone else here. I went over to Aubrey's shop. Told Avery where he was, I did. And then I came back. As good as any place to rest my head."

"So where is he?" the constable said.

Sid's eyes had turned calculating again. "What's in it for me? After all, I spent a day and night following this man. Time I could have spent earning some coins."

"You'll tell me now." Duncan's tone brooked no nonsense. "As a good law-abiding citizen."

Sid clammed up, his features taking a sullen look. "Don't have to."

This was getting them nowhere. Lucy decided to intervene. "What a clever lad you've been," she said to Sid. "Following that man to the Sparrow, following him to the magistrate's home, following him here. You've been ever so helpful. I'm sure Constable Duncan appreciates your help. He might even put in a good word for you, if you find yourself in a scrape." She looked meaningfully at Duncan.

"Of course," Duncan said, through clenched teeth. "Now out with it."

For a moment Sid was silent. Resentment and the grudging

wish for appreciation seemed to battle across his features. Lucy thought he might not answer the constable at all. Finally he spoke. "Over there," he said, pointing to a small crowd of men sitting on a low stone wall. They were huddled around a small fire. "The one on the end." He looked back at Lucy. "And I ain't no 'lad.'"

Peering at the men, Lucy tugged Duncan's sleeve. "I see him. It's him, I know it."

Duncan nodded. "Stay here." He walked over, Lucy on his heels, despite his order to the contrary. Looking down at the man, he said, "I'll have a word with you."

The man looked up, wary. He still bore a mark, now a great purpling bruise, across his face where Lucy had struck him with the branch the day before. Recognizing Lucy, the man looked startled. He made as if to run away, but Sid had already grabbed him from behind. A few of the other men who'd been sitting near him edged away, although a few continued to look on vaguely, seeming to welcome the break in the monotony.

"Going somewhere, soldier?" Duncan asked. "Not before you answer some of my questions."

Shaking free from Sid, the man slumped back on the wall, not making eye contact. Lucy wondered how Duncan had known he was a soldier. On closer inspection, though, she could see that the man bore the common wound found among many former soldiers. Injuries to the right forefinger and thumb, usually having been broken when muskets backfired during battle. She guessed this was what had happened to Avery, although he had lost his finger and his thumb outright.

Seeming resigned, the man looked at them. "What, Constable? What do you want to know?"

"Who are you?" Duncan demanded. "Tell me immediately, or I'll have you hauled off to jail for assault."

"Assault?" the man asked, but with little surprise in his voice. "I just wanted what's mine."

"You attacked me!" Lucy said angrily. "I could have been killed!"

"You did all right for yourself," the man muttered, rubbing the bruise on his head. " 'Sides, I wasn't trying to hurt you. I told you that already."

Duncan gave her a pained look. "Lucy, please." He looked sternly at the man. "Speak. What was your business with this woman?"

The man sighed. "My name is Ashton Hendricks." He jerked his head at Lucy. "I didn't mean to hurt her, but the brooch she was holding belongs to me. Same as the ring. I know she has that too."

"Well, that's a little hard to prove," Duncan said. "We have it on good authority that those items belong to Lord Cumberland. Not to you."

Hendricks's face first mottled, then paled. "To Lord Cumberland!" He spat. "My arse!" He then proceeded to let loose a string of profanities that shocked Lucy more than she liked to let on. Although some of it she couldn't even understand, giving his thick accent.

"Alright. Stop that!" Duncan said, holding up his hand. "You've admitted already that you attacked this woman yesterday. For that alone, you're off to jail." He pulled a whistle from under his shirt, and made as if to blow for a nearby bellman.

"No, please!" Hendricks said. He turned haggard eyes toward

Lucy. "Please, miss. I humbly beg your forgiveness. I never meant to hurt you. I just needed to talk to you!"

"By dragging her into the trees?" Duncan said. "Scaring her half to death?"

"Miss, I truly am sorry," Hendricks said. "I have—had—a daughter myself. About your same age, she was. I'd have near killed any man who dared lay a hand on her."

Behind her, she could hear Sid snort. Duncan made a similarly dismissive sound. Lucy laid a hand on the constable's arm. Something about the man seemed so pitiful. Besides, it seemed important to hear what he had to say.

"I'm sorry you lost your daughter," she said. "Did she die in the plague?"

"No, she was in Carlisle," he said. "The plague was light upon us, thanks be to God. Some families in York did succumb." He nodded respectfully at Duncan, having correctly identified his place of origin. Lucy looked at the constable, momentarily distracted. She wondered again if he had lost family in the great death.

"The toll was nothing like it was in London," Duncan said, not giving up his line of inquiry. "Tell me why you've been harassing the Earl."

"I don't know what you mean," Hendricks said, faltering.

"The Earl said you tried to kill him," Lucy pointed out, taking a step back, having retained a healthy fear of murderers. "That you've made several attacks on him over the last few months. You loosened the reins of his horse, took a shot at him."

"And I saw you throw rocks at him last night! Right outside the magistrate's home!" Sid volunteered.

Hendricks sighed. "I never tried to kill him. Scare him a bit, 'tis all."

"And to get back what's yours?" Lucy asked. "The brooch and the ring, you said."

"You're a long way from home," Duncan said. "Just to reclaim a little treasure that you lost gambling."

"They belonged to my daughter. She died, just a few months ago. In childbirth." Hendricks looked heavenward. Lucy thought for a moment he was praying, but then saw him blinking back tears. She shivered. So many women died that way, in the throngs of delivery. Even the most skilled of midwives could not always save them. "What about the babe?" Lucy asked. "Did it survive her travail?"

Hendricks glanced at her. "He's alive. A wonderful blessing he is too. I've got a wet nurse tending him these days, but I've already been gone longer than I would've liked. He's the only family I have left, you see. My wife, my poor child's mother, died long ago."

Lucy thought back to what she had gleaned about the card game from Tilly and Jacques Durand. "You put the brooch into the card game," she said slowly, "which you then lost. We know the Earl put in the signet ring. We know you had already left the game, but stayed in the tavern, watching the game from another table."

"So it would seem that neither the brooch nor the ring are yours," Duncan said sternly. "Yet you've claimed them as your own."

"The brooch belonged to my daughter!" Hendricks said, his voice becoming a bit wild. "I had to watch it get bid again and again! I want it back! I need it back!"

"The brooch didn't exactly *belong* to your daughter though, did it?" Lucy asked. She tried to adopt the magistrate's tone when he questioned a witness. "Wasn't it, in fact, *made* from your daughter's bones?"

At her question, Duncan looked taken aback. She hadn't had a chance to tell him what she had learned from Dr. Larimer about the brooch.

Mister Hendricks's eyes had welled with tears. "Yes. I had the brooch made shortly after she passed. It was the last thing I have of my precious Amelie. I thought," here he stumbled, perhaps seeing the disgust in their faces, "that her child deserved to have something from his mother. Something beautiful. I thought, a brooch . . ." His voice trailed off.

"Well, why then would you have gambled it away?" Lucy asked. Truly, the man's actions made no sense. "That scarcely seems like something you should do with such a treasured piece!"

"I hardly know why." Hendricks paused. "I suppose I wanted to remind Cumberland of who I was. What I had lost."

"Why ever would you do that?" Lucy asked. "Who is Lord Cumberland to you?"

To this, the man remained silent.

"You've explained the brooch, but not the ring," Duncan pressed. "You've no claim on that ring."

"Oh, but I do. That ring belonged to my daughter too."

Duncan looked disbelieving. "Thinking she's noble, is she? What, you have a clinch with her mum? The Earl would have recognized her as his daughter then, wouldn't he? His wife hardly seems cast off."

"No!" Hendricks said, aghast. "My daughter's me own."

"How can that be then?" Lucy asked, her mind flashing through a number of possibilities. "You mean the Earl gave the ring to her? Why ever would he have given your daughter such an expensive piece? Was she his—?" She couldn't bring herself to say "mistress," the man looked so openly distraught.

"Not the Earl. His son," Hendricks said through clenched teeth. "The less-than-honorable Master Clifford."

"Lord Cumberland's son," Duncan stated, looking suddenly weary. "He dallied with your daughter."

Lucy detected an accusing note in the constable's tone. Hendricks also seemed to hear it too, and flushed. "I was away, you see. Fighting for King Charles in Holland. Fought against the French too." He paused. "I thought I had placed Amelie in service at a good home before I left. She was a ladies' maid for Lady Cumberland. That's where she met their son."

What happened next was heartbreakingly obvious. Lucy stiffened, sensing Duncan's thoughts from the way his eyes flicked toward her. Gentry don't marry servants, they just use them for their own pleasures. Lucy felt sick. The master of the household was expected to protect his servants, but as was so common, the younger, comely women were often abused in the households of the very men who had promised to protect them. She had a stack of ballads in her pack that sang about this very moral tale.

Hendricks went on. "About four months ago, I received a letter from Amelie. She was so happy! She was bearing Clifford's child, but thought it would be all right because the young man intended to marry her, she said. In secret. But why keep it secret? Made no sense to me."

"They could have had a good reason!" Lucy said, digging her toe in the dirt.

Both men looked at her, with pitying expressions. "No, lass. He didn't have a good reason. He was just a flippery fellow, afraid to stand up to his parents," Hendricks said. "It took me almost two months, but at last I managed to get temporary leave from my captain, and I raced home, hoping it was not too late. Of course, it was. My daughter was already eight months along in her confinement by that point. The Countess had ousted her out of the household, claiming she'd thieved from them. Branded her a whore too. Dismissed without a reference, she was. My daughter, heartbroken and sick as she was, she couldn't bear to tell me of her shame." He wiped his eye. "Thanks be to God, my dear lass had found a home in a Quaker household to spend her last days. The women there were taking care of my dear child, who was already suffering greatly." His voice caught a little in his throat. "She was so frail and pale when she saw me. Yet still so happy about the babe. She swore to me, and the midwife who had attended her, that the marriage had happened, but neither the cad nor his parents would acknowledge either her or the babe." He sighed. "Labor came early, but lasted too long, and no one could save her. Why he would no longer acknowledge it, I could not understand. She died, holding the babe—Ambrose—in her arms."

Hendricks's face and voice grew hard. "I was determined to get justice for my child, and her son. Right now, unrecognized, my grandson's considered a bastard, not legitimate. I went to see Cumberland and his blasted son soon after my daughter died, but neither would see me. Not too long later, the ring was stolen from my possessions. I know it was the Earl who took it! His hench-men at least!"

He pounded his fist into his other palm. "I just wanted what was mine. I would never have put Amelie's dear brooch in that wretched game, except I wanted to see his face. I knew he would know what it was. What it meant. What his son's arrogance had done to my family."

"Then what happened?" Lucy asked. The man's distress was hard to bear. Against her will, she found herself believing him. Almost.

"The Earl took that bloody signet ring off his finger and added it to the stakes. He was taunting me, you see. He's as good a player as that damn card sharp, Jack. He knew he'd win it back. I never played cards myself. Lost everything right away. Every-thing! I watched them pass the brooch around for a while—fingering it with their damnable dirty fingers! Though I had to leave the game, I couldn't bear to leave the tavern. I set back to finish my pint to wait out the game. I suppose I had it in my mind that I might approach the winner at the end; try to get the brooch back privately."

"So you were there when the poem got read?" Duncan asked.

Hendricks nodded. "Put in by the dark foreign gent. I saw him start to yell at Jack too. But when I heard the bells ringing I knew something dreadful was happening nearby. I went out the front door of the tavern, smelled the smoke." He straightened up. "I'm a soldier, you see. Knew I had to report in for duty. I left, knowing there was little else I could do."

He continued. "I spent the next few days trying to help the fire brigade control the fire. Blew up a few buildings too. That blaze was mighty indeed. I hope to dear God that we must never suffer such a thing again." Rubbing his eyes, he seemed trying to control himself. "A few days passed before I heard that the Cheshire Cheese had burned down. I assumed the Earl still had everything. It wasn't until I heard this lass here"—he nodded at Lucy—"read that wretched poem that I realized the brooch and ring might have survived the fire too. I began to wonder if she had the ring and brooch. I just had to have them back. I'm dreadful sorry, miss, for frightening you." Hendricks looked at Duncan. "Are you going to arrest me?"

"That's up to Miss Campion here."

Lucy could not stay angry at the man any longer. "I don't wish to press charges."

The constable drew her to the side by the arm. It seemed as if he wanted to shake her. "Lucy, he dragged you behind some trees and assaulted you," he said, searching her face. "I cannot let you forgive him for this."

She shook herself free of his grasp. "I know. But I hit him over the head as well. I might have killed him."

Duncan scowled, but allowed her to lead him back to the man. "Well, since Lucy has decided to let the matter go—and I hope you appreciate what that entails—and since I have no direct evidence that you were the one who assaulted the Earl, I will give you leave." Duncan looked at him sternly. "Stay away from the Earl, and Lucy. Do you hear me?"

Hendricks slumped a bit. "Thank you, miss. Again, I'm dreadfully sorry for frightening you."

Lucy nodded without looking at him again. Suddenly his humility, born of sorrow and shame, were too hard to witness. She watched him lurch away. A sad man, to be sure. Yet was he truly so innocent? They only had his word, against the word of an earl, even if that earl had already shown himself to be less than reputable. What was the truth of the matter, she wondered, watching him pass stiffly down the dusty street.

Duncan turned back to Lucy. "You've been taking a lot of risks." There was a question in his voice. "I understood when you took risks when your brother's life was at stake. But now?" He looked at her intently. "For a stranger?"

"You don't approve?" Lucy said, feeling weary. She pulled her cloak around her shoulders.

"I just don't know anyone else like you." He seemed to be searching for words. "Any woman like you, that is. Because you do remind me of soldiers I've known." Then he corrected himself. "Except soldiers are trained to follow orders. You don't truly follow orders, do you?"

"Not so much," Lucy said, looking back at him over her shoulder.

·14·

A few days had passed since Lucy had encountered Hendricks at St. Martin-in-the-Fields. The urgency she'd been feeling about the puzzle had subsided, under the comfortable reliability of her everyday work. Lucy no longer feared getting her fingers caught in the press, and had grown quite adept at setting the type. Master Aubrey had even published another broadside she had written, about the cleanup of Fleet Street. But now she was quite disappointed with what he was telling her.

"I don't understand why you won't print it!" Lucy said again to Master Aubrey, trying hard to keep her tone in check. "It's like any other penny ballad we sell."

"I'm sorry, Lucy," the printer said. He read the title out loud. "'Robert Hubert, A Watchmaker Wrongly Accused.' I just can't print it."

"But why not?!" Lucy pleaded. Last night, she'd worked 'til

midnight on the piece, despite being exhausted by her day's labors.

Master Aubrey rubbed his ruddy beard. "People need to blame someone for the Fire. Hubert claimed to have set it. If we print this," he said, shaking Lucy's paper in his hand, "we're liable to see our own shop torched to the ground."

"I'll print it myself! I won't put your name on it," Lucy said, her voice rising. "The truth deserves to be out."

Master Aubrey's fleshy face grew mottled, a sure sign he was losing patience. "You'll be out on your ear if you do, without a proper reference." He wagged his finger at her. Lucy could not help but flinch. This was the first time she'd ever seen the printer look truly angry. "No more of your pretty wheedling ways. We can't print this, and that's final."

She received no sympathy from Master Hargrave either, when she asked him about it later that evening. She'd gone over to the Hargraves's household under the guise of seeing Annie, but with the will to seek out the magistrate. "It's out of my hands, Lucy," the magistrate had said, somewhat sadly. "The watchmaker seems determined to have himself killed. He has confessed several times to starting the cursed conflagration."

"But three of the Fariners paid to be on the jury!" Lucy protested. Even as she spoke, she felt a bit sick. This was the closest she'd ever come to arguing with the magistrate. Nevertheless, she went on. "Isn't it a bit convenient that the owners of the bakery were on the jury?"

"Convenient? Of course it is." The magistrate sighed. "What a wretch that man is. So eager to part with his life."

"But his wits are addled. The Fariners are using his illness for their own ends," she said tearfully. "I've heard you and Dr. Larimer both say so. Adam too."

The magistrate just patted her hand. "My dear, some battles just cannot be fought, I'm afraid."

Finally, she turned to Adam when he arrived home an hour later. They were standing together in the drawing room, on one of the rare nights he'd not worked late with the surveyors. "Lucy," he said, after listening to her explain the piece she wanted the printer to publish. "It's as Father says. There is nothing we can do for the poor man—except hope that he comes to a speedy end. Let us think happier thoughts."

Without warning, Adam had moved to embrace her then, something he had not done since the day after the Great Fire. Without even thinking, Lucy stepped away from him, causing him to drop his arms to his sides. She just knew that the look of bafflement that crossed his face mirrored her own. She could hardly explain why she had stepped away, except that she was so disappointed that he was not standing up for the watchmaker. She remembered a time when he had braved a dog-baiting ring to stop an atrocity from occurring. Why he would not intervene now, she could not understand.

"Adam, I—" she began, even as he cut her off.

"It's getting late, Lucy." He sounded tired. "You should get going. I'll have John accompany you, so that you're not stumbling about in the dark."

The next morning, Lucy set to making a batch of ink—a hot, smelly process—trying unsuccessfully to keep her uneasiness at bay. Thinking of last night's conversation with Adam only made her feel worse. In part, she was indignant that he was letting a grievous injustice go untended, and in part, in her deepest heart, she knew her pride was hurt. She did not have the power to persuade him as she thought she might.

"Silly git," she berated herself, softly though so that Lach would not overhear. Noisily, Lucy set a pot of water boiling, stirring in a bit of pine oil, and some other odd things that singed her nose and stung her eyes. Master Aubrey had entrusted them to make enough ink to fill several large pottery jugs that he kept in the cellar. As always, Lach was bossing her around.

"Easy, lass," Lach said. "You're liable to spill that pig vomit all over the floor."

"Pig vomit?" She gingerly laid the blue pottery jar back on the table. "You're jesting, right?"

Lach shrugged. "Who can tell?"

Certainly, Master Aubrey kept most of the ingredients for making the ink secret, having left instructions to add this amount of brown ground powder, and that amount of green stuff from small clay pots under the workbench by the front window. When the concoction was bubbling, the vile stench assaulted her nose, causing her to double over, nearly retching out her morning porridge.

"Open the shutters, why don't you?" Lach said, looking a bit green himself.

Lucy gave him an annoyed look. "Can't trouble yourself, can you?"

"I'll do you one better. I'll leave the door open on my way out." He grinned cheekily.

"Where are you going? What am I supposed to do with all this?" She gestured at the bubbling pot. "This mess?"

His hand on the door, the apprentice turned back for a moment. "Go get the jars from the cellar. Wait until the ink is nearly cool, and then use that spoon there to ladle into each jar," he explained, snickering. Lach clearly enjoyed bossing her about. "Mind you don't put the lids on until the ink has completely cooled. Then, put them all back in the cellar until Master Aubrey needs it. I'll even wait until you come back up." His last statement was spoken with excessive generosity, as if he were doing her an enormous favor.

Sighing, Lucy descended carefully into the cellar. There was a grated window just above the street that let in some daylight, so she didn't need to carry a candle. She hadn't been down here much, but she found the empty jars lined up on some wooden shelves. As she started to fill her arms, she noticed some stacks of old pamphlets and broadsides dumped in the corner. She'd not seen these before.

Curious, she knelt down and began to look through the pile. A quick glance at the printer's mark showed they were not Master Aubrey's, but rather from competing printers. Many seemed to be from other countries, including Germany, Holland, and France. There was also a great stack of newssheets called the *Mercurias Caledonian*, which seemed to have been printed in Edinburgh in the 1660s, just after King Charles's restoration to the throne. When she went back upstairs into the shop, she asked Lach about the sheets.

"Oh, yeah," Lach said, taking off his apron. "Master Aubrey has agreements with other printers in different countries, and other counties. He likes to see what they're doing. Sometimes he trades them for a woodcut he likes too." He showed her one. It looked like a rooster coming from a devil's mouth. "And here's another—"

"I see he has *News from Scotland*," Lucy interrupted, not wanting Lach to get needlessly diverted. "Do you think he has anything recent?"

"I think he may have brought some back from his last trip up north." Lach gave her a sharp look. "More about the plague, hey?"

Lucy smiled, but didn't say anything more when he left the shop. Let him think that's what she wanted to look at them for. Suddenly she was glad Lach had left her alone. After a minute or two, when she was positive the apprentice would not return, she bolted the shop door and returned to the cellar.

Sure enough, Master Aubrey had collected news from Edinburgh, Leeds, and York, many from earlier in the year. Rifling through the hodgepodge from York, she found the usual recipes for true love, reports of highwaymen, some speeches from the King. She was about to set them aside when a tract caught her eye. *A True and Horrible Account of a Good Preacher, Ill met by Vandals.*

Glancing at the text, Lucy saw that a parish priest in a little town outside of York had been found dead, a blow to the back of his head. Although she knew from experience that clergy were not always the most godly of men, to murder a priest seemed a most profane act.

Had he deserved it? A little voice inside her could not help but ask. Even as the terrible thought crossed her mind, Lucy tapped on a low-hanging wooden beam, saying a quick prayer, hoping God would forgive her. She continued to piece through the woodcuts, not sure what she was looking for. Before long, the title of a broadside stopped her. *A True Account, of a most terrible poysoning in Carlisle. The first born son of the second Earl of Cumberland, had been found poysoned, in his own bed.*

Quickly, Lucy read the rest of the account. Someone had slipped some arsenic to the young man, the guess was in his lamb stew. His mother, the very same Lady Cumberland who had dined at the Hargraves, had come to look for him after he missed their afternoon ride, and found him convulsing in his bed. The local apothecary had been called in, just in time to administer a soothing remedy. It was later discovered that a jar of arsenic, intended to be mixed with vinegar and chalk for Lady Cumberland's face cream, had disappeared from her dressing table. Lucy knew from reading Dr. Culpeper's guide to a woman's healthy complexion that such a mixture was common to whiten a woman's skin and to remove blemishes. Toward the end of the account, some rumors were mentioned that a maid from the household, who had been let go for an earlier theft, had been suspected of either adding the poison to the stew herself or giving it to the person who committed the act. Nothing had been proved, and the matter had been dropped.

Thoughtfully, Lucy tucked a few of the tracts in her pocket. She spent the next hour ladling the vile ink into the jars, swearing at Lach the whole time for abandoning her to such an unwholesome endeavor. "Errand, my foot!" she muttered. On her way out, she ran into Lach, who had timed his return carefully.

"Shop's all aired out now," she taunted. "So your delicate nose won't be offended."

Lach just gave her an infuriating grin. "No pack?" he asked, seeing her empty arms. "Where are you off to now? To see your sweetheart?"

"If you must know, I'm off to see Constable Duncan. There is something I must relay to him."

She hurried out, to forestall any more questions from the smirking printer's devil.

"I was thinking," Lucy said to Duncan some ten minutes later. She'd arrived at the makeshift jail to find the constable and his bellman wrestling a drunken man into one of the cells. "About Lord Cumberland."

"Ugh, I'm a bit busy at the moment, Lucy," he said through gritted teeth. The drunk was throwing anything he could get his hands on. He looked strong enough, and full of enough spirits to rip the wood frame right off its nails, if they could not restrain him. Since the Fire there had been much more public disorderliness, caused mainly from too much drink and not enough to do. Though athletic in build, the constable certainly looked to have his hands full.

"It's just that, don't you think it was a bit odd for a man of his means to be staying at The Sparrow?" Lucy asked, neatly avoiding a tin cup hitting her in the ear. "Hardly a place for gentry, I'd say."

With a final grimace, Duncan wrenched the man's hand from the prison bars and shoved him into the cell. He turned back toward Lucy, arms crossed over his red uniform. "It might not mean anything. Furthermore, we have no evidence to conclude that he's staying there. He might be meeting a business acquaintance there." He coughed slightly and she knew by "business acquaintance" he no doubt meant a lady-bird, but did not want to say. "Particularly since we know he has brought his wife to the City. He might wish to not involve her with his—" Again, he sought for words. "His business transactions."

"You're suggesting that he has a lady love on the side," Lucy said impatiently. "I've never had need of a nursemaid, and I don't need one now. Believe me, I understand something about how nobles behave." Catching a whiff of the drunken sot, Lucy added, "Whew! He's had a bit of ale, hasn't he?"

Duncan nodded at the drunken man now laying senseless on the floor. To the bellman he said, "Keep an eye on him." He led Lucy to a bench. "What brought you here anyway?"

"Look at these accounts," she said, pulling out the penny pieces she'd found in Master Aubrey's cellar. "What do you make of them?"

Duncan read through them quickly. "May I keep these for a bit?" he asked. "I'd like to read the details more carefully."

Lucy hesitated. They weren't hers to give away, but she nodded anyway.

"You've got to get back," he reminded her. "I can't let Master Aubrey think you're shirking your duties."

When Lucy returned to the printer's shop a short while later, she found Lach waiting for her. "Your lordship Master Adam stopped by," he said with a mischievous wink, handing her a folded piece of paper.

"Adam came here?" Lucy asked, sounding more eager than she intended.

"Yeah. He waited for quite some time, but neither of us thought it would take you so long to have your piece with the constable. He wanted me to pass this note on to your ladyship."

Lucy felt an odd sinking feeling in her heart. With slightly trembling fingers, she opened the note, reading Adam's elegant script. *"Lucy,"* he had written. *"I was hoping I might find you available but you seemed already engaged."*

She put the note to her chest. "Oh, Adam. What are you thinking?" she murmured, before continuing to read.

"I wanted to tell you that I did write a defense on behalf of Master Hubert, your beleaguered watchmaker, giving him words to speak at the trial. I truly hope that he will see sense and proclaim his innocence. I am not the heartless fellow you see me as these days."

After that, Adam had scribbled out some words before he'd added his customary signature. With a pang, she noticed he hadn't concluded with an endearment. She tried to make out the words he had crossed out. She thought it said, "I hope we can meet soon."

Lucy tucked the note inside her secret pocket. She was warmed by the knowledge that Adam had tried to help the watchmaker, especially since she knew the action stemmed from her plea. At the same time, everything between her and Adam seemed so strained lately. She reread his words. *I am not the heartless fellow you see me as these days.* Why ever would he write such a thing? He seemed distant, but not in the way he'd been when she'd first lived at the magistrate's household as a chambermaid. Then, the distance had stemmed from their relative positions, and certainly he'd always been courteous. Over time, she knew his regard for her had grown. The night of the Fire he'd admitted to her that he felt the gap between their stations had been bridged.

Lucy smiled for a moment, remembering that desperate, wonderful moment when Adam had pronounced his love for her. In the moment, life had seemed uncomplicated. Uncorking a small vial of ink, she started to write a note, asking if they could meet on the morrow.

Her good mood dissipated though when Master Aubrey returned to the shop a few hours later. He'd been hawking out by Westminster, where he learned that the watchmaker had once again proclaimed his guilt in burning down London. The man had begged to be hanged in the morning, and naturally the courts had happily obliged. It seemed that Adam's defense had come to naught.

"There's nothing else to be done for Master Hubert, I'm afraid." The bookseller moved to pour himself some ale from a large jar on the wooden table. Seeing Lucy clench her fists, Master Aubrey patted her awkwardly on the shoulder. "London doesn't need a martyr, Lucy," he said, "but it does need blood."

·15·

Lucy brushed away some of the dried leaves that had blown into the printer's shop, and took a deep breath. A week or so had passed since the witless watchmaker had been executed, and a little bit of life seemed to be returning to London. No longer did people seem to be rootless, like so much drifting fog. Indeed, the beginning of October had proved to be quite pleasant, and the heavy smoke smell that had long lingered over London seemed finally to be lifting as well.

Lach and Master Aubrey were both out selling, so it was a rare day that the press was not going. Lucy was about to shut the door, to keep more dirt and leaves from blowing in, when a woman called her name. It was Rhonda Water, looking slightly more disheveled than Lucy had ever seen her. Her fine gray traveling gown looked wrinkled, even a bit stained, as if she'd been moving roughly. Looking closer, Lucy was surprised to see a trickle of sweat on her forehead, a far cry from the collected woman she'd seen before.

"Miss Water." Lucy kept her tone civil, although her cheeks burned a bit from the memory of the gentlewoman calling her a pauper in the Oxford churchyard. "Is there something you want? Something I can fetch for you?"

Miss Water twisted her skirt a bit in her hands. "You were right. I knew you were right. May I sit down?" Without waiting for Lucy to respond, she plopped heavily down on the low bench by the printing press. "As you walked away that day, outside the church, I knew you were right. Tahmin deserves more. He was a good friend."

Without warning, tears began to flow down Miss Water's cheeks. She accepted the cup of chamomile, sprigged with a bit of lavender, which Lucy pressed into her hands. Smiling weakly, she said, "You always tend to me. Thank you."

"You look exhausted," Lucy said. She felt a little less miffed than she had when Miss Water first walked into the shop, but she still did not feel overly courteous. Pauper indeed!

"I am, at that," Miss Water said, setting the cup down. "I've not slept well since you left. I could not help but wonder, not just who killed Tahmin, but—"

"What happened to Darius," Lucy finished. "You've not heard from him, I take it?"

Miss Water shook her head. "I fear, you see, that he died in the Fire too. Why else wouldn't he have tried to contact me? I cannot send word to him myself. Indeed, Tahmin was the one who arranged our correspondence. Nor can I send word to Tahmin's family. I thought perhaps I could contact the local imam—he is similar to a parish priest—who might be able to pass on the sad ending for their son. But there are many imams in Isfahan, where they both lived. I wouldn't know where to start. And of course, I cannot ask Father." She looked around the shop, her eyes taking in the half-folded sheets. "I'm afraid that I am keeping you from your work."

"Miss Water, what can I do for you?" Lucy asked again, trying to keep her impatience from showing. She began to lay the text for their latest tract, a sermon titled *A Good Minister's Intonation to the Ungodly Sort.*

"Well," Miss Water said, "you've spoken with some of the people who were at the tavern the night Tahmin was killed. It occurred to me that perhaps one of them would remember something about Tahmin that would indicate where Darius is." She looked hopeful. "Does that make sense?"

"Possibly. One of them could also be the murderer," Lucy pointed out, as she began to sort through the italic type. She was trying to find a fifteen-point letter "U" to completely the word "Ungodly," and all she could find were twelve- and sixteen-point letters.

Miss Water looked crestfallen. "You're right, of course. I should have thought of that."

Seeing Miss Water's disappointment, Lucy hesitated. "I need to sell by St. Martin's today. Perhaps we could stop in to see Constable Duncan along the way. He might have some news."

Within a few moments of locking up the shop, they arrived at Duncan's little jail and headquarters. Today, he had a few ladybirds in the cell, two of them looking a bit haughty and defiant, their lips and cheeks reddened with berries and their eyelashes darkened with kohl. A third young woman, clad oddly in sackcloth and ashes, stood a few steps away, wide-eyed but not overly fearful of her cell. A Quaker, no doubt, picked up for disturbing the peace.

Seeing Lucy and her companion, Duncan came over right away. "Ladies!" he said, his eyes darting over to Lucy. "What brings you to my little jail?"

Lucy presented him to Miss Water, who looked a bit wide-eyed herself. Clearly, this was the closest the demure young woman had ever come to the criminal world, and she didn't know what to make of it. Lucy wondered if she'd ever had that same innocence, and then decided she hadn't. Or at least not in the four years since she'd left her family farm in Lambeth. Living in London changed a person, and hardly ever for the better.

Upon hearing what they wanted, Duncan was silent for a moment. Then, he pulled out an iron key from a cord around his waist, and unlocked a metal box atop his simple wooden desk. He withdrew the small bag found at the Cheshire Cheese, and emptied the contents.

"May I?" Lucy asked. When Duncan nodded, she began to sort the items into four piles. "The cards belonged to Jacques. Tahmin put in the rook and the letter to Miss Water. The Earl put in the ring, and maybe a few of the coins."

Miss Water stared at the items for a moment, before picking up two of the copper coins. "These are called *pul,* or *kasbeki,* and they are as common as our penny. Each region of Persia has its own *kasbeki.* See the imprint of the lion? These are from Isfahan, Darius and Tahmin's city. That is the main city of commerce and trade. They are worth very little." She slid the small silver coin along the table until it fell into her cupped hand. She held it up to the light. "This one, however, is worth much more. It is called an *Abbas,* named for the Shah."

Miss Water then touched the little green rook. "Dear Tahmin. Faithful friend." She dropped her hand.

Lucy pushed the brooch to make a fourth pile. "Ashton Hendricks put in this brooch—said it belonged to his recently deceased daughter. He said he wanted the Earl to look at it, to understand what the Earl's son had done to his family. Unfortunately," Lucy continued, watching Miss Water slide her finger along the delicate flowers of the brooch, "we think Hendricks had the brooch made from his dead daughter's bones."

Miss Water jerked away her finger. "Why would he defile her in such a way?" She looked like she was going to spew whatever she had eaten for her noon meal.

Lucy shrugged, having wondered the same thing many times over.

All three fell silent. Clearly, they were at a standstill. "Is there nothing else?" Miss Water asked, her voice showing her intense disappointment. "I had thought there would be something more. Something that would help."

"I did discover something," Duncan said, pulling out the tracts Lucy had given him the week before. "This past week, I journeyed to Carlisle." He tapped on the broadside that described how the Earl of Cumberland's son had been poisoned. "I wanted to learn more about the circumstances around this act."

"Did you talk to the Earl's son?" Lucy asked eagerly.

Duncan shook his head. "No, he was no longer in Carlisle. Apparently he's here in London. While I was there, however, it got me thinking about Hendricks's claim that the Earl's son had married his daughter. Had to be in secret, of course, since the Earl won't acknowledge the marriage. So, I thought I would check the marriage registers at the local parish churches. Seems a few of the churches had been broken into recently, and a priest had even been murdered by thieves." He pointed to the other broadside Lucy had given him. *A True and Horrible Account of a Good Preacher, Ill Met by Vandals.*

"Oh, I remember reading that piece," she exclaimed. "Do you think this priest's death was connected to the secret marriage? Did the church have a marriage certificate?"

"None that I could find," Duncan replied. "But when I looked in the parish register, where the priest records weddings, burials, baptisms, and the like, I could see someone had torn out all the pages from the last few months. If I had to guess, I would say that the marriage did occur, and someone else was trying to hide all evidence of that fact."

"So who murdered the priest? The Earl?"

Miss Water, who had been silent during Lucy and Duncan's exchange, gave a disbelieving little laugh. Clearly, in her world, earls did not go about committing acts of murder. Especially against men of the cloth. "I should hardly think so. Whatever would have been his motive?"

"Perhaps the Earl didn't murder the priest. I don't know," Duncan said. "He certainly did not wish to see the marriage acknowledged. To what extents he would go to preserve this secret, I cannot imagine. I do believe, however, that the Earl's son did give Hendricks's daughter that ring. Just as Hendricks claimed. This means, according to local inheritance law, the ring, as a piece of movable property, would pass to her son, upon her death. As such, the ring would be held in the care of her father until her son came of age."

"Why do you believe this?" Lucy asked. "You said the records had been destroyed."

For the first time since they had stopped by, Duncan grinned. "Just went to the local tavern. Bought a few rounds of drinks, and I got them talking soon enough. Found out they didn't consider the babe to be a bastard. No one claimed to have witnessed her wedding, but she wasn't a harlot, no matter what Lady Cumberland had said."

That was interesting. Lucy knew enough of small town beliefs to know that the young woman would surely have been shunned by their neighbors if they thought she'd lost her virtue, and had a babe out of wedlock. This certainly suggested they believed she had been wed before bearing the child. She said as much, and then asked, "Did they know who the babe's father was? Whom she had married?"

"No one would say for sure, but there were some hints that she had married a gentleman, but without the priest's word or the parish register, she could not be buried in hallowed ground." Duncan responded. "It appears she did not talk to people much, particularly after she took ill. The Quakers who took her in certainly weren't going to talk to me. All I know is that they buried her themselves, in a Quaker churchyard, with only her maiden name upon the stone."

Lucy nodded slowly. She knew the Quakers tended to be a close-lipped bunch, particularly around the authorities. She felt they were at an impasse.

"If only we could talk to the Earl's son," she said. Then she remembered what he had said a few minutes before. "You said he was here in London! Where?"

Duncan smiled at Lucy. "At The Sparrow, no less."

"I knew it!" Lucy snapped her fingers, not feeling all that surprised. "So not the Earl, but his son," Lucy mused. "I suppose his son has his reasons for not wanting to lodge at his parents' home in London?"

Duncan opened the door, and let out the Quakeress, looking like a little gray dove freed from a fox's snare. Once again, Lucy was reminded of Sarah. She hoped that America was kinder to conventiclers than they were to them here in London, although she'd heard enough stories to know that was unlikely. Stocks, if they were lucky. Tar and feathers if they were not. And in some cases, hanging, like poor Mary Dyer in Boston.

On a whim, Lucy placed a tuppence from her own pocket into the Quaker woman's hand. "Godspeed," she whispered. "I pray you do not see the stocks anytime soon." Seeing Miss Water eye her curiously, she spoke airily to the rest of the room. "I must get back to work." Lucy said, gathering up her pamphlets and woodcuts. "Master Aubrey won't be too keen to find out I've not peddled these. Thameside today, I think."

"Of course, Thameside," Duncan said. "By the Embankment. Rather near The Sparrow too, wouldn't you say?"

"Is it?" Lucy asked, blandly. "I had no idea."

Lucy had scarcely taken a few dozen steps down the street when she realized Miss Water was striding after her, seeming not to be hampered by her long skirts. Lucy quickened her pace, even though Miss Water easily matched her steps. She sighed. "What are you doing?" she asked.

"You can't go alone," Miss Water said.

"Miss Water, I don't think you should come with me," Lucy said. "Thameside's no place for a lady such as yourself."

"Fine enough for you though?" Miss Water asked. "Why is that?"

Lucy glanced down at her tattered skirts. They contrasted sharply with Miss Water's more elegant traveling costume, which despite its mild stains, still marked its wearer as gentry.

"How do you plan to talk to him?" Miss Water persisted. "That's what you're planning, isn't it? And what if it turns out that he murdered poor Tahmin? What will you do then?" She touched Lucy's elbow. "Do you fancy being trapped inside an inn with a man you do not know? I hardly think Constable Duncan would approve."

She said the last in a teasing way, but Lucy whirled around. "Why should I care what Constable Duncan thinks of me?" she demanded. "Believe it or not, I'm already betrothed."

Even as the rash words flew from her lips, Lucy flushed painfully. She looked around, hoping no one had heard her. For a moment, she stared helplessly at Miss Water, knowing the next questions would be ones she couldn't answer. *Who are you bethrothed to, Lucy? Have the banns been read? When are you getting married?*

But Miss Water surprised her. "Forgive me, Lucy. I was speaking in jest. My concern is only for your safety."

Lucy started to walk again. "No, you're right, Miss Water. Many times I've been told I'm too foolhardy. Headstrong too. I've no wish to be trapped inside the inn with a murderer. We've no reason to think the Earl's son murdered Tahmin though."

"It's always a possibility," Miss Water insisted. As they walked, the smell of the Thames grew stronger. A combination of dead fish, smoke, and the moldy stench of the river itself hung heavily in the air.

Lucy glanced at the stately woman walking beside her. Her face had whitened slightly and seemed to be taking teeny breaths. Clearly, she was ill at ease in their surroundings. Miss Water's eyes were slightly puffy. Yet she seemed so resolute, Lucy was unwittingly stricken with a flash of admiration. "Tell me about him," Lucy said, touching Miss Water's arm. "About Darius."

A jolt of emotion flooded Miss Water's face, and her eyes misted over in memory. For a moment, Lucy thought she was not going to talk at all. Then the woman smiled. "We had been at the Shah's court only a few days, Father and me," she began. "Everything was so strange there. My maid could not stop crying at the strangeness of it all. So Father dismissed her. He couldn't bear her weeping, you see." Hearing Lucy's choked cry, she hastened to explain. "No, pray, do not look so stricken, Lucy. He arranged for her safe passage back to her home in London. Even he would not be so heartless as to leave her stranded in a foreign land."

"Yet he left you alone," Lucy murmured, edging around a pile of horse manure still steaming in the road. "Without anyone to attend to you." She tried to imagine how her former mistress would have fared in a foreign land, without a maid. Not well, she thought. "What did you do?" she asked.

"Father did procure me a maid, to dress my hair and look after my clothes. Her name was Amah. She was how I came to

meet Darius." Miss Water needed no prompting from Lucy to
continue. "She was hired, in part, to help me understand the cus-
toms of the land, and to finesse my Persian. Yet her English was
not up to the task, and Father needed me to help with some
translations. So he arranged for Darius to tutor me. He was one of
the Shah's scribes, I think. I know he also served as a translator
and would accompany the Shah on diplomatic missions. I never
knew for certain his exact position in the Shah's court." She blushed.
"His English was exquisite."

A potter's cart rumbled by them, the pots clanking in every
direction, making a considerable din. Miss Water did not seem to
notice, fully gone in her reminiscing. "Darius was so handsome,
so kind, simply different from other men I'd known. The poems
he would recite to me, from Rumi and others, spoke so eloquently
of grace and beauty. Our English poets, save the good bard of
Stratford, never could compare." She smiled distantly, longing in
her voice. "Every day, when we met, I'd show him the passages I
was having trouble with. After he'd helped me, he'd have me
close my eyes. Then, he would slip something wonderful into my
hands—nuts perhaps, sometimes a piece of fruit, but most often
flowers, clipped from the Shah's gardens. And he'd write me the
most delightful letters—" her voice trailed away.

"What did you know of Tahmin?" Lucy asked. "Did he ever
come to your meetings?"

"Tahmin nearly always accompanied Darius. Yet he always
stayed a respectful distance away. We did not speak to one another directly, other than pleasantries." Her face had turned rueful. "I wish I had gotten to know him better. He seemed a strong

kindly sort. There were a few occasions when Darius couldn't meet me, and Tahmin would bring me the note. That's how I knew about the rook, you see."

"What did you know of Darius's family?" Lucy asked. "Didn't you ever ask him about them?"

Miss Water looked embarrassed. "He never wanted to talk much about himself. He always wanted to know more about me. My childhood, my life in England, that sort of thing." She paused. "I suppose I'd never had anyone take that kind of interest in me before." She fell silent, her eyes blinking away tears.

Lucy nodded. That made sense. Seeing Miss Water's distress, she decided not to press the woman any further. Within a few moments, the women came to The Sparrow, a rambling structure that would never have withstood the Fire, should the winds have shifted. A single bony mare was tied at the hitching post out front, and the whole inn had a bit of a forlorn air. The two women stared at it for a while.

"You think the son of the Earl has been living here?" Miss Water whispered. "Why ever for?" Her shocked expression once again betrayed her gentle upbringing. It was scandalous— unnatural even—for an Earl's son to be housing himself deliber- ately in such a hovel.

"I don't know, but I aim to find out," Lucy said, eyeing one of the malt barrels in front of the inn. No doubt the innkeeper was waiting for a new shipment of grain from which to make beer. Crossing her fingers that the lid of the empty barrel was not rot- ted through, she scrambled easily on top.

"What are you doing?" Miss Water asked.

"Just wait and see. I'm going to bring him to us." She began her customary call. "Love potions! True warnings! Monstrous doings! Get your penny press here!"

Moments later, a few servants and men began to trickle out of the inn, plying Lucy with coins. In an aside to Miss Water she whispered, "I would guess booksellers don't make it down here so much."

As she sold the pamphlets and broadsides, Lucy looked at each customer carefully, noting in particular their manner of dress, their stature, and especially their skin and hands. None seemed quite right. Most seemed to be hale and hearty servants used to hard work, or local townsmen, not sickly, recently poisoned nobles. Miss Water stood a few steps away, watching Lucy. She still wore the same puzzled look, but Lucy didn't have time to explain.

Instead, Lucy peered into her bag. What penny pieces did she have left? *A Watchmaker Loses Time?* Robert Hubert's confession and his hanging. Lucy hated to call that one. She hopped down to fill her tin cup with water from the trough.

"Maybe he's not here?" Miss Water murmured.

Lucy didn't answer, having spied a man drying his hands on a towel as he stepped out of the inn. "Are you the innkeeper, sir?" she asked him.

The man gave her a tired smile. "Yes. Name's McDaniels. I'm not going to run you off, lass, but none of your trade inside."

"No sir. How about a pennypiece for free? I didn't mean to take all your customers."

"This lot?" McDaniels waved his hand toward his customers. "They'll all be back in, soon enough."

"Do you think I did get all your customers?" Lucy smiled,

adding a wheedling tone. "My master will be none too happy if he sees I didn't finish my pack."

McDaniels picked out two of the pennypieces. "I'll take two. To make up for any business lost." Seeing her face, he added kindly, "Nah, there's one gentry sort who's been living up in the rooms." His voice took on a bit of disgust. "Has us send up food every day. You won't get that one, lass. Mind you run off soon."

"I will," she promised, watching McDaniels return to his tavern. A number of the revelers returned too, now armed with merriments and small pleasures to share from the ballads and broadsides.

"So, there is someone still in there," Lucy mused. Holding up her left hand to hide what she was doing from everyone but Miss Water, Lucy pointed with her right finger at a room on the second floor of the inn. A curtain had been drawn back, and the sash lifted, and the faintest outline of a figure could be seen just inside the window. The front-facing room on the second floor was usually an inn's "best" room, typically held for whatever swell the innkeeper could reel in. "Maybe he hasn't heard a story that captures his fancy."

"What do you mean?"

"Hear ye! Hear ye!" Lucy cried, winking at Miss Water. "True news from Carlisle! A most terrible story of a young maid, who after dallying with the master's son, did steal several precious items from the household! Upon being caught and dismissed for theft, hear how this young woman took a deadly vengeance upon her master's household!"

Through the side of her mouth, she said to Miss Water, "Is he still there? Did he come down?"

Miss Water made a questioning gesture with her hands. Lucy decided to embellish her tale. Still in her loud singsong voice, she called, "Hear how the young woman sought to bring revenge on the family who threw her out!" With a quick wink at Miss Water, she went on. "She did steal arsenic, intended for her lady's fine complexion. But rather than adding beauty to her fair mistress, she sought to kill the whole family! Yes indeed! By adding a large dose of arsenic to their Tuesday soup!"

As Miss Water nodded her head vigorously in encouragement, Lucy went on with the tale, adding dramatic flourishes as she went. "The nobleman's son, having bestirred himself to drink more bowls than the others, took gravely ill. Only the intervention of a most gifted apothecary, with an antidote administered right quick, saved the poor man from a most outrageous death!"

Lucy looked expectantly toward the inn's door, hearing a clamor from within.

"Where in heaven's name did you hear this dashed story?!" A well-dressed young man raced out of The Sparrow's medieval threshold. "Shut your confounded mouth!"

Despite his thick brogue, which made him sound like he had said "shu' yer confoinded muth," Lucy got his intention clearly enough.

The man brandished a handful of King Charles II's newly minted silver crowns. "I'll buy the lot."

"Good story, isn't it, sir?" Lucy asked, trying not to look impressed by the man's obvious wealth. She made a great show of looking in her satchel instead. "Alas, I've none more of that piece to sell. Perhaps I could interest you in this piece about Robert Hubert, Destroyer of London?"

The man stood there, confused. "I don't want that dashed story. I want the other one. The one you just told it! How did you hear it?"

Lucy was at a loss for words, but unexpectedly, the noblewoman surprised her. "Pray tell," Miss Water asked the man prettily, "why is this story, that this lass tells, so interesting to you? Such occurrences happen everywhere—the revenge of a maid dismissed for theft? A young maid who dallies with the master's son?"

Glancing at Miss Water, the man seemed to note her fine dress, for he tipped his hat before slumping against the wall. "You're quite right, of course. I don't know what got into me. Good miss, forgive my brash words."

Seeing that he was about to head back into the inn, Lucy added, "Carlisle, London, all much of the same, don't you think?"

The man turned back around. "Carlisle? You did say Carlisle! I thought I heard you!"

"Yes, my master has received several accounts from there in recent months. A man poisoned by his servant. A parish priest murdered in his own church. Terrible news, indeed."

The man's already sickly pallor seemed to become even more gray. "A priest murdered, you say?" He gulped. "Do you know his name?"

"Yes, it's right here." Lucy produced the pamphlets she'd gotten back from Duncan. Thinking of Master Aubrey, reluctantly, she added, "Three pence, sir."

The man, who she was quite sure now was Lord Cumberland's son, read through the True Account. "Oh, this is terrible. The poor man."

"Was he your parish priest?" Lucy asked, watching him closely.

"Mine? No. I—er—" He stopped.

Lucy took a deep breath, "Master Clifford. Sir. Did he marry you to the woman in this tale?"

"How did you know my name?" asked Francis Clifford, his identity now confirmed. He began to back away, retreating toward the inn. "How do you know about that? What do you want?"

"We just wanted to talk to you—" Lucy began.

"Did my father send you?" he interrupted. "I've told him I'm not going back! I can't live there again!"

"Because someone tried to murder you?" Miss Water asked, with a quick glance at Lucy. "We know you were poisoned."

"Murder me? Ha!" The Earl's son scoffed. "I took that dashed poison myself. I should have used a pistol! Done the job properly." His jaw jerked shut. Clearly, he had said more than he intended.

Lucy could not help but feel a bit shocked. Self-murder! That was a sin indeed, but not one she could contemplate now. How desperate the man must been.

To her surprise, Master Clifford continued. "The maid dismissed from the household was Amelie, a woman whom I once held dear. When my mother first informed me that she had dismissed her for theft, I couldn't believe it."

Clifford's deep melancholy was difficult to witness. The dark rings around his eyes were a testament to the weight of his grief. He hung his head. "Then she sent me a letter, saying that she had never loved me and did not want to see me again."

"She could write? The note was in her hand?" Lucy asked, surprised. Many servants were not able to easily write letters for themselves.

"How should I know? What difference does it make? Maybe she hired someone to write it. All I know is that she told me she had taken up with someone else. Told me she had"—he drew a ragged breath—"cuckolded me. The depth of her betrayal was immense, I assure you." Master Clifford slumped down on the barrel that Lucy had abandoned, seeming glad to shed a heavy burden. "I could not live, you see. Even though she had betrayed me. Then I heard that she had died." His eyes took on a glassy distant look. "So I left. I could not bear to be there."

Clifford looked upward toward the sky, his eyes for a moment lost and unseeing. "I've been here since before the Fire. Watched London burn. I never left. Fate decided that I should live, I guess." He shrugged. Indeed, the effort he had taken to speak seemed to have expended itself. He barely seemed able to keep himself upright, a portrait of pathos and despair.

Taking advantage of the man's lowered defenses, Lucy continued. "You were married to her, weren't you? To Amelie?"

Francis Clifford made a gesture, cutting her off. "You have evidence of this marriage?" he asked, his face reddening in anger.

Lucy gestured to the broadside he had crumpled in his fist. "Is he the priest that married you?" she tried again. "Funny thing about him having been murdered. The parish records were stolen too. As if someone were trying to cover something up."

Master Clifford blanched. "What you're suggesting is ludicrous. I had nothing to do with that man's death!" He turned to go.

"Her father is grieving too, you know," Lucy said, a bit desperately. "He soon must return to the army."

Clifford looked weary. "I've seen her father around here. He must have figured out where I've been living. I think he's been trying to kill me." Clifford rubbed his stubbly face. "Although maybe I should have just let him. I don't know."

"He's trying to do right by his daughter's memory," Lucy said, trying to be patient. "He wants you to acknowledge his daughter as your wife, because—"

"I wish to hear no more! I know what he thinks! Amelie was pregnant, but she told me herself—later—that the babe was not mine! She mocked me, she did. Now she's dead! It's all over, and I've no wish to speak of it again!" Before heading back inside The Sparrow, he turned to look at them fiercely. "I don't know what brought you here, but I suggest you cease trying to dredge my family's misfortunes. My father does not take well to people who try to cross or blackmail us."

He stomped back inside The Sparrow, leaving Lucy and Miss Water staring after him.

"So he knew Amelie was with child," Miss Water said softly. "And he abandoned her, and the baby."

"If the child was even his," Lucy sighed. "For all we know, she *had* taken up with someone else." She tapped her foot impatiently. "Did you see his face when I asked him about whether he had married Amelie? I think they were married, and he was ashamed of the marriage. More so when he thought her to have been a thief. I'm sure that someone broke into those churches and murdered that priest to hide the marriage record."

Miss Water nodded. "So where does that leave us?" she asked.

"Not one whit further," Lucy replied. "Not one whit."

·16·

The next morning, Lucy woke up bleary-eyed from a fitful night's sleep. Over and over she had woken up, recalling Master Clifford's face when he spoke of Amelie, his belief in her betrayal, and his own abandonment of his wife and child. The full truth of the story was still unclear, but poor Amelie's plight was hard to bear.

When she walked out of her chamber though, her dark mood shifted abruptly when she laid eyes on a small package wrapped in twine, Will sitting by the table proudly waiting. "It's my birthday!" she said, slapping the side of her head. "However could I have forgotten?" She shook the package expectantly.

"Open it!" commanded Will.

Lucy untied the strings on the cloth bag. Inside, she found the softest bit of leather, folded carefully. "Take it to the cordwainer," her brother said, smiling. "He will make you some fine new shoes. All those hours walking, 'tis a wonder your shoes have not become more riddled with holes!"

That was not her only gift. To her surprise, when she descended to the shop, Master Aubrey handed her a pot of ink and a newly sharpened quill. "For all your ramblings," he said, gruffly. "Maybe the next one will be worth printing."

"Thank you, sir," she said, admiring the quill. "I hope so." For a moment she was quite overcome by the gift. She hadn't expected Master Aubrey to know it was her birthday, much less give her a gift. She had indeed been fortunate in her employer.

From his place by the woodcut cabinet, Lach snorted. "I hope you didn't think I got you something. I barely make two bits together."

Master Aubrey swatted his apprentice with a rolled-up piece of paper, blowing back his red hair. "Never you mind this scamp," he said. "He's made it so you can have the morning off, didn't you, lad?" He pushed into him again.

Lach frowned. "Yeah. I guess I can do your work *and* my own," he said reluctantly to Lucy.

"Truly? Oh thank you, Lach!" She then proceeded to startle them greatly, by embracing first Master Aubrey and then Lach, kissing them both on the cheek. "The morning off! That's wonderful."

Seeing Lach's face turn the shade of a sheared sheep, incongruous with his red hair, she giggled.

Master Aubrey patted her arm. "Mind you're back for supper."

———

Without much care in the world, she popped off to see Annie and found her readying for market. Within a few minutes they had found their way to Covent Garden. As they walked about, Lucy picked out a bit of cod, and Annie a bit of tongue for the evening's meal. As Lucy expertly inspected each bit of produce, Annie sighed. "I wish you could go to market with me every day. Cook scolds me so! 'Why can't you bargain like Lucy used to?' she always says. She misses you! I do too."

Lucy looked into Annie's basket. "You've certainly learned to find nice trimmings though," she teased. She pulled out two purple ribbons from the top. "Are these for *another* dress?"

"Can't blame a girl for trying to put together a hope chest, can you?" Annie asked plaintively, like a kitten seeking milk.

"No, certainly not." Lucy paused, a bit uncomfortable now with conversations related to dowries and the like. "Do you have someone in mind?" she asked with a touch of trepidation.

"No, no," Annie murmured, a bit too quickly for Lucy's taste. They stopped to select some cheese from a funny little cheeseseller, who with his yellowish face and bright red apron looked remarkably like the red and yellow Leicestershire cheese on his cart. "Sid's still been working for the magistrate," Annie commented, sniffing a piece of the chard.

"Indeed?" Lucy's heart sank a bit though, for she found Sid's name came up quite frequently in Annie's conversations these days.

"Yes. He's not been thieving anymore. At least, none I can see."

"I should think not," Lucy said. "The magistrate would not take kindly to a thief in his household." She'd reminded Annie of this before, but it bore repeating. She sought to change the subject. "How is the magistrate faring?" Lucy asked. "I worry he is working too hard at the assize sessions. We should think of some way to ease his burden."

"Oh, I wouldn't dare," Annie said, sounding a bit awed by the prospect. "He's a kind master to be sure, but I'm not like you, Lucy. I cannot talk to him as you do. He's so fond of you."

Lucy smiled at her young friend. "I'm sure he's quite fond of you too, Annie. We are his family. That's why we must help him. But how to do that?" A moment later, she clapped her hands. "Perhaps you could pick something out for the magistrate's supper tonight. Cook could make a tasty dessert." She mused for a moment. "Would he like a cheese tart? No, that's not fine enough."

"I've been wanting to try my hand at an apple pie," Annie ventured, licking her lips. She pointed to a nearby fruit merchant's stand. "Let's try there."

Lucy was about to say apple pie was not what she had in mind for the magistrate either, but she could see Annie had her heart set on developing her cooking skills. As Annie picked through the apples, Lucy poked around, peering into the merchant's row of covered straw baskets. They each had a picture of the fruit or vegetable inside—rutabagas, carrots, some roots and herbs. One Lucy didn't recognize. Lifting the lid, she saw what looked like some dried brownish-yellowish chunks. She sniffed. The aroma was delicate and sweet but she could not place the scent.

"What's this?" she asked the seller, when he was done placing cabbage in a young woman's basket.

"Dried pineapple," he said, wiping his hands on the front of his shirt. "All the way from the New World, these are." Seeing that no one was at his cart, he seemed more than happy to tell the pineapple's trip to London. "I'm the only one who sold them, even before the Fire. I always have the best fruits." He waved his hand expansively around Covent Garden. "Those markets aren't even around anymore. Everyone's coming here. But no one but me can afford these finer bits."

Annie came over to pay for her apples. When she sniffed the pineapple appreciatively, as Lucy had done a few minutes before, the man seemed pleased. "Want to try a tiny bit?" he asked. "Just a taste, mind you," he added hastily.

"Oh yes!" Lucy and Annie exclaimed in unison.

The seller winked. "Thought you might. Just so long that you don't tell anyone I'm letting the customers sample my wares for free."

"We won't tell anyone!" Lucy said. Annie echoed her words, hopping up and down in excitement.

The fruit-seller handed them each a small chip of the pineapple. Annie ate hers straightaway. "Oooh," she sighed in satisfaction. "That was delicious."

Closing her eyes, Lucy put hers on the tip of her tongue, experiencing a great rush of sweetness. Rather than chewing, she sort of rolled the pineapple about in her mouth, savoring the taste, thinking about the odd bit of fruit. She could almost feel how the warm breezes from the New World had touched it, could feel the weight of its four-month journey, as it traveled in crates across the Atlantic. Her thoughts drifted to the magistrate's daughter, wondering how Sarah had fared crossing the ocean to the New World. Where was she living now? What was she doing? She knew that Sarah, traveling to the Massachusetts Bay Colony, was unlikely to have been anywhere near the origins of this pineapple, but she felt a momentary closeness to her far-traveling friend.

Then, something Annie said snapped her back to her present surroundings. "What did you say?"

"I just said," Annie repeated, "that ever since we read that poem from the Fire, I've been wanting to try a pineapple. And the other thing too, but I can never remember that one."

"Pomegranates," Lucy said distantly, her mind suddenly racing. "The poem mentioned pomegranates."

The fruit-seller shook his head. "No pomegranates here."

"Pineapples too!" Annie insisted. "I remember it distinctly."

"No, no. That is so!" Lucy said, realizing Annie was right. She turned back to the fruit-seller. "When do pineapples bloom, do you know?" she asked, following a different thought.

The man frowned, as he took some coins from a woman buying some herbs. "I don't know exactly, but I think I have something here—" He began to rummage through a much-worn leather bag hanging at the side of his cart. "Hold on a moment, I can tell you exactly." He pulled out a stack of folded papers, which Lucy immediately recognized. All pamphlets and broadsides. It was like looking in the jumble in her own pack.

"Are you a bookseller too then?" she asked with a smile, watching him thumb through the flimsy pieces.

He grunted. "Wouldn't touch such a livelihood. Prefer my honest fruits and vegetables to the nonsense and frippery they push. Don't need no stories of horned women or monstrous births. Just pick these up from time to time. Useful stuff about herbs and plants. Oh, here it is!" He pulled out a small pamphlet with pictures of plants and vegetables.

Lucy read the title out loud. *"The Garden of Eden, or, An accurate description of all flowers and fruits now growing in England."*

The fruit-seller glanced at the book. "This fellow Hugh Plat says pineapples must be planted in August. They bloom in spring and summer. These here they dried and packed in sugar. Otherwise, they wouldn't make the long trip."

"So they don't bloom in 'the first freezes of autumn.'" Lucy thought about the poem again. "Are many pineapples grown in England?"

"As far as I know, only in one hothouse, outside Cambridge." Seeing Lucy's puzzled face, the fruit-seller explained, "Hothouses are special places where they can grow plants not natural to England. They grow things from the New World and the Indies. I got a mate there who sold me a fresh one a few months back. I was quite famous for a while. Someone even wrote a ballad about me." He chuckled at the memory. His chest pressed out slightly. "Everyone knew me, Elias Greenleaf. The seller of pineapples." He gestured to his stall. "Greenleaf, green leaves, you get it?"

He moved over toward a woman holding out a coin and some apples. "You can look at the penny piece," he said to Lucy over his shoulder. "Just leave it here when you're done."

Lucy read through Plat's description of pineapples. He seemed to be quite a knowledgeable gentleman. Other than learning more about the pineapple's size and appearance, though, she discovered nothing more than what the fruit-seller had already told her.

Annie tugged at her sleeve. "Lucy, aren't you due back to Master Aubrey's?"

Thoughtfully, Lucy laid the tract under a basket of rosemary so that it would not blow away in the gentle autumn breeze. On a whim, she pulled out her treasured half crown. "How much pineapple can I get for this?" She glanced at Annie. "Perhaps Master Hargrave would like to try it."

Master Greenleaf grinned. "For such appreciative young ladies, I'll give you the lot. Perfect for a fruit cake. I'd say a treat made for a king, but King Charles himself has not yet had this delicacy!"

Pushing their way past all the people milling about, Lucy finally found a bit of grass under a spreading oak tree whose leaves had not yet fallen. "Let's rest here for a bit."

Annie immediately began to gnaw on a bit of bread, following the servant's common habit of eating whenever there was a break in duties. She seemed put out about something, but Lucy wanted to focus on what was puzzling her. Pulling out the poem, which she always kept in her hidden pocket, she read the last part aloud. *"My rose will bloom, among the hearty pineapples, even in the first freeze of autumn. Rose, my love—Even kings can wrong a fey duet."*

Annie scratched her head. "Still fiddle-faddle," she said, impatiently. "I need to get home. Shall I bring Cook the pineapple?"

"No, let's keep it a surprise for the family. I do not want to burden Cook. How about I make the fruitcake and bring it over myself, after supper? I'll see if Will can bring me. I don't think Master Aubrey will mind, so long as I get his supper ready." Finally she took in Annie's hangdog expression. "Wait, what's wrong?"

"I wanted to make the magistrate a special apple pie. Your fruitcake will be better than mine."

Lucy groaned at her own blindness. Of course Annie wanted to make something special for the magistrate. "I won't make the fruitcake then. I'm just bringing the pineapple." Seeing Annie still looking down, she added, "It's just an excuse, Annie. I just need to speak to the magistrate."

"Master Adam won't be there, you know," Annie said bluntly.

Lucy flushed. "I know that." She had a moment's misgiving, then shook herself. "I truly want to speak to the magistrate." She said again firmly, giving Annie's shoulders a little hug. "You'll make a wonderful pie, I know it."

Annie shrugged, unconvinced. "Whatever you say." Yet she looked a little more pleased, and Lucy hoped their conversation would soon be forgotten.

A few hours later, Lucy arrived at the magistrate's kitchen door, carrying the basket of pineapple. Not Will but a fairly grumpy Lach had accompanied her for the long walk after supper. Will had gone off to see one of his ladyloves, a habit Lucy hoped he would tire of soon. Only the promise of a bit of Annie's apple pie had convinced the redheaded apprentice to trot along beside her, and he had grumbled nearly every step of the way. He held his tongue only when they arrived at the relative grandeur of the magistrate's household.

As always, Cook and John were glad to see her, although neither showed it directly. Thankfully, the magistrate had no visitors that evening, and he had taken his supper in his little study. With great pride, Annie showed Lucy her apple pie, which she had yet to slice.

"It's beautiful," Lucy breathed, admiring the plump slices as they fell onto the plates.

"I thought for sure I'd forgotten an ingredient, but for the life

of me I could not think of what," Annie chattered happily under
the admiration of the other servants. She held up *A True Gentle-*
woman's Delight, a pamphlet of recipes that the late Mistress Hargrave had long ago purchased at the market. "See, I followed it
exactly. Take apples and pare them. Chop them very small. To the
rosewater, I beat in the cinnamon, a little ginger and some sugar,
uh oh!" She looked up in despair. "I think I forgot the sugar!"

"No, dear, you didn't," Cook said reassuringly, standing behind Annie. Catching Lucy's eye, she pantomimed how she had
added the sugar when Annie wasn't looking.

Lucy stifled a giggle. Thank goodness Cook had realized the
missing ingredient in time. She was grateful, too, that Cook had
spared the sugar, as it's cost from the grocer was dear. But the
master, they'd discovered, had a sweet tooth, and they all liked to
please him.

"Shall I take the pie to the master?" Annie asked, picking up
the small silver tray.

"May I come with you?" Lucy asked, carefully filling a goblet
of Master Hargrave's Rhenish wine. On a second plate, she placed
a few pieces of the pineapple.

When she knocked on his study door, the magistrate's eyes
widened with real delight when he saw Lucy. He glanced at Annie then, his brows rising slightly when he took in her anxious
eyes, her hands tightly gripping the tray. He looked back at Lucy
for an explanation.

"Annie made you her first apple pie," Lucy said, carefully
unloosing Annie's fingers from the tray, and setting it down on
master's table. "I'm sure you will find it delicious."

"Indeed!" the magistrate exclaimed, picking up his fork. "Let me make haste!" He took a bite, and both Annie and Lucy watched him carefully. "Delicious, just as you said. Thank you, Annie." Lucy beamed under his warm words, as if she'd made the pie herself. She was glad he understood what his words would mean to the lass.

Annie bobbed, her face bright and happy. She backed out of the room, no doubt back to the kitchen to flirt a bit with Lach, who'd been clearly bewildered by her ways.

The magistrate smiled at Lucy. "I thought for a bit she sought to poison me, she looked so frightened of putting the tray down before me." He took in her basket. "Have you something else?"

Lucy set down the small plate. "A bit of dried pineapple. I bought some at the market today. It's not nearly as nice as fresh apple pie, mind you. I thought you might like it," she said.

Standing up, the magistrate surprised her by clasping both her hands in his, before saying in his grave way, "Thank you, my dear. Please join me." He pulled the other chair next to his.

Sitting back down, he took a bite. Like herself, he savored the first bite without chewing it straightaway. "Pineapple! Delicious! Thank you, Lucy. This was quite kind of you. I've heard the King himself has not yet tried this delicacy. To his credit, he made it clear that he is waiting to try the pineapple until his colonies in the New World can produce it. If that is true, he is truly missing out, for this dessert is fit for a king!" He paused. "I seem to recall a fresh pineapple had been sold here in London."

"Yes," Lucy said eagerly. "In Covent Garden. It came from a hothouse in Cambridge. It seems that Master Greenleaf was quite famous at one point!"

"Ah, I see." The magistrate took another careful bite, and then another. Lucy watched him fondly as he took the last crumb of the apple pie from the small silver salver, and laid his fork down with satisfaction. "My dear. Thank you. Now, before you tell me why you've actually come, I have something for you."

To her great surprise and delight, Master Hargrave pulled out a small leather-bound book and set it in front of her. "I happen to know that today is your twenty-first birthday. I thought you might enjoy this piece."

Lucy picked up the slim volume carefully. "*The Two Gentlemen of Verona?* Shakespeare? You're giving this to me?" She felt her throat catch. "That is very kind of you, sir. How can I accept it?" She could hardly put it down, wanting to tear into it straightaway.

"Ah, Lucy. 'Tis no kinder than you stopping by to cheer an old man with a bit of pineapple." He rubbed his hands together. "Now tell me, why do I suspect this was more than a social visit?"

Lucy had to hide a smile. How preposterous it was that a former servant would ever call on a magistrate. And yet, wasn't that what she was doing? As always, her heart warmed a bit when she regarded the magistrate. He certainly had never held her lowly station against her.

Lucy pulled out the *London Miscellany* again. Seeing the well-worn piece again, the magistrate shook his head slightly in wonder. "I declare, Lucy. I can't remember anyone ever as interested in sorting out puzzles as you."

"Excepting yourself, sir." She rushed along. "I just think there's more to this poem than what we've seen." She pointed to the line about pineapples. "I think he was telling Miss Water something."

"About pineapples? Are they usually available in the 'first

freezes of autumn?'" The magistrate looked at the poem again and then squinted at Lucy. "That may be true, but we'll never know. Wasn't this poor man killed in the Fire?"

"Oh no, sir! As it turns out, that man was not Darius at all, but rather his manservant, or something like that—Miss Water wasn't sure. His name was Tahmin and—"

"I see there's a bit more story here." His eyes twinkled. "Let me first have another piece of this most excellent apple pie."

He rang for Annie, who brought him another large slice of apple pie and some more wine. Her smile was wide and happy. When Annie left, Lucy told him everything she had learned over the last fortnight. As always, the magistrate listened attentively, his eyes slightly closed. She knew from seeing him at court that this was how he listened to testimony after testimony, seeking the truth from the great mounds of evidence that came before his bench.

When Lucy finished recounting everything, the magistrate remained silent for a moment. Then his eyes opened. "You think there is one more puzzle in here?"

Lucy nodded. "I know it sounds odd. I think Darius was telling her something specific, without her father discovering their relationship. He had to disguise his words, in case his poem fell into the wrong hands."

"Which it did."

"Which it did"—Lucy sighed—"when I asked Master Aubrey to print it."

"Are you telling me that you think this love poem is a real invitation? Not just a reminder of their romance, but a real reminder to her? Why ever do you think so? Forgive me, but the verse is a bit vague."

"I think when he wrote 'I'm here,' he wanted Rhonda, Miss Water, to know he was in London. The fruit-seller mentioned that there are some hothouses near London that grow pineapples, which is the only way they might be able to bloom in autumn."

"Ah, I see." Master Hargrave sat back in his chair. "You believe that Darius was telling Miss Water where to meet him? Interesting." He spooned some tobacco into his clay pipe from a small silver box on his desk. Unlike other men of his acquaintance, he had not yet taken to snuff. "How could she possibly know when?"

The magistrate looked at Lucy with a half smile. She got the feeling he already knew the answer to the question, and wanted to see what she had figured out. "The last line," she said. "I think there is another puzzle here. 'Even kings can wrong a fey duet.' That doesn't sound right, does it?"

"Well, perhaps. Let's look at that line a little more closely. Bring that candle over, would you, my dear?"

After Lucy set a second taper down on the table, he smoothed the much-wrinkled verse. "First there is the notion of a king, and then a 'fey duet' being wronged. He may have been apologizing for something he did."

"What do you mean? Is that referring to His Majesty?" Lucy asked. "I don't see anything about an apology."

"No, I shouldn't think that by 'king' he was referring to our king of England. Darius was the name of a fifth-century Persian king. Perhaps he was alluding to a wrong he did to her, to ruin their 'fey duet.'"

"So, you think the letter was simply an apology? That he wasn't

planning to come at all?" Lucy suddenly felt disappointed, thinking about Miss Water, whom she knew missed Darius terribly.

"No, let's not jump to conclusions." The magistrate took a sip
of his wine. "Indeed, I think you are right. There is one last message hidden here, even if there was also an outward apology. Another anagram, perhaps."

"That's what I was thinking!" Lucy said, regaining her earlier
excitement. "I don't know where to begin."

"Well, let's ascertain your first guess. You said that the pineapple was grown in a hothouse outside Cambridge. Perhaps the
name 'Cambridge' can be found here. Why don't we see?"

Just as he had done before, when they discovered Miss Water's
name hidden in the first line, Lucy carefully copied out the last
line. *Rose, my love—Even kings can wrong a fey duet.*

She then crossed out the letters C-A-M. She stopped. "There's
no "B" in this line. So not Cambridge." She thought for a moment.
"Maybe the word London is here. L-O-N-D-O-N," she spelled.
"The letters are all here!"

"And what letters remain?"

Lucy read them out loud. "R-S-E-M-Y-V-E-E-V-E-K-I-C-A-
N-W-R-O-N-G-A-F-E-Y-U-E-T." She looked at the magistrate
doubtfully. "That's a lot of letters still. And 'London' seems so
vague." She thought back to her conversation with the fruit-seller.
"Wait a minute!" she exclaimed. She grabbed the quill again with-
out thinking. The magistrate watched her as she worked it out.
"The fruit-seller said pineapples had only been sold in Covent
Garden, even before the Fire." Carefully she crossed out C-O-V-E-
N-T-G-A-R-D-E-N.

"All the letters are here. That must mean something."

"Perhaps it means something, perhaps it doesn't," the magistrate warned her, but she could hear the rising excitement in his voice too.

She looked at what was left in the sentence. "That's certainly a lot of letters. What could they spell? A date?" Her face fell. "The date may have already passed."

"Well, we won't know unless we figure it out. Shall we try each month?"

"May!" Lucy exclaimed. "Look, here's May!"

"As well as the first few letters of August and November. Any dates?" the magistrate said. "Let's see, I see the numbers 'one,' 'four,' 'five,' 'seven,' 'nine.'"

"And I see 'eleven,'" she sighed. "But nothing like 'first,' 'second,' or 'third.'"

Finally, seeing how the candle had burned nearly to the quick, Lucy reluctantly laid down her quill. "Maybe we're trying to find something that isn't there," she said, carefully replacing the stopper in the magistrate's inkwell.

"I'll try to keep thinking about it," the magistrate promised, although Lucy knew he was quite busy. "Let us not give up."

As she was leaving, he surprised her by taking her hand for a moment. "Lucy, I do not truly like these investigations you are taking on yourself, and I know Adam does not either." He released her hand. "Indulge an old man, will you? Please. Be careful."

·17·

The next afternoon, Lucy stood before The George, seriously displeased. For mid-October, the weather was a bit warm, even though the morning had started off chilly. She loosened the faded green scarf she'd crisscrossed on her body. Now she could feel sweat trickle uncomfortably down the insides of her dress. She'd barely sold any penny merriments, let alone the longer—and far duller—chapbooks and pamphlets. She had no true accounts of murders or any last dying speeches left with which to tempt the crowd, although she had one piece detailing a monstrous dog, and a bawdy tale of a man thrice cuckolded. Londoners just didn't seem to be buying today. As Master Aubrey would say, "The crowd can be fickle as any false-hearted lover. What they want today, they'll forget tomorrow."

As she hefted her still heavy pack back onto her shoulders, Lucy got the queasy feeling she was being watched. She peered at the crowd, passing around her, trying to see if anyone was indeed looking at her.

Straining her eyes, she looked between a soap-seller and two young women eagerly sniffing at her pots and jars. Sure enough, Ashton Hendricks was standing there. She didn't know how long he'd been watching her. When she marched right up to him, he didn't seem too surprised.

"Why in Heaven's name are you following me?" she asked, trying to look more angry than afraid. "Are you planning to drag me somewhere again? I'm going to scream for the constable, if you don't tell me this instant."

"Why did you go see the Earl's son?" Hendricks demanded. "I saw you there, speaking to him."

"Have you been following me since then?" Lucy countered. "You still haven't told me what you're doing here."

They stared at each other fiercely for a moment.

Then Hendricks gave in, sighing a bit. "No," he said. "I haven't been following you. I saw you, and I needed to know what you were up to."

Lucy shrugged. "I suppose I'm a bit nosy."

"Hoping to add some gold to your pocket, are you?" His yellowish teeth and skin took on a fierce, feral quality. "Trying to make a few coins?"

Lucy stepped back. "No! Whatever do you mean?"

"So, you weren't the one who sent me this?" He brandished a piece of paper in her face. "I just received it."

Lucy read the letter over quickly, the base quality causing a sickening feeling in her stomach. The author threatened to tell everyone that Amelie had been prostituting herself and had not even known the father of her son. The last line read "Just Ten Sovereigns, or I will Publish her Deeds for the World to Know."

"I swear to you," she said, handing it back to him. "I had nothing to do with this. I never even knew you." She frowned. "So someone was blackmailing you about your daughter. I wonder if anyone else was being blackmailed."

But Hendricks wasn't interested in her musings. "Tell me, then, what you wanted from that bloody son of Cumberland. If you weren't there to blackmail him, then why?"

"I'm hoping to find out who killed the man in the Cheshire Cheese. His name was Tahmin."

Hendricks blinked in surprise. This was not what he was expecting. "The Arab?"

"He was Persian, actually."

The distinction seemed lost on Hendricks. "Why ever do you care?"

"He was a—" she sought to explain, then stopped. Who was Tahmin to her, anyway? "Friend. Of a Friend." He was a friend of a friend of a woman Lucy scarcely knew. Not for the first time she wondered at her own drive for the truth.

Hendricks leaned back against the stone wall. He seemed to be trying to think. "There were only a few of us there that night."

Lucy nodded. "That's right. You. Lord Cumberland. Jacques—he was the card sharp. Tahmin—the man who was killed. Tilly, the barmaid. And you said you heard the bells tolling the Fire soon afterward." Lucy continued. "Tahmin must have been killed soon after you left."

Lucy saw him open and shut his mouth without speaking. "Yes? What is it?"

"I only just thought of it," he muttered.

"Yes?" Lucy felt a surge of excitement.

"Your friend. Tahmin—was his name?"

"Yes."

"I saw Tilly whisper something to those men. While he was arguing with Jacques. I thought this was odd you see."

"Odd? Why?"

"She looked like she was pointing that man out."

"Pointing him out?" Lucy repeated. What had Tilly told them? She had to find out. She wheeled abruptly on the balls of her feet, nearly catching her skirts on a piece of wood as she passed.

"Hey, where are you going?" she heard Hendricks call, but she did not stop her mad pace.

Lucy raced the mile to the Fox and Duck without stopping, not heeding the staring passersby. When she reached the tavern, she doubled over, gasping for breath. She untied her scarf to breathe more easily. Once she had stopped panting, she walked in, without thinking through what she was going to say.

As before, the tavern was rather dark and dreary, with little light streaming through the windows. There were only a few people in there, gulping beer from their mugs. Right away she saw Tilly, dressed in a drab blue dress, wiping down tables with a bit of a rag.

"Tilly!" Lucy stormed over. A few people looked up. "*You* killed him! It was you!"

Startled, Tilly knocked over a half full pewter mug. Rather than wiping up the mess, she drew herself, planting her meaty hands on her hips. She looked wary, as much like a fox as the sign above the bar. "I don't know what you're talking about."

Lucy stood right in front of her. "You killed Tahmin!"

"Never heard of him," Tilly said, picking up the pewter mug. She dropped the cloth on the wood floor, swabbing up the spilled beer with a swish of her foot.

"The Persian man. You told the other men something about him." She grabbed Tilly's arm. "At the Cheshire Cheese. You set those men on him."

"Aw—what's she on about, Tilly?" one man said, hunkering over his pint.

"You kill someone?" slurred another.

"She's a madwoman, she is," Tilly said, to no one in particular. "Escaped from Bedlam, didn't she?"

Lucy pulled on Tilly's sleeve. "You pointed Tahmin out to those men," she repeated. "Why? Why did you do it?"

Tilly jerked her arm away. "I didn't like him."

"Why? Because Tahmin bluffed about the value of the contents of the bag? Jacques—or shall I say 'Jack'—didn't like looking like a fool? Maybe he didn't take too kindly to being outbluffed."

Tilly turned back to Lucy then, so that the two women only had a half-step between them. "See here. Those men had been tippling down. I heard them talking dirty stuff, about French papists and the like. I got the feeling they were waiting for a foreigner, all right? I didn't know what they were planning, and I didn't truly care. I just didn't want it to be Jack. You got that?"

The barmaid leaned in then, and deliberately burped in Lucy's face. Lucy gagged, the acrid smell from her breath a bad mixture of stale beer, old cheese, and garlic. Seeing her advantage, Tilly then seized Lucy by the arm and hauled her bodily through the back door and through the kitchen. In passing, she saw an old woman with milky eyes cock her head, and then spit into the boiling pot. Lucy looked away in disgust, even as Tilly threw open the door and pushed her out into the alley.

"You'd best be leaving well enough alone!" the barmaid said, as they stood out in the alley. There were slops all over the place. Clearly the raker didn't come back that way all too often.

Lucy stepped forward, trying not to smell Tilly's bad breath. "Did you do it? Did you set those men on him?"

Tilly shrugged, a hard, cynical gesture. "Maybe I did. Look, I didn't know they would kill the poor sot. I've just seen people turn on Jack before, just for being French." She leaned in toward Lucy. "You should leave now. You should feel lucky no one has been set upon you."

"Are you threatening me?" Lucy asked.

"Nah," Tilly bared her teeth, a chilly semblance of a smile. "Just a reminder, friendly like, you understand. Don't come around this way again."

·18·

"Then I left the Fox and Duck," Lucy concluded an hour later, having related the entire encounter with Tilly to a very bored Lach. The apprentice was seated on the printer's bench, a bowl in his hands. When she had returned from the tavern, still blistering from the exchange, she'd found only Lach there, looking miserably at the printer's stores, trying to figure out what he could eat for supper. The printer was off on a short journey to see the licenser, a trek that always returned him in an angry and contentious mood. Will was nowhere to be found. So as Lucy had fixed supper for Lach and herself, she had angrily related what had happened at the tavern.

"Tilly never actually struck me, 'tis true, but she did hurt my arm," Lucy said, pulling up her sleeve to inspect her forearm. She didn't see any bruising. "I think she knows something. Maybe I went about it the wrong way."

"Serves you right. You're lucky she didn't wallup you," Lach said, not too sympathetically. "I don't think you'd fare too well in a skirmish. Tilly sounds tough." He cocked his ear. "Is someone at the door?"

Lucy gestured toward their shuttered window. "See if it's Will. Master Aubrey would use his key around back." She began to scrape the last of her bowl into the slop bucket.

Grunting slightly, Lach peered out the window onto the street below. "Not Will." Taking a deep breath, he shouted, "We're closed! Come back tomorrow!" He threw up his hands. "Honestly!" he muttered. "*A Lady from Leicester-shire* can wait!!"

Then an angry voice—one that was quite familiar to them both—boomed out with authority. "It's Constable Duncan. Unlock this door at once. I need to speak to Miss Campion. Now!"

"Be right there!" Lucy called, hurriedly taking off her apron. She smoothed her skirts as she crossed the room.

Behind her, Lach clambered up, quick on her heels. "Look how she jumps when her constable calls!"

"Hush!" Lucy glared at him.

Lach crossed in front of her, so that he reached the door first. For a moment he barred her way. "Now why ever would our dear constable wish to speak to you? At this time of the evening, no less."

"Open the door, Lach," Lucy said through gritted teeth.

"As you wish," he said. But as he unbarred the door, the apprentice began to loudly sing the disparaging words of an anonymous ballad he'd been hawking earlier. "The Devil take the constable's head, if we beg milk, bacon, butter or bread . . ."

"Shh! He'll hear you!" Lucy hissed at him.

"Nah, he won't. He's too busy being important." He tugged on the bar. "Gimme a hand, will you? This bar's heavy."

"Now!" the constable shouted from the other side of the door. His proximity to them made them both jump.

Lucy scrambled to help Lach raise the bar that kept the shop door barred from outsiders. The constable strode in, and looked around. The larger bellman was with him. Neither looked very friendly.

"Duncan, what's wrong?" Lucy asked.

"Miss Campion." He frowned at her. "Tell me where you were this afternoon."

"I-I was here," she stumbled, wondering at his unexpectedly formal tone, "at the shop, printing several almanacs and then I was hawking at the George—"

"The George, alright." Duncan waved his hand to stop her. "Did your master send you somewhere else?"

"Yes, I mean, no. He didn't send me anywhere."

"So are you denying you were at the Fox and Duck in Smith-field?"

Lucy swallowed. What in heaven's name was going on? She wondered. "Well, no. I was there."

"You just said you were here. Which is it?"

"You asked if he *sent* me somewhere. He did not."

Constable Duncan looked around. "Where is he now?"

Lucy stared at him, but answered the question. "Master Aubrey's away, on a journey. He had an appointment to see the Licenser of the Press, Roger L'Estrange. He must have taken lodging overnight. He's done that before." She paused. "What is this about?"

The constable did not answer her. "What was your business at the Fox and Duck earlier today?" he countered instead.

Lucy's mind began to reel, remembering her skirmish with the barmaid. Had the wench complained about her public accusation? If so, she needed to make sure Duncan understood why she'd blame her. "Tilly!" she blurted. "I went to speak to Tilly."

"So I gather. Why?"

"It was something Ashton Hendricks said." Lucy sank down on the printer's bench. Dimly she noted that Lach had spilled some ink and had not scrubbed the area clean with lye, as he was supposed to. Master Aubrey would not like it; he could be quite particular about the cleanliness of his shop. Sometimes she wondered if the printer held cleanliness a bit higher than he held godliness.

Duncan rapped his knuckles on a low fixed timber just above his head. "Which was?"

"Tilly pointed Tahmin out to those men. She said they'd been talking of killing a foreigner. She thought they might be after Jacques. I suppose she was trying to protect Jacques? Made up that story . . . ?"

The constable made an exasperated gesture. "What are you talking about? Speak sense, lass!"

Lucy did not like his tone and apparently neither did Lach. He had retreated to the corner, but was watching them warily. For once he'd dropped the mocking look.

"I think Jacques was the one who was blackmailing Lord Cumberland," Lucy said. "Or maybe it was Tilly. I'm not sure. She was definitely trying to protect Jacques." Lucy stopped. She looked at the constable. "What are you doing here?"

"You left something of yours at the tavern." He produced her green scarf. "I know this is yours. I recognized it."

"Oh, I wondered where I had left it!" Lucy said, standing up. She was frantically trying to remember when she'd last seen the scarf. It must have slipped off when Tilly chased her out, she thought. Then she felt indignant. Tilly, that harlot, must have kept it.

"Thank you." When she reached for the scarf, he held it above his head. She frowned. "May I have it back, please?"

She could see Lach narrow his eyes. The apprentice shared most Londoners' distrust of authorities, especially those with the ability to haul a fellow off to jail for having a bit of fun.

"Tell me, Miss Campion," the constable waited, still watching her.

"Yes? What?" She dropped her outstretched hand.

"Tell me why your scarf was found with Tilly Baker's dead body."

"What? Tilly Baker was murdered?" Lucy sat back down abruptly. "No! That can't be true."

"You argued with her, from what I hear." Duncan watched her closely. "Close to blows, you were."

Lucy fanned herself with her hand. Suddenly the shop seemed unbearably warm, even though she'd already banked the fire. "Well, clearly she was killed after I left."

"After you argued with her. Don't even try to deny it. Several people witnessed your argument."

"They didn't witness me kill her!" Seeing the bellman's eyebrows raise, she added, "You know what I mean!"

"Tell me then."

Lucy quickly described her meeting with Tilly. "Constable," Lucy said, winking back tears, "you know that I did not murder Tilly."

She saw the bellman shuffle his feet. Duncan did not meet her eyes. "I need to consider the facts," he said. "Several witnesses will state in a court of law that you were seen scuffling with her, and then you continued your fight outside the inn. Shortly afterward, Tilly Baker was found dead. Do you deny this?"

"No. I mean, yes." Lucy stopped, confused. "Surely someone must have seen her alive after our—" she cast about for a term, "disagreement." She thought back to the people at the inn. "There was a woman in the kitchen. The cook, I guess. She spit in the stew—"

Duncan interrupted her. "I'm here to enforce the law. That's what you prefer, isn't it?"

Lucy began to breathe heavily. She knew only too well how gossip could be shaped into truth. She tried to speak evenly. "Constable, you yourself said some time back, that you promised yourself not to jump to conclusions again and—"

Duncan cut her off. "Are you here alone? Aside from this nitwit, I mean?" He gestured toward Lach, who let out an indignant and decidedly unmanly squeak. "You said Master Aubrey is off to the licenser's. Where's your brother?"

Lucy didn't want to admit that as usual she didn't know where her brother was. The constable must have read it on her face. "You're coming with me."

Against her will, Lucy's eyes filled with tears. "Are you arresting me?" Even though Newgate had been destroyed in the Great

Fire, the thought of being hauled off to jail sickened her. That he was accusing her of murder truly stung.

"I'll give you five minutes. Collect your things."

Exactly five minutes later, Lucy found herself walking up Fleet Street between the constable and the larger bellman, still silent. When she retrieved her cloak, she'd spent a few minutes pleading with Lach to take a note to the magistrate, but the apprentice had refused. First, she threatened him. "You'll have to do all the chores if I get locked up." When that didn't work, she tried pleading. "I'll do all your duties for a week!"

"It's near curfew," Lach stated flatly. "For sure the bellman will be tolling nine on my way back. I'm not getting arrested for breaking curfew. The magistrate can get you out in the morning."

Lucy did not say a word to Duncan as they walked up the street to the jail. It seemed that he was walking very slowly, as if he wanted everyone in all of London, or at least everyone coming from market, to take notice. Thankfully, he had not brought around the cart to haul her away, although there were still enough gossips on the streets to notice them. Walking with the constable would damage her reputation, no matter what people thought. She could see her neighbors, returning home from their long day's laboring, scrutinizing her, whispering behind closed hands.

Throughout the embarrassingly long walk along Fleet Street, Duncan kept his her hand on her elbow, a subtle reminder that he would grab her should she try to run. Lucy kept her head down, focusing on putting one step in front of the other. The initial shock past, her mind was starting to clear, reviewing her encounter with Tilly.

When they arrived at the jail, Duncan murmured something to the bellman who stepped into the cell and wiped the dirt off the bench. Still in shock, Lucy didn't quite catch it. She numbly accepted the blanket that Duncan thrust in her arms, before stepping back out.

She watched him sit down at his table, his back to her. She would have cast the woolen pieces away, but she remembered from her visits to see her brother in Newgate how cold the bench could get. Luckily, there were no other inhabitants, human, rodent, or otherwise, within the cell. The bellman left, to go call the hour and walk the streets. Curfew was nigh.

Lucy stomped inside the cell, and crossed her arms. She expected Duncan to lock the door behind her, but he didn't. Seeing the back of his head made her even angrier. He could at least give her the dignity of looking upon her. "You truly think that I murdered that woman? Why in the world would I do that?" She tapped her foot angrily, waiting for him to answer. "You believe a bunch of drunken sots more than you believe me?"

At that, Duncan looked up. "Are you more mad that I don't believe you, or that I locked you up? I can hardly tell."

"You didn't lock me up," Lucy pointed out. "It seems I could just walk straight back to my home, should I please."

Moving quickly, Duncan barred the entrance before she could make good on her threat. "I wouldn't do that, Lucy." Vaguely, she noted that he had referred to her again by her first name, no longer the overly formal speech he'd used before. He nodded toward the small table in the corner of the room. "Why don't you come sit down? How about some hot cider? You seem cold."

Without waiting for her to answer, Duncan poured some steaming cider into a mug that had been hanging from a peg on the wall. He set it on the edge of his desk. Lucy frowned at the gesture. Being a bit cold though, Lucy soon flounced over to the chair and sat down. She picked up the mug, not wanting to look particularly interested in its contents. Nonetheless, she couldn't help but notice small leaves floating in her cup. She sniffed. Nutmeg. A costly spice. She looked back at the constable. "Am I under arrest?"

To her surprise, Duncan laughed. "Hardly."

"Then why—?"

"It's safer if people think you've been locked up for Tilly Baker's murder."

"Safer how?" Lucy glared at Duncan. Unable to help herself, she took a deep sip. The cider was good and she felt warmer, less dazed.

"Safer than having the real murderer come after you."

Lucy set the mug abruptly down on his desk, not caring that a few drops spilled on his papers. "Why ever would the murderer come after me?"

"Look, you've gotten yourself mixed up in something. Again. I can't take the chance. This way at least, you're protected. The true murderer will be satisfied to have you swing for Tilly's murder."

Lucy shuddered.

"Believe me. For now, this is the best way to protect you." He checked his timepiece, a surprisingly elegant little affair. Idly, she

wondered how he'd been able to afford it. He pulled on his coat.
"Don't worry. The bellman—Hank—will watch over you. He's
just outside."

"You're leaving me?" She could not keep the slight note of fear
out of her voice. "Where are you going?"

"There's been a murder, Lucy," he reminded her, speaking as if
she were a babe being dandled on her mother's knee. "I must
track the monster down."

This was too much. "You're not leaving me here. I want to go
home."

"No, Lucy. I can't let you stay home alone. You'll be protected
here. Tilly's murderer won't come after you if he thinks you've
been arrested. He probably thinks he's in the clear."

"I can stay at the magistrate's house," she said stoutly. "He'll
protect me."

He looked at her steadily. "I have no doubt that the magistrate,
good man that he is, would seek to protect you. What about him?
You would put the magistrate in that position? Sheltering an al-
leged murderer? Isn't it bad enough that he's got that pickpocket,
Sid, in his occasional employ?"

Again, as much as she hated to admit it, deep in her heart she
knew the constable was right. Duncan was about to say something else when they heard a horse whinny outside the window,
and the sounds of a cart drawing up on the gravel. The constable
glanced out. "Miss Campion. Lucy, please! Into the cell, if you
would. We must maintain pretenses."

Lucy stepped into the cell, trying not to flinch when the metal
door clanged shut behind her, and the constable turned the key
in the lock. "Why, who's coming?"

A moment later, the outside door swung open and Lucy could see for herself. Hank was standing there, accompanied by a straggly unkempt man. He looked grizzled, his beard was uncombed, and his shirtfront was stained with what looked to be an indiscriminate partaking of grease and food. When Lucy caught wind of the man she nearly swooned from the stench. The smell of decay, coupled with all manner of rotting garbage. From the hallows of his eyes, Lucy fancied for a dark moment that his very soul was drifting toward her. She recognized him, or, at least, she knew his smell. He was a raker, one of those godforsaken sorts, commissioned with removing slops, animal remains and sewage, and all else that everyone tried to ignore. He spoke, his words raspy. "I got the body. Where do you want it?"

"Oh, no, Constable," Lucy taunted. "Dr. Larimer will be none too pleased that the body's been moved."

Constable Duncan looked annoyed. "I gave strict instructions that the body was to be left till the morning."

The raker shrugged. "The owner of the tavern—the Fox and Duck, was it?—he wasn't wishing to lose no business. Said I had to take the body, or he'd chuck it himself." He held out his hand. "That's a half-crown. Else I dump it in Hounds-ditch."

Reluctantly, Duncan passed the raker the coin. The next few minutes the three men were busy with the body, while Lucy watched the proceedings with great curiosity from her bench in the cell. First, the constable produced a table, upon which they laid Tilly's body. They steadily regarded the deceased barmaid while the constable lit several lanterns to better view the body. The tavern miss was still dressed as Lucy had last seen her, wearing her faded blue dress, sleeves still rolled up, revealing her plump dimpled elbows. Except, now, dried blood seemed to cover much of her upper torso.

Lucy saw the raker crook his finger behind his back, bringing down an ancient blessing from the heavens upon Tilly's soul. Something about that small gesture warmed her to the bedraggled man. Then he left and the bellman stepped outside, having been given orders to bring a note to Dr. Larimer. The next instant she heard the raker rattle off in his cart, leaving her and Duncan alone with Tilly's body. He unlocked her cell again, and set to work.

The constable moved several lamps closer to the corpse. Lucy flinched, able to see now what she had not been able to see before. Tilly's face was a terrible mottled purple, and it looked like her tongue was swollen. They both regarded the corpse solemnly.

"Was she strangled?" Lucy asked. "I mean, it's obvious she was stabbed."

The constable shook his head. "Maybe poisoned. I'll need the physician to say for sure."

Lucy leaned forward, squinting. "Hey, look at her hand," she said. "There may be something there."

"Oh, Lucy," the constable sighed. "Do you truly think her finger is pointing to the murderer? You must admit, there aren't too many possible candidates here, unless you want me to drop the pretense and keep you locked up for real."

Lucy rolled her eyes. "No, I mean, look in her hand. Something's in her fingers." She stepped out of the unlocked cell and toward the table.

"Oh." The constable seized Tilly's hand, and with a quick sickening gesture, pried open her fingers. Carefully, he pulled out a piece of paper. Glancing at it, he frowned.

"What is it?"

He passed the paper to her. "What do you make of this?"

Lucy took the scrap, rolling it in her fingers. Not a very rich quality, to be sure. The paper was rather pulplike, as from one of the newer paper mills. It was certainly not vellum, or the finer grade of paper that the magistrate and Adam used. She said as much to the constable.

"What about the writing?"

Lucy scrutinized the words more closely. She could only make out the end of a sentence. Three words, all capitalized, as was common in letters. ". . . Expect it To-Day."

"That doesn't sound good," Lucy commented, holding the paper up to the candle. The script was not that of an uneducated barmaid, but rather by someone with a well-practiced hand. The flourish of the "D" somehow seemed familiar. She snapped her fingers. "Do you still have the items from Tahmin's body?"

"Right here." He pushed the leather pocket across the table, and watched her open it up.

She pulled out the three cards that bore Jacques's scrawled signature, comparing the letter "D" in each. "They look the same, do you think?"

The constable nodded, pulling a blanket over Tilly's head. "Could be from Durand's hand," he conceded. "What of it?"

"This suggests that the card sharp was blackmailing someone. Tilly? Since the note was in her fist." Lucy shook her head. "However, I can't make any sense of it. Why on earth would he have blackmailed Tilly? He truly seemed to care for her."

"It would not be the first time a person was deceived by one whom they loved."

Lucy looked at him in surprise, but said nothing, allowing his fervent words to hang heavily in the air. He coughed, as if to dispel the strange moment, and went on. "Or more likely, Tilly and Durand were working together. Maybe the person being blackmailed was the one who set upon her."

Closing her eyes, Lucy tried to work out the sequence of events, unconsciously imitating the magistrate. "First, I had my conversation with Tilly this afternoon."

"Where you got into a scuffle."

"Yes and then I left," Lucy stated firmly.

"Alright!" he said. "I don't think you killed her. Tilly was found behind the tavern. By the empty barrels. We found her slop pail nearby. So what happened in the hour or so between the time you left her and the time she was killed?"

"Was she killed by someone they were blackmailing, or someone else altogether?" Lucy asked.

"Or someone who suspects she may have brought about the death of her friend." His insinuation was clear.

"Not Miss Water!"

The constable looked at her, almost pityingly. "How well do you know Miss Water, Lucy?"

Lucy stopped, considering the constable's question. Not well at all, if she were to be strictly honest. Certainly, Miss Water had not been completely straightforward herself in sharing information. Not deceptive exactly, but she hadn't been completely forthcoming about her relationship with Darius, and then with Tahmin. "I can't believe it was Miss Water," Lucy said thinly. "What—she went to the Fox and Duck, and then killed Tilly after I left? I can't believe that! It must have been someone else."

"Who stands to gain?" Duncan asked.

"Well. The person being blackmailed, of course." She slammed her hand on the table. "Hendricks! He was being blackmailed! He just told me so! He even showed me the note." Her voice trailed off, seeing the constable's thunderous expression. "I forgot about it, with the excitement of being arrested and seeing the body and all."

"Hendricks was being blackmailed?" Duncan asked, tapping his hand on his leg. "Tell me everything."

Quickly she told him what she knew. "You'll need to talk to him."

"Yes, I gathered that."

"And you'll need to speak to Durand again," Lucy offered.

"Yes, Lucy. I gathered that as well. First thing in the morning."

"I thought you were leaving," she commented, still a bit annoyed.

"Well, now that the damn raker delivered my body, there's not much for me to do. As such, even I must obey the mayor's curfew. This means I must also snuff our candles."

Lucy looked back in the cell, eyeing the hard bench and tattered blanket doubtfully. She'd faced worse. But with Tilly's corpse, rotting on the table beside her. And without even a candle—

Seeing her shiver, Duncan sighed. "Come with me."

After barring the outer door, the constable beckoned her to follow him down the corridor. He opened another door into a set of rooms to reveal a small kitchen, an eating area, and a sleeping area. Like Master Aubrey, the chandler had probably once slept in a large room nearby to easily tend to his shop. She could see another room that an apprentice may once have made use of as well.

He pointed to a pallet in the larger room, by the unlit fireplace. "You can sleep there."

"Where will you sleep?"

He pointed to a small side door. "Back there." He handed her another blanket. "That's it, so don't ask for anything else."

"Is this place where . . . you *live?*"

If he heard the shock in her voice, he chose to ignore it. "Currently. And Lucy, for your sake, don't even think of leaving. There are a lot of highwaymen about, and scant protection. Not to mention a murderer on the loose."

When the constable stepped away, leaving the door open between them, Lucy removed her outer dress, shivering in her woolen shift, wishing the fire could have been lit. The gray blanket she had been holding had a funny smell, and she wondered for a moment whether it had ever been wrapped around a corpse. She laid the gray blanket on top of the blue one, so that when she crawled in, the one closest to her face was the one that had already been spread across the pallet. For one moment, Tilly's mocking face flashed before her. She screwed her eyes shut, trying not to think of Tilly lying out there, exposed and alone.

Huddling under the blankets, Lucy thought she would not be able to fall asleep, but the pallet proved far more comfortable than she expected. She could hear Duncan's breathing from the other room. On a whim, she called softly to him. "Good night, Duncan."

His breathing stopped for a moment, as if he had taken a deep breath. "Good night, Lucy," he said. "I'll see you in the morning."

She put all thoughts of Tilly aside, allowing the fatigue of the day to catch up with her, and she quickly drifted off.

·19·

Murder. No doubt about it." Dr. Larimer put down one of his metal instruments. The physician had arrived early in the morning to examine the corpse, accompanied by a tall, gangly young man who had been introduced simply as "James Sheridan, my assistant, if he can hang on." Finally spying Lucy, who'd been sitting demurely in her cell, the physician lowered his spectacles in a questioning way.

"I've been accused of this woman's murder," Lucy told him brightly. "I didn't do it, of course. The constable thought I would be safer here, in case the real murderer came around." Catching the constable's dour look, she added, "What? Dr. Larimer knows I didn't kill her. There's no use pretending otherwise."

"Lucy?" Dr. Larimer scoffed. "I should think not." The physician gingerly pulled back the dirty blanket covering Tilly's body. He selected a pair of sharp scissors from a collection of metal

instruments that he'd laid on a tray prior to beginning the dissection. "May as well examine the body here," he grumbled when
he arrived. "Since the body's already been moved." After cutting
through the front of her frock, he'd spent the next thirty minutes
carefully examining her. From time to time, he'd murmur something to Sheridan. Lucy looked on with considerable curiosity. During her time working at the magistrate's household, she'd heard
the physician describe findings he'd gleaned from dissecting a
corpse. Certainly, she had never seen such a thing performed, and
she couldn't help but feel a bit intrigued, if a little sick, too.

After Larimer's comment that Tilly had been murdered, the
constable started to say something. The physician held up his
hand. "Let me finish my observations."

Murmuring something to Sheridan, the two men carefully
flipped the corpse on her stomach. The physician cut away the back
of her dress, to better see the murdered woman's death wound. The
constable looked away, she was glad to see, preserving some of
Tilly's dignity. Lucy noted with faint satisfaction how the assistant gagged when he took a deep breath.

The physician peered down at him. "Steady there, lad. You've
got to be made of sterner stuff if you ever hope to join my ranks.
Look at Lucy there. She's not fainting and carrying on, is she?"

"Stabbed, of course," Larimer said after a cursory examination.
He looked up, just in time to see his assistant holding a sachet of
dried flowers to his nose. Without missing a beat, the physician
plucked the posy from his assistant's fingers. With a grimace, he
dropped the dried flowers to the floor, grinding them under his
heavy black boot. For a moment, the sweet smell of lavender and
rosemary filled the air. "Sheridan, what do you make of that?" He

pointed to two large purpling discolorations that extended across her back. "It seems her blood pooled twice. That's what those discolorations indicate."

"Well, ahem—" Sheridan's ears grew red, as he struggled to answer the physician's question. He looked helplessly down at the ground petals on the floor of the dirty jail, up at the crack on the ceiling, anywhere but at Dr. Larimer's expectant gaze.

"It means the body was only moved once," Lucy called from her cell. "It pooled the first time where she died, behind the tavern, and then again when she was moved here on the cart."

All three men turned to look at her. Lucy smirked, but didn't say anything about how she'd acquired this surprising bit of knowledge. Living through the plague, Lucy had learned something about death and what it did to the human body. Not to mention, she'd heard Larimer himself describe such scenes when he spoke to the magistrate. Indeed, she had heard quite a lot about how the doctor determined death, since Master Hargrave always asked detailed questions and the physician would give detailed replies in return. Certainly, the men were far less guarded when ladies were not present, and the physician had never shown any qualms sharing sordid details before a servant innocently passing around salvers of cheese or filled goblets with wine.

"Just so." The physician pulled the blanket back over Tilly's face. He looked at the constable. "Well, Sheridan here can write up the report. Poisoned, then stabbed."

"Poisoned, then stabbed. That's odd." The constable rubbed the stubble on his jaw. "How many times was she stabbed?"

"Twice," the physician said. "It looks as if she was bent over, and her assailant struck her twice with a short knife."

The constable nodded. "She'd have been retching from the poison, no doubt. Bent over double."

Something else had occurred to Lucy. "Was she stabbed in the stomach before or after being stabbed in the back?"

Still stinging from being mocked for his vapors, Sheridan smirked. "Did you not hear Dr. Larimer, girl? This here woman was struck in the back."

"Then what accounts for all the blood on her shirtfront?" Lucy responded, hotly. "I saw it when her body was brought in. She most certainly did not have that blood when I saw her at the inn."

"She was not stabbed in the stomach. There are no wounds there at all." The physician picked up Tilly's cast-off skirts, and scowled. "This blood does not match up with her wound."

"Animal blood, then?" Sheridan offered. "She was probably slaughtering a chicken or a pig in the kitchen. Got the blood on her waist."

Here Lucy scoffed. "Not Tilly's job. Would be the cook's."

"You seem to know a lot about her job then." Sheridan looked meaningfully at her cell. "Perhaps there's a good reason you're in there."

The physician scowled again. "This is why I do not like the body to be moved from the original crime scene. There are many things to be learned. We must go back to the Fox and Duck to discover the truth."

"You'll need me," Lucy stated. She didn't know what had made her say it. She bit her lip. "You do."

Sheridan threw up his hands. "Why would we possibly need you?"

The constable looked resigned. Sheridan was about to protest until the physician spoke. "You're quite right. Lucy's got a shrewd sense about her. And she was there, just before the murder occurred. She might see something we don't. By all means, Constable, bring Lucy along."

On the way to the Fox and Duck, Lucy left word with Lach about what she was doing. Will had never stopped back, having gone straight to the smithy's that morning from the arms of his lady-love. Master Aubrey still had not returned from the licenser's, for which Lucy was grateful. "I'm going to write the True Account on Tilly's death. Master Aubrey will like that," she said, more to herself than to Lach.

"If you say so," he grumbled.

She had to promise that she would do all kinds of chores when she got back before he gave his grudging consent. She needed to run a bit to catch up with the physician, Mister Sheridan, and the constable. Along the way, she listened as Dr. Larimer peppered Mister Sheridan about different types of poisons, and what one could do should they come across a soul who had been poisoned. "What would Nicholas Culpepper tell us to do?" the physician asked.

"Prepare an emetic, sir. Something to make the sufferer forcibly vomit the contents of his stomach and restore his humors. Grind up some white hellebore, I should think."

The physician nodded. "Although some of these poisons work frightfully quick. Mustard seed, or a bit of rosemary might work in most cases, I should think. Assuming we were to happen upon the poor soul in time, that is."

The two men spent the next quarter of an hour conversing

about the relative strengths of different poisons and their antidotes. Soon, they had reached the tavern. The Fox and Duck
looked much as it had the day before, only more crowded if anything. Word must have spread about Tilly's murder. Master Aubrey's wry observance that "everyone loves a murder" never seemed
so true.

"Let's check around back," the constable said.

There they found the bellman waiting for them. Lucy thought
the alley smelled even worse than yesterday, if that were possible.
She curled her lip in disgust when she saw the remnants of several small animals and birds, half picked away by other rodents
and cats.

Although it was nearing mid-morning, the sky was overcast
and cloudy, making the alley appear as if it were dusk. The constable ordered the bellman to bring some lanterns to better light
the area.

"The body was found about here, sir." Hank pointed to a dung
heap, next to the tavern's empty barrels. Lucy eyed them warily,
thinking about Tahmin's body falling out of a barrel similar to
those lined up before her. Bringing the lanterns over, they all
studied the spot carefully.

"There!" the physician said. "That's vomit. And that's blood.
Both fairly fresh." He peered closer. "Shine the light here."

They could make out a dark stain. "Her wound would not
have bled very much," Dr. Larimer commented, carefully stepping through the rubble to protect his fine laced shoes from the
muck. "I think someone else was here, bleeding out. Although it
could have been an animal of course."

The constable, who had been pacing, suddenly snapped his

fingers. "Wait a minute! I'm Tilly, feeling sick, having just taken some poison, unbeknownst to myself. Not wanting to vomit or carry on inside the tavern—knowing I'd be dismissed for sure by the innkeeper—I stagger out of the kitchen." Here he proceeded to do so. If it were not so serious, Lucy would have laughed.

"I enter the alley then, and then—?"

"You're set upon by an assailant," Sheridan said. "Obvious."

"She had no defensive wounds on her hands. She was clearly struck from behind" Dr. Larimer reminded them.

"Perhaps she was vomiting," Lucy said. "Still doesn't explain the blood on the front of her dress. The blood must have come from somewhere else. Or someone else."

Duncan resumed his play-acting. He feigned retching. "So I vomit and see what—?" Here he pantomimed Tilly's look of despair.

Lucy stepped forward. "Let me. I'm Tilly. I've spied someone. Lying on the ground—" She gestured to the constable to lay on the ground. "This person's bleeding. It has to be someone she knows, maybe even someone she cares about. She goes to him. He's bleeding. Maybe he's dead." Kneeling beside Duncan, she put her hands on his shoulders. "She begins to weep, and she throws her arms around him, getting his blood on the front of her dress—"

Before she could finish her charade, Lucy heard Dr. Larimer's slight dry cough above her, and she recalled herself. Standing up, she finished, "And that's when she's killed by her attacker." Lucy didn't look at the constable, who had also returned to his feet.

"Two assailants?" the physician mused. "One who poisoned her, and then one who stabbed her? Could be the same person, I suppose."

"What happened to the other body?" Sheridan asked, shaking his head. "If Tilly really stumbled over someone."

"We need to look for blood splatter," the constable said. "If there was another body then—"

"Look!" Lucy pointed. They all peered closer. They could make out what looked like a smear of blood drops that led to the door next to the tavern.

Dr. Larimer touched the drops gingerly. "Fresh. From a rather deep wound, I'd say."

"A cooper's shop," Hank said, opening the door. "I talked to the shopkeeper yesterday, to see if he'd heard anything."

"And had he?" Duncan asked.

The bellman shook his head. Lucy was busy following the drops. "They lead this way." She moved quickly down some steps. "Into the cellar."

"Let me go first," Duncan said. "Please, Lucy."

Reluctantly, Lucy stood aside to let the constable and Dr. Larimer press past her. The next moment, they heard a faint moaning beyond the cellar door. Duncan tried the handle, but it appeared to be locked. He gestured to Hank, and he and the bellman pushed together on the door, cracking it open.

They held up their lanterns to find a figure laying prone on a bit of straw and dirty matting. His upper body was bare, wrapped only in a bit of cloth stained with sweat and blood. As the man's eyes caught the candlelight, he blinked and tried to shield his face.

Lucy gasped. It was Jacques Durand.

The physician moved quickly to the injured card sharp, Lucy

right at his heels. The Frenchman looked gaunt, and his face was dirty and unshaven. A grimy pus dripped from the open wound in his shoulder. Lucy looked away, taking in the cellar where Durand had obviously been hiding for at least the night. Evidence of the cooper's profession was everywhere—rough-cut oak, bevels, and half-formed barrel frames—laying about in a seeming disarray. No doubt, the cooper would just throw misshapen barrel parts into the cellar, maybe intending to reuse the wood for new barrel frames.

Despite his obvious pain, the card sharp put on a bold front. *"C'est un plaîsir de vous revoir,"* he said. "It is a pleasure to see you again." His words were gallant but his tone conveying quite the opposite sentiment.

"Who did this to you?" Lucy cried. "Who killed Tilly? Was it you?!"

Unexpectedly, Durand's eyes filled with tears, and he sank back. "Tilly!" he murmured.

"Pray, quiet yourself." The physician pulled back the rags wrapping Jacques's upper arm, and sniffed it. "This wound seems to be infected. I must tend to it at once. Sheridan, fetch my bag."

"Why don't you tell us what happened?" the constable said. "The physician can tend to your wounds while you talk." He bowed to Larimer. "That is, if that's all right with you, sir."

"Quite so, quite so," Larimer said. "Bring me the lantern."

Seeing the card sharp still struggling to speak, Lucy ran up and filled her own little cup with water from the well she had spied outside the Fox and Duck. When she returned, Jacques took a grateful sip. "I was set upon by two scoundrels in the alley. I can only assume they were the ones to kill my dear Tilly. *Mon Dieu*. If I could lay hand on those foul-mouthed villains, tear them from limb to limb, I would."

"So you knew Tilly was dead, but did not see her killed?" Lucy asked, trying to work it out. "How could that be?"

"I don't rightly know," Jacques said, licking his lips. He took a sip from the small tin cup Lucy was holding to his mouth. "I came out, was set upon, and I must have fainted at that point. When I awoke, I found Tilly collapsed upon me. She was dead."

"Why didn't you get help?" Lucy asked.

Jacques sniffed as if he had inhaled something unpleasant, but did not answer her.

The constable sneered in return. "He's a coward."

"*Oui*," Durand admitted, wiping away a wayward tear. "I knew she was dead. I would not be so foolish as to go to the law, to run the risk of being tossed into one of your wretched prisons!"

"You hid here, among the rats and the vermin." Duncan gestured at the Frenchman's shirt. "With Tilly's blood still upon on you. Do you think that makes you look more or less guilty?"

"Can't prove it was Tilly's, now can you?" Durand snapped back. The tiny effort seemed to exhaust him, and he sank back.

Seeing the men reaching an impasse, Lucy jumped in. "You were the one blackmailing Lord Cumberland's son?"

Durand clutched the blanket. "I did no such thing," the card sharp replied. He glanced at the physician, who had finished binding his wound. "Monsieur Physician, I implore you. Tell me how I may take care of this painful wound. I feel weak."

"He cannot stay here," the physician agreed. "He must be

moved to the hospital." For the next few minutes, the constable and Sheridan occupied themselves with creating a makeshift sling from boards and a bit of blanket they had found in the cooper's cellar.

Lucy remained, kneeling by the injured man. Indeed, Durand looked quite pathetic, but Lucy did not want to let go. "Tilly could not have written those notes to Master Clifford and Ashton Hendricks. We know you wrote them," she whispered.

He sighed, giving in. "Tilly, rest her hardened soul, had a way of finding out secrets. She convinced me that no one would be hurt. Her unfortunate demise proves how wrong she was."

Still whispering, Lucy asked. "What truly happened at the Cheshire Cheese? What did you know of Tahmin? Why did she turn those men on him?"

"I am not proud of that. I was angry with Tilly for that deception. It was petty, and I told her so. She wanted to protect me, with little thought to the harm she would do to that innocent man. She was a blackmailer, you understand? Her victim must not have known for sure who had been blackmailing him, but only knew to pay the bribe to someone at the Cheshire Cheese. Sometimes, she must have realized this victim planned to kill his blackmailer, so she pointed out that stranger—Tahmin?—to divert the attention from us."

Jacques crossed himself, returning his gaze to the ceiling. "Tilly was greedy though, and continued to blackmail this person, arranging to get the bribes at different places. Alas, she has paid for her wrong many times over. The victim must have followed her to the Fox and Duck and, well, you know the rest."

"Who?" Lucy whispered frantically. "Who was she blackmailing? You must know! The Earl? Was he the one who killed Tahmin? One of his men?"

Jacques only shook his head, laying still, not even moaning. It was clear he was not going to say another word. Perhaps he really didn't know.

Despite her frustration, Lucy wiped his forehead with a cool cloth. She stepped back to allow the other men to transfer Durand to the sling. The physician carefully checked that the man was tightly secured, so that he would not slip when they transported him up the rickety cellar stairs into the alley and into the waiting cart. Lucy followed them up the steps. A sudden thought occurred to her. "Wait!" she called to the three men in front of her.

The constable and Sheridan shifted uncomfortably with their burden. The card sharp seemed to have passed out. His eyes were closed again, but now his breathing was shallow and his flesh was looking gray.

"What is it, Lucy?" Duncan asked.

"Will he be safe at the hospital? Whoever tried to kill him might try again. And you may need him alive for a trial. Also," she floundered, "I think he was the one doing the blackmailing, even though he says otherwise. You could imprison him later."

"I'm not taking him on as a private patient," the physician said. "This mess has taken me long enough from my other obligations." He sighed. "Still, I think Lucy's right."

"I suppose we could keep him at the jail." The constable looked around. "I've no time to be a wet nurse though." He looked at Lucy.

She hesitated. She *had* done some nursing in the past, but she didn't think Master Aubrey would take too kindly to the idea.

Thankfully, the physician intervened. "Sheridan here can take care of him. He needs a bit of real experience with this type of wound. Mind you don't kill him, Sheridan." He laughed at his apprentice's dour expression. "Doctoring's not all about tending the delicate ailments of winsome young ladies, despite what you might have learned at Cambridge."

"Yes, sir," Sheridan muttered, though clearly aghast at the suggestion.

The physician laughed again. "Well, I'll be off then. I'll send around Sheridan's report for the inquest. I'm to dine at the Hargraves this evening."

For a moment, his gaze seemed to rest meaningfully on Lucy and she shifted uncomfortably. Did the physician know about her close friendship with Adam? She knew he would not despise her for it, but he'd likely be uncomfortable with the idea.

"Well, we're off then," Duncan said abruptly, swinging his end of the card sharp's sling into the cart.

"Careful, man!" the physician admonished, checking the man's eyelids again. "He's in enough pain as it is!"

Duncan looked a bit chagrined. He turned to Lucy without meeting her eyes. "There's no room in the cart. I'll accompany you back to Aubrey's."

"Of course," Lucy said. She watched the cart rattle off. She looked up at Duncan. "Does this mean I'm not under arrest anymore?"

"I suppose." He grinned. "You know I never truly arrested you.

But you can tell everyone you are still under suspicion of Tilly's murder. I am still collecting evidence."

"You no longer think the murderer will come after me?" Lucy asked. "Even though you did before?"

Duncan ran a hand through his hair. Suddenly he looked much younger, less sure of himself. He started walking, and remained silent for most of the walk. As they approached Aubrey's shop, he said, "I just wanted to make sure someone was protecting you. You said Aubrey would be back today?"

Darting a glance at him, she caught a look on his face that she'd seen more and more frequently. Her voice caught. "Yes. I'd best be off. Master Aubrey will be waiting for me."

·20·

The next evening, Lucy set one of her new quills back in a little ink jar, appraising the scribbling in front of her. She had just finished writing a true account of Tilly's murder and she didn't completely know how she felt. Satisfied, that she had captured the story in a way she hoped would engage her listeners. Sad, that even a mean and blackmailing tavern maid like Tilly had her life cut short. But perhaps the story would serve as a means to memorialize Tilly in some way, and perhaps it would even be the means to avenge her death. Master Aubrey would be sure to print it.

Lucy frowned. That is, if the printer did not mind reading through all her scratched-over words. "Best copy it again," she sighed. The physical act of writing still hurt her hand a bit, and her script was nothing like the elegant hand of the magistrate or his son.

She was still copiously copying the words onto a new sheet of milled paper when Will arrived home from work. She eyed him. At least he'd come home instead of returning to his most recent sweetheart. Laurel, she thought Will had said her name was, but truly it was hard to keep straight.

"What are you writing?" her brother asked, as he seated himself on the low bench by the fire. He pulled out one of his tools and began to polish it with a bit of soft sheepskin.

"Oh," Lucy hesitated. "A True Account." She wasn't sure how to bring up Tilly's murder without also mentioning the fact that she'd spent the previous night in jail.

Luckily, she was spared from having to offer more details because someone began to knock loudly on the shop's shuttered windows. Flinching, Lucy could not help but remember the night before, when Duncan had appeared at the shop. Could it be the constable again? She wondered. Tonight's pounding was equally insistent.

When she didn't move, Will went over to the window and peered through a crack that Lach had cut in the shutters.

"Hmm," Will said, with a backward glance at Lucy. "One of your suitors." He then went over and pushed up the bar that kept the door shut. "Come in, Sir."

The visitor turned out to be Adam. Barely acknowledging her brother, he came straight over to Lucy, who had stood up in alarm. "What in heaven's name have you been doing?" he demanded. "I just learned from Dr. Larimer that you'd been arrested for murder?!"

"What?" Will slammed the door shut and stared at Lucy. "What in God's name are you talking about?"

"I was going to tell you—" Lucy began.

Adam cut her off. "He also said you spent the night in jail?

You visited the site of that poor woman's murder? Lucy, what is going on?"

Will was looking increasingly confused. "Hang on. Who was murdered?"

"Tilly Baker," Lucy and Adam said at the same time.

Will scratched his head. "Tilly Baker? Tilly Baker? That name's familiar."

"Well, you met her," Lucy reminded her brother. "Remember? The barmaid at the Fox and Duck."

"Ah, that one. Right, I remember." Will eyed his sister. "You didn't actually kill her, did you?"

Lucy rolled her eyes. "No, I most certainly did not. Moreover, Duncan didn't truly arrest me." Seeing Adam cross his arms, she added hastily, "Duncan thought I should stay at the jail for my own protection. He was concerned that the real murderer might come after me, but if it were known that I was the one who had been arrested, well, then the murderer would be able to relax, maybe let his guard down. While keeping me protected at the same time. Apparently," Lucy added with a smile, "he did not think much of Lach's abilities to protect me, should the real murderer come my way."

Will protested. "I'd have taken care of you."

"You weren't here," she said gently.

Her brother had the grace to flush when he discerned her meaning. "Oh, right. Sorry."

"I could kill that constable," Adam said, glaring at them both. "Why in heaven's name didn't you send word to Father? He'd have had you out of that bloody jail in an instant!"

Lucy tried to explain. "Lach was afraid to break curfew, afraid to carry a note to your father. Moreover, Duncan said that we should not put the magistrate in the position of looking like he was harboring a murderess in his household. I have to say I agreed with him." She stuck out her chin, even though her body betrayed her by trembling. Her actions no longer seemed to have made as much sense as they did the night before, in the light of Adam's anger.

Adam frowned. "I can't say I like it, but it was certainly smart," he admitted at last, grudgingly. "Still, were you planning to tell me?"

"Or me?" Will echoed. "You've been a little mouse, tonight, haven't you? Keeping this tidbit to yourself?"

Lucy gestured to the broadside she had been writing. "I was going to let you read my True Account," she teased, holding up the paper she'd been writing, trying in vain to lighten the tension in the room. "You'd have found out soon enough when Master Aubrey set this piece for tomorrow's printing."

"You-were-going-to-let-us-read-your-true-account?" Will said in a strangled voice. He and Adam exchanged an incredulous glance.

Both men stood shoulder to shoulder then, joined in their indignation toward Lucy. That was the first time they had ever looked alike. Will so fair, Adam so dark, but akin in their shared ire. Lucy wanted to giggle, but refrained. "Yes, it's all here. Quite fascinating, if I may be so immodest."

"This isn't a lark, Lucy." Adam frowned. "Murder's no jest."

"Of course it isn't!" Lucy snapped, suddenly weary. "I suppose you think I enjoyed being escorted by the constable to the jail? I could see them staring. Everyone, as we passed them in the street. Do you think I liked being in the jail? All night?"

"He locked you up? In the jail?" Adam glanced at Will, both of them remembering the terrors of Newgate. She could read their thoughts. Even a makeshift jail was likely to be quite awful.

"Well, no, actually." She hesitated. "I slept in Duncan's—the constable's—bed, in his rooms. He was very kind." She searched Adam's face, which had grown cold again.

Hearing Will tsk-tsk, she glared at her brother. At her searing look, he edged backward, retreating to his seat, far in the shadows. This was clearly a conversation he no longer wanted to take part in. She looked back at Adam. "Duncan stayed in another room, of course." She rushed on, "The next morning, Dr. Larimer performed the dissection and then he wanted me to come with him and—" she broke off, seeing Adam's perplexed expression. "What is it?"

Adam sighed, a weary sound. "Lucy, I'll be honest. I'm confused. Why did you feel you had to speak to Tilly again at all? Why didn't you just go tell the constable about your suspicions? Why in the world did you confront her? What if she had killed you?"

"Adam, I—" She stopped. The pain in his voice chastened her. She had not meant to worry him so. Distantly, Lucy heard Will quietly go upstairs. "I'm sorry. I didn't even think before I went to Tilly. I don't know why I did it."

"Well, I do know why. It's because you care about people. And you care about justice. I like those things about you. I'm just afraid you're going to get yourself killed."

She touched his hand. "I'm sorry," she repeated.

He took her hand and gave her a weak smile. "Enough about that. You may as well tell me the rest. Dr. Larimer performed the dissection and—?"

Eagerly, Lucy told him all about what they'd learned about Tilly's corpse, their visit to the Fox and Duck, and finding Jacques Durand. Adam sat down on the low bench, watching her face, occasionally asking her questions, but mostly listening. Throughout, Adam's expression was thoughtful, reminding her a bit of the magistrate.

When she was done, to her relief, Adam smiled at her fondly, his earlier annoyance now dissipated. "I've no doubt, if you'd been born a man, you'd be a constable yourself. Or a lawyer. I believe you truly enjoy puzzling through the minds of criminals."

Lucy smiled back, gesturing at the True Account. "And writing about them too. I don't want their victims to be forgotten, just because they may be without family, wealth, or connections. Tahmin and Tilly deserve better. As do the living. Miss Water. Mister Hendricks. They all deserve justice."

"I understand, Lucy. Truly, I'm beginning to understand."

She gazed into his deep blue eyes, warming at their renewed closeness. It seemed a very long time since she had last been able to look at him in such a way.

Adam broke the silence. "Father told me he gave you a book the other day," he said, changing the subject. "For your birthday."

"Oh yes!" Lucy said. "*The Two Gentlemen of Verona.* I will treasure it."

"I have the feeling that he felt he had to remind me about your birthday," he said. "As if I'd forgotten." He paused. "I do have something for you. I'm sorry it's a little late. From his pocket, he withdrew a silver bracelet, which he clasped around her wrist. "I just wanted to give it to you in person."

"Oh, Adam, it's lovely," she breathed. "Thank you."

When she touched his cheek, he held her hand there for a moment, gazing down at her. "I truly regret being unable to see you on your birthday," he said. "Our survey work has been overwhelming, Lucy. So much misery. So many people who have lost so much. I don't like to speak of it, because I would shield you from such suffering if I could."

She shook her head. "Adam, you can't shield me from such things, nor should you. I'm no fine lady eating grapes on a pedestal."

"Eating grapes on a pedestal?" He laughed. "Is that what fine ladies do?"

She swatted at him, but then became serious once more. "Adam, I share your need to help others. That's why I can't rest until I see their murderers unmasked," she said, picking up her True Account again. "I believe the Earl had something to do with Tahmin's death. Maybe Tilly's too. We know the Earl was being blackmailed. We know Tilly wrongly pointed Tahmin out to the Earl's men the night of the card game. Perhaps he had Tahmin killed."

Adam sat up straight, still not letting go of her hand. "You think the Earl had something to do with these deaths? Lord Cumberland? Oh, sweetheart, that's a grave accusation to make."

"Yes, I understand that. I think there is something odd about the Earl. Your father thinks so as well. I just know it. I think we should talk to the Earl, find out what he's hiding." She held up her hand. "I know that you think this is the constable's duty, and you are right. Yet you know as well as I do that Duncan will never be able to gain admittance into the Earl's house."

Adam nodded. His lips twisted ruefully, as he fingers tightened over hers. "I take it you have a plan?"

Lucy squeezed his hand in return. "As a matter of fact, I do!"

Lucy's plan was simple. So simple that Adam didn't even think it would work when she first told him. Neither had the constable, but he hadn't said not to do it. Indeed, she knew that if he didn't come up with something soon, he would have to drop the investigation altogether. "I'll be nearby," he told her. "This may be foolish, but you might be able to get some useful information."

Now, two days later, she was standing outside Lord Cumberland's London residence beside Adam, with Miss Water at her side. Master Hargrave had sent a note around to the Earl, asking if his son could call on them. The Earl had responded readily enough, inviting them to dine that Saturday evening. And here they were. Bringing Miss Water in had been easy enough, although Adam had objected to Lucy's suggestion that she pose as his fiancé. "What about you?" he had asked. "Why can't you pose as my wife?" She had smiled, patting his arm. "Miss Water is more believable. It makes more sense that I'd be her maid. Besides, this way I can speak to the servants."

They stared at the Earl's home. The place was grand enough to be sure, but had a neglected, cast-off feel.

Miss Water seemed to be thinking along the same lines. "The Earl doesn't visit here very often, does he?" she said in a low voice.

"Let's just get this over with, shall we?" Adam said, reaching for the elaborate lion's head door knocker. He rapped smartly.

Lucy felt a momentary misgiving when Adam and Miss Water were welcomed by Lady Cumberland, as they stepped through the great stone doorway together. If not beautiful, Miss Water was elegant and kind, and Adam had decided to be charming. Excitement had brought a shine to her eyes and a flush to her cheeks. Lucy felt downright dull in comparison, clad neatly in her servant's gray wool dress. The feeling worsened when Adam slipped Miss Water's wrap from her shoulders, as her betrothed would, and handed it to Lucy.

"I see you brought along a maid. I hope you did not think we would be short-staffed," Lady Cumberland said, her smile tight. She looked as sallow as she had when she had supped at the Hargraves, yet even more pinched, if that were possible.

"No indeed," Miss Water responded, smiling sweetly in return. "I find even these short journeys to be taxing, and no one comforts me so well as my own dear Reenie."

She nodded at Lucy, who kept her head ducked down. Lucy was hoping that Lady Cumberland, like most nobles, had not looked too closely at Lucy when they had come to dine at Master Hargrave's household those few weeks before. Calling her "Reenie" they hoped would secure the illusion.

Lady Cumberland waved a lace-clad sleeve toward one of her own servants, a plump young woman with carefully bound red hair and an abundance of freckles. "Sulwen will look after your girl, give her something to eat. She can help with supper and clean up later, I suppose."

Taking Adam's proffered arm, Miss Water nodded at Lucy. "Go along then, Reenie. I'll ring if I need you."

Bobbing a quick curtsy to Lady Cumberland, Lucy followed Sulwen meekly to the kitchen, not daring to look at Adam as she passed into the cold dark entranceway.

As they walked through the passage, Lucy looked about curiously. While the walkways were swept, no one had taken care to wipe away the cobwebs or to sweep away the crumbs that had dropped from an earlier meal. Lucy shuddered. They may as well invite the rats to come take up residence. A faint unpleasant smell hung in the air, as if some meat had been left spoiling in the sun. When they passed the grand drawing room, she could see that no one had cleaned out the fireplace in some time. Even the kitchen, larger than Master Hargrave's current home, contained surprisingly few servants.

In fact, she saw only one woman, for just an instant. The woman stooped a bit, glanced at her, and then disappeared up the stairs.

"Do the servants have the night off?" Lucy asked Sulwen, as they passed down the long dusty corridor. It was unusual for servants to be allowed off on a Saturday night, to be sure, but sometimes a more benevolent master would let them go if there was some rare merriment to be had, such as at Michaelmas, or Bartholomew's Fair.

Sulwen looked at her in surprise. "Nay, we are but four servants here." Like her master, her voice contained a bit of a brogue that marked her from the distant northwest.

"Four servants for the entire household?!" Lucy was shocked. Even Master Hargrave used to have five servants, and his was not even so grand an estate as the Earl's London residence. Moreover, the magistrate most certainly was not an earl.

Sulwen shrugged, her lips wrinkling slightly. "The master's tight with his money."

Tight with money could mask a number of things. Debt, shriveling finances, failed business ventures. Or even, in some cases, a rare Puritanical streak, although judging from the Earl's propensity to gamble, she did not think this last to be the case. "Who was that woman, who just passed upstairs?" Lucy asked.

"That's Theresa. My lady's personal maid. She was her nursemaid when she was still a child, and has stayed with her ever since. We also have Jones, Theresa's nephew I think, who attends to the Master, and Burly, who is our all-around jack. I think he's also related to Theresa, too. I'm not sure. I don't talk to them much." She looked at Lucy, a bit defiantly. "That's all we need."

Though doubtful, Lucy nodded. Something still seemed off. Once in the kitchen she watched Sulwen carefully prepare the plates for supper. She searched for an opening gambit. "Have you been with the Earl very long?" she asked.

Sulwen fished a stray hair out of the soup. "Not very long. Just a few months now." She hesitated. "I was hired to replace a girl. She'd been dismissed from Lord Cumberland's household."

"Oh?" Lucy asked offhandedly. She didn't want to make Sulwen suspicious with too many questions. "Now, how can I help you? Give the pot a stir? Bone some fish?"

Sulwen checked a small chicken that was roasting on a spit. "No fish tonight. Just the fowl. If you could do the carving?" She pulled the chicken off and laid it in front of Lucy. "If you would, Reenie."

"Of course," Lucy said, glad she had remembered the false name she had given. She set to carving. No fish? That surprised her too. The magistrate's son was not one to skimp for. Although Master Hargrave no longer entertained very often, he always ensured both fish and fowl appeared on his table when he invited acquaintances to dine. Adding to her surprise, Sulwen poured some water into the wine, something the magistrate would never allow.

Seeing her look, Sulwen giggled. "My lord does not like my lady to have strong spirits. He thinks they do not agree with her."

Though skeptical, Lucy smiled. "I'm sure watering down the wine is a very good idea then."

As they filled platters full of food, they heard a distant knocking at the front door. "Oh!" Sulwen said. "I didn't know Lady Cumberland was expecting any more guests." She looked doubtfully at the meal, which was looking decidedly meager. "Oh, what else can I serve?" She began to peer fretfully at the shelves.

Lucy felt sorry for her. In some households, the mistress would beat her servants if they embarrassed her in front of her guests. No matter that the mistress had given her servants insufficient coins to make the table plentiful—a good servant, as was well understood, was one who knew how to make do.

Frowning, Sulwen peeked her head into the hallway. "Oh, it's the Earl's son," she said, visibly relaxing. "Master Clifford's not the picky sort. I wonder what he's doing here? I haven't seen him around for some time now."

"Oh? He doesn't live here then?" Lucy asked casually, pretending that she did not know that the Earl's son had taken up residence at the Sparrow.

"No, he lives elsewhere in London; I'm not sure where. Odd, he's not being one for socializing or fancy dinners." She brightened. "Betcha anything he stops in here for a nibble." At that, Lucy had to smile. Young men always seemed to find their way to the kitchen, often to flirt with the maids, but just as often to get an extra tidbit.

Seeing that it was almost time to serve, Lucy didn't want to miss her chance. Hurriedly, she tried to get back to the topic they'd been discussing before. "What did she get dismissed for?" Lucy asked, giving the pot a stir. "The girl you replaced."

Sulwen glanced at her. Lucy could see the desire to spill the household secrets warring with her sense of duty and loyalty.

"We had a girl put out for theft once," Lucy lied, hoping to encourage some confidences. "I'm not even sure she took the thing."

"Yeah?"

"A trifle. A necklace. Not even a very fine one at that." She waited for Sulwen to respond, and when she didn't, Lucy pressed a bit more. "Is that what happened to the miss you replaced?"

The desire to gossip won out against any sense of loyalty to the Earl. "Amelie, her name was. I don't rightfully know, to be honest. I think though," Sulwen stopped, pausing for effect. "I heard she did something dreadful, but that's not why she was sent off."

Lucy lowered her tone. "What did she do?"

Sulwen looked around, the gesture furtive and cautious. "They said she tried to murder the Earl's son, but I don't think that's true."

Something in the way Sulwen said those last words caused Lucy to peer at her. "You don't think so?"

"Some people said the young master had his way with her, and then cast her off. But I can't see it in him. He was so melancholic. Lacking in life. Like he'd lost the very will to live, the will to breathe. And the girl died, you know. I heard that later. I feel so very sorry for him sometimes."

Lucy took a deep breath. Sulwen still had the air of someone who knew more than what she wanted to say. "Perhaps their affair . . . they left something behind?"

Sulwen looked at her sharply. Lucy kept her face vaguely interested as if she were just passing the time with idle gossip. Sulwen seemed satisfied and continued. "A baby. I knew a girl who was the babe's wet nurse. No one was saying much, but we knew. I heard the girl said she'd been driven out by my lady. Bit of a terror, ain't she? I might be leaving service myself." Then the girl smiled. "He's a good healthy babe, that's for sure. I've seen him around." She looked down the hallway. "We've got to make haste," she said briskly. "Don't tell anyone what I said. About the babe. They might let me go and I can't leave 'til I get a proper reference."

Lucy nodded, placing some dishes on a tray. "I'll help you serve."

To their dismay, however, when Sulwen pushed open the door, they found Master Clifford standing there, looking stricken. Maybe he'd come to the kitchen to get a bit before supper as Sulwen had thought. From his expression, it was clear he'd heard every word. "Amelie's baby was mine?" he asked, dully. "I thought she had lied about that. Cuckolded me, ran off to be with her real love. Could that be true?"

Sulwen's freckled face flushed a deep, unbecoming shade of red. "Sir!" she cried. "Begging your pardon, Master Clifford. I should not have repeated such gossip. To a stranger, no less."

Master Clifford did not seem to have heard her. His eyes swept over Lucy. She ducked her head so that he would not recognize her from the Sparrow, but she didn't think he'd even noticed her presence. Beside her, Sulwen twisted her hands anxiously. "Sir, I—" she broke off.

As they watched, he stumbled backward out of the kitchen. Through the open door they saw him enter a different room and shut the heavy wooden door behind him.

"That's my Lord's private room," Sulwen said. She glowered at Lucy. "If I get let go because of you . . ."

"We'd best take these trays in," Lucy interrupted. As they walked to the dining room, they heard the door open behind them.

Master Clifford stepped out, one arm clasped oddly behind his back. "Mother!" he shouted. "Mother! I need to speak to you!"

Lady Cumberland opened the drawing room door. "Francis!" She hissed through gritted teeth. "Stop that shouting at once! Supper is ready, as you can see." She glared at Sulwen, who had backed up against the wall. "Why are you cowering there, girl? Set the supper on the table!"

As Lucy walked in with Sulwen, her eyes met Adam's. He, Miss Water, and Lord Cumberland had all risen at the ruckus.

Seeing the question in his eyes, Lucy mouthed "baby." For a moment Adam looked confused, then his brow cleared. He looked wary.

Ignoring the guests, Francis Clifford turned toward his mother. "Mother, tell me at once. What truly happened to Amelie? You told me that she'd lied to me about the baby being mine!"

Lady Cumberland gasped, paling noticeably. "What a thing to say!"

"Is it true?"

"Francis! This is hardly the time to—"

"It is the time, Mother! I want answers!" He moved closer to his mother, who had recovered herself and was standing proudly by a great silver urn. Everyone else was still frozen. He asked his mother again. "Did Amelie have my baby? I know you know. I could never understand why you dismissed her."

"That young woman stole from us, I told you so!"

"No! I don't believe you!" Master Clifford shouted. "And to tell everyone that she had tried to poison me! Mother, why did you do such a thing? You know that I took that poison myself!"

Lady Cumberland sniffed. "If that harlot was with child I'm quite sure she had no idea who the father was. I had to dismiss her, before she spread tales, and ruined our good name." She looked at her husband. "William, please take care of Francis."

Lord Cumberland nodded slowly, his face suddenly strained. He looked at Sulwen, who still looked white-faced and stricken. "My son is . . . unwell. Get Burly—he'll be at the neighbor's stable, seeing to my horse. Mind you tell him to hurry."

Sulwen bobbed a quick curtsy, and fled the room, her eyes

wide. This would be quite a tale to tell when she moved on to her next employment.

Without warning, Frances Clifford pulled a small flintlock pistol from behind his back and aimed it at his mother.

They all froze. "Son," Lord Cumberland said warily. "Put the gun down."

Master Clifford jerked his head at Adam and Miss Water. "You two! Sit down. Over there!" He pointed to one of the embroidered benches that ran the length of the table.

"Hey, there," Adam started. "There's no need for this."

Master Clifford swiveled back to face Adam. "One more word from you and I'm going to shoot one of you." He waved the flintlock at Lucy again. "You, go stand over there."

Lucy did as she was told, warily watching the pistol. Even though she hadn't seen too many guns with her own eyes, their effects were everywhere, found in the injured older men like Avery, who had fought in the King's battles with Cromwell when she was young. She also knew he'd only have time to fire once before needing to reload, but she didn't want anyone to be hurt, or worse.

She moved to stand next to Miss Water, putting her hand on her shoulder to steady the shaking woman.

"She was beneath you," Lady Cumberland said to her son. Lucy winced at her tone.

"Martha!" her husband whispered hoarsely. "Stop talking."

"No, Father," Master Clifford said. "I should like to hear what Mother has to say. Amelie was my wife! Yes, that's right." He said to his father. "I married her. I did. I'm ashamed now that I kept it a secret."

The Earl sank back, a blank look on his face. "You married a servant?" For a moment he seemed quite overcome. Then he drew a great breath. "Your wife!" he shouted, no longer heeding the loaded gun in his son's hands. "Lower our name in such a fashion! Reduce our circumstances! I didn't build this family name up for years only for you to wreck it by marrying my maid!"

Lucy flinched at his words. She didn't dare look at Adam. The Earl wasn't directing his speech at her, but he may as well have been. He went on, shaking his fist at his son. "We expected you to marry a baroness, or a viscount's daughter. How dare you cast aside everything we gave you?!"

"How dare *you* cast away my Amelie! I was just," he gulped, "biding my time. I knew you and Mother would never approve!" He thumped angrily on the table. "Do you know, I thought we would run off, start a new life. I never cared about the title, or my inheritance. But she did not want me to cast myself from my family! She thought I would regret it! So we married in secret."

"That priest had no right to marry you!" his mother exclaimed. "I told him so! Right before—" She broke off, clapping her hand involuntarily over her mouth.

"Right before you struck him across his head?" Lucy finished, without thinking how it would sound. "That was a fatal blow!"

"Mother!" Master Clifford exclaimed, looking aghast at his mother. "*You* killed the priest?"

"Certainly not! That was Burly! He acted to protect us. He heard me trying to reason with the priest. The man kept saying he wouldn't tell anyone, but I could not trust that he would keep silent about the marriage. It seemed better to scrub out all traces. So when he turned away, Burly knew what to do."

The Earl stood up then, trying to quiet his wife. "That's enough, my dear!" He looked at Adam and Miss Water. "She doesn't know what she's saying."

Master Clifford was looking at his mother, dully. "How did you find out about our marriage?"

Not heeding her husband's attempts to keep her from speaking, Lady Cumberland answered the question. "I saw the harlot with your father's ring around her neck, and I accused her of stealing. Imagine how surprised I was when that vixen declared that the two of you had married." His mother's voice grew more shrill. "Your father gave *you* that ring, so that you would feel pride in what he had done! You threw everything we worked for away! We, who started with nothing!"

"I knew you had stolen that title!" Master Clifford replied. "I knew my father was no rightful heir! That's why I told Amelie it mattered not that we got married."

"You gave up on the bitch quick enough," his father said cruelly, "when we told you she was a thief, and that she was carrying the babe of another man!" With a sniff, he turned away.

"You who would commit self-murder," his mother spat at her son. "I did this to protect you, to save your father's name! That title was hard-won! I wouldn't see you losing everything that we had gained. Not for a whore! Her own father blasphemed her body after she died! Carved a brooch out of her bones! We could not be associated with such madness!"

"A brooch?" Master Clifford asked, his face growing paler as he tried to fathom the idea. "He made a brooch from her bones?" His despair seemed unbearable. But his grip on the pistol remained true.

The room was still. Then, the Earl whirled around to face Lucy, his rage barely contained. "Who are you? How did you know about the priest? Were you one of the scoundrels blackmailing me? Tell me! Were you working with that guttersnipe from the tavern?! I suppose you want to end up like her!"

Lucy shook her head, starting to tremble. From the corner of her eye she could tell Adam was trying to signal something to her, but she could not understand what he was trying to communicate.

The Earl went on. "I must have been in my cups one night, talking a little too much about my life before I inherited my title. That card sharp Jack was there, and so was that blasted wench from the tavern. The next thing I knew, I was being blackmailed. Getting malicious notes, claiming my title was not legitimate! Saying that my son had secretly married the village whore!" He moved closer to her. "Was that you?"

"No! No! I didn't blackmail you! That was all Tilly!" Lucy cried. Then she stopped, realizing what he had said. She hardly noticed when Adam edged off the bench and was moving carefully along the short end of the table. Miss Water was still sitting as she had been, trying to contain her own shaking. "Wait! You knew that it was Tilly who had been blackmailing you!"

Trying to keep them from paying attention to Adam, who was sidling closer to Master Clifford, Lucy asked the Earl. "Who was it that killed Tilly? You? Or, like your wife, did you have one of your servants do your treacherous deeds?" Lucy paused. "Only Tilly was poisoned first." She had a sudden image of the old woman spitting into the soup at the Fox and Duck. She turned back to Lady Cumberland. "You *did* send your servant! Theresa! Theresa poisoned her, didn't she?"

"Why must you interfere?!" Lady Cumberland screamed, an odd garbled sound. The next instant, she lunged toward Lucy, her outstretched fingers reaching for her neck.

At that same instant, Master Clifford pointed the gun at his mother and pulled the trigger. It clicked, but did not fire. Taking advantage of the delay, Adam hurled himself on Master Clifford. This time, the pistol's delayed shot went off with a terrible roar.

After a stunned second, and with her ears ringing from the gun's loud report, Lucy thrust Lady Cumberland from her. As she did, she caught sight of Adam reeling backward, blood streaming down the side of his head and Master Clifford slumping silently to the floor, not moving.

"Adam!" she screamed, leaping toward him. "Adam!"

Lucy flew to Adam's side. Mustering every bit of strength she had, Lucy forced herself to check if he was still breathing. The left side of his face was covered with black gunpowder, and blood was streaming from the side of his head. His eyes were closed and he appeared to have passed out. He was, however, breathing and his heart was beating determinedly.

"Thank God," she gasped. She began to tear patches from her petticoat, holding the straggly bits of material to the part of his head that seemed to be gushing the most blood. Lucy felt herself growing faint. She glanced over at Miss Water, who was still half-crouched, as if her mind could no longer remember what her body had been doing when the gunshot rang out. "Miss Water!" Lucy shouted, even though they were separated only by a few lengths.

"You must get help. Find Duncan—he should be nearby! Adam needs a physician straightaway! There's no time to lose. I do not know how badly he's been hurt."

Darting a quick fearful glance at Adam, Miss Water raced out of the room. Like Lucy, she'd spent a lifetime taking orders from others, mainly from her father. Lucy patted at Adam's face, trying to wipe the blood and gunpowder from his face with a bit of wine from the pitcher.

To her relief, he opened his eyes. "I'm all right," he said, his jaw clenched in pain.

"You're not all right," she said. "But you will be. I will summon Dr. Larimer."

Behind her, she could hear Lady Cumberland calling out to her son. "I did it for us! I did it for us!" Lucy heard her moaning. "The scandal would have been too great. We'd only just been accepted by Society."

Forcing herself to look, she could see that Master Clifford was still laying in the same unnatural position. She could not tell if he was dead or not.

The next moment, the door burst open. The Earl strode back into the room, followed by two large men. Jonesie and Burly, she assumed. Sulwen, she could see, was peering behind them, her hands to her mouth in shock. "Master Clifford?" She gasped, her eyes darting fearfully at the Earl. She whispered, "I think he's dead."

Hardly sparing a glance at his son, the Earl went over to his wife. "Martha," Lucy heard him murmur, "there's nothing we can do for the boy. We must go." As he straightened up, he said to the men, "Take care of this," gesturing expansively to everyone in the room. "I'll pay you well, never you fear."

Lady Cumberland stood up, still imperious, even with her half-crazed eyes and tear-stained cheeks. She kissed her husband on the cheek. "You go. I'll be with Theresa upstairs." Though she'd regained her composure, her expression looked like that of a trapped animal. She swept from the room, the Earl on her heels.

Lucy looked up at the two men, who were still staring in confusion at the scene around them. Wildly, she hoped they wouldn't understand the Earl's message.

That hope disappeared when Burly picked up a large water pitcher. Hefting it in his hands, he felt the weight. "I'll take her," he said. "You take him."

Jonesie nodded, pulling out a large knife from his belt that had been hidden by his jacket. As they began to advance, Lucy stood up, hoping to be able to ward off the impending attack.

To her great relief, though, she heard shouts in the hallway. Duncan raced into the room with two bellmen, followed by Miss Water. They stopped, trying to decipher the madness before them. Pushing past the men who were now bending over Master Clifford's body, the constable rushed to her side. "Are you alright?" He looked at her anxiously.

"Duncan! Thank God!" Lucy exclaimed. "Adam needs help! Those men are murderers! And they were trying to kill us!" She pointed at Jonesie and Burly. "Grab them!"

The bellmen leaped on the two men. As they fought to subdue them, Lucy breathlessly explained. "They killed Tilly. They were told to do it by the Earl. Or maybe Lady Cumberland. Only she's not a lady. And he's not an Earl." She could hear herself babbling. "She's upstairs with her servant, Theresa. I think the Earl has run off!"

After hearing her accusation, Duncan was barely listening. "I'll see to the women upstairs."

Lucy watched the bellmen wrestle Jonesie and Burly out of the house. The room was quiet except for the muffled sound of Sulwen weeping into her hands. "We're a pair, aren't we?" she whispered to Adam. "Always getting set upon by murderous sorts." The flow of blood seemed to have staunched a bit. Grimly, Lucy pulled off more of her petticoat. As she continued to wipe his face with the wine-soaked cloth, she could see great burns starting to appear by his ear. "Cook will make you a special salve," she said softly. "Don't you worry."

Duncan shouting her name from somewhere upstairs broke through her rising hysterics. "Lucy! They've taken poison! We need an emetic."

"What?"

"Lady Cumberland. As well as her servant. That old woman. They both took poison."

Lucy's mind flew to the conversation Dr. Larimer had with Sheridan, concerning Culpeper's antidotes to poison. "Sulwen! Have you mustard seed! Or rosemary?"

"Yes, miss. We have both. In the kitchen!"

"Stay with Master Hargrave," she ordered Sulwen. "Hold this cloth to his head, just so. Do *not* leave him, do you understand me?"

Though she hated to leave Adam's side, she rushed to the kitchen. Murmuring a quick thanks that she'd paid attention when the physician had questioned his assistant, she began to grind up the rosemary and mustard and dissolved it in a bit of hot water that Sulwen already had on the fire. Lucy poured the brew into two cups, and returned to the dining room, a steaming cup in each hand. Miss Water was kneeling anxiously beside Adam as well.

As she passed by, she heard Adam groaning. "I'm alright." He was already struggling to sit up. "I'm just having some problems hearing you."

"Sulwen!" Lucy said. "Take this cup and come with me." Seeing Sulwen's dull eyes, she stamped her foot. This was no time to go into shock. "Now! Do you want your lady to die?"

Sulwen took the second cup, and her eyes seemed to clear.

"This way!" Duncan shouted. Lucy and Sulwen raced up the stairs, being careful not to spill the brew. As they neared the top of the stairs, they could hear terrible groaning and moaning behind a room at the end of the passageway. There they found Lady Cumberland and Theresa both clutching their stomachs and turning a nasty shade of purple.

Remembering how she'd seen Dr. Larimer force brew down the throats of ailing people, Lucy grabbed Lady Cumberland by the hair, yanking her head back. "Down her throat! Quickly!" she called to Sulwen, pouring the brew between the struggling woman's clenched lips. Saying another quick prayer that she was not hastening Lady Cumberland's death, Lucy placed her hand over the woman's mouth, forcing her to swallow the concoction.

Despite the woman's contortions, Lucy managed to get it all down her throat. She released her, laying her down.

"Oh no!" She heard Sulwen cry. To her dismay, she saw Theresa had knocked the cup out of Sulwen's hands.

"Sulwen, there's more in the kitchen! Get it!" But the girl still didn't move, so entranced was she by the old servant's convulsions.

Quickly, the emetic starting working on Lady Cumberland as she began to wretch violently, heaving out the contents of her stomach. Within a few moments, she stopped and lay on the ground, panting heavily and glaring at Lucy.

"Theresa!" Sulwen said. The servant stopped contorting and lay back, her face a terrible purple and her tongue black. She was dead.

·22·

Within thirty minutes, Adam, Lucy, and Miss Water were on their way to Master Hargrave's home. Duncan had requisitioned a hackney cab for them with surprising swiftness, before he set off with his bellman to capture the Earl. The two-mile ride to Master Hargrave's home was grueling. Adam's head had stopped bleeding, but he seemed very groggy. "What happened to him?" Miss Water asked Lucy, watching her cradle Adam's head against her shoulder to absorb the shocks of the road. "It happened so fast! Was he struck by a bullet?"

Lucy shook her head, trying to keep the tears from flowing. "I think the pistol exploded. That's why he has gunpowder all over his face. His head might be damaged. I hope Dr. Larimer received the message from the bellman that Duncan sent! We need him desperately." She sighed in relief when she saw the physician and Master Hargrave awaiting them in front of the magistrate's home.

As the bellman helped Adam inside to his bedchamber, Lucy gave as succinct an account of his injuries as she could. She could barely stand to look at the magistrate, whose face had grown drawn and anxious.

For a few minutes she was not allowed in the room while the physician completed a cursory examination. She gave a quick account to Cook and Annie. Without a word, Cook set to making a salve for burns, and Lucy showed Annie how to make bandages by stripping an old sheet.

When the physician opened the door to Adam's room, Lucy was standing there, with a basin of warm water and some clothes. "Cook is making a salve," she said, peering into the room.

Dr. Larimer nodded approvingly at Lucy. "Good girl," he said. "You've certainly been helpful."

Lucy felt like she'd been punched in the gut. If it hadn't been for her, Adam wouldn't have been injured at all. She felt her eyes fill with tears, which she blinked quickly away. The physician didn't speak again as he bandaged the left side of Adam's head, except for a few murmurs here and there to Mister Sheridan.

They also, to Lucy's surprise, bandaged Adam's right hand. He must have caught a bit of the gun shrapnel when he raised his hand to protect his head.

"Adam's hand will heal in time," the physician explained to the magistrate. " 'Tis the blow to the side of his head I'm more worried about. He seems to be having trouble hearing. Until the swelling goes down, we will not know if there has been any permanent damage."

Still sitting on the edge of Adam's bed, Dr. Larimer turned to Lucy then. "How did you know to create that emetic?" he asked. "A folk remedy from your mother?"

Wearily, Lucy shook her head. "Culpeper. I was there when you discussed it with Mr. Sheridan, remember?"

"Indeed. Very quick thinking. I'm not sure my good man Sheridan would have been so handy," he said, trying to sound hearty. "He'd still be looking for the white hellebore in the kitchen stores, I'm afraid."

"Yes, Lucy's a good lass," the magistrate said, distracted.

The sickening feeling that had been bubbling in Lucy's stomach threatened upheaval. She fled, and collapsed to weep in the old bedchamber she had once shared with Annie. The shock of the last few hours finally overwhelmed her, and she fell asleep.

When Lucy awoke, she was disoriented. Looking out the unshuttered window, she could see the moon. Someone, probably Annie, had pulled a blanket over her body as she slept. Her thoughts turned to Master Aubrey, and her work in his shop. Would he dismiss her for not having returned, she wondered. To be honest, she didn't know if she even cared. Right now her only concern was how Adam was doing.

She slipped quietly down the steps to Adam's bedchamber, and knocked softly.

"Come in," she heard Master Hargrave reply in a low voice. When she entered, she found the magistrate seated in a chair by Adam's bed, an unopened leather-bound book in his lap, and a solitary candle lit on the table. Seeing her, he smiled. "Did you get some sleep?"

Lucy nodded, biting her lip. He continued, "I sent John over to Master Aubrey's a few hours ago, to let him know you were here. I didn't say much about what had happened, but I asked him to give you some leave during this family crisis."

The enormity of the gesture almost overwhelmed Lucy. "Oh, thank you, sir. I appreciate your kindness, even though I don't deserve it."

Master Hargrave glanced at Adam's sleeping form, then back at Lucy. "Why ever don't you deserve it? I wouldn't want Master Aubrey to release you from his employ. I know you've been an excellent apprentice, and keen on the work."

She gulped. Tears threatened to overwhelm her. *This is all my fault,* she wanted to scream, but she couldn't speak.

"Lucy, dear," the magistrate said, alarmed at her tears. "You've been through another terrible ordeal." He handed her his handkerchief. "Pray do not weep. I would appreciate if you could help me understand what transpired this evening. Adam's condition has made me rather remiss in asking questions, yet I must endeavor to understand. If you would?" He indicated a small, embroidered footstool beside the bed.

Sighing, Lucy sat down before him. Earnestly, she explained all they had learned before the pistol had exploded in Master Clifford's hands.

The magistrate closed his eyes as she spoke, listening intently to her halting narrative. When she paused, he opened his eyes. His smile a bit sad, he said, "As always, my dear, I'm enthralled by your tales." He paused. "So let me see if I've gotten this straight.

The luckless Amelie, a servant in the Earl's household, and young Master Clifford fell in love and at some point she became pregnant with his child. He then took her to a small chapel in Carlisle, where they secretly wed. He gave her his father's signet ring as a symbol of their troth. Is this all correct so far?" At Lucy's nod, he continued. "Lady Cumberland saw the ring around Amelie's neck and confronted her as a thief. Amelie told her the truth, and our Countess promptly threw her out of the house, because she could not bear the scandal. She spread the word that Amelie was a thief and told her own son that he had been cuckolded, that the babe was not his own. Rather than talking to his wife, Master Clifford opted to believe his mother's wicked tales. In the meantime, Lady Cumberland had her husband's manservant kill the priest who had performed the marriage. I'm not sure what happened next."

"Then, not too long later, Master Clifford, in his despair, took the poison," Lucy explained. "Lady Cumberland used this story to further hurt Amelie's reputation." Here, Lucy could hardly hide the contempt in her voice. "She let it be known that Amelie had tried to kill the young master, or helped someone else do it, in her anger at being cast from the house—I read the broadside that said so." She swallowed before continuing. "I didn't know Amelie, but I would wager that she was so sad with the faithlessness of her lover, and so weakened by her condition, her heart just broke." Lucy sat silently for a moment. "When Ashton Hendricks returned, just before his daughter died giving birth to the baby, he went mad with grief himself, and began to try to bring down the Earl and his family, in a desperate attempt to seek revenge on his daughter's behalf. I believe at that point he began to follow the Earl, making several failed attempts on his life."

Master Hargrave stroked his chin thoughtfully. "You said that Tilly and Jacques were blackmailing the Earl and his son, is that correct? How do you suppose that came to be?"

"Jacques said he invited the Earl to the game, knowing of his fondness—weakness, truly—for gambling," Lucy said, recollecting her earlier conversation with the card sharp. "The Earl said that when he was tippling down, he might have said too much. Tilly was the sort to seize upon such knowledge when a man had been taking spirits, and seek to use it to her own advantage."

"Well, that brings us to the Cheshire Cheese, and perhaps to Tilly's murder."

"I think that Lady Cumberland sent Theresa to poison her, just as she had the priest killed. Maybe Burly and Jonesie were there to finish the job." She sighed. "Hopefully the constable can sort that out."

"But we still don't know who killed Tahmin, do we?" the magistrate asked gently.

"Burly and Jonesie, I imagine," Lucy said, and she explained about the Earl's bodyguards. "Durand said Tilly had set the men on Tahmin, to let them think he was the one blackmailing the Earl. I'm certain they killed Tilly. They must have figured it out when she blackmailed them again, I suppose, and attempted to kill Durand too."

"Perhaps," the magistrate clucked softly. "Somehow that explanation doesn't seem sufficient to me. But I'm tired. Maybe nothing makes sense to me in this state."

"I'll stay with him, sir. Please, get some sleep."

She began to dab softly at Adam's face, wiping away some of the beads of sweat that had formed. Behind her, she heard the door close as the magistrate headed to his own chambers down the corridor.

In the morning, Constable Duncan stopped by with some news. Lucy was in Master Hargraves drawing room, writing a letter to the magistrate's daughter Sarah, even though she didn't know exactly where to send the note. The last she'd heard, Sarah was still in the Massachussetts Bay Colony with the other Quakers. They could only hope that good winds and a fast ship could bring her word in a timely way.

"You'll be glad to know that Lady Cumberland is recovering from her attempt to poison herself, thanks to you," Duncan said.

Lucy set the letter aside. "She is? I just wish we had been able to save Theresa as well."

"Well, Lady Cumberland is fit enough to stand trial, even though Dr. Larimer thinks her insides are burned a bit from the poison. I'll be honest, I can't say I'm too sorry she's in pain. Just enough to torment her 'til she swings on the Tyburn tree. Killing a man of the cloth! Bloody hell! Burly and Jones will be standing trial too."

"Oh, is that so?" Lucy asked.

"Indeed," the constable explained. It seemed that Burly, the dumber of the pair, had confirmed that Theresa had poisoned Tilly first. "They claim they hadn't meant to kill Tilly, just scare her a little, as they did Durand. Burly just struck Tilly a 'mite too hard.'"

"Do you believe that?"

"No. Lady Cumberland had made it clear that she wanted the blackmailers dead. They're probably hoping to escape Tyburn."

"But why have Theresa poison her first?"

Duncan shook his head. "I'm not sure. I suspect that Lady Cumberland thought Burly and Jonesie would botch the job. Maybe it was just insurance that the job would get done."

"What about Tahmin?" Lucy asked eagerly. "Did they confess to his murder too?"

"I tell you, Lucy. 'Tis the damndest thing." He paced back and forth. "Surely they know they're going to swing for killing Tilly, and attempting to murder Durand. Yet they both swear up and down they did not kill Tahmin. Roughed him up, they said. Still, they didn't kill him. Do you believe it?"

She shook her head. "I don't know what to believe." She paused. "What about the Earl? Have you caught him yet?"

"Not yet," Duncan said grimly. "But we will."

Over the next day, Lucy stayed beside Adam as much as she dared. Dr. Larimer said that it was important that someone keep an eye on him. "Sometimes, when a man is concussed, he can slip away," the physician warned. Moreover, despite Adam's protests to the contrary, it was obvious he was in a lot of pain and felt quite nauseous from the blow to his head. Master Hargrave had wanted to hire a woman to nurse his son, but had not said another word when the servants gently insisted that they could take care of him. John, Mary, Annie, and Lucy all took turns being beside him.

That evening, as it approached midnight, Lucy drifted off while sitting on the floor beside the bed, holding Adam's hand in her own. She'd woken to find Master Hargrave shaking her shoulder. Jerking her hand out of Adam's, she struggled to stand hastily. "Forgive me, sir. For all of it. It's my fault he was injured."

"No, Lucy," he said firmly. "Francis Clifford wielded that pistol. He is to blame, God rest his soul."

"But Adam would not have been there if I'd not dreamed up that silly scheme."

"Yes, I'm the one who requested that the Earl invite you to dine. So by your reasoning I am equally, if not more, at fault." He touched Lucy's arm. "The Earl and his wife will be the ones to stand trial."

"If they find the Earl." Looking at Adam, she sighed. His face was still heavily bandaged on the left side. At least his color was no longer that ghastly gray it had been after they first scraped away the gunpowder.

The magistrate looked at her kindly. "Lucy, dear. I'm not blind. To your feelings. Or to his." He sat down on the bed beside Adam's sleeping form. To Lucy's surprise, he took her hand and laid it back on top of his son's still hand. "I hope you know I do not oppose the match. Indeed, I could not imagine a dearer daughter-in-law."

Lucy smiled tiredly. "Thank you, sir. I'm afraid, though, there are those who would shut their doors to him should he marry a chambermaid." The Earl's words to his son still burned a bit in her ears. *You would have ruined this family by marrying her!*

"He is not afraid of closed doors, any more than you have been," the magistrate said, after a slight pause. "You, my dear, have proved Aristotle right. 'The educated differ from the uneducated, as much as the living from the dead.'" He chuckled. "I can see that you're barely upright, which means you need to get a few hours sleep. I will stay with him." Seeing her protest, he added, "I will let you know if anything changes."

Lucy felt her head had barely been on the pillow a minute when she heard a flurry of activity in the household. The full morning sun was streaming through the windows of Annie's tiny room. When she came down, she met Master Hargrave coming out of his son's chambers.

When he saw Lucy, he smiled. "Adam's faring much better and he'd like to see you, Lucy. You may go in."

"Thank you, sir."

Giving a little knock, she walked in. Adam was sitting at his little table, fully dressed. He still had the bandage around his ear, but his color looked much better than it had three days before.

"Hello, Lucy," he said. "Got ourselves in another scrape again, didn't we?"

Shakily, she nodded. "Yes, I guess we did. How are you feeling?"

"Like a gun exploded in my face," he said wryly. He gestured to the other chair. "Please, Lucy, will you sit down? I've something to say."

When she sat down, he reached across the small table and took her hands in his. "Lucy, these last few months have been overwhelming. Truly. The things we've seen. What we've gone through. The plague, the Fire. So much death. So much violence.

Sometimes the world around us seems so completely mad. I've never been so aware how short life is."

Lucy nodded, searching his face. "I know."

"But when I'm with you," he went on, "none of that matters. Life is fine. I've told you before that I want to spend my life with you. No, please," he said, as she started to speak. "Let me finish. My father told me about your worries about your station. You must believe me," he tightened his hands over hers, "even if I ever thought that way, I do not now. And I would never let such a thing stand in the way of our happiness."

"Adam, I—" Lucy tried to speak again.

He smiled at her. "I'm almost done. Then it's your turn, I promise. But these last few months, I've realized something too. About you. How contented you are in your new position, working with Master Aubrey. You so enjoy being a printer's apprentice, writing books and selling them. And I think you're good at it." He laughed, fondly. "And you like solving puzzles. I could never take you from that. Both Father and I agree. Sometimes we think you can do anything you set your mind to, and we'd like to see what lies ahead for you."

"I would like to own my own press one day," Lucy whispered, her eyes tearing a bit. She'd never even admitted this to Will. "Create my own books. I don't know if I can ever be licensed, but Master Aubrey told me that the only reason he could even take me as an apprentice at all is because the guild rules have been growing soft. Certainly there have been other female apprentices, but they may not agree to let me in. I'd have to prove myself to them first." She touched his arm. "But you know how deeply I care for you. How much I would like to be your—" she could not bring herself to say the last word. "Wife."

Adam nodded, looking slightly sad but not surprised. "Let us wait a while. Stay on with Master Aubrey. I'll court you properly too, when you're ready. I can't let that constable think you're available. When I saw him around you, I didn't know what to think." There was a strong undercurrent of feeling when he said this last part.

"He knows I'm not available," she whispered, sounding more confident than she felt. She quickly kissed Adam's cheek as she stood up to leave. "I should probably get back to Master Aubrey's then. What he must think of me!"

As she turned to go, Adam caught her hand and raised it to his lips in farewell. "Lucy, I *will* see you soon."

·23·

You've swept that same spot three times now," Lach said to her over his shoulder. He was seated at the printing press, carefully laying letters. "We've got lots to do before Guy Fawkes festivities tonight, and you're not helping too much."

"What? Oh, right," she said, returning the broom back to its customary place in the corner.

More than a week had passed since she left the magistrate's house. Although she felt gratified that Adam had been so understanding, there was a tiny ache inside her, as she wondered how long he would truly want to wait for her.

Lucy tried to keep her mind on her work, but to no avail. Stacks of pamphlets, still unfolded, were strewn about her workspace. All day she'd managed to fill only two bags. Master Aubrey would not be pleased when he returned tomorrow from his journey to Kent. Because she'd missed so much work this past week, tending to Adam, she felt she owed Master Aubrey some good sales. Besides, she really didn't feel much like celebrating Guy Fawkes Day, a reminder of the day Parliament had nearly been blown up by a papist.

"Here's a new ballad," Lach said, bringing over the stack he'd been cutting. He handed her a broadside. "You'll have to tell me what you think of it."

"An Earl's Bloody Disgrace . . ." she read the title aloud. "What?" Quickly she scanned the bit of doggerel. The ballad described, fairly accurately, Lady Cumberland's hand in the murders, and the Earl's disgrace. His gambling debts had been quite severe it seemed, and this scandal had closed him off from his normal avenues. The ballad also suggested that the Earl had forged his inheritance. "Not noble born, just a gent roughly shorn."

Jonesie and Burly played a role in the ballad too, the henchmen who did the Earl's bidding. At this point, she looked up. "Whoever wrote this piece?"

Lach shrugged. "Anonymous. As usual."

"Wait a minute," she said suspiciously, pointing to the last bit of doggerel, which she read aloud. " ' 'Twas all due to a young printer's maid, that these crimes were unearthed! No thanks to the bumbling constable, who only provided mirth . . . !' " Lucy threw the paper down. Reaching over she grabbed Lach's thumb and forefinger of his right hand. There was the same telltale mark she often wore on her own hand. *"You* wrote this!" she exclaimed. "Admit it!"

"Can't prove it was me! Came under the door, like usual." Lach grinned cheekily. "Even though I think this 'Anonymous' chap is a mighty discerning fellow. After all, *you* did do all the constable's work."

"That's not true!" Lucy protested. "Anyway, I can't sell this!"

"I'll sell it then. Make a pretty penny too, I will." Lach laid them in his pack and set off. "I'll see you later. No curfew tonight, so I'm aiming to have a bit of fun after I sell these."

As Lach walked out, he tipped his hat cheekily to Miss Water who was entering the shop.

"I've come to see how you are," the woman said, "and how Adam has fared since our ordeal."

For a moment Lucy wanted to confide in her, but she just couldn't. "Better. I suppose," she said. "He's having trouble hearing, but the physician hopes that he will soon improve."

Miss Water looked at her shrewdly and then grabbed her arm. "Come on. Let's go outside. We can eat at the Cross Keys. The Lord Mayor lifted the curfew, just for tonight. That tavern will have some life in it, that's for sure."

Lucy gestured at the pile of work on the table. "I can't. I still have all this. Master Aubrey won't be happy if I don't bring back some coins." She looked at the darkening sky. "Although it's so late already." She sighed. "I don't want to go too far."

Miss Water folded the last few pieces rapidly and stuffed them in Lucy's sack. "Done. Where are we going?"

"Oh, maybe St. Martin-in-the-Fields again, I suppose. So many people taking up residence over there. Hopefully I can sell a few right quick."

"Wonderful," Miss Water said. "If I could relieve myself first?"

Lucy gestured to the back room, where they kept the refuse bucket. "I'll wait in front."

Standing in the doorway, Lucy watched a cart pass by full of effigies to be sold at market. Officially, of course, the Lord Mayor had banned the effigies, for fear of fire, but no one seemed to be heeding the ordinance. Off to Covent Garden no doubt, for the evening Guy Fawkes bonfires and dancing. As a cool breeze chilled her, a line from Darius's poem unexpectedly crossed her mind again. *Hearty pineapples, even in the first freeze of autumn.*

The first freeze of autumn. Surely, he meant around this time of year? Because she'd thought so much about the poem, the next line followed, unbidden. *Rose, my love—Even kings can wrong a fey duet.* Suddenly, a preposterous thought occurred to her. She went back inside the shop, taking one of Master Aubrey's quills and a bit of ink from his desk. Then she proceeded to write the entire poem by memory, her fingers flying in her excitement.

As she'd done before, Lucy removed the letters spelling out "C-O-V-E-N-T-G-A-R-D-E-N." All of them were there. She stared expectantly at the letters that remained. Thoughtfully, using the method Master Hargrave had taught her to solve anagrams, she spelled out G-U-Y-F-A-W-K-E-S. All the letters containing the doomed papist's name were present. Four letters remained. "I-N-N-E."

In her mind, she rearranged the letters. Nine! "Nine o'clock!" she said out loud. Was it possible that Darius would actually be there, waiting for his love? After crumpling up the piece of paper, she wrote a quick note to Duncan, telling him what she had deciphered. She put that note in her pocket. In that instant, she didn't want to show the last part of the anagram to Miss Water. No need to get her hopes up. "Ready!" she called to Miss Water. "I changed my mind! We're going to Covent Garden!"

When they arrived, great throngs of people were already milling about, buying and selling wares. Except for the darkness, it could have been a mid-morning Saturday market. Tall torches started to be carefully lit, casting odd flickering shadows on the merry-makers below. Lucy was glad to see that more soldiers than ever were on hand—the first night without an early curfew was not one to be taken lightly.

As they strolled about, Lucy sang "True News from Tewksbury," keeping a careful eye out. She didn't know exactly what she was looking for, but she thought the best thing to do was to keep Miss Water as visible as possible, should anyone be searching for her. She didn't see the constable. He hadn't been at the makeshift jail when she stopped by, but Hank was there, guarding two rough sorts, and he'd promised he'd give the note to Duncan. "Nine at Covent Garden. Near the man who sells pineapples!" she'd written quickly.

The bellman called seven o'clock and then eight o'clock. The crowd had been steadily growing, and Guy Fawkes effigies were starting to be tossed about. As Lucy had suspected, not everyone was going to heed the Lord Mayor's ban. Peddlers and hawkers were still selling their wares, not wishing to lose the rare night of free spending and carousing.

Miss Water, she was grateful to see, seemed happy enough to help her exchange coins for the penny pieces. At one point, Lucy thanked her for her help.

"If Father should see me now," Miss Water sighed. "I don't know what he would do to me."

Lucy stopped short. "By all means, please cease your assistance to me. I shouldn't like to see you in trouble."

"Truly, Lucy, it's the least I can do for you. Right now I feel

you're my only friend." She flushed in embarrassment. "I suppose
that's not the sort of thing a lady should admit to another."

"Perhaps *ladies* do not speak of their feelings, but friends certainly do." Lucy paused. "I hope you know I always try to be true
with you." Glancing at the sky, she thought it must be nearing
nine o'clock. Her heart started pounding nervously. "I've sold everything, and I'm craving some refreshment. Let us go this way,"
she said, pulling Miss Water in the direction of Master Greenleaf's fruit cart. "I've the oddest hankering for a pineapple."

"You are a strange girl." Miss Water laughed. "Alright, I've yet
to try such a delicacy although Darius told me once I should . . ."
Her voice trailed off. She stopped. "Covent Garden. Pineapple.
You know something—?"

Shifting her pack to her left arm, Lucy linked her free arm in
Miss Water's. "I did figure something else out," she whispered.
"Guy Fawkes Day. At nine." She faltered. Master Greenleaf's cart
was in view. "I don't know if he'll be there . . ."

But Miss Water didn't heed her words. Instead, she clutched
Lucy's arm. "Lucy! Is that—? I think that's . . ." her voice trailed
off. A man was standing quietly by the fruit cart. "Darius!" she
whispered. "Can it be? Lucy, can it be?"

As if he heard her little sigh, the man turned around. "Nasrin!" he called, holding his arms wide. Wordlessly, Miss Water
walked into Darius's arms.

Lucy turned away from the pair, a slight mist covering her
eyes. Seeing the lovers reunited was almost too much to bear. She
could hear Miss Water crying. "For so long, I thought you were
dead! Now, here you are!"

"I did not know if you would decipher my riddle." Lucy heard

Darius say to Miss Water. "I have not heard from that rascal Tah-min for almost two months now. What was I to think when I did not receive your reply? I told him to return with your message. Then, when I heard of the Great Fire, I feared the worst. But I could not leave Persia, you understand, until my obligation to the Shah was complete. That's why I sent Tahmin."

"Oh Darius!" Miss Water pulled away slightly. "We must talk. No, Lucy, wait!" she said, seeing Lucy start to move away. "Please help me explain to Darius all that has happened." She gulped, a pleading look in her eyes. *Please help me tell him what happened to Tahmin.*

The young man turned toward Lucy with a gentle smile. His wavy hair and eyes were black, and his skin was darker than that of most people of her acquaintance. He reminded her somewhat of some of the Arab traders she'd met before at market. When he spoke, his voice was deeply cultured and rich, sounding even more refined than Master Hargrave.

"Nasrin, I should very much like to meet your friend. Miss—?"

"Campion," Miss Water supplied.

"Miss Campion," he said to Lucy with an elegant bow. The gesture made her smile; she'd never felt so important. A breeze blew again, and both women shivered.

"Let us go near one of these bonfires. We can talk there easily enough," Darius said. He also bought them mugs of steaming wormwood from a man ladling the drink from a small cauldron over a small fire.

Sighing, they sat down on the ground, still close by Master Greenleaf's fruit cart. All about them revelers strolled or danced about with their effigies and bonfires.

Darius grinned at them, his white teeth gleaming in the light of the fire. "When I wrote you that letter, dear Nasrin, I never truly imagined Covent Garden would be like this. How long did it take for you to decipher my anagram?"

Miss Water gulped, looking helplessly at Lucy. She seemed incapable of speech.

"We just figured the whole message out," Lucy said slowly. "Just a few hours ago."

"Just a few hours ago? How can that be?" Darius asked, looking from Lucy to Nasrin in surprise. "Tahmin was supposed to let you know which lines held the clue, in case you could not sort it out. Where is Tahmin anyway?" He looked around, as if expecting his old friend to emerge from behind a vendor's stall.

Reluctantly, Lucy explained all that occurred since the night of the Fire, what they had pieced together of Tahmin's last hours, of the aftermath they'd experienced when Lucy innocently published the poem. As she spoke, Darius's face grew ashen, and for a moment he seemed quite overcome. Lucy looked away, while he laid his face on Miss Water's shoulder.

"I'm sorry," he said. "I never suspected this would happen."

"Why did you say you were here? In your anagram?" Miss Water asked, pulling away slightly. The first few blissful moments were forgotten as evidently she remembered her months of distress and worry.

"My intention was to come with Tahmin, but I was delayed by affairs at the Shah's court. He was dying, and I could not leave him." He paused. "Forgive me, my dear. Forgive this little game I had planned. It's just that I've had a surprise long planned for you. I had heard of the famous Covent Garden from an English ballad that was passed around at the Palace." He looked ruefully about. "What can I say? I thought we might try pineapple together." He leaned toward Miss Water. "I had heard of your Londoner's love of this Guy Fawkes celebration, and I thought I would be here by then."

"You just couldn't stay away, could you, Darius?" A figure stepped into the light of the bonfire.

Miss Water gasped, pulling away from Darius. "Father! What are you doing here?"

"What do you think?" Master Water held up a careworn copy of *From the Charred Remains*. "Child's play. I deciphered Darius's poem months ago. After I heard you and Miss Campion here talking that day in Oxford, I knew that Tahmin was simply the messenger, and Darius your *lover*." He spat the last word out at them. "I never dreamed you'd figure out the rest of the poem on your own. I thought I would be able to just meet Darius myself."

Darius stood up, his chest heaving with emotion. "Do you know who killed Tahmin?" he asked Master Water, the pain at asking that question evident. "Did *you* kill my friend?"

Miss Water turned a shocked face toward Darius. "Darius! That's not possible! Why ever would you ask my father such a dreadful thing?"

"Because I asked him to send your father a letter in Oxford when he arrived in London, asking to see him." A shadow crossed Darius's face. "I told him to say that he would like to pay his respects personally, but not to say that he was there on my behalf." He stared at Master Water. "*Did* you meet him?"

"No, that's not possible. Tell him, Father, that's not possible," Miss Water exclaimed again. "You weren't at the Cheshire Cheese that night! You weren't even in London!"

"But he was," Lucy said slowly, remembering what she'd learned about that ill-fated game from Tilly, Durand, Mister Hendricks, and even the Earl.

Out of the corner of her eye Lucy noticed Constable Duncan moving toward them. He had received the note she had left with the bellman. Giving him a slight warning flick of her hand, she raised her voice a bit. "*You* were the other man who didn't play the game of cards at the Cheshire Cheese that night! Tilly told us there was another man who watched the game intently." She stared at Miss Water's father. "*You* brought Tahmin! You knew he had the gambling sickness."

"Yes, that's right," Master Water said, ignoring his daughter's gasp. "What was I supposed to think? Tahmin had informed me he was coming to London. Told me he wanted to see me. Having seen my daughter embrace a man in the shadows of the Shah's garden, I could only assume one thing. He'd made this trek to see her. Maybe even try to run off with her. This I could not allow."

Beside her, Darius put his hand to his face, a deep pain crossing his features. "Tahmin had come on my bequest. Indeed, to see your daughter, but also to convey my best wishes to you." Darius sighed. "Tahmin was a deeply honorable man."

Master Water continued, his words tumbling out more quickly now, as if he couldn't keep them in even if he had wished. Lucy was glad to see that Constable Duncan was taking in every word. "Tahmin wanted to play a game of cards," Master Water said. "I knew I could not let him see you, my dear." He gazed at his daughter, who was staring at him wordlessly. "I certainly couldn't take him to one of my regular establishments, couldn't run the risk of meeting any of my acquaintances." He gazed at a bonfire for a moment. "I'd heard tell of the Cheshire Cheese.

"My worries were confirmed when that poem was read out loud. I knew it was intended for you, my daughter. Rhonda— Rose. I could not let him court you."

"Why ever not?" Miss Water exclaimed. "You told me that you admired them."

"Let you marry one of them? Live among them forever?" Lucy winced at the disdain in his voice, his upper-class breeding showing. "I jolly well don't think so."

Miss Water looked like she'd been slapped, and she clutched Darius again. For a long moment her father and Darius stared balefully at one another.

"What happened at the Cheshire Cheese?" Lucy asked, still trying to learn what had happened to Tahmin.

Master Water sighed. "I heard him called a blackmailer, and I egged on his beating. When those louts left him outside the tavern, I nearly left him. But then I thought of him, in the shadows, in the garden, embracing you. Taking your honor. *That's* when I drove my knife in."

Miss Water's face crumpled. "You *did* kill him?"

Master Water regarded his daughter with a mixture of sadness, exasperation, and even a bit of defiance. "I just could not think. I stuffed him in the barrel. When the Fire happened, I thought my crime would never come to light. I'm not proud of what I did."

Darius drew her toward him then, so that she turned her stunned face to his. "Please let me bring you back to my land. At the court, you will be revered, not disrespected for taking up with, how do you English say it, 'a foreign gent'?"

Constable Duncan stepped up, placing his hand around the scholar's arm. "Master Water, you are under arrest for the murder of Tahmin—" He looked at Darius. "What is his surname?"

"Abbas," Darius said, wiping a tear from his eye. "His name was Tahmin Abbas." He put his arm around Miss Water then, for she had begun to tremble. The full weight of her father's crime was starting to sink in.

"Father?" she asked, her voice wavering. "What will happen to us?"

Master Water looked at her with profound sadness. "I have made an egregious error, one I can never rectify. I can only hope in time for your forgiveness." He embraced her swiftly, then released her, and she nearly collapsed. "Get me out of here, Constable."

Duncan gestured to his bellman, who stepped forward to lead Master Water away. Miss Water sobbed softly against Darius's shoulder.

"Please show me where my friend died," Darius said quietly, after pulling slightly away from Miss Water's tight grasp. "Please, Miss Campion?"

Duncan frowned slightly. "It's dark. Can you not go in the morning?"

"I should like to go now," Darius said. He inclined his head. "But if you feel I will be endangering Miss Campion, then by all means we can wait."

"I think we will be all right," Lucy said to Duncan. "Truly."

"I know you'll be fine." He flicked a bit of ash from her shoulder. "You always come out on top."

The intensity of his gaze made her remember what Adam had said about the constable. Feeling slightly flustered, Lucy bid him farewell. Picking up two torches, she turned to Darius and Miss Water. Handing one to Darius, she said, "This way."

Together, the trio walked along Fleet Street, toward the site of the Cheshire Cheese. "You're more than a scribe, aren't you?" Miss Water asked, with slightly misty eyes. Her eyes widened when he leaned down to whisper something in her ear. The rubble there had been cleared for the most part. Lucy pointed to the location where the barrels had been, near the old stone wall. "Just there."

Darius broke his silence. " 'The Truth stands before me,' " he said softly. " 'On my left is a blazing fire, and on my right, a cool flowing stream.' " He looked down at Rhonda. "I think Rumi would tell us to find the flowing stream. Come." Holding hands, they walked over to the remnants of the wall and knelt down. From the distance, Miss Water appeared to be saying a prayer.

Lucy turned away. A cart stopped beside her on the street. "Lucy?" someone called.

Surprised, she turned around. The magistrate and Adam were sitting in the cart. Lucy stepped quickly over, her mind racing. Master Hargrave was smiling kindly down at her. "We deciphered the last bit," he said. "I see you did too. We stopped by Master Aubrey to tell you, and we found this." He held up the

crumpled piece of paper where she'd scrawled the complete message. "We then went to see Constable Duncan, and found him
locking up Master Water. He told us what had happened. He also
told us you had found Darius, and that the three of you were
coming here. I think he was feeling a bit anxious for your safety,
but I can see you are all right."

"Three different stories," Lucy said, her eyes a bit misty. "Poor
Tahmin! The Earl thought he had found his blackmailer, and set
Burly and Jonesie on him. Master Water thought he was protecting his daughter. Truly, he was simply Darius's messenger, charged
to bring a lighthearted puzzle to Miss Water." She smiled wryly.
"Who could have imagined that printing a simple poem would
have brought all this to light?"

"Indeed." Master Hargrave looked at Darius and Miss Water.
"That's Darius, is it?" he asked. "Over there, with Miss Water?
He's a regal sort."

"Yes," Lucy hesitated. His secrets were not hers to share. "I
don't think he's the court translator."

Master Hargrave raised his eyebrows. "No, I shouldn't think
so. A translator is hardly likely to have the wherewithal to send a
message by hand to a young woman in a far-off land. Even a dear
friend might think twice about such a mission, but Tahmin appears to have been quite devoted."

Lucy smiled. Trust Master Hargrave to boil a mystery down
in such a fashion. "Just so," she agreed.

They all watched Darius whisper something in Miss Water's
ear, and they could see the responding pleasure in her face in the
flickering light of the lantern.

Lucy looked at Adam who was smiling at her in approval.

"Well done, Lucy. Well done! You've helped right a terrible wrong. Perhaps they would never have found each other, had it not been for your perseverance."

She smiled back, unconsciously stroking her silver bracelet. She did not expect him to repeat what he had said in the intimacy of his bedchamber. In that moment, she knew all would be right between them, even if it took them a while to find the way forward.

Lucy turned back then, to where Miss Water and Darius still knelt. As she watched, Darius took out a small silver dagger, which he raised high in the air, clearly paying tribute to Tahmin. He then dropped the dagger into a hole he had dug in the ground. Seeing the blade, Lucy had a sudden memory of the two little boys playing with the armor they'd found. Sir Dungheap and Lord Lughead. Their play had started this tale, but there had been far more twists than anyone might have imagined.

Together, Miss Water and Darius pushed the dirt over the dagger and stood up. The Persian man kept his arm around her protectively.

"They have found each other, I see," the magistrate said. "The trials they have suffered do not seem to have driven them apart." He sighed. "Although they will have much to bear when her father's crime comes to light."

Adam glanced at Lucy. "Indeed." Grimacing, he touched the side of his head. "Father—I—"

"You must rest," Lucy said quickly. There would be other times to talk. "Please, sir, take Adam home."

The magistrate smiled down at her kindly. "Take care, Lucy. We'll see you soon," he said, with a firm set to his jaw. "And Lucy?"

"Yes?"

"No more dead bodies for a while." Master Hargrave clucked at the horses and shook the reins. As they drove away, he called back, "Find some time for the living, Lucy! London is rising from the ashes, and so must we!"

HISTORICAL NOTE

In writing this novel, I had to occasionally reimagine historical details in order to tell the most compelling story I could.

Sometimes this reimagining allowed me to question established historical narrative. For example, beyond the puzzle of the murdered man, there is a larger and far more real mystery that forms the backdrop of my story: the so-called "miracle" of the Great Fire of 1666. Despite the fact that thousands of homes and businesses were destroyed in the three-day blaze, contemporaries such as Samuel Pepys and other chroniclers from this time period only noted a handful of deaths overall. More significantly, the *Bills of Mortality,* which had carefully documented all deaths from the plague and other misfortunes in the 1660s, did not describe any great numbers after the Fire. This lack of evidence has led historians to long believe that the death toll was quite low; hence, the so-called miracle.

How could this be? Just imagine, as I've tried to do, the mayhem, the panic, the crush of humanity. Could the elderly, the infirm, the drunk have fled so easily? And what about the inmates of Newgate prison? It's unlikely the wardens of that dreadful place would have thought through a systematic evacuation plan. The scholar Neil Hanson has made a compelling argument that thousands may have perished in this blaze—in direct opposition to the commonly accepted view. This is why I had Lucy pose the question that has perpetually bothered me: what happened to all the people?

On other occasions, I took creative license on certain historic points to keep the story moving easily. For example, I simplified the language to make the prose more accessible to the modern reader. (L'Estrange's *Anagram on the Citie London* suggests something of the speech of this era.) Similarly, since there was no established police force at this time, I gave Constable Duncan a bit more scope and authority than he would have truly had at this time. I also consolidated much of the bookselling trade; in reality, authors, booksellers, printers, paper makers, bookbinders, etc., might have all worked separately, but it worked better for the story if Master Aubrey and his apprentices could handle all of these processes themselves. For the sake of the story, too, even though there were strict injunctions against burning effigies in November 1666 for Guy Fawkes Day (because of fear of fire), I figured that some people would surely disobey the authorities.

In contrast, some details were true but might not be believed to be so. For example, there was a tavern called Ye Olde Cheshire Cheese that burned down in the Great Fire, but I changed the name because the original one sounded contrived. The Fariners who owned the bakery where the Great Fire started really were paid members of the jury who convicted poor Robert Hubert. There was an Earl of Cumberland, but his line died out in the 1640s. As far as I know, however, no one has tried to illegally gain the title.

Lastly, I released Lucy from some of the constraints that would likely have bound her, given her class, gender, and station. But I thought about this very carefully as I developed her character.

While it's true that most servants or apprentices might not have had her freedom, and indeed, might have lived with masters who beat them or took advantage of them, there is much evidence to suggest that many employers believed that sparing the rod was better for cultivating loyalty and good service in their employees. So it's not farfetched to me that both Master Hargrave and Master Aubrey might have treated Lucy well, particularly at a time when Enlightenment ideas were starting to bubble up in England. Moreover, in smaller households, too, it was quite common for servants to seem like members of the family; the distance between "upstairs" and "downstairs" was not nearly so pronounced as it may have become in later centuries.

It's clear, too, that in the mid-1660s, after the plague and Great Fire, there was unprecedented social mobility, when servants could become masters with no one around to gainsay their claims. Indeed, many women became apprentices, helped their husbands with their trades, or even owned businesses in their own right. So it seemed reasonable to me that, in this brief moment, Lucy might feel that she had more options than women in previous decades might have had. Moreover, only noblewomen married young; for the most part, female servants didn't marry until about age twenty-five, after they had put together a dowry and felt they could afford to marry. And that's my story, and I'm sticking to it!

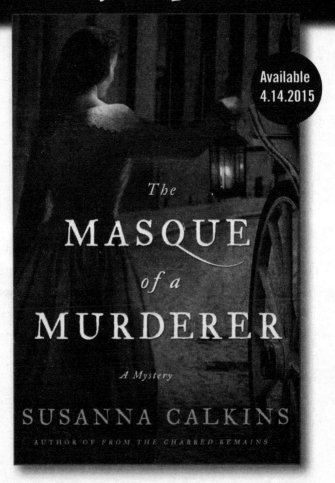